the ROSE
and the
THISTLE

Books by Laura Frantz

The Frontiersman's Daughter
Courting Morrow Little
The Colonel's Lady
The Mistress of Tall Acre
A Moonbow Night
The Lacemaker
A Bound Heart
An Uncommon Woman
Tidewater Bride
A Heart Adrift
The Rose and the Thistle

THE BALLANTYNE LEGACY

Love's Reckoning
Love's Awakening
Love's Fortune

the ROSE
and the
THISTLE

A Novel

LAURA FRANTZ

Revell
a division of Baker Publishing Group
Grand Rapids, Michigan

Published by Revell
a division of Baker Publishing Group
PO Box 6287, Grand Rapids, MI 49516-6287
www.revellbooks.com

Printed in the United States of America

Library of Congress Cataloging-in-Publication Data
Names: Frantz, Laura, author.
Title: The rose and the thistle : a novel / Laura Frantz.
Description: Grand Rapids, Michigan : Revell, a division of Baker Publishing Group,
    [2023]
Identifiers: LCCN 2022014279 | ISBN 9780800740672 (paperback) | ISBN
    9780800742669 (casebound) | ISBN 9781493439713 (ebook)
Subjects: LCGFT: Novels.
Classification: LCC PS3606.R4226 R67 2023 | DDC 813/.6—dc23
LC record available at https://lccn.loc.gov/2022014279

Scripture used in this book, whether quoted or paraphrased by the characters, is taken
from the King James Version of the Bible.

Published in association with Books & Such Literary Management, www.booksandsuch
.com.

Baker Publishing Group publications use paper produced from sustainable forestry prac-
tices and post-consumer waste whenever possible.

23   24   25   26   27   28   29   7   6   5   4   3   2   1

Dedicated to
Tawny Brown Ramsperger, Sarah Sleet,
and our eighteenth-century Humes of Wedderburn Castle
in the Scottish Borders

Historical Note

In 1707, the two kingdoms of Scotland and England were united, much to the ire of those who supported the Jacobite cause. The Jacobites were supporters of the deposed James II, who reigned from 1685 to 1688, and his descendants in the long-reigning Stuart dynasty. (*Jacobus* was derived from the Latin form of *James*.) His son, James Francis Edward Stuart, attempted to reclaim the throne his father had lost. This resulted in the Rising, or rebellion, in the year 1715, when George I was the reigning monarch of Great Britain.

Glossary

a-crow: to tell or proclaim
auld: old
Auld Reekie: Edinburgh, on account of its smoke and stench
aywis at the cow's tail: always last, behind, or lagging
barmy: crazy
blether: chat, gossip
braisant: bold
braw: handsome
brose: soup
bumbazed: confused
burn: brook or stream
canna: cannot
close: passageway or courtyard
collieshangie: dispute, uproar, disturbance
clype: gossip, spread tales
crabbit: in a bad temper, out of humor
crankie: unsteady, undependable
crivvens: an exclamation of astonishment or horror
doesna: does not
douce: sweet, pleasant, modest, agreeable
dowie: sad, melancholy

dreich: dreary, cheerless, bleak
dyke: low wall made of stones
endie: selfish, attached to one's own interests
faither: father
fankle: tangle, snare
frichtsome: fearful, terrifying
guid: good
haar: a cold sea fog
haver: babble, gossip
heidie: headstrong, rebellious
ill-scrappit: abusive, rude, bitter
ill-willy: bad-tempered, mean
isna: is not
jings: exclamation of surprise
kelpie: a water spirit
kirk: church
laird: lord or landowner
limmer: a woman of low morals
lykewake: the watch kept over a deceased person
Merse: a luxuriant part of the Scottish Borders
Michaelmas: a day in May when servants were hired or terminated
nae: no
peely-wally: sickly or wan
sair: sore
sassenach: foreigner
scourie: shabby, poor in appearance
sculduddery: unchaste behavior
selkie: magical creature
shelpit: thin, puny

slippit awa: slipped away

smirr: a fine rain or drizzle

sonsie: engaging or friendly in appearance or manner

tae: to

tapsalteerie: upside down, confused, disordered

trittil-trattil: nonsense, foolishness

ugsome: inspiring fear or dread

unco: unfamiliar, strange

unweel: unwell

vauntie: proud, boastful

weel: well

wheest: exclamation of surprise or chiding

Whitsunday: May 28, one of four Scottish quarter days when contracts could be terminated or renewed and servants could be hired or dismissed

wynd: a narrow lane, street, or alley

yer: your, you're

We are persons of quality, I assure you, and women of
fashion, and come to see and be seen.

BEN JONSON

April 1715
Château de Saint-Germain-en-Laye
France

Struck by sunlight, the sprawling château was a blinding, rose-hued white. It reminded Lady Blythe Hedley of home, of her family's Northumbrian castle with its pink harled walls, a pearl in an emerald-green meadow. Tipping her straw hat slightly forward, Blythe glanced up at the royal apartments and terraces on the second floor before turning toward the River Seine and the château's famous gardens.

Her companions walked ahead of her. Were they finally tired of flirting with the officers of the Gardes du Corps who stood watch? Only Lady Catherine Stuart tarried, linking arms with her old friend before continuing down the gravel path, their maids following at a discreet distance.

"How fetching you look in your pale green gown, La Belle Hedley. Akin to a stalk of celery," Catherine teased, knowing Blythe didn't give a fig for fashion and lamented her height, exceeding most of the court's gallants. "And though you may roll your eyes at me for saying so, there's no doubt you are the best-dressed woman here and have set French society afire."

'Tis not my fashion sense but my mother's reputation that has done so. "I would rather spend it all on books than silks and ribbons," Blythe replied. But her dear father wouldn't let her. The duke was far more matrimonially minded than she. And given she lacked any outward beauty save her garments, fashion was her one asset.

"You are unquestionably à la mode." Catherine openly admired Blythe's flawless coiffure styled into pale coils over one bare shoulder and adorned with beribboned rosettes. "I've heard the Duchess d'Orleans covets your hairdresser while Mary of Modena covets your gems." Her hazel eyes slid to the choker of sapphires around Blythe's throat and the ones set in silver and pearl adorning her ears. "Not paste gems but true brilliants. I suppose they were your mother's. Such a blinding, bewitching blue."

Blythe touched an earring absently. "But how ridiculous I feel in red heels." She looked down at her new slippers in bemusement before reaching into her pocket. With a practiced snap of her wrist, she unfurled a painted fan encrusted with tiny precious stones, a gift from Catherine's aunt, lady of the queen's bedchamber.

Blythe tallied how many days she'd been exiled to—*visiting*—France. Sixty-three?

She and Catherine strolled on with no apparent aim beneath the strengthening spring sun, their hooped, colorful skirts swaying in the breeze. "We've walked these paths for weeks now." The lament in Catherine's tone was telling. "And not one glimpse of my kindred, the ousted prince."

Blythe's gaze swept the manicured grounds as though James Francis Edward Stuart would materialize before their eyes. Charming and highly polished, the would-be James III of England and James VIII of Scotland was the catch of the continent—if he could only regain his crown.

"His Royal Highness remains in Lorraine," Blythe said quietly. Much could be learned by listening, as gossip and intrigue buzzed at every turn. "He seeks a royal bride. One who is wealthy and polished and—"

"That would be *you*." Catherine cast her a knowing look.

"Alas, I lack the requisite curves and double chin, plain as I am," Blythe replied with a flutter of her fan. The foremost courtiers were voluptuous, sensuous women with heavily rouged cheeks and lips, sporting beauty patches in myriad places.

"Ha! Beauty is in the eye of the beholder, is it not?"

"Most men of my acquaintance seem preoccupied with face, form, and fortune, in that order. Yet I long to be loved for myself and nothing else."

A shadow passed over Catherine's porcelain-perfect features. "Though you profess to being plain, there is no denying you *are* the Duke of Northumbria's daughter."

Blythe squinted as the sun strengthened. Not just his daughter. His only daughter—and only child. The whole weight of the Northumbrian fortune and future was upon her. If she failed to marry, failed to provide an heir . . .

"Alas, a duke's daughter of scandalous lineage."

Catherine raised slender shoulders in a shrug. "'Twas long ago and best forgotten."

"Then needs be I find a man of dim memory and even greater purse than my beloved father."

"How few nobles fit, including our impoverished if dashing Stuart prince." Catherine sighed. "I fear we shall all be branded spinsters if we leave France unaffianced."

"Marriage is not a right, nor is singleness a curse." Blythe's fan fluttered harder. "I've been pondering other paths, like becoming a nun and joining a convent in Flanders or Chaillot. Perhaps a contemplative order like the English Augustine nuns at Bruges."

"Don't you dare!" Catherine gave a vicious pinch to Blythe's arm as if to bring her to her senses. "You have too much to offer to shut yourself away so."

Stung but in no mood to argue, Blythe made no reply. They'd

reached the river's parterre with its tall hedge walls that led to the renowned grotto rooms, raising the gooseflesh on her arms. She always felt she entered a magical, otherworldly kingdom amid its rushing fountains, water-spewing dragons, moving statuary, and automated music. Cool as a cave, it was.

Cool as England in the rain.

She paused before a whimsical fountain of twittering birds, their song caused by unseen waterworks that made them spin and trill. Other waterspouts were hidden, sometimes erupting to spray visitors and mimic a tempest, complete with thunder and wind. It wouldn't be the first time Blythe got a soaking, but she wouldn't mind a whit.

"The musicality of this place never fails to delight me," she said.

"I prefer the automaton carriage and company of soldiers," Catherine said, moving on. "Or the musical theater that enacts an opera in five parts."

Blythe lingered by the birds, feeling a trifle homesick for her own pet sparrow at Bellbroke Castle. Was Mrs. Stanhope taking proper care of Pepys?

Ashiver from the grotto's mist, she tapped Catherine's arm with her fan as she overtook her. "The sun suits me better." She raised her skirts and hastened up marble steps over which water cascaded, soaking her gaudy, red-heeled shoes.

Together they moved along to the Grand Terrace as Catherine's younger, giggling sisters joined them, their maids still in pursuit.

When strolling, a lady should be reserved and demure.

Blythe slowed her steps, ever mindful of French etiquette. For all she knew, the exiled dowager queen, Mary of Modena, was peering out the castle windows, wondering why her English guests were in such a hurry. And for what? Multicourse suppers preceded by endless music, games of lansquenet and portique, court balls and royal birthday celebrations, theater, and endless other amusements. Save the servants, one did not do anything resembling work here.

Everything seemed devoted to beauty. The perfumed court was ever abloom with the lushest flowers, the gilded salons perpetually fragrant. Blythe raised her fan and hid a yawn. Though her days were astonishingly full, her mind was empty. She sought solace in the sedate order of morning prayers, private meditations, and daily mass followed by vespers and the recital of the rosary. 'Twas a relief to practice her Catholic faith openly here when it must be hidden in England. Time spent on her knees grew. So much needed praying for.

The English Queen Anne had recently died, and the throne had been usurped by a foreign Hanoverian named George who spoke no English. All hopes for a Stuart restoration seemed at a standstill, as the displaced British court was all too content to linger in France instead of fighting to regain the English throne. Meanwhile, Louis XIV, the long-standing French monarch who financed the exiled Stuarts and royal household, lay ill. Would his successor be as generous in regard to his poor British relations?

"We must not dally," Catherine said, consulting her watch. "Tonight is the ball, remember. And we must look our very best."

They hastened on, intent on the château.

"Mademoiselle." At the door of their apartments stood a liveried footman, a letter clasped in his gloved hands.

"Je vous remercie," Blythe murmured, taking the post and noting the intact seal.

She pocketed it, feeling a dozen eyes upon her. The exiled court was rife with spies and informants. Letters were oft written in codes and ciphers to protect their privacy, though hers to and from her father were hardly worth intercepting. Tepid at best, they were simply the terse musings of a widower and his homesick daughter. Hardly the stuff of secrecy and intrigue.

Once inside their apartment, Blythe closed the door and leaned against it. The foolscap opened with a crisp rustle, and for a time the gilded halls of St. Germaine gave way to the north of England, the beloved landscape of home.

Bellbroke Castle
Northumberland
6 April 1715

My dearest daughter,
    I pray this finds you in excellent health and spirits. Our Northumbrian hills are now awash with your favorite bluebells. Bellbroke is hardly the same without you, and even the servants and tenants are asking about you. You will no doubt delight in the fact I have finally heeded your homesickness. The time has come for you to return to England . . .

2

I can make a lord, but only God can make a gentleman.

KING JAMES I

Edinburgh, Scotland

Edinburgh was as dangerous as it was odiferous.

If someone had predicted that he, Everard Hume, Lord Fast, would soon be meeting the Duke of Northumbria in an oyster cellar, he'd have roared with mirth.

But this was no laughing matter.

The duke's renowned dour disposition hardly sweetened the task, nor did the anticipation of ale and oysters to come. Everard wound his way through Old Town's wynds and closes as all grew inky and the gloaming snuck in, his manservant, Boyd, on his booted heels. Flickering candle lanterns glowed outside shopkeepers' doors, proclaiming eight o' the clock.

They went into the King's Wark, which was so crowded it seemed cheek to jowl. The auld tavern had a storied past. Once a royal residence and armory, it now crowned the shore of Leith's celebrated oyster beds. Discarded oyster shells crunched beneath Everard's leather soles as he made his way to a far corner where the duke's penned summons said he'd be waiting.

"A shame we've not come in October when the best oysters are

17

to be had," Boyd said above the din. "But at a mere two shillings, I'll not complain."

They moved past the large central table piled high with raw oysters and endless pots of ale. Nearby a fiddler ground out a spirited tune while a few well-dressed couples danced. Rich and poor alike came here, so it was no surprise the duke had chosen the King's Wark.

Did Northumbria like oysters? Everard didn't.

His gaze swept the crowd, alighting on what looked to be a valet standing behind a seated gentleman, both looking straight at him. Northumbria? Everard hadn't seen Musgrave Hedley in years.

To Everard's surprise, the duke pulled himself to his feet, dwarfing his manservant. There was no reason to rise, but mayhap that was part of the ruse, as was the duke's humble appearance. He was kitted out in the hodden grey of commoners, his thinning flaxen hair disguised by a simple, unpowdered periwig, his silver-buckled shoes his only vanity.

Everard came to a stop before the bare table. Though he was a head higher, the duke still cut an imposing figure. "Your Grace."

"Lord Fast."

So, the duke had not forgotten him. Still . . .

"I was expecting your father." Northumbria sat down again and gestured to the seat opposite.

Everard slid onto a bench, grateful ale was promptly served. "My faither is unweel, so I have come in his stead." Reluctantly, even unwillingly. And at considerable trouble. The fifty or so miles from Wedderburn Castle had been in rough weather, the spring rains heavy, the muck up to their ankles. Away from home at such a time was chancy if the auld laird took another ill turn.

"I am sorry to hear it." Northumbria's stern features softened briefly before turning to stone again. "I am seldom in Scotland. Nor do I venture near London lately."

Was he referring to the recent rioting there? The unrest following Queen Anne's death and a Hanoverian ruler in her stead? Nae doubt.

The duke's eyes roamed the room even as his voice dropped. "You'll convey to your father all that I tell you here with the utmost secrecy? The utmost urgency?"

Everard swallowed a sip of ale. "Depend on it."

"Very well. The matter involves my daughter."

Their eyes locked, and Everard read a steely resolve most men only carried into battle.

"As you may know, there are plans in place for the House of Stuart to rise again, starting with a possible landing on the Northumbrian coast. I am under suspicion by the new government. Diverse threats have been made against me by unknown persons."

Everard gave a curt nod. "You are concerned for your daughter's safety."

"I am more than concerned. I fear for her life."

Everard paused. What the deuce was his daughter's name? Did it even matter? "Is her ladyship at Bellbroke Castle?"

"Nay. She has been in France with the Stuarts of Traquair House since Candlemas but will soon be on her way home."

Everard nearly groaned aloud. The Stuarts of Traquair were no safer. Courtiers and kin to the exiled Stuarts, they were arguably the most unsafe Scots in the country, at least on British soil. In France where Catholicism ruled the day and the French king was a cousin, 'twas somewhat less dangerous.

"While she is safer there, she is pining for England," the duke said. "In truth, she despises France and feels besmirched by the excess and endless frivolity. And I, in truth, am missing her company. Lately, she has been threatening to join a religious order. That I cannot conscience. She is all I have, understand." He leaned in, his long, narrow fingers curled around his tankard. "However, once she returns, if matters continue dangerous, I would send her to a remote location far from any upheaval. Wedderburn Castle should suit."

Everard arched a brow as the fiddler switched to a rousing jig, though he hardly heard the hubbub around them. The tension between him and the duke was palpable, ratcheting higher with every word. What would his father say to this surprising proposal?

Northumbria motioned for more ale. "Your parents—God rest your dear mother's soul—are my daughter's godparents."

Everard swallowed, reaching into the past when the Hedleys and Humes were tightly knit. Once upon a time there had been a Catholic christening, a shadowy affair long forgotten. Something scandalous, if memory served. "My parents have long since left the Catholic faith."

"Nevertheless, as godparents they are charged with my daughter's well-being. Such a commitment has no end, at least till her death or she weds and is in the safekeeping of a husband."

Her death—or my faither's? Everard focused on his replenished ale. He knew little of christenings and less of godparents. It seemed he and the duke had crossed swords. Their politics were at odds, as was their faith, the Humes being Protestant Scots and Whigs, the Hedleys Romish Tories. What had they in common other than the lass now in question?

"A husband . . ." Everard echoed.

For a moment, the duke looked aggravated. "Unfortunately, she has no matrimonial prospects."

Wheest. A damning indictment for an heiress. The flicker of sympathy Everard had felt changed to vexation. "What would you have me do, Your Grace?"

"Convey to your father my fears. Send word to me his answer. If his is a mortal illness or injury, I leave the matter with you, his heir."

The eleventh Earl of Wedderburn.

Everard made no reply. There was no arguing with a doting father, even if a lass was not in danger.

3

I see no point in reading.

Louis XIV

Château de Saint-Germain-en-Laye
France

French court etiquette swam through Blythe's mind like the teeming carp with golden chokers in Versailles' ornate pools. *Do not address someone of higher rank than yourself. Never turn your back on royalty. One must curtsy to the king's portrait if he is not present. One must not knock at a door but scratch. Do not leave the room until an usher opens the door. As soon as you are seated for supper, remove your gloves and place your serviette across your lap, your gloves beneath. A lady never holds hands or locks arms with a gentleman . . .*

Tonight was Blythe's last court ball at the Château de Sceaux, hosted by La Duchesse du Maine. It would be a violently late night followed by a hideously early morning.

Tomorrow—could it be?—she'd begin the long journey home to England. But for now she was too distracted to dwell on the delight of it.

Lady Catherine and Lady Mary Stuart hovered around the dressing table with their French maids, painting their faces with fashionable white lead powder, rouging their cheeks into scarlet dots,

21

and coloring their lips beetroot red. Their elaborate wigs eclipsed Blythe's, though her own flaxen hair was teased into a rather large, unrecognizable pouf. She shied away from the glittering gold, lilac, and blue powder that came next.

"But, mademoiselle"—the French maid looked aghast—"you may be the only woman in the room so unadorned!"

"Is it required by the king?"

The maid pursed her lips. "Non, but . . ."

Blythe simply smiled and stood back as the Stuart ladies received the coveted, colorful powder by way of a small bellows. They sneezed prettily into their lace handkerchiefs when all was said and done.

Alas, the price of beauty.

Blythe gave silent thanks there was none of this foolishness in Northumbria or even the rustic reaches of Scotland where the Stuarts' Traquair House held sway. But it seemed her friends wanted to make the most of their French experience, even donning the exaggerated hoop panniers that stretched several feet wide and required the utmost care maneuvering. In her own smaller petticoats, Blythe looked quite deflated beside them. If she *were* an influencer of fashion, she would hasten this ridiculous extreme to its deathbed. No gallant could get near enough to press his suit!

Eye on the clock, Blythe slipped a hand into her pocket, which was cleverly disguised beneath the ball gown's petticoat to hold essentials. Spectacles. Handkerchief. Watch. Pencil case. Her father's latest letter. Even a tiny book of verse. Nary a mirror, scent bottle, comb, or snuff box to be had. Vain trinkets, all.

———⊗⊗⊗———

Blythe danced with an aged, half-blind count and then a young, balding silk merchant while the ladies of Traquair never lacked handsome, willing partners. Was it her imagination, or did these people regard her with a sort of veiled derision—a haughty superiority—as if she were shadowed or stained, her very garments besmirched or marked by Clementine Hedley's scandalous history?

She drank two cups of punch, all the while inching her way nearer a small door, no easy feat given the press of people and panniers on all sides. Finally, she made her escape into a crimson-and-gold antechamber and up a back stair to she knew not where. A footman eyed her departure warily.

She might be plain, but she was not timid, nor was she above using her standing when it suited her purpose, including roaming another's château at will.

Voilà! At the top of the stairs was an open window. Leaning in, Blythe breathed the blissful fragrance of magnolias and the pink-blossomed trees she'd seen from the coach but had no name for. If she closed her eyes, she could almost believe she was in Bellbroke's garden, the stone walls holding in the scent of age-old roses. White roses foremost, her mother's favorite, cultivated in honor of the Jacobite cause and her family's allegiance to the Stuart kings.

Blessedly alone, Blythe sought an upholstered bench in a little alcove where she was hidden from sight, uncaring about the crush of her violet taffeta skirts. Her mind was on dusty roads, a water crossing, cramped carriages, lukewarm cuisine, and questionable coaching inns.

She took her father's letter from her pocket and smoothed the paper's creases. The ducal seal bore a coronet, knight's helmet, and quiver and arrows, each as familiar as his handsome, scrolling hand. She reread the last lines.

Perhaps I erred in sending you to France, though I sensed you needed a change, a respite from your books and papers. I misjudged how the frivolities and decadence found amongst courtiers even in exile are so contrary to your nature that you would feel a fish out of water. Though you rarely complain, I sense this has been more trial than holiday for you. And since you mention no suitor to sweeten your stay, thus ends the matter. Foremost, I beg you to dismiss joining a religious order once and for all. Your reasons for doing so are hardly holy.

How that last line stung. He sensed her desperation to quit this place. While she might have been dazzled by the French court as a girl of eight and ten, at eight and twenty she saw through the luster. Though the Stuarts had once reigned supreme, their royal trappings were now tarnished. They themselves were at the mercy of the French king, who stood to gain from his allegiance should the Stuarts be restored to the throne.

You asked in an earlier letter if you might tarry awhile at Traquair House with Lady Catherine and Lady Mary before your return home. By now you may know Charles Stuart has told me his daughters are to continue in France, going with the dowager Queen Mary to spend the summer in Lorraine.

I have a different plan in mind for you, which I will tell you about once we are face-to-face.

She looked out the window. A different plan? How odd that sounded. And how intriguing.

You shall cross the channel and come north up the English coast to Newcastle-upon-Tyne. Arrangements have been secured, and I caution you to stay close to Bell and heed the direction of Father Beverly.

She refolded the letter. Not Dover to Calais as she'd come, which was always the most direct, preferred route. Why the change? She disliked the rigors of travel, but in the company of her maid and her family's priest, she would make the best of it.

A footfall in the corridor made her press her back against the paneled wall. Someone hastened past, not bothering to look in the small alcove where she hid but stopping just beyond.

"How fortunate we are able to conduct business under the guise of a ball." The male voice was subdued and clearly British. "And in King's English too, though French shall forever be the language of intrigue."

Another man chuckled. "For now, let us anticipate the coming campaign. We've not had such profitable news in some time as we've had tonight. At long last, Royalist armies are being raised in the north country—one in Northumberland and one in Scotland, is that correct?"

"Aye. A fleet of French ships will soon be at hand."

"By June, 'tis said. Have you confirmation?"

"I do, indeed. Thrice. From Viscount Bolingbroke, the Earl of Mar, and the Duke of Ormonde. None better."

"Brilliant! The current riots and protests in London and Edinburgh against the Hanoverian king are in our favor."

"'Twould seem so. Still, his red-coated swine and a great many mounted government troops will soon be crawling all over the country."

"They dare not encroach on the Highlands. All the dragoons in the kingdom are no match for a Highland charge."

"Or a Lowland one if the Radcliffes and Swinburnes and Haggerstons have their way."

"Dinna forget the Blacketts of Newcastle and the Forsters of Bamburgh, all leading, loyal Jacobites."

Blythe listened with a sort of bemused detachment to the whispered names of powerful Catholic nobles she knew.

"And then there is the Duke of Northumbria, who has not only contributed so generously to the cause but stands to lose the most of any noble if the Rising fails."

At the mention of her father, Blythe went still.

The Rising. Spoken of with such gravity, as if the whole world hinged upon it.

What did that even mean?

4

I always admired virtue—but I could never imitate it.

KING CHARLES II

Edinburgh, Scotland

Pondering the Duke of Northumbria's predicament, Everard left the oyster cellar with Boyd, wishing his final destination was his family's elegant Canongate mansion rather than Edinburgh Castle on the distant, craggy hilltop. But first he must stop at Hume's Land on the south side of the High Street in the castle's brooding shadow. It was home to a city minister, a marchioness, a dancing master, a judge, and other tenants. David Hume claimed the eighth and ninth floors.

By the time they crossed the damp cobblestones and reached the familiar turnpike stair, Boyd was winded and belching, suffering the ill effects of too much ale and too many oysters. Everard felt a momentary qualm. Betimes he forgot his long stride equaled two of his valet's.

"If ye dinna mind, milord"—Boyd came to a stop, chest heaving beneath his bulging weskit—"I'll not go up just yet."

"Yer aywis at the cow's tail." With a sympathetic chuckle, Everard started up the stone steps, glad he'd sent word ahead of his coming. The butler would be awaiting him, a fire in the hearth and some whisky-laced tea near at hand. Just the remedy for a chill spring night, if not the duke's conundrum.

Everard raked his mind for what he knew of Lady Hedley. Precious little. Had they ever even met?

At last, he reached the top story, his pulse up a notch. Lantern light flickered across the tirling pin. As a lad, he'd moved the iron ring up and down, reveling in the rusty rattle that announced their arrival. But tonight, the butler was at the ready, denying him the boyish pleasure.

"Lord Fast." With a stiff bow usually reserved for the laird of Wedderburn, Simms opened the door, then stepped aside as Everard entered the inner hall.

From the large parlor came Mrs. Archer, no doubt anxious to learn word of his father. "How glad we are to see you, milord," she told him. "Though we are sorry to deny you the pleasure of the Canongate and your lodgings there."

He tried not to think of the much larger townhouse and its little luxuries. Rarely did he come up the hill. Like as not, they didn't quite know what to do with him. But this visit was all business, not pleasure.

As Simms took his damp coat and hat, Everard answered what was surely uppermost in their thoughts. "My faither continues unweel. More on that in the morn. For now, I'll retire to my chambers."

"Of course, milord," they said in unison. "If ye have need of anything . . ."

Everard passed into the large parlor. The wooden shutters were open, and the tall windows framed Edinburgh, which was all aglitter with candlelight below and starlight above. The castle seemed a great hunchback looming atop the city, its battlements and towers sullen and brooding and black.

A brocaded blue chair near the bank of windows had been his mother's favorite, overlooking the city she loved. He swallowed past the catch in his throat, which only tightened when his gaze hung on her portrait against a grey-paneled wall before falling to the leaping fire below. Woodsmoke and lavender still threaded the elegant room just as it had in Mariota Hume's lifetime.

He sought a seat by the hearth. The leather armchair bore his father's formidable imprint, the seat sagging from years of use. Tipping his head back, he watched light leap across the smoke-blackened beams painted with unicorns and thistles. Rarely did he come here. Not since the countess had died eight years prior. His brother David, second of the Hume sons, had moved in the year before with his new bride, Calysta. She preferred the bustle of Edinburgh to the boredom of Wedderburn Castle, she'd told them. But at the moment, she and David were in the Highlands visiting her kin.

God be thanked.

Davie the Devil, as he was oft called, had wed no angel.

A distant door groaned open, and he heard Boyd's voice. He'd no doubt head to his bed in the servants' hall after he paid court to Polly the kitchen maid. Boyd was here more oft than he, acting as courier between the Humes' houses.

To Everard's right a bottle of aqua vitae rested beside a steaming silver teapot. Lowland Scotch whisky, the taste smooth and light, as the laird preferred it to the smoky, peaty flavor of other regions. Everard added a dram to his tea, held the wide porcelain dish between his callused palms, and took a long, satisfying sip.

Mayhap the whisky would temper tonight's cares.

Cares that would only return in the morning.

———— ✺ ————

"Lord Fast, you wanted a word with us?" Simms asked from the study doorway as the mantel clock struck ten the following day.

At Everard's nod, the butler and Mrs. Archer entered, closing the door after them. Sunlight streamed through the windows behind the large mahogany desk, illuminating neglected papers and correspondence, the result of the laird's three-month malady.

Everard opened a cupboard, unlocked a strongbox, and withdrew two small pouches of five-pieces in gold. He turned toward the servants and handed them their due. "For your years of faithful service on behalf of my faither."

Mrs. Archer lowered her gaze, pleasure overriding her fluster. "His lairdship has ever been a generous man, even in his infirmity."

"Indeed," Simms said. "Please relay our deepest thanks. I'm hard-pressed to believe we've been twenty years in his employ."

Mrs. Archer bobbed her capped head. "The both of us hired on that long-ago Whitsunday."

They were looking at him expectantly, likely wanting more news of the laird, but he had precious little to give. "As for my faither, he remains abed. Another attack of the heart—his second in a sennight—has laid him low. His physicians hold little hope for his recovery, though I continue to pray otherwise."

"As do we," Mrs. Archer said, tears in her eyes.

"My faither also kens your patience has been tried with Mr. and Mrs. Hume. Have you need of more help here at Hume's Land?" Everard asked. "Word is you've lost a lady's maid of late." According to Boyd, the maid had quit over David's unwanted advances.

Confirmation was written all over Mrs. Archer's distressed face. "Well, milord . . ."

Simms stiffened. "I'll not be so timid. A great row erupted a fortnight ago over some small matter, upon which Mrs. Hume kicked off a slipper and flung it at an offending maid. The result was a rather severe nosebleed, which required a doctor be summoned."

A slipper. Hardly a bullet or bayonet. Still . . .

"Was the lass all right?" Everard asked.

"In time. But that was only the first incident," Mrs. Archer chimed in. "The second was a Highlander brought into service by Mrs. Hume herself who could not be kept in shoes and stockings. She soon quit after Simms raised an objection."

"Highland help is so rough-mannered," Simms said. "Though Lowland servants are little better. 'Tis a hard matter to know the mistress from the maid by their dress, so proud they are."

"Train your servants well and pay them enough to induce them to stay, as my faither says," Everard told them, hiding a smile. "But only if they remain fully clothed."

Simms snorted. "With your permission, milord, I'll contact Lawson's Intelligence Office as he supplies honest servants. With character references, of course. A second cook, kitchen maid, and footman are needed, as your brother and his wife like to entertain."

Everard took a seat behind his father's desk. "Who, perchance, is on the guest list?"

A tense pause. "Lord Drummond, Dr. Arthur, the writers Alexander Ramsay and George Boswell, even the Earl of Mar and Duchess of Gordon."

Jacobites, all. Everard felt a beat of exasperation. "Any keyhole conversations you're privy to?"

"We're kept so busy running and fetching, there's scarce time for any eavesdropping, however well intentioned," Mrs. Archer said.

"Nonetheless," Simms said, "we shall certainly make that a priority in future if necessary."

"When are Mr. and Mrs. Hume due to return?" Everard asked.

"We know not." Simms rubbed his high forehead, made higher by his wigless, balding head. "They are somewhat secretive about their comings and goings of late."

Everard sensed they were telling him only the half of it, but for now it was all he could stomach. "Mayhap they'll dally in the north and give you a needed respite."

The butler and housekeeper exchanged small, wry smiles.

"I've kept you from your duties long enough."

"When will ye be leaving, milord?" Simms asked.

Everard eyed the voluminous papers before him. "When I finish all my faither's business here."

Not nearly soon enough.

5

This blessed plot, this earth, this realm, this England.

WILLIAM SHAKESPEARE

Bellbroke Castle
Northumberland, England

Blythe stepped from the coach-and-six and felt like kissing the greening ground. Home at last.

She'd left for France on a dreary February day and now returned to jonquils blooming like sunbursts and a cloudless sky mirroring the last of spring's bluebells. The Palladian facade of Bellbroke's newest addition dwarfed the medieval castle at its end, transforming the rusticated pile into a palatial residence some hailed as the grandest in Northumberland. The approach leading up to Bellbroke was equally impressive, winding over a Palladian bridge past parterred gardens to crest a hill where the mansion overlooked a great forest.

Nearly holding her breath, Blythe reached back into the coach and retrieved her purse, which held a few heartfelt belongings. The interior smelled of overuse and was in dire need of an airing after so many miles.

A fortnight of travel marred by fickle spring weather had seemed endless. She'd been wretchedly seasick crossing the channel and continuing up the coast, then little better in the rough coach ride north over waterlogged, rutted roads. Since she, her lady's companion, Elodie Bell, and Father Beverly, her family's priest, traveled incognito due to highwaymen, they overnighted at shabby coaching inns, a shock to Blythe's system after the extravagances of the French court. Such humble circumstances sharpened her appreciation for common folk with little means and fewer privileges.

But all that was now forgotten, further pushed to the far reaches by the sound of Mrs. Stanhope's high voice. As Blythe and her small party started up the broad stone steps that led to the front door, the housekeeper hurried out of it, pleasure lighting her features.

"At last, Lady Blythe! I feared the French might woo you away forever!"

"No need to worry!" Blythe hugged their longtime housekeeper's ample figure tightly, conveying how much she'd been missed. "Truly home is where my heart is."

Drawing back, Mrs. Stanhope said, "I'm sure even Pepys will burst into song once he sees you!"

Blythe's gaze rested on a second-story window where her father's tall frame was outlined behind the glass. In a moment he disappeared. Blythe entered the grand foyer, certain he would soon appear.

"I'll draw you a bath, milady," Elodie said, clearly relieved to be back at Bellbroke again. She disappeared up the spiral staircase Blythe's father had just come down.

Forsaking her soiled cloak and gloves into Mrs. Stanhope's keeping, Blythe laid her head against her father's chest as his arms went round her.

"Welcome home, poppet. I've been counting the days . . . the hours."

"As I have, Father. All is well?" A new uncertainty crept into her query. For a few seconds she was cast back to the château alcove where she'd heard more than she wanted to, his name foremost.

"All is ready for your arrival." His smile seemed somewhat forced. "I've instructed the kitchen to prepare your favorite supper and the maids to cut as many flowers from the garden as they can for your rooms. From this day forward I shall have to compete with France, I suppose."

"France doesn't hold a candle to Northumberland." She looked to her soiled slippers, ready for a clean change of clothes. "Shall we dine together at eight o'clock as usual? I shall have tea before that to tide me over."

"Whatever you wish, milady." Mrs. Stanhope reached for a bell pull that traveled to the servants' hall below. "I'll have it sent up right after your bath."

Thoughts full of a steaming pot of hyson, Blythe started toward the stairs. Behind her, her father tarried with Father Beverly, whose rooms were in the old castle nearest the chapel, overlooking the old moat.

"No more salón de té for me," Blythe called over her shoulder, remembering the ladies' teahouses she'd frequented in Paris. "English tea is the finest. Besides, aside from the Mariage teas, the French prefer coffee."

Mrs. Stanhope smiled. "I'll send up some of your favorite lemon tarts too."

This spurred Blythe's steps. At the landing she turned down a shadowed corridor to her bedchamber overlooking the walled garden. Pushing open the door, she found Elodie busy preparing her bath behind a painted panel in her dressing room, the rose-scented bath salts wafting through the chamber on a warm wind. All the windows were open on so fair a day, and Blythe rushed to the nearest one, drinking in the garden like she soon would the tea.

Her beloved snowdrops of winter were no more, nor March and April's primroses and violets. Below, countless rosebushes flourished, awaiting summer's bloom, their fragrance permeating her rooms day and night. The garden's high stone enclosure faced north toward the Borders and Hadrian's Wall. She'd not been farther than Traquair House in Scotland, nor had she wanted to. All knew the Highlands were rife with danger, the clans murderous, the Lowlands little better. Father forbade travel north, other than to Traquair, and never to Edinburgh.

But that did not stop her from wondering about those places.

Blythe retreated behind the screen, soiled garments falling to the carpeted floor. She stepped into the tub and emerged half an hour later stripped of the journey's grime, her fair hair falling to her hips.

"Like Persinette in the French fairy tale," Elodie said, taking up a comb to free the tangles.

"Only I have no prince to invite into my tower," Blythe replied. "Not even Persinette's pet parrot, just Pepys."

They laughed, something they'd done little of on their journey. Once in her sultana, her damp hair arranged in a lovelock and tied with ribbon, Blythe passed through her dressing room to the chamber she'd most missed. Her writing desk sat beneath a large window, Pepys's cage of forged iron and gilt to one side of it.

Upon seeing her, the sparrow began to do an amusing little dance. After unlatching the cage, Blythe offered her arm. The tiny creature landed on it and burst into raucous song, complete with whistles and trills. Blythe cast a wary glance at the open window. On occasion Pepys would wing away and give her a fright, only to wing back in again.

Of course, she could not contemplate Pepys without another, less elevating memory swooping in. During the reign of King Charles, there'd been a Birdcage Walk near Kensington Palace, and her mother had been gifted a rare pelican by the Russian ambassador. Blythe abhorred pelicans.

She admired Pepys's chestnut plumage, his white speckles fading now that it was spring, his stout bill open, head tilted. "If only you were able to speak Greek and Latin as the philosophers of old once claimed your species could," she said. In a trice he'd nestled against her neck, his favorite spot. "I do believe you missed me."

She spoke to him in soothing tones, coaxing him back into his cage with seed. Then she locked him in and turned to her desk. It was much as she had left it, her favorite quills and inkwells for calligraphy in alignment, a few beloved books between globe bookends. Erondel's *The French Garden*. *The History of the Kings of Britain*. *Romeo and Juliet*. *Paradise Lost*. *A Book of Hours*. *King Arthur Pendragon*. Leusden's Hebrew Bible. Caedmon's *Paraphrase of Genesis*. All gathered from European booksellers in various languages and editions, their gilded spines lovely to look at, their pages tantalizing to open.

"Milady, which gown shall you wear?" Elodie stood in the doorway, arms full of a rose brocade and a daffodil-yellow taffeta.

"The yellow," Blythe said. "And please find my spectacles. I pray I've not lost them on the journey."

"Never fear. Your shagreen case is here somewhere. The footman has just brought up your last trunk."

Blythe rested her hands on the back of her desk chair, feeling the thrill of excitement her work always wrought. "I'm so giddy I want to do everything at once."

Elodie smiled knowingly before returning to the bedchamber. "Don't forget—tea is on the way. Perhaps there'll be time at your desk after that."

35

6

Princes and lords are but the breath of kings,
"An honest man's the noblest work of God."

ROBERT BURNS

Scottish Lowlands

The stench of Edinburgh, oft called Auld Reekie, soon left Everard's senses, even if his ire over his brother's affairs had not. Ever attuned to his mood, Boyd rode quietly behind him as they left Edinburgh for the Lowlands at first light. The weather was far more sonsie than when they'd arrived, not rain-slick and mud-ridden but fair. Pewter clouds rolled back as a mild wind dried the heavy dew.

Berwickshire—Siorrachd Bhearaig—was tucked in Scotland's southeast corner. Once a part of Northumbria in England, it stretched from the Lowther Hills to the North Sea, a land of sheep and bastel houses and a long, jagged jewel of rocky coastline.

If Lady Hedley were to come to Wedderburn Castle, she'd travel northeast, crossing the River Tweed and then the rolling, oft treacherous terrain of Borderland that marked the bloodiest valley in Britain's history, eventually landing her at their gatehouse. Had she heard the Hume history? Everard was not proud of it all. Even now the echoes of his ancestors' misdeeds seemed to linger.

No doubt Lady Hedley would rejoice that Traquair House was but forty miles distant in Peebleshire, easily managed by horseback. But was she an able horsewoman? Or cosseted and kept in a coach? He looked east toward the coast where the wind-worn ruins of Fast Castle clung to a cliff. The auld fortress was his, and there was no better place to seek solitude. His usual forays to Edinburgh skirted the sea, but this day he'd taken the shorter route, the urgency he felt regarding his father foremost.

Was the laird any better? Or any worse?

Though he wanted to hurry home, practicalities slowed them.

"The horses need water," Everard said as they came to the outskirts of Duns and headed toward Market Square. "And I need to make discreet inquiries."

"*Discreet*, milord?" Boyd chuckled, his russet beard nearly hiding his flash of a smile. "That isna how I would describe ye."

Everard slid to the cobbles before the busy tavern with a distinct thump, his boots stirring the dust. "Nae?"

Boyd studied him and scratched his whiskers. "Say I were tae take yer sword and cut ye doun at the knee tae a proper height . . ."

"To six feet or so?" Everard handed his reins to a stable lad who'd come flying toward them on bare feet, his ready grin tempering Everard's fractious mood.

Boyd winked. "Ye'd nae longer be the mightiest spear of Wedderburn . . . though ye'd still be the eldest and heir."

With a chuckle, Everard entered the Cockburn Arms, ducking beneath the low lintel. At his appearance, the smoky, ale-laced air held a distinct hush. A few bonnets were doffed, and then all seemed to sigh in relief as talk resumed. With government dragoons patrolling, one must be cautious. Which was why Everard routinely sent Boyd from village to village around the Borderlands to listen, question, observe. If King Geordie's men were indeed crawling about, he would ken firsthand.

Everard sought a corner table, his back to the wall and his eyes on the open door. Behind his left shoulder was a window into an alley that had been the sudden exit of a great many Scots in trouble with the law. Though he had no such difficulties, who knew when it might be needed? He was sometimes mistaken for his brother, though Davie was not quite so tall.

Boyd soon joined him after a quick perusal of the room. A serving maid bobbed a curtsy and brought ale, the pewter tankards chilled. Boyd swallowed a mouthful. Everard raised his tankard as two men at the next table did the same in a toast to "the king o'er the water," as the exiled Stuart was called.

"Plenty o' Jacobite feeling hereabout among common folk," Boyd said under his breath. "But has been for mony a year."

The tavern was full of coarse talk and laughter, black-faced miners from the coal pits crowding half the tables. It brought to mind Lady Hedley and her family's extensive collieries employing hundreds of miners across Northumbria. Word was the duke was an honest, generous laird, overseeing entire villages of miners' families.

Or was it simply hearsay?

Everard could find out. Quell his restlessness and ride south and learn firsthand. Trouble was, as Boyd jested, he could go nowhere unnoticed no matter how humbly clad. Word would soon travel about the sable-haired giant with the harmonic Borders lilt. Nor could he leave his father again. Rather he send Boyd in his stead.

"So, are you prepared for scouting Northumbria and leave nae stone unturned in regard to the duke and his daughter?" he asked Boyd.

"Och." Boyd set down his tankard, surprise sketched across his unshaven features. "Sae far? Ye must be jesting."

"Nae. If we're to bring the lass into the castle, needs be we find out how certain matters stand first."

Boyd took another drink. "But yer faither should make so weighty a decision, aye?"

Everard stared hard at him in brooding silence. Boyd, never guilty of a lazy intellect, surely read the reluctance in his master's eyes.

"Unless yer faither was nae longer here . . . then the matter would fall to ye." Boyd squinted as if weighing the possibility. "And ye dinna want to invite trouble beneath yer roof . . . or a traitor."

A fiddler struck a tune near the flickering hearth, the popular air "Katie Beardie." Everard tapped his toe beneath the scarred table, the wind rising as if aroused by the music and wafting through the window.

"Is it true what's said about roving fiddlers?" Boyd cast a glance over his shoulder. "That some are naught but Jacobite spies?"

"Aye, but like as not there are some who fiddle for King Geordie."

Everard drained his drink and brought an end to his toe tapping. "We'd best hie the two miles home. I've no inkling what awaits me."

7

*To conserve oneself in a Court is
to become an absolute Hero.*

JOHN EVELYN

**Bellbroke Castle
Northumberland, England**

The small dining room glittered with beeswax tapers, liveried footmen bringing dishes on quiet feet. Blythe sat to the right of her father at the damask-clad table that seemed somewhat foreign, she'd been away so long. Her stomach rumbled in unladylike fashion as grace was said. After so much rich French fare, it was heartening to see the table spread with many of her favorite Northumberland dishes—Cook's way of welcoming her home? Kippers and leek pudding. Stottie cake and clootie dumplings. Cheeses and cold meats.

"Have you ventured out much in my absence, Father?" she asked, placing her serviette in her lap. "You've always enjoyed making the rounds to our neighbors. I can't imagine you dining alone the entire time I've been gone."

Her father took a long drink of claret. "I've lately seen the Shaftoes and Forsters on business. As for entertainment, the Percys had a March assembly you missed."

"The Percys are such gracious hosts." She smiled, though her mind stayed fixed on what she'd overheard at the Château de Sceaux. "I recall you saying something about venturing to Lancashire."

"Ah yes, an occasional trip south to meet with certain gentlemen at the Unicorn Inn in Walton-le-Dale there. The Earl of Derwentwater and fellows."

She stilled at the young earl's mention. How casually her father spoke of him, as if he bore no painful association with her mother. The earl's own mother, in fact, had been rival for the king's affections, though she wasn't nobly born but a stage actress named Moll Davis.

Blythe shut the memory away. "I suppose your meetings have to do with estate matters?"

"Among other things." Father's mouth seemed sewn shut, her cue not to press the subject.

"I'm full of questions, being away so long," Blythe said, passing him a dish of dumplings. "My thoughts are with the villagers too. I've oft wondered how Widow Collingwood is faring with her eyesight nearly gone, and the Robsons' triplet babes who had fever. I suppose your factors bring you news of our neediest tenants."

He cut into his meat as she sampled the leek pudding. "They are all well, last time I inquired."

"Then there's little Jemmy Turnbull, who was run over by a wagon, and Mr. Elliot and the miners, who suffered firedamp from the last explosion."

Her father's thick brow raised. "How on earth do you remember such things?"

"I've a mind for details, much like Grandmother," she said, wishing he would address matters at home rather than abroad. What would he think of founding a society for the prevention of accidents in collieries? From his stern expression, she daren't mention it. Not yet.

Try as she might to pin him down, it seemed his thoughts ranged elsewhere, the silences heavy, even intimidating. How deep was he in this business of the Rising?

Taking a breath, she forged ahead. "Now that I'm home, I'm ready to resume riding and paying visits, something I missed amidst all my fan waving in France."

At last, a spark of interest lit his eyes. "There's a new foal sired by Galahad in the mews. A lively black filly with a white marking between her eyes."

"How delightful." She smiled. "What shall you name her?"

"That pleasure is yours. Something literary, I suppose." He sig-naled for a footman to bring more wine. "Borrowed from the hallowed halls of Camelot, perhaps."

"Then I shall go down to the stables in the morning." She cut a bite of fowl with her knife, a thousand thoughts galloping through her head. "Guinevere has been exercised faithfully in my absence, I hope."

"Of course." He set down his utensils though he'd eaten but half his supper. "I was expecting you'd rather spend time at your desk than gadding about the countryside."

"I read the post, then enjoyed two hours of calligraphy and a bit of Dante prior to supper. I've missed everything so much I shall likely flit about from place to place for a time."

"Then I must caution you against it." He leaned back in his chair, candlelight calling out weary lines about his eyes and the downward slant of his thin lips. In a few terse words he dismissed the servants and bade them close the dining room doors. "Now that you've returned, my fervent hope is to safeguard you from any danger."

So at last they came to the heart of it. She set down her own fork and looked at him, dread welling.

"Though we've lived quietly for some time, Catholic families such as ours are now being harassed with more fervor, even by our formerly civil Protestant neighbors."

Her lips parted in disbelief. "You've just provided new bells for Rothbury's Anglican Church and have been paying double taxes—"

"There's been talk Bellbroke could be searched, deprived of arms." His eyes grew grieved. "I could continue . . ."

"Nay." Appetite lost, she dotted her lips with her serviette. "'Tis not the homecoming I hoped for, though I suspect you sent me to France with the Traquair ladies to shield me from such to begin with."

"I did not want to make too much of it at the time, but now we are under such a threat I cannot keep silent nor allow you to ride about and resume your usual activities."

"So I must keep to home," she said, not wanting to add to his worry with a contrary attitude. "Of course, I have plenty to do at my desk. Perhaps this shall all pass quickly and we can live peaceably like before."

"You should know there are said to be government spies in our midst, working for the new Hanoverian king."

"Spies?"

He leaned in, nearly knocking over his wine glass in agitation. "They've been known to turn tenants against their own masters."

"But our tenants are and have ever been loyal. We've treated them fairly, even generously—"

"And how quickly 'tis forgotten if they've been threatened by outsiders—or bribed in some cases."

She took a drink of wine, her stomach churning. Beyond the windows the sun was setting, the rolling meadowlands to the south a brilliant reddish gold.

"How I hate to spoil your homecoming with such dire talk." He drummed his fingers atop the damask cloth. "But I could not wait another moment lest you slip out and bring harm to yourself in the coming days."

"You are talking about a coming rebellion, a battle over who will be king." Her mind assembled the pieces of this unwelcome puzzle. "I overheard your name mentioned by a gentleman at a court ball. It concerned the Northumbrian Jacobites."

"Matters are coming to a head. Though I pray without ceasing that peace will reign."

Peace? It seemed a fool's wish.

"How involved are you?" She had pushed the matter to the back

43

of her mind, not wanting to dwell on all the implications, but his intensity told her she could do so no longer. "I would know all of it, Father."

His beleaguered gaze roamed the blue silk walls and lingered on the closed doors. Did he suspect the servants of spying? In turn, she looked about, dismissing the portrait of her mother above the mantel, its very presence a testament to her father's forgiveness. Painted by the court artist Peter Lely, it captured the duchess in amber silk adorned with diamonds. Not the simpler portrait of her as a shepherdess, pretending to be something she was not, that once hung at Whitehall.

The gilded harlot, she'd been called.

Buried so many years, Clementine Hedley had no inkling of the turmoil in this dining room at present, though she'd caused a great deal of it in the past.

"Say no more, Father." Blythe's voice was flat and hushed with none of the animation of moments before. "I have no heart for it tonight."

8

It's difficult to draw pure water from a dirty well.

GAELIC PROVERB

Wedderburn Castle
Berwickshire, Scotland

E verard was home. But it didn't feel like home. Not with his father's life leeching like brose from a cracked bowl. Home as he'd known it for more than three and thirty years was past. On the other side of that ancient, battle-hardened facade might be grim news that would turn the world as he knew it tapsalteerie.

"I'll see to the horses, milord," Boyd told him as they dismounted before Wedderburn Castle's timeworn entrance.

With a nod, Everard passed through the castle's semicircular arch with its thick, iron-studded double doors to a small inner courtyard dominated by a gnarled rowan tree. Flagstones beneath his feet soon gave way to stone steps leading to the castle foyer, where a magnificent cedar staircase rose to a gallery. The wood's aroma mingled with beeswax and turpentine as it threaded the chill air. He began his climb upward, passing immense tapestries and portraits of prior Humes, intent on the door to his father's chambers that bore the Hume crest.

"Lord Fast."

Everard halted his climb and turned back, looking down on Wedderburn's diminutive housekeeper. Mrs. Candlish wore a bright plaid about her shoulders. She'd been in their service so long she even adopted their surname at times. "Welcome home, milord. Your faither is not in his chambers but in the old garden, I'm pleased to report."

A beat of hope took hold. Everard came back down the stairs, somewhat disbelieving. When he'd left, his father was bedfast, sleeping more than waking, and taking little meat or drink.

From a side corridor Munro entered the foyer clad in a black suit, a golden chain about his neck denoting his stewardship of Wedderburn Castle. His aged face wore a smile. "Ah, Lord Fast. I trust yer time in Edinburgh was productive."

"Aye," Everard said. "I'm eager to bring the laird news. But what of my brothers?"

"Orin is in the schoolroom with his tutors," Mrs. Candlish said quickly, as if not wanting to delay him. "Bernard has ridden into the village. And last I heard, Ronan and the twins were out hawking in the deer park."

"All is well otherwise?"

"Indeed, milord," Munro said with a nod.

Their apparent cheer put him at ease. "To my faither, then."

With deferential nods, they disappeared as he sought the passageway that would take him to the garden. There he found the laird in a wheeled chair, seated in a sunny corner, an attendant not far. The laird's silvered head was bowed, his eyes closed.

"Leave us," Everard told the maidservant, who gave a nod and hastened away.

His father raised up at the sound of his voice. Had he been sleeping? Everard knelt and clasped his father's enormous hand, the thin, wrinkled skin like crumpled linen paper, his grip limp where it had once been ironlike.

"Ah, my son." Pleasure warmed his voice. "You've come back."

"Nae better homecoming than to find you out here in the fresh air, Faither."

The laird gave a fleeting smile. "After so long a winter, 'tis good to feel the warmth. But tell me, what of your travels? You've returned sooner than I expected."

Everard let go of his hand and sat upon a near bench. "I did not want to leave you long. Besides, Edinburgh holds few charms for me." "'Tis the fearsome stench, I suppose. And hordes of folk all together." His father struggled to sit up straight. "But what I'd give to see it once more . . . feel your mither's presence and pleasure in the place she so loved. Her garden in the Canongate especially."

Everard blinked at the sudden sting in his eyes. Rarely did he soften or give vent to his feelings. Years of soldiering had bred it out of him. But seeing his father fade and struggle required a different kind of courage. "I bring you news about David and Calysta . . . and from your old friend Northumbria."

"I am anxious to hear it." His father brightened though his words came a bit breathless. "For the life of me, I cannot imagine the reason for the duke's summons. It's been many a year since we've crossed paths."

Everard lapsed into Lowland Gaelic. "You and Màthair were godparents to his only daughter, aye?"

"Och, once upon a time. I last saw her when she was a wee lass. A lively, enchanting child. Your mither doted on her, having all sons. But I would hardly ken her as a grown woman."

"'Tis the grown woman Northumbria is concerned with."

"Ah . . . Lady Blythe."

Blythe. Everard leaned back against a sun-warmed wall. A comely name. He'd never heard the like.

"She is not wed?" his father asked.

"Nae. Nary a suitor, Northumbria claims. Of late Lady Hedley is—or was—in France at Château de Saint-Germain-en-Laye."

"With the exiled Stuarts awaiting another restoration." The laird's snow-white brows knit together. "What news have you of the king o'er the water?"

Everard could not keep his mockery at bay. "That the French

47

court is in a chaos similar to that in Genesis before the creation of the world."

His father's chest shook with laughter. "God help the Stuarts. Though they seem the rightful heirs, one wonders. God Himself sets rulers upon thrones, does He not? And topples those He wills."

Everard paused. How to broach David's suspected Jacobite allegiance?

"'Let every soul be subject unto the higher powers. For there is no power but of God: the powers that be are ordained of God.'" His father's voice filled the warm air as thunderously as John Knox's himself. "'Whosoever therefore resisteth the power, resisteth the ordinance of God: and they that resist shall receive to themselves damnation.'"

Waiting for the familiar sermon to end, Everard fixed his eyes on a cluster of his mother's beloved tuberoses near his boots. Blue, the color she'd held dear.

His father cleared his throat. "Northumbria's last letter was a few years ago. I recall it if only because it was unusual."

"Unusual," Everard echoed. "I suppose her ladyship is not only sole heiress but the fairest rose of Northumbria."

"Nae, not beautiful. Brilliant. Which may explain her lack of suitors."

"What means you?"

"She's said to be something of a scholar, schooled like the royal women of old." Respect laced his father's words. "A linguist and translator. A writer of some merit."

Looking at the castle's foremost turret, Everard raked his mind for all the implications. Noblewomen were usually well educated. Schooled in affluence, at least. "She speaks fluent French and Italian, then."

"And Greek and Hebrew and Latin. I may even be overlooking a few."

"She sounds more fit for a religious order. Whoever she is, she's a damsel in distress."

"What is her faither the duke wanting?"

"A refuge. A hideaway here if things take a turn."

"If there's another uprising, you mean, and the Stuarts attempt to take the throne."

Everard gave an aggrieved nod. "Though he did not say it, I'd wager Northumbria is in league with Rebel leaders, supplying them with funds, mayhap arms and mounts, helping plan a landing on the coast nearest him. 'Tis nae secret he's a staunch Jacobite like most of the Northumbrian nobles surrounding him." He took a mental step back to the oyster cellar. "In Edinburgh, he voiced a fear a mob might storm Bellbroke and other neighboring Catholic estates suspected of supporting a Stuart restoration. In short, he fears for his daughter's life."

"She's had a hard lot of it, Lady Blythe, without a mither. And the only child of a cuckolded faither."

"What?"

"You've never heard the tale of the Duchess of Northumbria? Once it was the talk of Britain from the basest taverns to the loftiest palaces." His father paused as if wondering how much to tell. "Lady Clementine Hedley was lauded as the most beautiful woman in Britannia. But with the passing of King Charles and the retiring of his seraglio, it's been mostly forgotten." He shifted in his chair, a grimace of pain crossing his face. Or did it have to do with the memory? "They wed young, Musgrave and Clementine. 'Twas arranged by their families amid elaborate negotiations like so many noble marriages. The duke had yet to come into his own, with his faither still living."

Everard nearly winced. *The duke had yet to come into his own.* As had he. He looked at the ailing laird, wondering how much time they had left and feeling the tick of some eternal, unseen clock.

"Soon after they wed, they went to court, she as a maid of honor to the queen, he as a gentleman of the Duke of York's bedchamber. There they met your mither, who was another maid of honor. All the libertines and courtesans of the day surrounded them. 'Odd's

49

fish,' as the king used to say. Never was there a man so out of his element as Northumbria."

Everard tried to picture it. He ken what was coming before his father spelled it out.

"The duchess's fatal flaws were her face and figure. Everyone said she had no equal. Of course, she soon caught the king's eye. Nae beautiful woman escaped his notice, be it the orange girls and actresses at the King's Theater or the titled women at court. Charles took what and whom he wanted with nae thought to the consequences. The duchess's family said they were honored by the king's 'preferment' shown to their daughter."

"*Preferment?* A fancy word for adultery and debauchery."

"Sin oft comes disguised glittering and crowned, not reeking and clad in rags." His father took a labored breath. "Of course, Northumbria felt otherwise, but his opinion hardly mattered. Soon the duchess became Charles's maîtresse-en-titre and was given preferred apartments at Whitehall. A shrewd if unscrupulous woman, she was soon orchestrating affairs of state."

"What of her husband?"

"The duke returned to Bellbroke, and they lived apart till the king died, at which point the duchess was turned out of the palace and returned home to Northumberland."

"She had nae children with the king?" Everard asked. Charles had fathered a large brood, many of them born to women who'd gained lands, titles, and possessions still in evidence. But the "merry monarch," as he was called, had never gained a legitimate heir to the throne.

"She bore Charles a son who died in infancy. Lady Blythe was born years later after, she'd reunited with the duke. Due to your mither's friendship with the duchess when they were at court, and our own Catholicism at the time, we were chosen as godparents. I recall how distraught your mither was upon hearing the duchess had died soon after her daughter's birth. Clementine Hedley was but eight and twenty and had come to court a decade earlier. Your mither even sent word to Northumbria, asking him to consider letting us raise the lass."

Everard pondered it. His mother, surrounded by so many sons, wishing for a lass not her own. "But the duke refused and raised his daughter alone?"

"With the help of his mither, the dowager duchess, a fine woman known for her faith."

It seemed the only silver thread in a sordid tapestry that had led to the eventual downfall of the Stuart dynasty. Everard shook his head, hard-pressed to imagine it. An unfaithful wife. A dissolute king. A duke who stood by his duchess even when she'd cuckolded him before an entire kingdom.

"Your mither said the duchess died a broken, penitent woman."

Had she? Was that not the last Sabbath sermon? *Be not deceived; God is not mocked: for whatsoever a man soweth, that shall he also reap. For he that soweth to the flesh shall of the flesh reap corruption.*

Lady Hedley, a royal harlot—unlike the tawdry limmers on foreign soil. Those whisky-sated, hurried assignations among soldiers and lasses were brief and soon forgotten. Everard had asked the Lord's forgiveness for the one he'd had his first year afield. What came harder was forgiving himself.

His father continued as if telling an old story. "They oft exchanged letters, your mither and the duchess."

"Somehow I cannot imagine such," Everard said. His mother had been a lady in every sense of the word.

"But all that is history, and we are in the very pressing present." His father's gaze sharpened. "What say you about the matter?"

Everard lifted his shoulders in a shrug. "Northumbria begs you consider and send him word as quickly as you can."

"That is not what I asked you."

Everard met his father's faded blue eyes, his resistance roaring though his stoicism stayed steadfast. "Meaning if you were not here, what would I do in your stead?"

"Aye, that is the very heart of it."

Indeed it was, and Everard wanted no part of it. His hands and thoughts were brimful of David and Calysta, a complication he wanted to spare the laird. That tangle was worry enough. His father didn't need the thorny plight of an unknown noblewoman.

"I've rarely seen you at sixes and sevens, son." The laird cleared his throat. "What say you?"

"I say nae." Everard rubbed his jaw. "I want nae Catholic Jacobite lass here. And I am certain Lady Hedley has nae wish to be sent to the lair of Protestant Lowland Scots, all of whom are male. Such seems deadly dangerous."

"The duke is nae fool." The laird's frown gave way to a bemused chuckle. "Perhaps he has matrimony in mind more than her safe-keeping."

"Would a devout faither want such an unholy union? A Papist and a Presbyterian?"

"You realize Lady Blythe brings all the wealth of Northumbria as her dowry."

"A dowry neither needed nor coveted."

"Marriages are oft based on that alone." His father squinted in the sunlight. "You'd do well to consider such. My heir needs a wife and children. The Hume lineage must continue. I am, though I am loath to say it, not long for this world."

Everard stood, wearying of such talk even if his father showed a sudden, surprising rallying. "'Tis a Scots lass I seek, Faither. Not a sassenach. Not an Englishwoman."

9

Through his mane and tail the high wind sings,
Fanning the hairs, who wave like feather'd wings.

WILLIAM SHAKESPEARE

Bellbroke Castle
Northumberland, England

As a cock crowed in the courtyard, Blythe put her arms around her mare's silky neck. Guinevere nickered softly. The scent of hay and horseflesh was like perfume to a woman who'd been raised in the saddle, the earthy stables a solace. Never had Blythe imagined such liberties would come to a halt.

"I miss you, dear girl," she said in low tones. "For now, I cannot take you out, though a finer spring morn cannot be had."

She let go only to have Guinevere nuzzle her, much like the foal with its mother in a near stall. At the mare's continued nickering, Blythe reached into her pocket and brought out a wizened apple from the castle's cellar. The pippin disappeared with a few crunching bites, and Blythe moved down the dimly lit walk leading to the coach house.

There in a large stall stood a strange coach. Not the sleek black one her father favored with the Hedley arms on the door and a gilt crown on the roof, nor the subdued mourning chaise beside it used after her grandmother's passing. She'd never seen this contraption.

It was obviously newly made, the great wheels hardly showing a speck of wear. Standing on tiptoe, she peered into a window to find the interior finely upholstered in yellow silk, the twin lamps on the front corners sparkling and unmarred by sooty lights.

Curiosity overcame her normal reticence. She called to a passing groom, "What can you tell me about this coach, Billy?"

The lad approached, eyes on the object in question. "Built by a coachmaker in London town, milady. Smaller. Sleeker. To be kept in readiness should it be needed."

With a nod, Blythe turned away, hoping she'd never sit upon that silken seat. So Father had all in readiness should the worst happen.

She returned to the castle, finding Elodie sitting beneath an arbor near the house, altering a French gown Blythe had given her. Two of the gardeners were at work trimming and planting among the hedgerows a stone's throw away. Blythe looked past them toward the ponds and woods where she might have gone riding, trying to put down a niggle of discontent.

At morning prayers, she'd confessed her impatience and disappointment, her outright restlessness. By now she'd have been visiting the neediest tenants, gone into the village of Rothbury for market day, reacquainted herself with ploughland and meadow and woods.

As if sensing her disquiet, Elodie called to her, "Are you in need of anything, milady?"

My freedom.

Forcing a smile, Blythe turned in to the rose garden with a reassuring, "Nary a thing."

Perhaps by summer, when the roses were abloom and at their peak, matters would have settled down. In the night she'd lain awake trying to recall the Stuarts' tumultuous history. There had been rebellions before, but she had been too small to remember much. It hardly seemed likely there would be another, yet the exiled French court existed to honor the ousted Stuarts, hoping to return them to the throne. Instead, Britain had just crowned a Hanoverian named George.

Such musings seemed no more substantial than moorland mist, like the wandering Stuart prince. Yet she sensed in her father a heightened wariness, a secrecy she could not penetrate. He wanted to make her aware of the danger but would not burden her with details. And she dare not ask.

"Welcome home, milady." Armed with shears and shovel, the gardeners gave a little bow. Father and son, they might have been brothers but for a few wrinkles.

"I see no sign of Old Man Winter, thanks to your careful tending," she told them, admiring an heirloom rosebush that had seen a hearty pruning.

The elder disappeared and returned to hold out a hyacinth bouquet, a mass of purples and blues. "'Tis the Celestine variety, newly arrived from Holland. But I suppose ye had your fill of flowers in France."

She brought them to her nose, breathing in their sweet fragrance. Delighted, she thanked him. "These beauties are grown behind glass in château gardens all winter. But none are as lovely as ours out in the open."

They returned to their work, and she walked on with her bouquet, down stone steps to a wide fountain that spilled into a second and third before emptying into a small lake. Swans glided across the mirror-like surface, smaller cygnets in tow. The scene was idyllic. It bespoke utter peace.

Belying the whirlwind inside her.

Sitting down on a bench, she exchanged her bouquet for her grandmother's rosary. The glass prayer beads, bound by a knotted cord, were beloved, given to her at Elinor Hedley's death. Bending her head, Blythe made the sign of the cross as she clutched the tiny silver crucifix, the Latin words on her lips spoken countless times before.

"Salve Regina, Mater misericordiae, vita dulcedo et spes nostrae salve . . ."

The wind tugged at her skirts and the sun made her drowsy, but she prayed for long minutes, seeking calm, letting the beauty of her surroundings assuage her. Perhaps she needed to talk with Father Beverly, further pour out her heart, once he returned. He'd left before dawn, making his rounds to other Catholic families in secret. The Penal Laws against Catholics were harsh yet seldom enforced . . . but could be if the occasion warranted. Therein lay the threat.

They were no longer in France, where they could practice their faith in relative safety and security, not secrecy. If James Francis Edward Stuart was crowned king of Britain, would he allow for differences in faith? Was intolerance not part of the reason his father had lost the crown to begin with? The fact he was Catholic and a Protestant king was wanted?

Was any sort of successful Rising naught but a lunatic's dream?

10

I myself am best when least in company.

WILLIAM SHAKESPEARE

Fast Castle
Berwickshire Coast, Scotland

The jaunt to the coast was only a few miles, but for wee Orin Hume it no doubt seemed longer. Everard, aware of the lad's drooping spirits, purposed to remove him from the castle. Since his youngest brother lacked his own mount, he rode pillion atop Lancelot, his arms firmly around Everard's middle.

Slight of build—teasingly referred to as the twig of Wedderburn and not a spear—Orin was the essence of his Gaelic name. Fair. Pale. Light. Not dark and sturdy like his six older brothers but a mirror of the mother who had birthed him and died of a fever days after.

Dismissing the dark thought, Everard dwelt on the bannocks and cheese in his knapsack and the bond he and Orin shared.

"Brother, I am glad 'tis spring," Orin said. "My thoughts grow dark as the dungeon when winter overstays its welcome."

Everard chuckled at his poetic phrasing and prodded Lancelot forward, past Wedderburn's back gates and onto open moorland. Despite the air of frailty about him, Orin had an agile intellect. His tutors could hardly keep up with him. It made Everard proud even if his other brothers teased the lad mercilessly. And then there was Davie, who was downright cruel.

Orin continued, "'Be blyth in hairt for ony adventure.'"

Blythe.

Everard kneed Lancelot's sides as if to outrun the thought. Could the noble lass be like her name? Staunching curiosity, he slowed and returned his mind to Orin twisting uncomfortably in the saddle. "Would you rather walk awhile?"

"Oh, aye," Orin replied, already half off the horse.

Once on the ground, Everard grasped for a bit of verse. "'O, that that earth, which kept the world in awe, should patch a wall to expel the winter flaw.'"

Orin smiled, revealing a missing front tooth. "Act 5, scene 1. *Hamlet Prince of Denmark.*"

"Your tutors are to be applauded."

"I'm fond of the auld bard. Shakespeare goes easily into my head." He screwed up his face as if having tasted rancid cider. "Unlike Chaucer."

"But both are needed medicine, aye? To make a whole, well-educated lad?"

"So Faither says." Orin sobered, his bright eyes blue as forget-me-nots. "When he dies, will you send my tutors away?"

Everard looked hard at him. "What trittil-trattil is this? Would you forsake all your learning? Besides, Faither still lives."

"The servants say he'll be buried by Michaelmas and you'll be Lord Fast nae longer but the new laird."

Michaelmas was generous. He nearly winced. Would the dread of death never abate? "As for your tutors, they are needed awhile longer. Even Malcolm and Alistair keep at their studies, and they're older than you. Faither insists upon it."

"Well, I shan't forget Faither like I did Mither." The entwined regret and relief in the lad's tone was striking. An old soul, Orin.

"'Tis not that you've forgotten her," Everard said more gently. "You were newly born. You hadn't the chance to know her."

"Then tell me what you remember."

Everard weighed his answer. He'd been on the continent fighting when she'd sickened and died. Nor had he much to do with Orin, who'd been spirited away by a wet nurse till he was nearly two and kept to the castle nursery. When Everard returned to Wedderburn after the war, the lad hadn't even known him.

Once over the rise, Everard slowed and answered. "Mither . . . she was beautiful. Fair as you. Bright as a star. Her laughter filled the castle day and night." Lest his words sound too much like a fairy tale, he added, "She had a frichtsome temper at times."

The lad turned his freckled face to the sky, squinting in the sunlight. "Why did she die so young?"

"She was not so young, Orin. She was over twoscore years."

"Nurse says I will see her again in heaven and she will be even more beautiful. And she will remember me."

"Nurse speaks truth, aye. And when Faither joins her, they shall have a merry time of it. Though death is melancholy for us here below, 'tis more a celebration there."

Orin nodded, squaring his small shoulders as if staring down an unseen foe. "'If I must die, I will encounter darkness as a bride and hug it in mine arms.'"

Everard looked askance at him. "*Hamlet* again?"

"Nae." Orin's freckled face grew less somber. "*Measure for Measure*."

They walked on long enough to stretch their legs. "Needs be we ride the rest of the way," Everard said, returning Orin to the saddle.

In time, Lancelot came to a graceful stop at Everard's pull on the reins. Before them stretched the North Sea, the wind rifling the surface of the deep as it did Orin's silky hair, which fell in flaxen wisps about his thin shoulders. Everard preferred windless days when a hallowed hush held the coast captive. In midsummer, the sloped, grassy expanse to Fast Castle's ruins was smothered in a haze of purple heather. A ruined gatehouse on the landward end was his aim, but to get there one had to come down a long, barren slope and navigate the broken drawbridge before braving the thin path to the castle's beleaguered tower.

After dismounting again, Everard hobbled Lancelot and left Orin on the hillside.

"Is it true Mary, Queen of Scots, stayed at Fast Castle on the way to her wedding?" Orin called after him.

"She did indeed, but it wasna a heap of rubble back then," Everard said over his shoulder as he started down the hillside. "Someday you'll accompany me to explore what's left of it. For now, stand watch and take care lest the gulls rob you of your victuals."

With a nod, Orin dug into the knapsack as Lancelot tore at the greening grass a few feet away. Nearer the ruins, Everard felt a beat of caution as he began to cross the narrow, ancient approach, sending a rattle of stones over the twin cliffs that hedged him on both sides.

He came here only when his thoughts were in a tangle and needed unraveling. He came here to pray. He often left calmer, with steadier purpose and a clearer head. But now, with his father's death imminent, an errant brother at large, and a lady's fate to be decided . . .

He soon gained the castle's seaward end and keep, and he took his usual place, leaning against a window that still offered a stunning view. Though the sun was warm, the wind tore at him, pressing his bulk against the old stone that had such a turbulent history and whose name he bore.

How quickly fortunes—and families—rose and fell. Let this crumbling hulk be a reminder of all that was at stake. His father, too old and sick to make a decisive stand for either the new Hanoverian king or the old Stuart one, was a blessed bystander. David had, it seemed, thrown in his lot with the Jacobites. Coupled with his rash nature, that boded ill. As the second-born son, what would David's traitorous allegiance look like to the new Hanoverian king? Rather, what impact would it have on the Humes of Wedderburn?

If there was an uprising and Everard himself raised the Rebel standard alongside David and lost, his estates would be forfeited, his titles taken. Spared a hanging or a merciless drawing and quartering, he'd be beheaded instead. And his brothers, even if they did not take sides, would be left homeless and penniless. Destitute. Perhaps even transported to the American colonies or elsewhere.

But if the Stuarts won . . .

He folded his arms, his gaze on a kestrel's soaring flight. If the king o'er the water regained the throne, the Humes would be lauded for their allegiance, garnering more lands and titles, perhaps even a place at court, though the latter turned his stomach. Fawning courtier he was not.

Still, to royalty they'd ever been tied. The Humes had received a grant from King James I of Scotland in the year 1413 to become the strongest magnate in southeast Scotland. Yet Hume loyalties had wavered over the centuries. They'd even fought against James III in the uprising that led to his death.

"Brother!"

Orin's voice floated down to him across the vast expanse of land separating them, even over the roar of the sea. Turning, Everard saw the lad picking his way down the steep slope. Was he intent on the old drawbridge?

Och! In a trice, Everard crossed the rubble of the castle's interior to find Orin staring over the cliffside at the front of the old bridge. Despite his wee size, he had a manly curiosity.

"Come nae further!" Everard shouted, but the wind picked up his voice and flung it back to him.

Wariness stiffening his slight form, Orin crept nearer danger. Everard broke into a run, a dozen horrendous outcomes flashing through his head. If he shouted again and scared him, the lad might slip and fall . . .

Winded more by alarm than exertion, Everard crossed the thin causeway that led to the sunny hill. Orin's back was to him. With a final run, Everard snatched him up out of harm's way, crushing him to his chest. Burying his face in the lad's shoulder, he breathed a simple prayer. *Bethankit.*

"Dragoons!" Orin squirmed to be free. "British dragoons are coming from the south."

Everard stared at him even as he set him on his feet. "Not dragons . . . dragoons?"

A bit breathless, Orin said, "Sea serpents from the murky depths would be more welcome!"

Taking in the rise that cut off their view of moorland beyond and its red-coated soldiers, Everard clasped his arm. "I fear you might take a tumble. A great many slippery stones await even the surefooted."

"And thunderheads." Orin motioned toward a bank of clouds hovering to the west as they hurried up the hill.

The coming storm was as unwelcome as King Geordie's troops. But Everard refused to let Orin sense his concern. "Once, not so long ago, I saw lightning strike the castle's keep. Even a dragon would have been afraid."

"I wish I could have seen such," Orin said, holding tight to his hand. "Next time I want to stand at the castle's seaward end and be strong and brave like you."

"More foolhardy than brave, mayhap."

At last they reached Lancelot, who was sated and drinking from a watery hole.

"I saved you a bannock," Orin said. "And some cheese."

But Everard had no appetite. Once mounted, he looked back to fix the castle in his thoughts. He wasn't sure when he'd return, and his regard for the ruin never dimmed.

They cantered toward the main road leading to Eyemouth, the thunderheads amassing overhead like cannonballs. Moorland stretched in all directions, bare of all but a few trees along watercourses and scattered cottages—and a large number of scarlet-coated government troops, some of them on horseback, a great many afoot.

"Where are they headed?" Orin asked, his gaze steadfast.

"I ken not," Everard answered.

The British army was said to be widely scattered, with troops in Ireland and other riotous parts of England, especially London. Many of them were new recruits. Had they now crossed the border? Come to keep watch over the Scottish Rebels? All the while absconding with horses from noble stables and stealing provisions.

Schooling his disgust, a prayer on his lips, Everard turned away from the sight and headed another, safer direction toward home.

11

Make tea not war.

UNKNOWN

Bellbroke Castle
Northumberland, England

An invitation to tea at Wellinghurst Hall arrived for Blythe. But would Father let her go?

A few miles distant, the estate was home to a longtime Northumberland family like themselves. Sir Jon Wellinghurst was usually in London on business, though his family preferred the country. Blythe felt a qualm that she hadn't sent a note round to Charlotte, Sir Jon's daughter, upon her return. A dear friend deserved better.

"What have you there, milady?" Elodie came into the bedchamber carrying a newly beribboned bonnet, a spring creation smothered in silk violets and lace.

Blythe looked up with a smile. "An invitation to tea on the morrow at Wellinghurst Hall."

"No doubt Miss Charlotte has missed you and wants to hear all about your stay in France."

No doubt. But France already seemed like a distant dream, the present pressing in with all its messy complications.

"Usually we go riding together, but . . ."

Elodie nodded sympathetically. "Riding is frowned upon, but tea may be more welcome."

"I shall ask Father." She was used to doing as she wished, so the notion of asking sat strangely. "You'll want to accompany me, of course."

"Oh yes. Might you wear this winsome hat?" Elodie held the creation aloft.

"You're a wonder with millinery." Blythe admired it, particularly the flowers Elodie had stitched so cleverly they looked lifelike. "I've not seen anything to compare with your creations anywhere."

"I once had such a hat and have now re-created it. I was hoping you'd fancy it like I do."

"'Tis yours, then, since it has meaning for you. Only I might borrow it on occasion," Blythe said.

Elodie was no less than an impoverished gentlewoman, in their employ since Blythe came of age, the both of them now eight and twenty. Though Elodie's station had changed, her pleasures had not, and tea at Wellinghurst Hall was one of them. Blythe refused to address her by her surname, Bell, as was the custom. Elodie was a true lady's companion, not a servant, as evidenced by her genteel manner and speech.

Elodie's pale face creased in a smile. "Shall I ready a tea gown, then?"

"For the both of us, please. I don't think Father will object. Wellinghurst Hall is not far."

The ride to Wellinghurst Hall was executed with haste in the coach that lacked the ostentatious ducal arms.

Alone with Elodie in the carriage, Blythe ran a hand over the shiny, upholstered seat. "Though the coach is unmarked, the small army of grooms accompanying us is sure to draw notice and surely defeat Father's discreet intention."

Elodie seemed to work to suppress a wry smile. "I do believe every hand is riding along with us save the stable master."

"I suppose they are all armed." Blythe sighed. "'Tis rather embarrassing. The danger is exaggerated, much like rumors of Risings and such. Can we not go back to the way things were prior to our going to France?"

Elodie bit her lip. "Your father is a wise man, milady. And very protective of your well-being."

Elodie, on the other hand, had no family to speak of, forcing her into service.

"Forgive me," Blythe said. "Never for one moment do I forget how rare is the air I breathe."

As if to illustrate her point, they turned out of Bellbroke Hall's elaborate gates and soon passed the largest Hedley colliery—Allhallows—which belched smoke night and day. Countless stone cottages plastered with lime, their blue slate roofs distinct, were scattered on the hills surrounding the colliery and leased by the lead miners. Small villages for miners' widows had been built at her grandmother's insistence a decade before, beginning with Allhallows.

Other than a few older children moving coal out of the mines in wagons and carts, a great many proud, fiercely loyal men did the brutal, filthy work. The duke forbade women and younger children from laboring alongside the pitmen. Colliery explosions were feared, the Hedley pits having suffered a few such calamities. The memory of the worst disasters wrung Blythe's heart.

Their coach passed into dense forest, sycamores and oaks so old they seemed to have stood since the creation of time. Her father's timberworks were vast, but it was Cheviot Hills that stole her heart. The beauty of the uplands, thick with sheep and shepherds, moors and watercourses, stole her breath.

"Do you ever wonder what 'tis like far beyond Hadrian's Wall, milady?" Elodie was looking north out the coach window. "Are the Scots as uncivilized as 'tis said?"

"The Traquair ladies certainly aren't." A few less-than-complimentary opinions about Scots paraded through Blythe's head. Much that was desultory had been written about them—embellished, she'd always thought. "The Scottish courtiers in France were rather charming."

The coach rattled across a bridge and swung right, taking them uphill past an avenue of lime trees, terraced gardens, and statuary. The facade of Wellinghurst Hall was as grand as its name, sunlight striking the glass of its high Palladian windows. The same architect had designed Bellbroke's latest addition, thus both mansions bore striking similarities.

Once out of the coach, Blythe linked arms with Elodie. Charlotte's maid met them on the steps and escorted them to the gardens. "Since the day is so fine, Miss Charlotte thought tea in the folly would suit."

And what a folly it was—a white marble temple with pillars on all sides, in honor of Flora, the Roman goddess of spring. Reached by a meandering path and a little rise, the folly boasted a view of the formal gardens on one side and rolling meadowland on the other.

A tea table had been laid, and Charlotte was beckoning. Nary a servant was to be seen. Had she purposed to be private, out of the hearing of any help?

"At last you've come home!" Charlotte hurried down the marble steps to greet them, her yellow gown the very hue of the lady's bedstraw bordering the walkways. "I feared France would keep you."

"Forgive me for not sending word I'd returned." Blythe accompanied her and Elodie up the steps. "Our homecoming quite wore me out. But finally, here we are." She plucked a small vial from her pocket. "I've not returned empty-handed."

"Je suis ravi, merci!" Charlotte said, examining the gift before opening it and sprinkling some on her wrists. "White jasmine? It smells divine."

"From the perfumed court, where a great many ladies soak themselves in cologne rather than bathe."

Charlotte's amusement turned inquiring. "You do not miss it?"

"Nary a whiff," Blythe replied, her words meeting with their muted laughter.

"Come, the tea must not grow cold."

They sat down, the spread before them both savory and sweet. Dainty squares of bread and butter, jam, scones, and sweetmeats adorned crystal dishes, a silver pitcher of milk alongside silver nippers crowning the sugar bowl.

Charlotte poured the amber liquid into warmed porcelain cups. "So tell me, did you meet the would-be Stuart king? And is he as tall and handsome as 'tis said?"

"I know not. His Majesty had left St. Germaine," Blythe said. "He's rumored to be residing at Châteauneuf."

"He and his mother continue to be sorely bereaved about the passing of Princess Louise," Elodie added with a sigh.

Blythe took a sip of tea. Not even royalty was immune from the smallpox. "Perhaps that is why his mother is en route to join him for the summer. The Traquair ladies are in her retinue. When they return to Britain, I'm sure they'll tell us all about it."

"Lady Catherine and Lady Mary?" Charlotte stirred cream into her tea. "Seeking titled husbands at court, I suppose."

"Many are," Blythe said.

"But not you?" A shadow passed over Charlotte's face. "I still think John Manners, Duke of Rutland, wronged you. His family, rather."

Another reason Father had sent her to the continent, Blythe supposed. When marriage negotiations failed last winter, he'd wanted to spare her the embarrassment. The only saving grace in the entire debacle was that she'd not met the duke, so she hadn't a gentleman's face to haunt her, just a sudden inexplicable refusal.

Blythe shrugged. "With such a name, how could they possibly want to be blackened by the Hedleys' past?"

"Manners, indeed. They have none." Charlotte was forever loyal. "Surely there was a wealth of gentlemen at the French court."

Blythe darted a sheepish look at Elodie, who'd borne many a recounting of every failed suitor while in France. "I was beset by doddering old dukes, indebted earls, and a libertine or two. The pool of worthy Catholic suitors is quite small."

Charlotte took a scone. "There seems a frightful number of fortune hunters these days."

This was Blythe's ongoing worry, that her dowry—and her father's fortune—would be squandered. Given that possibility, however remote, she'd do all she could to prevent it from happening in the first place. "And you? You have both a face *and* fortune. But more than that, you have all the sterling qualities that will make you a wonderful wife."

"High praise from an old friend who's seen all my faults and foibles." The spots of color in Charlotte's cheeks only made her prettier. "It seems Father and his lawyers are considering a match with one of the Perkinses."

"Of Ufton Court in Berkshire?"

Charlotte's smile bespoke her pleasure. "I shan't meet Arthur till all is in order, of course. But he's known to be a gentleman of competent estate and good character, and a Catholic. He's even penned me a love letter of sorts . . . and sent a painted miniature." She reached into her pocket and produced a small oval. "He's rather handsome, is he not?"

Elodie and Blythe leaned in and studied the blond gentleman captured in watercolor. "Rather?" Blythe exclaimed just as Elodie said, "Undoubtedly!"

Charlotte blushed a brighter pink, and Blythe's gaze lingered on her honeyed hair and the charming cleft in her chin that marked all the Wellinghursts. "I'm happy for you. A worthy match, though I shall miss you sorely."

"And I the both of you. You've been the dearest friends I could ever hope to have."

"To the future mistress of Ufton Court!" Blythe raised her cup in a toast. "As such, you'll make many new friends but shan't forget the old. Once you're settled, Elodie and I shall come visit, I promise."

"Please do." Charlotte took out a lace-edged handkerchief and dabbed her eyes. "But let's speak of other, more pressing matters. Like how to dispose of doddering dukes and indebted earls and libertines."

"'Tis a simple matter." Blythe smiled, remembering a particularly amusing moment with one unsavory suitor. "I simply say I'm contemplating a nunnery."

Charlotte put a finger to her lips lest she laugh and spew her tea. After swallowing with difficulty, she said, "You jest."

"I should hope so," Elodie said, looking rather sad.

"On my honor. There's such peace to be had there. I could be content as a choir nun, singing the Latin office each day. The music within those hallowed, echoing walls is ethereal. Then I'd be free to further my studies and writings—"

"But you cannot sing, by your own admission," Elodie reminded her gently. "At least not well."

"And your father would be very much against it," Charlotte added with a frown.

The scone turned to dry crumbs in Blythe's mouth. Swallowing, she said, "While in Paris, I even met with the prioress at the Convent of Our Blessed Lady of Syon."

"Go on." Charlotte's eyes widened as she refilled their cups.

"She said she'd be praying about my becoming a novice mistress and teaching the young English girls schooled there."

"No doubt you'd be a splendid teacher, but . . ." Charlotte reached for the sugar. "Like my father, yours wants a suitable match. Grandchildren. Heirs."

How easy it was for Charlotte. Not only was she beautiful and well-born, but the Wellinghursts had eleven children, most of them sons.

"How I wish I'd been male to continue the Hedley name. The most I can do is marry well and give my father grandchildren." Blythe reached out a finger and touched a rose petal from the table's bouquet. White, of course, a subtle nod to the king o'er the water. "But in truth, taking holy orders and a life of religious devotion are far preferable to a husband I dislike or one that can't be found."

Charlotte nodded. "At least you'd be sheltered from any harm there. You do know what is transpiring all around us, do you not?"

Blythe hated seeing the worry in her friend's face. "Father told me there has been harassment and threats of late."

"There's even been rumors of recent searches made for priest holes in Catholic houses like ours, among other things."

"I pray 'tis only talk."

"You heard nothing about an imminent Stuart Rising in France?" Charlotte's eyes turned beseeching as if she hoped Blythe would put down any untruths. "An amassing of French ships and arms for a landing on our very coast?"

"I overheard such, yes, but gossip always flies about, ever since the last Stuart king fled England years ago." She finished her scone. "What I saw in France belied the notion. Courtiers seem altogether too comfortable to risk an invasion and their very heads along with it. 'Tis one thing to talk of war and altogether another thing to make it."

"Indeed—"

A distant shriek of laughter curtailed the conversation, followed by a nursemaid's caution not to tumble down the hill. Blythe and Elodie cast a look over their shoulders.

"Be on your guard," Charlotte said, setting down her cup. "We are about to be ambushed by my younger brothers and sisters intent on seeing you."

Blythe pushed away from the table and turned toward the mansion. Coming full tilt toward her were six small Wellinghursts in a flurry of petticoats and breeches, shouting her name and gamboling about like spring lambs without a care in the world.

Laughing and lighter of heart, Blythe opened her arms to them.

12

You must pardon me, gentlemen,
for being a most unconscionable time a-dying.

KING CHARLES II

Wedderburn Castle
Berwickshire, Scotland

Restless, Everard made his rounds, first to his father's bedchamber to find doctors hovering, then down a turnpike stair that led to the castle's kitchen, spence, and buttery. Servants scurried hither and yon, eyes wide and heads bowed at the sight of him. He paused near the wall of bells, each room of the castle plainly marked.

Great Hall. Cedar Room. Tower Room. Great Parlor. Upper Hall. Laird's Chamber. Dressing Room. Larkspur Room. Morning Room. Nursery. Even the Royal Room for personages of that ilk. Beside this was a slightly yellowed, framed list of household rules signed by his father.

He peered into the cavernous kitchen. The cook, a stout matron with copper hair fading to silver beneath her mobcap, stood looking up at him with a spoon in hand. She seemed near apoplexy at his appearance, and he wondered if it was time to change the rule that servants couldn't speak until spoken to.

"I don't mean to scare you," he said, as she was known for her formidable temper.

"Good evening, Lord Fast." She flushed bright as a beet. "'Tis rare to see any of the family here below, but I'm glad of it."

"I've scarce been here since I was a lad."

"Och! Ye and yer brothers were a bit like Jackie Horner, sneakin' belowstairs and puttin' yer thumb in the Christmas pie!"

He chuckled, his gaze sliding toward the kitchen, where a side of mutton roasted on a spit. "Little has altered."

"At least not since the countess, yer dear mither, was alive, God rest her." She pursed thin lips. "As for yer faither, ye dinna bring ill news . . ."

"Nae." Though he felt such was imminent. "I'm in search of Mrs. Candlish."

"She's not to be found in her sitting room, milord?"

"Nae." He took a step back, the sizzle of roasting meat filling his senses. "But go on about your business, as I'd rather have my supper than you hunting the housekeeper."

With a cackle, she returned to the large service table where a kitchen maid was beating something in a bowl and a scullery maid created a great clatter washing crockery in a far corner. Housemaids skittered past like mice, curtsying as they did so.

Everard continued down the corridor, intent on another back stair leading to the upper hall that served as the family dining room. Coming down the steps was the housekeeper.

"Mrs. Candlish," he began.

"Milord, what brings you below?"

"A word with you, if I may." Overseeing the house sat strangely upon his shoulders. He was usually outside castle walls, on the laird's business. Or hawking, fencing, throwing the javelin, riding. And at his leisure, playing cards and dice.

"Of course, sir." She looked befuddled, as though torn between alarm and the pleasure of his company, if it could be called that. "My sitting room is private and near at hand."

She gestured to a half-open door leading to a chamber where she managed the affairs of the household. Spacious and tidy, it bespoke efficiency, even an austere elegance. Mrs. Candlish's father had been a bonnet laird from Inverness, but when he'd died, she'd been left with little recourse but to seek a life of service.

After shutting the door, she took a chair near the hearth, a low fire casting flickering light on a faded Turkey-red carpet. Everard remained standing, looking briefly out a window into the kitchen garden, where the late afternoon sun slid behind the castle's high west wall. How to begin? The whole matter was as unsavory as the day was long.

"When I was last in Edinburgh, I learned three of the servants at Hume's Land are wanting positions here at Wedderburn instead." He paused, wondering how his father would manage the matter. "A housemaid, a footman, and a lad-of-all-work. What say you?"

She hesitated, clearly surprised. "'Tis a great change, milord, from town to country. But it seems to come at a providential time. One of our housemaids will soon wed, and a footman has recently sought military service. How soon can they come?"

"I'll send word tomorrow, and you can likely expect them in a sennight."

"Very well, milord." Her voice dropped to a mournful tone. "We'll soon have need of them." No doubt she was thinking of the looming funeral and all it entailed.

"Needs be we prepare the house for blacking and coffining." He looked to his boots, mud-toed from his afternoon ride about the estate. "My faither's physicians feel it won't be much longer now."

She sighed. "I am sorely sorry to hear it."

"Expect a great many guests, the customary feasting and funeral dance." Everard spoke of the usual mourning customs with authority, though it seemed odd to talk of the dead before they were so. "My faither has requested nae expense be spared."

"Of course, milord."

Funeral costs were usually enormous, often crippling smaller estates. Thankfully, Wedderburn would not be set too much aback by it. The laird deserved a proper burial. All of Berwickshire expected it. As heir, Everard would see it well done. Still . . .

Lord, let my faither rally and live on, if it pleases Thee.

His voice grew hoarse with emotion. "Warn the servants there's to be nae stopping the clocks, nae shrouding of mirrors and foolish talk of omens." His mother had abhorred such, feeling it invited in the darkness. His father, steeped in old Scots tradition, turned a blind eye to the superstitions. "Such nonsense reeks of the medieval."

"Of course, sir."

"Needs be we summon a tailor and seamstress from the village to fit out those who lack proper mourning garments, including the servants coming from Hume's Land."

"I'll see to it right away, milord." She went to a cupboard and produced a booklet. "I'm thinking you may need this—a manuscript of household regulations penned by a steward of old. Munro, under your faither's oversight, never saw fit to change it, though 'tis subject to your will."

Everard took the tattered auld book from her and stared down at the title. *A Form for the Earl of Wedderburn's Family in Berwickshire.*

He moved toward the door, noting the mantel clock hurrying toward supper. Though he did want to gather with his brothers, he was suddenly in no mood to eat.

The Upper Hall was hushed, the laird's ornate mahogany seat at table's end empty, as was the countess's place to the right. Everard took his seat to the left, all seven chairs arranged in order of oldest to youngest. He eyed the door the footmen would soon come through. The journey from the ground-floor kitchen to the second floor was long and winding, the food not always hot depending on the season, but it had been so for hundreds of years and remained the same.

Mightn't he change that?

Bernard was the first to enter. He was dressed for dinner, though Everard knew he'd been out riding. He came through the door with his characteristic joie de vivre, though it faded at the sight of Everard unsmiling and leaning back in his chair.

Three years younger, Bernard was so opposite him in looks 'twas hard to tell they were brothers. Their temperaments were poles apart as well.

"How was your ride?" Everard asked as a footman appeared with wine.

"I completed the usual rounds," Bernard said. "The peas and wheat are flourishing despite so much rain, and the men are just now harrowing for the beer crop then the oats. A heavy sowing is in our favor and looks to yield a bountiful harvest."

"I've been studying granary accounts from all four factors," Everard said. "Needs be we crop oats most heavily in the outfield. Faither also spoke of raising the ploughmen's pay along with the acremen's."

At the mention of the laird, they paused. Bernard sat down as a ruckus was raised in the corridor. Alistair and Malcolm shoved their way into the room, then sobered upon seeing their two elder brothers. At six and twenty, they were too old to behave like schoolboys, as their father oft said, but they continued to roughhouse despite reprimanding. Though they'd seen heavy fighting during their time soldiering on the continent, they retained a merry spirit. They were known around Berwickshire as the Black Twins on account of their dark looks.

Everard welcomed their merriment. Their usual antics helped relieve the gloom of their circumstances. Waiting for someone beloved to die was . . . excruciating. He knew not how to act. How to stay atop his fractured feelings.

Ronan came in next, Orin on his heels. Coarse-featured like Bernard and almost as tall as Everard, Ronan was as dark in coloring as the rest of them while Orin was fair, a star amid the blackness. If not for their mother's light looks, some might have questioned Orin's lineage.

Ronan was suddenly as serious as a magistrate. He stared at Everard, a telling wariness on his face that bespoke but one thing. Even before he uttered a word, Everard knew the whole of it.

"It seems Davie has returned from his Highland stay," Ronan said. "His coach has just passed the gatehouse."

13

*Honor's a good brooch to wear
in a man's hat at all times.*

BEN JONSON

It took a full fifteen minutes for the coach to pass the main gate-house and arrive at Wedderburn Castle's entrance. Fifteen minutes for Everard to school his surprise and make peace with his brother's coming. No doubt David had bypassed Edinburgh and continued south to the Lowlands because he'd received word of their father's expected passing. Everard had only to look at Orin's down-cast face as he took his chair at table's end to gauge the tenor of this unexpected visit.

"Go ahead and sup without me," Everard told his brothers, signaling a servant to serve dinner.

He left the dining room and took a back stair leading to the stable courtyard. The staccato tap of hooves met him as the coach pulled to a stop before the castle's fifteenth-century watchtower.

Calysta emerged first, stepping down in a flurry of scarlet. She looked straight at him, her gaze hard as pewter. Without waiting for David, she sailed toward Everard with sullen petulance on her face.

"Lord Fast, I am undone. Our coach lost a wheel and landed us in a ditch outside Duns." With the theatrical flair he'd never grown used to, she brought a handkerchief to her powdered brow as if covered in dust. "I desire hot water and something other than unpalatable coaching-inn fare."

How glad I am you inquired about your faither-in-law's health.

Staunching the caustic thought, Everard stepped aside as Mrs. Candlish came forward to attend to Calysta, as deferential as he was disgusted. "Mrs. Hume, though your arrival is unexpected, your rooms are in readiness."

David strode toward Everard like a thundercloud, swearing beneath his breath. "I came as fast as I could. How is Faither?"

"Follow me." Everard returned inside, David on his heels. They reached the laird's rooms without speaking further.

Bracing himself anew, Everard opened the door. Around the immense box bed were four physicians. With an inward wince at the stench of camphor, all the bloodletting equipment, and their grave expressions, he stood by while David approached their father.

In a surprising show of deference, his brother dropped to one knee near the head of the bed. The laird's eyes were closed, his unshaven face pale and sunken as it had never been when he was on his feet. The barely perceptible rise and fall of his chest testified he still lived. But for how long? At least his second-born son had come in time.

But did he even ken David was present?

A physician murmured, "His lordship hasn't taken any food or drink for three days now. Nor has he opened his eyes."

David straightened to his full height, any mournfulness replaced by a slight scowl as he surveyed the array of lancets and scarificators on a near table. "I canna abide bloodletting. For a man so weak, have you nae other remedies?"

"Sir," the senior physician said, distress in his tone, "'tis a centuries-old practice that balances harmful bodily humors. Lord Wedderburn has not responded to any of our other treatments."

With a last look at the bed, David strode out. The silence in his wake was unsettling. But such was David's way. Death was near, its cold shadow felt. Everard had witnessed it in countless camps and on battlefields, the grit and anguish and irreversibility of it all. At least his father lay still and could die in the dignity of his own bed, not on foreign, inhospitable ground.

"We've nae need of all four of you." Everard stepped nearer the physicians. "Surely there are other matters to deal with, other needful patients in the parish. Only one of you will remain. Decide amongst yourselves who that will be, then report to the steward before you leave."

A murmuring. The senior physician stepped forward. "But, Lord Fast—"

"The matter is decided," Everard said.

By the time Everard returned to the dining room, all chairs were empty save David's. He was swiping a piece of bread about his plate, only bones remaining. Motioning to a servant, he requested more Canary wine. Calysta was not present, keeping to her rooms, likely. Everard took his seat, and a servant filled his own wine glass.

David sat back, the groan of his chair a testament to his bulk. He was stouter than he'd been a few months ago when last at Wedderburn, having lost the leanness that once marked him in youth. Excess sat upon his once spare frame—the result of Edinburgh's many enticements?

"Did you already dine, Brother?" he asked Everard.

"I've nae appetite." Everard wanted nothing more than to go to his own rooms, but there needed to be an accounting first.

He'd not informed his father what was told him at Hume's Land lest he upset him and make dying more difficult. Now the weight of the coming confrontation pressed down on him. But mayhap David would be more obliging than usual with his belly full.

Everard kept his tone even. "Now that you're here, I need a reckoning of how you are spending your time in Edinburgh."

With a shrug, David downed the contents of his glass in two swallows. "The servants are complaining about me, then." He cast a contemptuous glance Everard's way. "Hume's Land be hanged."

"Hanged, aye, though we nobles are allowed the axe, not the noose. And such might well be your fate if the king's men have enough of your Jacobite company."

"Meaning there are government spies as plentiful as rats in Auld Reekie."

"Not only Edinburgh," Everard said, thinking of the dragoons near Fast Castle.

"I find Jacks far better company than King Geordie's ugsome allies and minions."

Everard's gaze was unwavering. "Will you declare for the Stuarts and take up their standard? Or does simply dallying with dangerous Jacobites amuse you?"

"Crivvens!" David spat. "There's nae law against the company I keep."

"I question your allegiance nonetheless. The Stuarts, all told, made abysmal kings."

"And you think the jabbering German will be better?" David motioned for more wine, then took the entire bottle from the footman's hands. He refilled his glass to the brim, splashing wine onto the tablecloth.

Everard watched him with mounting aggravation. "I would also caution you against any hard drinking."

With a snort, David rubbed his bearded jaw. "Already playing the part of the laird and Faither has yet to breathe his last."

Everard took a long swallow from his own glass, trying to keep his temper as the footman retreated on fleet feet. "As your older brother, I can do nae less than caution you."

"Hoot! If I wanted lessons, I'd return to the schoolroom. I'm a grown man, free to do and go and act as I please. I'll not have you badgering me." He waved a hand as if brushing aside a swarm of midges. "We're not bairns any longer."

"Have you any thought of your kin? If not us, your wife?"

"Meaning I might slur the renowned Hume name."

"Aye, slur and jeopardize our very titles and holdings, not to mention our honor. There is more to be considered here than you, Brother."

"Faither never naysayed me."

"Mayhap he was hoping you'd change your ways. As it stands, his silence may well have opened the door wider for your questionable conduct."

David emptied his glass and poured more wine, ever more surly. And now unquestionably drunk.

"I've been going over Faither's accounts," Everard said. So many accounts it was a wonder he and Munro kept abreast of them all— including a great many frivolous expenses from Edinburgh, some of them Calysta's doing. "As laird, I'll not pay your debts, Davie."

The dining room door swung open and Orin entered, eyes going wide with surprise. Had he thought Davie was with Calysta? Suddenly looking downcast, he hurried toward Everard, giving Davie wide berth. In his hands was a paper, which he placed before his eldest brother.

Cupping his hand around his mouth, he whispered overloudly in Everard's ear, "'Tis the story I promised you. The one I've been writing about kelpies and selkies and Fast Castle since you last took me there."

"Ah, the one you mentioned earlier." Everard took the paper and noted the small childish hand, the spilled ink and effort. "I'll read it as soon as I'm done here. And hope for more of the tale in future, aye?"

Darting a skittish glance across the table at David, Orin nodded.

"Are you still dithering with nursery rhymes?" David asked him. "At eight I was out hawking and riding about, not scribbling in the nursery."

Orin stilled as if struck.

"Speak up, lad!" David reached for the empty wine bottle. "I asked you a question. Can you not answer it?"

Everard stood, motioning for Orin to leave just as the bottle was hurled in the lad's direction. Wide of the mark, it hit the table's edge with a jarring thud before falling to the floor and rolling from the carpet to the planks.

"Kelpies and selkies, indeed!" With a low growl, David rose from the table like a lumbering bear. His wine-garbled shout resounded to the four corners. "Out of my sight! You took our mither's life!"

Orin fled as Everard crossed the distance to David in four short strides. Grabbing him by the sark, he fisted the fine linen fabric and shoved him against the paneled wall. A footman peered into the room from a doorway, alarm scoring his features.

Keeping his voice down, Everard could not restrain his fury. "Hold your ill-scrappit tongue lest ye pay Hades right here."

David grabbed at him, but big as he was, he was still half a head shorter and no match for his brother's battle-honed strength. Everard twisted David's cravat like a noose, keeping him to the wall till his face grew an ugly, mottled red. "Do we have an understanding?"

David attempted to get away without success, cold fire in his eyes. "For now . . . at least while Faither still draws breath."

14

*To make women learned and foxes tame has the
same effect—to make them more cunning.*

KING JAMES I

Bellbroke Castle
Northumberland, England

T he day after tea at Wellinghurst Hall, Blythe sat at her writing table, quill pen poised in her right hand, gaze falling to her sleeve where white roses were embroidered inside the silken fabric. The same roses were stitched into her dress hems and handkerchiefs, a feminine flourish showing the Hedleys' support of the Stuarts. Despite his zeal to diminish or hide any outward affiliation, Father had said nothing about this. Perhaps embroidered roses were too small and insignificant a detail to matter.

A stray drop of ink fell, splattering the half-empty page before her. Sighing, Blythe set the quill aside and took out a book instead. She'd been writing to the Traquair ladies in France but needed to return to her studies. Yet her mind refused to attend to the task, trailing this or that way like a flustered partridge on the hills. The open window before her was another distraction, the view of the formal gardens enticing. And Pepys. He sang and trilled, fluttered and squawked near her desk. Annoyed rather than amused, she drew the fabric over his cage, at last quieting him.

With renewed determination, she arranged what was needed to resume her work and applied herself to her task, assembling quills and texts, blotter and sand. Her tidy desk soon cast her back to the schoolroom with her many tutors. The work that set her soul on fire might appear deadly dull to others. Betimes even her father seemed to wonder what kept her rooted to her desk.

She had a fondness for—nay, a fascination with—translating Latin texts into English. 'Twas like a puzzle. Sometimes she undertook a double translation and included Greek. When she grew weary of that, her back sore and hand cramped, she would walk the length of the room, her overburdened bookcases staring down at her, and relax by reading Plato's *Phaedo* aloud.

Usually Pepys strenuously objected. Was he not fond of Plato, or was it the whistling tones of Greek? Something always seemed to agitate him, his feathers a-flutter. Nor did he like any of the Romance languages, whereas the more methodical Latin put him to sleep.

"Lady Blythe, what will you be wearing for supper?"

Blythe turned toward Elodie, who hovered in the doorway of the adjoining bedchamber. She hadn't a clue. Fashion seemed the least of her worries. "I believe Father is going out tonight. If so, I'll not change at all but have supper in my rooms."

"As you wish."

Father was attending another meeting. Blythe sensed it had to do with his fellow Jacobites.

"Has Father said anything about my garments? Stripping them of roses or ceasing to embroider them?"

"Nay, milady." Elodie gave her a fleeting smile. "It might not be long before the Stuart rose is again worn openly and proudly."

Blythe studied Elodie. She seemed quieter of late, as if she had more on her mind than her usual tasks. "Are you all right?"

"Just a bit weary." Elodie touched her brow, the cloudiness in her eyes troubling. "I believe the long trip has caught up with me and I've not got rid of my headache." She did suffer so, oft requiring a tonic.

"I'm sorry," Blythe said. "Must you be on your feet?"

"Work distracts me. And I've never been one to loll about."

"Nay, lolling is not how I would describe you. You're in need of the cucupha." Blythe pulled on the bell cord to summon a maid, then retrieved the quilted head covering into which healing spices were sewn. "Some peppermint tea may help too."

"Tea always soothes, yes."

"You look lovely in that gown, by the way," Blythe told her, handing her the cucupha. "The color matches your eyes."

Even wearing the quilted hat, Elodie was lovely. So lovely, in fact, she set the menservants all a-titter no matter what she wore. Raised in a genteel household, she'd not lower herself to flirt but held herself to a higher standard. Blythe had long gotten past the dismay she'd first felt upon introduction, if not the lingering hurt of overhearing servants contrast them unfavorably.

Ye'd think her ladyship wouldn't want a mere maid to outshine her!

Does she not realize the contrast they make? The one so fair and the one so plain?

A homely companion would have suited far better.

Pushing the remarks to the back of her mind, Blythe said, "Offering you some solace is the least I can do for your faithful service. 'Tis been ten years this autumn, has it not?"

"Indeed. Ten blessed years." Elodie smiled, sitting down on the chaise longue at Blythe's urging. "I don't know of many in my circumstances so fortunate."

"You are very good at putting up with my moods and whims when they arise." Blythe moved toward the door. "Have you seen Father Beverly of late?"

"Nay, but he works tirelessly *not* to be seen." Elodie lay back and closed her eyes. "I do know he's been especially busy making his rounds beyond our walls."

"I feel I need to visit the chapel even in his absence. While I'm there, please rest. Tea is coming."

Blythe took a back stair and made her way to the small chapel that had served the Hedley family for generations. The wooden doorway gave its customary high squeak, the scent of all things ancient welcoming her. As a child she'd been especially drawn here, sensing the history and even the mystery within its stone walls.

Here she'd been christened and had come daily with her grandmother to pray from the time she could walk. Often she'd failed to keep her eyes closed, awed by the stained-glass windows that told colorful stories. Here it was always cool. Hallowed. The vault where her grandmother and mother were buried wore a perpetual fresh bouquet in summer and dried everlastings in winter, placed there unfailingly by the servants at her father's command. The sight never failed to make Blythe melancholy, and she averted her eyes, focusing instead on the silver chalices, the Host box, and the statuary at the altar.

She knelt, her knees cushioned by a velvet bench. Once, the hush of solitude was heavenly. After the fuss and rush of the French court, she'd craved aloneness. But lately, inexplicably, she felt lonely. She did not sense God's nearness. Her prayers seemed to reach no farther than the fan-vaulted ceiling. And their family priest was hiding and in disguise lest he lose his life.

She reached into her pocket, withdrew her rosary, and crossed herself. Perhaps solace could be had by saying the words she'd learned by heart long ago, when she was but a child and the world was brighter.

15

To all, to each, a fair good night,
and pleasing dreams, and slumbers light.

SIR WALTER SCOTT

Blythe's nightly ritual rarely varied. When dusk descended, Elodie drew her a bath in a copper tub behind a silk screen in her bedchamber, a practice she'd adopted after studying Hebrew and the ritual cleanliness of the Jewish people. That she was an oddity did not concern her. Cologne and vials of hartshorn and smelling salts would only go so far. She would be as clean as her peers were filthy. Fine clothes didn't disguise a foul-smelling body any more than a silk purse did a sow's ear.

"I've added your favorite bath salts," Elodie said, adjusting the screen to give her complete privacy.

Blythe sank down into the aromatic water up to her chin, eucalyptus steam swirling. Though it wasn't a miqveh or ritual immersion like in the Old Testament, it brought comfort, even peace, and some of the normalcy she craved. Tilting her head back, she closed her eyes, the cooing of doves beyond the window equally soothing.

Heavenly Father, please grant me sleep.

Perhaps a long bath would help. She'd been increasingly restless and sleepless since returning from France. Had it been but a fortnight ago she'd left there?

"Your father is now home, Lady Blythe." Elodie's voice came from near the window. Had she seen him come up the drive?

"I'm glad of it. He's been away so many evenings of late. Is he alone?"

"But for his manservant, aye."

"Perhaps we can breakfast together tomorrow. I've hardly seen him."

Yet for all his wandering about, he insists on keeping me home.

If Father let her resume her usual activities, she was sure to rest better. Being cooped up was neither healthy nor of benefit to anyone. She had new sympathy for invalids who must keep to their rooms.

Half an hour later, prayers said, she lay down and drew her bedcovers up to her chin, for the night was unusually cool. She turned on her side and pillowed an arm beneath her head, her nightly braid tangling around her, and listened.

The doves had stopped their cooing. A wind was rising, stirring the drapes. Though her father wanted the house shuttered after dark, she'd left one second-floor window open. 'Twas spring, after all. The wind seemed to carry the scent of the awakening garden, the roses especially.

She finally dozed, but it was a hazy half sleep full of shadows and dark feelings. Why did her mother haunt her dreams so? One recurrent dream in particular?

They were floating on the long lake in the deer park, taking tea in a boat. But not just any boat—the swan boat Mama had sailed in with the king on the canal at Hampton Court Palace. Mama was smiling at her, her eyes as bewitchingly blue as the deep water. They both held royal porcelain dishes edged with a gilt band and the royal arms. When the lake grew strangely restive, tea sloshed onto their skirts. Her mother cried out, and Blythe tried to clean up the spill with a lace handkerchief, but the stain kept spreading and burning . . .

Mumbling, Blythe turned over, caught in the gauzy veil between asleep and awake. Voices pressed in, further rousing her. Who was shouting from the dreamy lakeshore? Such a fuss.

Beyond her window came a great noise. Footsteps. More shouting. A wave of something out of sorts—and terrifying. Eyes wide open now, Blythe sat bolt upright, sleep sloughing off like water. She stumbled on the linens as she got out of bed, then rushed to the window and stared down at the section of formal garden that had been so carefully cultivated. It was lit by a great many moving, flickering torches. Someone was banging on the doors below. The shattering of glass bespoke much.

A mob!

"Milady!" Elodie burst through the bedchamber door, fully dressed and in such furious haste she nearly collided with her mistress, snuffing the candle she carried. "Away from the window!" She closed the shutters with a bang. "Put on your sultana quickly. You can further dress in the coach."

Heart a-hammer, Blythe groped about in the darkness, her hands shaking. "But why are these people storming the house—"

"Hurry! Say nothing." Elodie moved to the bookcase by the fireplace. The priest's hole?

A secret spring opened a concealed door in the wall, which led to a precipitous stair. Elodie all but shoved Blythe through the opening before drawing the door shut. On the steps before them were satchels. A lantern flickered on one stone wall. Elodie relit her taper, then helped Blythe snatch up the bags before leading the way down the winding steps.

Blythe stared at her maid's bent back, her skirts clasped tight in one hand. Bile crept up the back of her throat. She leaned into the wall, fearing she might cast up accounts.

Elodie whirled on her, never so beseeching as now. "I beg you, milady. Pray, collect yourself and follow me."

Through the darkened corridor they moved, the candle flickering from not only the drafts but their haste. If their light went out, how would they continue? The cold, ancient passageway seemed to close around them, chilling Blythe to the marrow. She had on no shoes, her bare feet numb against the uneven flagstone.

Holy God, Holy Mighty One, Holy Immortal One, have mercy on us!

The prayer came from her heart but failed to take root in her head. She could not hear the shouting of the mob here, deep inside the house. Had the agitators gained admittance? Would they somehow find them as they fled?

Soon they reached the labyrinth's end, the cave-like corridor connecting to the stables. The scents of straw and horseflesh filled her swirling senses. Quickly, Elodie snuffed the candle and steered Blythe to an open coach door, half a dozen silent men surrounding it. Grooms? The dark denied her knowing, but she saw the glint of moonlight on gunmetal.

Still shaking, she was hustled into the coach, stubbing her bare toe on the iron footplate. A wounded cry escaped her, loud as a gunshot in the night's stillness. In seconds, the conveyance was in motion, pulling down a tree-lined road behind Bellbroke. Elodie sat across from her, the moment's terror holding them in spellbound silence for several tense minutes.

Toe throbbing, Blythe took hold of the facts. "Where is Father?"

"Facing down the mob . . ." Elodie's voice trailed off.

Oh, Father. Save yourself.

Elodie took a breath. "He is not to accompany us but gave strict instructions as to how to proceed."

"Can we trust the postillion and driver?" Blythe wondered aloud, her voice wheezy with breathlessness. "The men riding with us?"

"I pray they stay loyal. If so, we are bound for the Borders."

"The Borders?" Blythe sat up straighter. This was another realm entirely, and she doubted much safer. "Is this Father's doing? What secrets are you keeping?"

"Oh, milady—" Elodie's voice broke. "We have returned from France to such danger. Father Beverly was killed while making his rounds. Tonight the mob outside our very door is tenants and colliers. They broke into the blacksmith's and gardener's sheds and took up tools as weapons, intent on doing us harm."

The frightful facts tumbled over in her benumbed mind as if she was still abed dreaming. Blythe drew her sultana closer as Elodie took out a coach rug and settled it around her. Father Beverly—killed? *Murdered.* Could it be?

She could barely choke out another question. "The Borders . . . are we bound for Traquair House, then?"

"Nay, 'tis no safer there. No Catholic estate is our refuge. We are headed toward Berwickshire in Scotland. To the Humes of Wedderburn. The earl has sympathized with your plight and agreed to take you in."

16

Look back, and smile on perils past!
SIR WALTER SCOTT

Wedderburn Castle

E verard fisted his aching right hand. His sword hand. Had he truly penned fifteen hundred funeral letters in three days' time?

The dull cramp in his fingers told him so. Notices of his father's death were spread across the breadth of the immense desk, penned on black-edged, foolscap paper and sealed with the Hume arms. A great many magistrates, town council, and clergy all over Berwickshire and beyond were to be notified, including important personages in Edinburgh. All must be invited to the funeral.

While he himself had hardly come to terms with the loss.

Alexander Hume had breathed his last with a noteworthy final flourish. Though sapped of all strength, he'd struggled to sit up shortly before midnight, asking who the white-robed men were sitting alongside his bed—those smiling beings who said nary a word but were such agreeable company of late.

The lone physician, a religious man from Jedburgh, paused briefly before saying with admirable certainty, "Angels, milord. Surely sent to welcome you to the celestial city, the New Jerusalem."

His father nodded as if agreeing it was so, then closed his eyes again. And died.

Watching the shadowed scene play out, Everard, ringing the bed with all six brothers, could barely breathe past the tightness in his throat. Could it really be so simple? Was death simply walking through a door as if passing from one room to the next?

Calysta gave a great cry near the foot of the bed, turning Everard's grief to vexation. She had hardly been the doting daughter-in-law. God be thanked his father was now beyond such hysterics. He couldn't abide a wailing woman.

Now, snuffing the candelabra as the clock struck midnight, Everard left the study and retired to bed. He was weary yet oddly awake. Supper sat uneasily in his gut. Since the hour of his father's passing, he'd eaten without tasting, listened without hearing, spoken without weighing his words. Was that grief too?

Once he'd undressed down to his sark, his feet bare and hands a-fumble, he poured himself a dram of whisky. It trailed down his throat like a flash of fire. He wanted to sleep as much as he wanted to escape Orin's sobbing himself to sleep in the adjoining chamber. Och, how the lad's bare sorrow rent his heart.

He passed into his brother's smaller room, more at ease with battle cries and bullet lead. Sitting down, the feather mattress collapsing beneath his weight, he reached out a tentative hand and found his brother's shuddering back.

He stayed till Orin's sobbing quieted to hiccups. Unable to offer much comfort, Everard dressed again, then lit a lantern and went to the stables where a litter of just-weaned pups cavorted in the straw. He scooped up the bonniest, a furry black bundle, and returned to present it to the bereft boy, gaining the intended effect. Momentarily pulled from his grief, Orin embraced the squirming creature, his face paler than usual in the candlelight.

"Can I sleep with him?" he asked, no doubt Nurse's displeasure in mind. "You're the laird now. We all do as you bid us."

All but David, who remained under their roof in the guest wing with Calysta, a continual burr.

"Bedsheets can be laundered, carpets cleaned," Everard replied with a shrug. "What will you call him?"

"Wallace," Orin said, the pup's tiny pink tongue finding his tear-stained cheek.

"Verra weel. He'll like as not keep you awake, but better company than tears, aye?"

Satisfied, Everard left the door open between their rooms and lay down again. He stared up at the oak bed's crewelwork canopy, moonlight from a bank of windows to his right bridging the inky darkness. The only sound was the shrieking of a distant fox.

Lord God Almighty, grant me sleep, if it pleases Thee.

And so he slept the sleep of the dead. Hard, snoreless sleep. He didn't remember his head hitting the pillow nor the pup's noises. In time—how many hours?—an insistent voice met his ear. Boyd?

"She's here, milord." The urgent words threaded through the fog of sleep, then thundered through his conscience.

She?

Had his kin already begun arriving for the lykewake?

Everard threw back the bedcovers in exasperation. "What means you?"

His manservant stood before him, candle held aloft. "The duke's daughter—Northumbria's. Lady . . ."

Lady . . . what?

Sleep-addled but sensing he must do something, Everard grabbed for his breeches. The taper's flame danced about the drafty chamber, casting wan light on a mantel timepiece. Three o' the clock.

Nearly cursing, Everard pulled on the boots Boyd had hurriedly brought. *Lord, forgive me.*

Forgetting his unkempt state—his unbound hair and untucked sark—he strode toward the door. "Where is she?"

"In the front hall, milord. Her coach-and-four has just gone round to the stables. The horses are foundered."

Everard left his room, Boyd trailing. Betimes the castle seemed to take an age to traverse, especially in the wee small hours. But someone had lit the hall sconces—Mrs. Candlish? Surely she was near at hand, seeing to their untimely guest.

Below, half a dozen people stood near the castle entrance, all looking up at him. Mrs. Candlish, Munro, Atchison, and a footman whose name he couldn't recall.

Plus a bedraggled pair of women.

No one spoke. His boots sounded heavy on the stairs. Finally he came to a stop atop the black-and-white marble floor and faced the woman he guessed to be the duke's daughter. She was dressed, or barely. A flattened gown without hoops, hair falling to her hips in a frayed braid, her face ashen. She appeared to wear no stockings, just slippers.

He forgot the obligatory bow. Nor did she give the slightest acknowledgment, not even an obliging nod. Her eyes were wild. Weary.

"Who are ye and why are ye here?" he asked, his sleepy query resounding about the dimly lit hall.

"I am Lady Blythe Hedley, the Duke of Northumbria's daughter. And this is my lady's companion." She straightened as if gathering her misplaced dignity, the lift of her chin a rebuke to his bluntness. "And you, sir?"

"I am Lord Fast—or was. The laird of Wedderburn's oldest son."

She thrust a paper at him, her hand trembling. From fear or fury?

He took what looked to be a letter—the seal broken—from her outstretched hand, the last vestiges of sleep and surprise sloughing off him. He motioned Boyd nearer, needing his taper. Candlelight danced upon the crowded, ink-filled page. His father's handwriting, that he knew. But the message? He squinted in the low light, flummoxed, furious. 'Twould take an age to decipher. And broad daylight.

"Milady . . ." He gave in to his ire. "Yer as welcome as water in a holed ship."

The lass's maidservant gave a little gasp.

Undeterred, Lady Hedley stepped nearer, her hands outstretched in a plea that failed to move him. "Your father the earl bade me come."

Grief reached in and squeezed hard. "My faither slippit awa."

17

Wherever the storm carries me,
I go a willing guest.

HORACE

Slippit awa.

What means you? Blythe wanted to ask, but she was too busy fighting weariness and tears to trust her voice. It didn't help that Elodie, usually the soul of composure, cried quietly in the shadows behind her.

Blythe stared at the Scots giant, mulling his porridge-thick brogue. Despite his obvious ire—and outright insult—he managed to look mournful when he spoke. For now, he continued to peruse the letter his father had penned to hers.

She focused on his unshaven face as discreetly as she dared, knowing at any moment he might look up and meet her searching gaze. She wondered the color of his eyes. In his present mood, they would be stormy no matter their hue. She took in the downward sweep of dark lashes above well-defined cheekbones. A Grecian nose. The taut line of his full mouth. His loose hair fell like black ribbons against his untucked linen shirt. She'd awakened him from a sound sleep, no question. And he was as obliging as a bear roused from its den with a sharp stick.

Something else seized her attention. It wasn't just his face but his form that commanded notice. Remarkably tall, he had the bearing of a soldier. His powerful presence seemed to fill the hall as much as his voice—more a medieval knight within these castle walls. Sir Galahad or Richard the Lionheart. Or Edward the Black Prince. It took all her willpower not to curtsy before him.

At last he looked up from the letter, crushing it in one fist. "Ye moost be weirrie and fu' o' keer." To the mob-capped woman near at hand—the housekeeper?—he said, "Gie'r tae the toor. I hae nae tyme fer sech tonycht."

Blythe stared at him uncomprehendingly. With a deferential nod, the woman instructed the maid and footman to gather their guests' satchels. Without another word, she led them down a corridor, a lantern in her hand. Skirts trailing, Blythe glanced back to see that her black-haired host had disappeared.

Though curiosity clawed at her, she was too worn to take notice of her surroundings. The housekeeper slowed. She took out a clanking set of keys and unlocked a hulking door. Here they seemed to step back centuries. They went up a turnpike stair that held the dank chill of winter and the dust of disuse.

Gie'r tae the toor.

Had he meant *tower*? Undoubtedly, for that is where they were. In the donjon or keep, the oldest, most heavily fortified part of any castle. Bellbroke Castle's round-shell keep with turrets was more art than defense, but this sprawling edifice on the fractious Borders seemed more a prison.

The turnpike stair climbed higher, built clockwise so it could be defended by a right-handed swordsman. Tiny slits of windows barely let in light or air, deflecting a volley of arrows from a bygone age. Another thick wooden door was opened. The lantern cast light onto a chamber that seemed to have belonged to the Dark Ages. That box bed—it made five of her own at home. By day, the chamber might be brighter. By night it was . . . ghostly. Ghastly. And unaccommodating.

The housekeeper seemed kind, though her speech was no more

understandable than her master's. The footman began laying a fire while the maidservant put their satchels on a settle. Blythe longed for a brazier to warm them while they waited, but alas, this antiquity of a place might never have even heard of such. Tea was brought just as dawn seeped through the tower's slits.

"Take care not to show yerself," the housekeeper told them, slowing her speech as if realizing they struggled to understand her. "Keep closeted till the laird decides what's to be done with ye. This is a house of mourning, first and foremost."

Mourning? Had the earl died?

She went out, silence in her wake. Blythe's exhaustion settled in her bones. She sank into a chair and listened. Outside came the sigh of the wind and the rhythmic croaking of frogs. And something faint but almost chilling . . .

A violin?

The music lent an air of civility to their rustic surroundings. She looked to Elodie already dozing in a chair, giving in to the tumultuous events that plagued them. The music ebbed and flowed, a sonorous symphony on a sole instrument. And clearly a lament. How fitting to her mood. And how expertly played, every note bittersweet and resonant. Whoever it was, Blythe's soul gave silent thanks.

———⊗⊗⊗———

They huddled by the fire in old chairs that were oddly comfortable, sipping tea and eating oatcakes as dawn flooded the room with soft yellow light. Elodie had dried her tears and seemed more composed, a bed rug covering her shoulders. Blythe pulled her own rug about her, a dull headache pulsing between her temples. Though exhausted, she could not bring herself to lie down on the strange bed, not with their world on end as they awaited Lord Fast.

"I am loath to be thrust upon the Humes, especially if the earl has just passed," Blythe said in low tones, wondering if the tower had peepholes as Bellbroke did. Her eyes roamed the cavernous chamber from the beamed ceiling to the faded, threadbare carpets upon the floor. At the hearth, a large copper kettle steamed on a trivet in the coals, their one consolation. "I can scarce take it in."

"I fear the former Lord Wedderburn is no more." Elodie tucked a strand of unpinned hair behind her ear. "Lord Fast may well be the new earl."

"And we've intruded on his mourning." Blythe sighed. "Harkening back to what he said, I've never been made to feel as welcome as water in a holed ship."

"In hindsight, 'tis rather amusing." With a chuckle, Elodie took another sip from her humble earthenware cup. Hardly the stuff of Scottish nobles. Rather, reserved for unwanted guests? "He's a bold one, however he styles himself."

Blythe frowned, recalling the humbling moment. Would she ever forget it? "'Tis all akin to a bad dream." She took another sip of tea. Hyson. A reminder of home.

Truly, the events of the night seemed more nightmare. Father Beverly had met a dismal end, though Elodie could provide few details. The dark hole in Blythe's heart widened. And what of Father? Had the mob gotten hold of him once she and Elodie escaped through the priest's hole? Not knowing gnawed at her, filling her mind with the most dreadful implications. What of the Wellinghursts? Had the mob gone there too?

The coach ride had been a blur—hours and hours of speeding over back roads and byways, stopping only to change horses, then being slowed again by a group of riders just south of Wedderburn Castle. Hadn't the clansmen identified themselves as enemies of the English?

The coachman spun a fine tale of hastening them to the Borders, where one of their kinsmen lay dying. Blythe abhorred untruths, but the coachman's lies flowed smooth as melted butter. Such was their welcome to Berwickshire.

"Filthy Borderers," one of the grooms had said, spitting upon the ground in the dust of their departure. "No better than highwaymen."

Remembering it now, Blythe made up her mind. "I shall speak to the earl about returning home immediately."

Elodie regarded her mournfully. "*Immediately* is not what your dear father had in mind, milady. The trouble that drove us away shan't be resolved anytime soon, and the duke said so."

"But we cannot remain here with a man who is clearly unhappy with our coming. It was not even he who authorized it. I fear he who did so is dead!"

"'Twould seem so, yes." Elodie massaged her temples, clearly beset with another headache.

"And now we've been closeted in this musty tower away from the main house so we won't be seen. I feel akin to a prisoner." Blythe knew she was talking in circles, but she could not help it, grappling to make sense of it all. "Lord Fast's countenance was stormy enough, but I scarce understood a word of what he said. He and his household speak as if their mouths are full of mush. And how unusually he says *lady*. It becomes *leddy* instead."

"If you think Lowland Scots is hard on the ears, Highlanders are said to be completely unintelligible."

"I pray I shan't hear them ever. As for accommodations, I'd rather lodge in the town nearest us—what is it called?"

"Duns, I believe."

"I would rather lodge in a tavern or coaching inn than stay where I am unwanted." Too distressed to sit still, Blythe set down her cup and crossed to the nearest shuttered window. Which way was Duns? She would walk there if she had to. But there was the unmarked coach they had come in. "I shall find the stables and see about our leaving posthaste."

"By what means shall we lodge or leave? We have no funds."

The cold reality of being penniless was like a dousing of ice water. "For all his planning, Father failed to supply us with coin enough to do anything at all?"

"Hardly an oversight, I'm certain. Your father is not a foolish man."

Blythe turned away from the window and stared at Elodie. Had Father left her without a farthing, knowing she would try to leave Scotland at the first opportunity? Biting her lip to stem her frustration, she threw the shutters open. Cool, moist air rushed over her. Daybreak's view, even to her begrudging eyes, was breathtaking.

Clearly, Wedderburn Castle was situated for defense with a strategic command of the Borders. Lush fields rolled away from the castle walls for miles in all directions, the sunrise spreading pale light upon a patchwork of greens. Jade. Sage. Mint. Emerald.

They'd been lodged in what was known as the sunroom of the keep, the top floor that allowed the most windows. For that Blythe could be thankful. Her gaze roved to an adjoining closed door. Dare she open it?

She simply wanted *out*.

18

Silence, maiden; thy tongue outruns thy discretion.

SIR WALTER SCOTT

Everard took in the seventy or so servants assembled. They fanned out about him in staid rows as he stood in the Great Hall—all clad in sable as befitted those in mourning. He himself wore all black. One glance in the looking glass this morn assured him he looked the devil himself.

He certainly felt like it.

"I expect each of you to prepare for the days to come like a soldier for battle. Rise early with your wits about you, armed for whatever the hours may bring." He cleared his throat, in need of a dram of whisky. "A great many guests, most of them strangers, will be flooding Wedderburn to pay their respects. Take care of their needs as best you can and see that none make off with the silver."

Though they worked hard to remain solemn, a few fresh-scrubbed faces bore smirks. And there were a great many obliging nods.

"If you encounter any trouble, Munro will be on hand, as will Mrs. Candlish." Everard examined the lot of them to gauge any shirkers. "I will be near as well. For now, go about your duties, though I beg a word with Atchison and Graham." His gaze swept to the maid and footman who'd seen the arrival of the duke's daughter in the wee small hours.

The servants dispersed, all but the two. They approached him, heads down, as if still cowed by his tirade of last night. Or were they already guilty of what he was about to warn them against?

"A word of caution to you both." He continued slow and low, letting every word sink in. "Mrs. Candlish assures me you have sworn secrecy to this matter of our unexpected English visitors, aye?"

They nodded vigorously. Atchison he was confident of. Graham, new to Wedderburn, he was less sure of.

"Their safekeeping requires the utmost discretion. If I hear even a word of tattle about the matter, all babblers will be dismissed. Have I made myself clear?"

More vigorous nodding. Though he kept his tone steady, the steel of it, sharpened by sorrow and exasperation, could not be missed.

"You're dismissed."

Ten o' the clock. Was her ladyship still abed? Everard doubted, given the tumult, she'd even slept. Nor had he, given the chain of events. Weighing what he was about to say, he walked a seldom-used passage to the castle's keep, a labyrinth of corridors needed to reach the sole turnpike stair that gained access to the top floor. A wise placement, given her ladyship's circumstances and the fact that David and Calysta were beneath the same roof. He didn't trust them or what they would do if they learned of her presence. For one, it wouldn't be a private matter any longer.

He knocked at the door, struck by the irony of seeking entry to his own residence. The door was opened by a lass who was bonnier than a lady's maid had a right to be. She curtsied, then looked up at him in a perturbed fashion, expression wary.

"I'm here to see her ladyship," he said. *If she's fit to be seen.*

Bell—was that the name mentioned in the duke's letter?—glanced back over her shoulder, clearly torn. "Very well. If you'll grant me a moment, Lord Fast."

"Wedderburn," he corrected, though his courtesy title was a hard parting.

The door closed in his face. He went to the opposite apartment, letting himself in with a skeleton key. He left it dangling from the lock while he entered what was once the laird's apartments in the fifteenth century, namely a library. The dusty-sweet smell of countless tomes overcame him, distracting him momentarily from his mission.

Though the servants kept the auld tower clean, time was no friend. The faded tapestries held centuries of dust and the furnishings bespoke another age entirely. Glastonbury chairs, enormous chests, ornate oak tables, and uncomfortable settles. Even a gilded chair for an overlord before the fireplace.

A rustle of skirts bade him turn. Lady Hedley stood behind him, her maidservant in her wake. He gestured for her ladyship to enter, then shook his head at her maid.

The lass looked aghast. "But, milord—"

"Nae need for your presence. Our Borders' ways are less stringent than yours. But for what it's worth, I promise not to rile your English sensibilities." He could not help the hint of mockery in his tone. "And if her ladyship screams or you suspect anything untoward, by all means rush in and rescue her."

He removed the key from the lock and shut the door, noting Lady Hedley had moved away from him to stand before a bookcase that made her look small when she was in fact a tall woman. Gone was the braid that had marked her arrival. Her hair, hidden by shadows the night before, was fair as flax but bore a reddish tint. It peeked out from beneath her white lace cap, long curls spiraling over her left shoulder. He moved to open a shutter, letting in light enough to aid her momentary perusal of the books.

And his perusal of her.

What had his father said? She was not beautiful but . . . brilliant.

For all that she was not, she had a queenly carriage. And she was slim as a willow switch. Not a hint of cinnabar or lead paint or vermillion on her flawless face. No pomatum or powdered hair. She'd shed her ill-scrappit gown of last night and now wore a wrinkled rose one with sleeves of tiered lace. When she turned round and faced him again, he gestured to a chair.

A shake of her head declined his offer. Did she expect him to be brief so stayed standing? A shaft of light called out her intelligent eyes. Pale green and more serene than he'd expected them to be. She joined her hands at her waist, pressing them against her ornate stomacher.

"Milord . . ." Her voice was soft. Dulcet, even. And aggravatingly aristocratic, even a tad arrogant. "Allow me to express my sincere sympathy for your loss."

He gave a nod, taking the seat she had declined. He faced the open window, glad for fresh air. "Did you sleep, milady?"

"I did not." Her eyes showed surprise at his candor. "My fears for my father would not let me." She stared at him pointedly. "That—and a violin—kept me from my rest."

So, she'd heard Munro's playing? The fiddle, despite thick walls, had a voice all its own. "Do you not care for music, or is the hour your complaint?"

"On the contrary, I play the harpsichord. It pairs beautifully with the violin whatever the time."

He hesitated. One moment she was tetchy, the other douce. She was obviously unsure of him. "Tell me what sent you fleeing Northumberland."

She looked down at her joined hands as if collecting her thoughts. Soon the tale poured forth. Her return from France and her father's caution and keeping her to home. The moonlit night that saw a mob storming Bellbroke and sent her and her maid fleeing toward the Borders in an unmarked coach.

"I met with your faither in Edinburgh, so your arrival was not entirely a surprise to me," he said, crossing his arms. "But I was not privy to my faither's agreement, as he told me nothing of his own letter to the duke before he died."

She sat down on a settle, facing toward the window as he did. "I do not want to burden you by staying on here. I intend to return to Northumberland as soon as possible. I must know how my father fares. Bellbroke is my home. I desire to be nowhere else."

"Is such wise, milady?"

Again that prolonged pause as if she weighed his every word. Or did she struggle with his Scots speech? "Wise, milord? Given your conduct last night, 'tis not prudent to remain."

"My conduct?" Despite a barb of guilt, he continued lightly, "'Twas the dead o' night. Did you expect me to greet you with banners and trumpet fanfare?"

"Ha!" she said, her serenity shattered. She turned flinty eyes on him. "I expect to be treated as a duke's daughter by the new Earl of Wedderburn, no matter the circumstances."

"Och, I accept the rebuke, but I am not one to suffer any mincing airs."

"Airs? I am speaking of mere manners."

"Then take the mettle from your tone, milady." He passed a hand over his whiskers. "Dinna get yerself in such a fankle."

"A *fankle*, is it? What sort of speech is that?"

"Solid Scots. An assault on your exalted upland ears, nae doubt." He studied her, her chin raised another notch. "Dinna direct your anger toward me. 'Tis our faithers who bear the blame, God rest the one and mayhap the other."

She looked away from him, her profile caught in the wan light, hands fisted in the folds of her skirts. "I beg your leave to have my coach readied and—"

"Your coach departed with fresh horses at dawn."

"Departed?" She flashed him a look of fiery disbelief. "So I am your prisoner?"

"Only if you wish to be. More a grudging guest." He stood. He would not tell her he'd sent word to her father along with the coach, inquiring as to the man's welfare and asking for a speedy reply. "I'd recommend you make the best of your stay in Berwickshire, Lady Hedley, however long it shall be."

He strode out, leaving the door open. Her maid stood in stricken silence in the hall as he passed. "See that your mistress becalms herself as befits a lady of her station."

19

We must dare, and dare again, and go on daring.

GEORGES JACQUES DANTON

Before Blythe recovered her composure and left the library, Mrs. Candlish and the black-clad maidservant, Peg, arrived with hot water for a bath and the promise of a meal.

"I'm not sure what yer ladyship partakes of. Surely not our hearty Scottish fare," Peg told her almost apologetically. "But Cook has done what she could to try to tempt yer appetite, so I'll have dinner brought up next, then tea to follow at four o' the clock."

Thanking her, Blythe watched as she finished filling the copper tub placed near the hearth, leaving a quantity of soft soap and towels. Blythe's mind was so full of the laird's conversation she could hardly attend to the matter at hand.

"Dinna get yerself in such a fankle."

His admonishment had struck like a whip. No one had ever spoken to her so, nor given her such searing glances. Those eyes of his— blue as the fierce, lace-frothed waves that battered their boat when crossing the channel from France, leaving her reeling and ill.

Surely sensing her discomfiture, Elodie began to lay out another gown, this one pressed, then sent the garments they'd worn upon coming to Wedderburn to the castle's laundress by way of Peg. As Blythe sank into the tub up to her chin, her teeth chattered unreasonably. The fire's warmth seemed to extend no farther than the dog irons, a scuffed brass pair in dire need of polishing.

Once bathed and dressed in a plain chintz gown and underpinnings, Blythe sat down at a table that replaced the hip bath. Clearly, the Scots lived about their hearths. One was in danger of courting frostbite indoors otherwise, no matter the season.

"I'm sorry about the rude fire, milady," Peg said, poking the feeble flames with an iron rod. "Peat nor coal nor wood hardly heats this auld tower."

Blythe bit her lip. Was her displeasure so plain? Or had other ears overheard her outburst with the laird? She tried to smooth out her countenance, surprised to find a damask napkin and silver utensils upon the table. A half dozen covered dishes were unveiled, the mingled aromas foreign but tempting. With a proud flourish, Peg explained each. Barley bannocks. Beef pie. Spring greens. Cock-a-leekie soup with an entire fowl sitting in the tureen's center. Ewe's-milk cheese. And a dish of the tiniest, reddest strawberries Blythe had ever beheld.

Prisoners or no, they would not go hungry. Once grace was said, Elodie drew a spoon through her soup as she sat opposite. Tasting it, she murmured, "Delicious."

Blythe followed, sampling each dish though she had little appetite. Heaven forbid Cook tell the new laird she'd refused their offerings. She gave a halfhearted stab at the beef pie, as robust as the man who'd sparred with her an hour before.

What was Lord Wedderburn doing now? And where?

Peg bustled about, bringing this or that, clearly charged with their well-being. It wasn't until she left with a promise to return that Blythe felt free to speak.

"Did you hear mine and his lordship's conversation?"

Elodie plucked a strawberry from the dish. "I could not help but hear it. 'Twas rather . . . heated."

Heated was an understatement. His distinct voice had carried far and crackled with intensity.

"I must admit his speech has a beguiling, musical quality." The glint in Elodie's eye was most unlike her. "Rather charming, in fact."

Blythe looked hard at her. "His gibberish, you mean." Yet she could not deny that the more they conversed, the more her ears adjusted to the rhythm of his strange tongue.

If one could get past the sheer force of his presence.

Aye, that was the gist of it. He had a vehemence—an authority—that rivaled a Puritan preacher. He belonged on the battlefield if not in the pulpit. Had he been a soldier? She would find out. Whatever and whoever he was, he was no foppish gallant sporting lace ruffles and snorting snuff.

"I fear more heated conversations are forthcoming since we are without a coach or funds to carry us home." Blythe sampled a bannock, finding it dry. She eyed the butter and what appeared to be marmalade. "I know not what to do."

"Why not enjoy the hospitality of the house?" Elodie's wry smile bordered on a laugh. "Or, as Lord Wedderburn said, 'See that your mistress becalms herself as befits a lady of her station.'"

"I overheard him and fail to see the humor in it." Frowning, Blythe leaned back in her chair. "I shall ask him to send word to my father. If I knew he was all right I might be less . . . restless."

Elodie's levity vanished. "Last night was such a fright. I've never seen so many tenants so angry all at once and intent on harm. They came through the gardens like one of the king's armies and may well have destroyed it."

Blythe recalled the rush of flaming torches and breaking glass. Had the house suffered further damage? Given the hostilities at home, what more could they do but wait for word—and pray?

"I am trying to see reason," she said, taking a drink of tea to wash down the bannock. "Needs be I think of Lord Wedderburn's loss too. I know naught about Scottish funerals, do you?"

"Nothing except these Scots seem to do everything in a raucous manner, the Traquair ladies aside."

Ah, Lady Mary and Lady Catherine, utterly genteel and safely sequestered in the northeast of France. Blythe wished she had never left there. Her eyes roved the dark chamber, lingering on the bed. Stifling a yawn, she wondered at the time. Nary a clock could be seen, which further added to her befuddlement.

When Peg returned to collect the supper dishes, Blythe stood. "Might I speak with you in the other room?"

Elodie looked up in surprise where she sat finishing her meal. Peg seemed surprised as well—and a little concerned. "Was the fare not to your liking, milady?"

"'Twas delicious. My compliments to the kitchen," Blythe said with a small smile to reassure her. "'Tis another matter entirely I wish to discuss."

Peg's obvious relief changed to outright worry. "Of course, mem."

They exited the room and went into the one filled with books. The laird's memory—even his Castile soap scent—returned larger than life as Blythe shut the door and glanced at where they'd sat.

"Please," she said, gesturing to a chair. "I won't stand on formality, and this might take some time."

With a nod, Peg perched on the very edge of the chair, looking glad to be off of her feet even if it was an unusual request.

Blythe took a bracing breath. "If I'm to impose on the hospitality of the Humes, I should like to honor the former earl's memory. Have you a black dress I might use?"

Peg drew back a bit. "None that would suit a lady such as yerself, mem."

"I see you and the housekeeper clad in mourning. I assume the whole household wears sable. Surely I should observe the custom as well, perhaps as a token of respect to the new Lord Wedderburn. 'Twould help me blend in if I happen to be seen."

"As ye wish, mem. I could summon a mantua-maker from Duns—" Peg shook her head. "But such would give ye dead away and the laird would have my hide."

"No need. I was hoping to borrow a garment."

Peg's face became a stew of confliction. Her voice faded to a whisper.

"The countess's wardrobe has no' been touched in eight years, milady. My sister, Sal, was her ladyship's maid. I could ask her. She's waiting on Mistress Hume here at the castle of late."

"Mistress Hume?" Blythe's brow raised. Here was a missing piece of the clan's puzzle.

"Calysta Hume, mem. She is David's—the second-born's—wife. They're usually at Hume's Land in Edinburgh, but the coming funeral keeps them at Wedderburn, ye ken."

"Of course. Please ask your sister for me, then. I wouldn't keep the dress, of course. Only borrow it."

"What's good enough for the countess might be good enough for a duke's daughter, aye?" Peg's mouth pursed as she appraised Blythe's person with the eye of a seamstress. "The countess was uncommonly tall like ye, mem. But stouter."

"A small matter my maid can easily remedy as she's skilled with a needle."

"Then I shall ask Sal and fetch ye a proper gown posthaste."

"Tell no one. But if we're found out, lay all the blame at my door." She wouldn't risk Peg's or her sister's good standing in the household. She knew how hard servants were to come by and how easily they could be dismissed.

"Never fear, milady. Sal and me, we ain't ones to go clyping about the countryside."

"Clyping?"

"Telling tales," Peg said. "We won't be found out, mem. None go into the countess's chambers anymore. Not since her death. Now if she'd had a daughter, it might be different. As it stands, few would know what went missing, not even Mrs. Candlish. And being men, the laird and his brothers willna remember one dress from the next."

"Glad I am to hear it." Blythe admired the bookcase that lined an entire wall, tempted to spend the remainder of the day right here. "When will the funeral be?"

"Sennight's end, milady. I believe Lord Fa—the new laird—named Saturday next."

Laird. She'd heard the Scots term but never dreamed she'd use it. Blythe bit her lip, unsure of what day it was. "Oh, and I shall need a black bonnet. And veil."

Peg nodded, a sly gleam in her eye. "Very well, milady. Ye shall have them. And a pair o' black shambo gloves, besides."

20

Noble fathers have noble children.

EURIPIDES

Everard entered the Great Hall, a two-storied, oak-paneled chamber seldom used except for large gatherings. Underneath his feet was a marble-tiled floor embedded with the Hume coat of arms, which stretched expansively from a hidden entrance beneath the minstrel's gallery at the far end to open double doors at his back. Lofty windows overlooking the gardens let in plenty of natural light, and a massive fireplace tall enough for a man to stand in was to his right. The hearth, lit only for winter use, invoked images of his Elizabethan ancestors gathered about on rugs and rushes near its welcoming warmth.

For now, the lykewake was in progress, the hall packed cheek by jowl. Those eager to pay their respects spilled out into the courtyard and lined up outside Wedderburn's front entrance, more coming up the long drive on foot, on horseback, or by conveyance. Humble, great, stranger, friend, kin, even enemy—all mingled here. Servants threaded in and out of the throng and paid homage to the auld laird as they went about their duties.

In an antechamber adjoining the Great Hall lay his father, the oils and frankincense used for the coffining the least of the expense. Alexander Hume had always loved a great gathering. Of all the bounty provided for consumption, the whisky, brandy, claret, and ale were being consumed with the usual gusto, accompanied by an endless repast of beef and oxen and moorfowl spread upon numerous tables alongside sweetmeats and confections.

All was in hand, though David's laugh was overloud, a telling sign he'd drunk too much. Calysta mingled with a knot of women, mostly kinfolk, near the hearth. Filling their ears about Edinburgh? They resembled a murder of crows in their black garb.

Their guests were not black clad but had turned out in their finest. Such celebrations could extend upwards of three weeks, but given the exorbitant outlay, Everard refused to feed the entire parish for longer than a sennight.

Saturday's funeral was at hand—coffin, hearse, and adornments settled. A suit of clothes for the minister was doled out, the fees for presiding paid, right down to the bellman who walked the streets of Duns, proclaiming the laird's passing.

"Won't ye have a drink, milord?" Boyd stood beside Everard, raising his cup in invitation.

"Nae, I need my wits about me," he said, though he'd had a dram with his porridge at dawn.

"Yer a far cry from Davie," Boyd muttered, eyes pivoting to Everard's irascible brother. "I'll keep my sights on him. His new man-servant is not much better. From Auld Reekie, I take it."

"Iron doesn't sharpen iron in this case."

Boyd took another drink. "Nae, it doesna." He moved off into the crowd with a canny eye, his genial smile a foil for his duties as keeper of the peace.

A trio of fiddlers began to rosin their bows in a far corner, and the tune "Maggie Lauder" soon burst forth, rising to the rafters and raising spirits. Everard's own mood shifted as he spoke with two bonnet lairds who'd come to pay their respects and then with the sheriff and magistrates, who expressed their sympathies and seemed to be enjoying themselves. For the next hour or so he worked his way across the immense hall, greeting guests and answering a question or two. As he was solitary by nature, such gatherings taxed his spirit and left him wanting fresh air. He'd not been riding or hawking in—what? A fortnight?

Looking up, he spied Orin, Wallace the pup in arms, high in the minstrel's gallery. Everard winked, gaining the lad's smile. Passing through a hidden door resembling paneling, Everard climbed up the gallery steps to join him. No better place to watch the lykewake than hidden away with an eagle's view.

"I hear fiddle music." Blythe moved nearer a window, feeling she'd worn a hole in the carpet with her pacing.

"Quite lively too." Elodie didn't miss a stitch as she worked to alter Blythe's mourning gown—formerly the Countess of Wedderburn's—taking in the bodice and adjusting the sleeves.

Peg had delivered the garment as promised during the night, including a comely veiled hat and gloves. Blythe rued forgetting to ask about shoes. She supposed her French slippers would have to do. Though a suitable black, the red heels were distracting. But with the press of so many people, would anyone notice? Peg had explained the lykewake and what was to come, but Blythe could hardly believe it. Dancing at a funeral? Feasting? The Scottish kirk apparently frowned upon it, but time-honed tradition prevailed.

It cast her back to her grandmother's death, where they'd given all mourners white chamois gloves and other tokens, then partaken of a holy and orderly funeral mass with glittering candlelight and lengthy prayers. Would she do the same for her father if . . .

"Don't look so glum, Lady Blythe. 'Tis so bright a day despite the, um, lykewake." The odd word rolled off Elodie's tongue, though not as melodiously as it did Peg's. "And I've nearly finished this gown. I do wonder though, given the laird's canny nature, if he won't suspect something if he spies you wearing it."

"I don't think we have cause to worry. His hands are full of a great many guests, and he's avoided us these three days past."

Blythe passed into the next room. Not once had Lord Wedder-burn darkened their door since his setdown of her in the library. That still rankled. Or was it her wounded pride that struggled to recover? She grudgingly admired his directness. He did not mince words or indulge in frivolous pleasantries. Whatever his faults, he was not dull or dithering.

She'd softened slightly at the sight of him clad in mourning. He was grieving. Assuming an earldom. And having to deal with two women thrust upon him from England—a complication he did not welcome or warrant. She looked toward the place where he had sat turned toward the window. The room seemed somewhat lacking without him.

Shrugging, she went to the bookcase, which required a ladder to reach the top shelves. Dare she? Clutching her skirts in one hand, she grasped a rung and began her ascent, studying titles on the way up. Some she knew and many she didn't. The old tomes had been cleverly arranged, books shelved beneath small portraits of the authors. A charming detail.

Did the castle have a newer library?

One title leapt out at her. *The Missing Duchess*. Intrigued, she looped her arm around a rung to anchor herself, albeit precipitously, freeing her hands to open to the first page.

When a knight of heroic standing falls in love with a noblewoman . . .

The door opened. Peg came through, something clutched in her hand. Seeing Blythe near the ceiling, she gave a little gasp. The vehement shake of Peg's capped russet head underscored her warning.

"Och, milady. Come carefully down. The laird wouldna like ye to harm yerself on his watch. I've something important for ye."

Blythe snapped the book shut, then made it safely down the ladder. Peg held out a letter.

From Father?

117

Had it been almost a sennight since their departure? The longest stretch of time in her life.

"The laird said to give ye this immediately. The courier just left."

Blythe broke the black seal with a swipe of her finger. "Lord Wedderburn" was penned in Father's familiar script, though he'd omitted her own name, nor did he sign his own. If the letter fell into the wrong hands, none would be the wiser. The game was to keep her whereabouts secret. But could it be done? And for how long?

Despite the night of turmoil and destruction we suffered of late, I am unscathed. But the danger remains. I trust you have in your possession my dearest treasure and will guard and keep such until I send word for its return. You will be rewarded handsomely for your trouble.

Alive, then. *Thank You, Lord.*

So unlike Father. So heartbreakingly brief. His "dearest treasure" could be none other than herself. "Trouble" certainly described her, at least where the laird was concerned.

Peg's sharp eyes never left her. "The laird said to burn it when yer done."

Blythe nodded absently, chilled. There was no fire lit here, only in their bedchamber. "I suppose Lord Wedderburn was too busy to come himself." He'd sent a servant in his stead, a common enough occurrence. Why did she feel a bit let down?

"Did ye want me to carry a word back to him, mem?"

Puzzling over her disappointment, Blythe refolded the letter. "Nay, I won't bother him. 'Tis the lykewake, after all."

"Och." Peg heaved a sigh. "The castle's walls are about to burst with so many mourners."

Blythe hid a smile. She'd never heard so many mourners make merry.

She looked to the letter again. In the time that passed between Father's posting and their receipt of it, had something happened to him? If so, who did she have? Not the Hepburns or Percys, who considered them a liability because of their Catholic Jacobite standing, not to mention her mother's reputation . . .

"Are ye all right, milady?" Peg dug in her pocket as if about to fetch smelling salts or whisky.

"I'm just overtired," Blythe said, hearing the distant lilt of a fiddle again. "I believe I shall go lie down."

21

Hours are Time's shafts,
and one comes winged with death.

SCOTTISH PROVERB

Blythe took to her bed for the next two days. Elodie hovered nervously, the altered mourning gown hidden away in a musty-smelling wardrobe. A clearly befuddled Peg came and went on fleet feet, bringing stillroom remedies and copious pots of tea. When she mentioned a physician, Blythe protested.

"But ye look peely-wally, mem," Peg said.

Blythe sensed this was no compliment. "Sleep is the great restorative, is it not? And I promise you the laird shan't have a malady or another death on his hands. I don't require any special tending. I am simply missing home, my father, and my work."

That very afternoon a surprise ensued. Blythe was sitting by the fire, feeling more rested, when Peg and the footman sworn to secrecy came in, arms laden. Standing, Blythe faced them, her mouth falling open as a familiar squawk met her ears.

Pepys?

Peg toted the covered cage, looking like she might laugh. "Where would ye like the contrary creature, mem?"

Blythe hesitated, then gestured to a window. "Pepys prefers light and fresh air."

In a quarter of an hour several trunks were brought, including a load of her papers and books, quills and ink. Father had overlooked little, at least the essentials. Her elation was tempered by the evidence that this meant a prolonged stay at Wedderburn.

What did the laird think of that?

"Thanks be to the lykewake, nobody thought anything of yer belongings coming in at the service entrance," Peg said. "Only a few ken yer in hiding. Just me and Rab Graham here, Mrs. Candlish, Munro, and now Sal. Even Cook believes she's just sending a tray to a guest. One of many in residence right now."

"So 'tis truly a secret."

"Aye, and yer sparrow can squawk all he likes. Nobody can hear him, shut up in the keep as ye are with walls seven feet thick. Not even with a window or two open. If anyone should ask, Mrs. Candlish said to tell them we're simply airing out the rooms now 'tis spring."

Blythe studied her, wondering if she went straight to the laird with a report of all Blythe said and did. Dismissing the uneasy thought, she bent over her trunk of papers and books. "How thoughtful of Father to send what he knows are most important to me. The gowns and fripperies I can do without, especially in a house of mourning. But I am half-alive without my work."

Peg dug in her pocket, then presented a shagreen case. "Yer spectacles, milady."

Thanking her, she took them, noticing Peg still staring. "Would you like for me to try them on?"

"I've ne'er seen a lady in spectacles, mem."

Blythe obliged, slipping them on so they hooked round her small ears and rested near the end of her nose. "'Tis necessary for book-work and reading."

"Yer a learned lass, to be sure. I canna read nor write." Peg looked at the three trunks that needed unpacking. "Where should we begin, mem?"

"I don't expect you to unpack, Peg. Surely you have better things to do in a castle overflowing with guests. Besides, I am restless and need something to occupy me. Think no more of it."

"Very well, mem, but if ye should change yer mind . . ." Peg worried her bottom lip. "With the funeral on the morrow, my hands are full, aye. All the servants are nigh run ragged with all the folks coming and going."

"I can only imagine." Mourners continued to come up the driveway at all hours. Blythe had finally stopped looking out the window. "I do have a last question."

"Of course, mem."

"Since it appears I'll be staying on longer, I would know more about Wedderburn Castle and the Humes. What is the new laird's name and title? The formerly styled Lord Fast?"

"The young laird, mem?" Peg drew up proudly. "Everard Hume, the most noble laird of Wedderburn, Viscount Ninewell and Marchmont, Baron Polwarth . . ." She trailed off. "I forget all the rest."

"No worries. And the new laird has brothers, does he not?"

"Aye, mem. There's Mr. Hume, or David, who lives in Edinburgh, then the third-born, Bernard. Next comes Ronan and then the twins—Alistair and Malcolm—followed by wee Orin."

Blythe repeated each name to etch them into memory. "How old is wee Orin?"

"He is but eight." Peg's face clouded. "Though his brothers are braw and stalwart, he's not cut o' the same cloth. But a more charming lad ne'r lived, and we'd all be heartbroken should anything happen to him."

Blythe's heart tugged. "And is there a Countess of Wedderburn in the making?"

"Och!" Peg's smile widened and revealed yellowed teeth. "Now there's a tale to tell. Many a lowly lass and wellborn lady in Berwickshire and beyond have their eye on the young laird, but he's bumbazed them all with his soldierin' and bein' gone for so long. He came home just two years ago."

"He fought on the continent, then? Against the French and the Spaniards?"

"Aye, mem. Under the Duke of Marlborough himself."

"Ah, Marlborough. I confess I know little of the war except the Battle of Malplaquet was brutal." How had Lord Wedderburn lived through that?

Elodie stopped her unpacking as if intrigued too. Blythe wasn't fazed when Pepys began squawking, though she quickly covered the cage to hush him so they could continue the conversation.

"Are there no women at Wedderburn Castle other than Mrs. Hume?"

"Crivvens!" Peg's face hardened, conveying how she felt about the woman. There was no artifice or subterfuge with these Scots. Did they all wear their feelings on their sleeves? "Mr. Hume is the only one who's married, aye, mem."

"Very well, Peg. I believe I shall keep all these Humes straight now."

With a slight nod, Peg seemed herself again. "Time for tea, mem. Cook has made enough oatcakes to feed an army."

22

*Jolly dogs! A Scots burial is merrier
than our weddings.*

ENGLISH DRAGOON QUARTERED AT FALKIRK

The funeral procession was about to begin, four Spears of Wedderburn bearing the walnut coffin the two miles to kirk. All the servants assembled in the castle's courtyard, a small army standing shoulder to shoulder, before the journey began. Looking out the castle's front entrance, Everard paused. It seemed everyone in Berwickshire lined the sunlit road all the way to kirk. As chief landowner in the district, he was not surprised. The laird had also been patron to the present minister, Reverend Johnston, a man of no small merit and a true shepherd to his oft wayward flock. Today there weren't many parishioners sober.

Sending a prayer heavenward, Everard took a step. Had he forgotten anything? Straightening his shoulders, he adjusted his cocked hat and motioned Boyd nearer for a final caution, remembering the debacle at his mother's burial.

"When the time comes to lower the casket, see that nae one is overcome by spirits and falls into the vault."

A grimace creased Boyd's weathered face. "Aye, milord."

Everard walked onto the drive where his women kin and a number of other ladies lined one side of the road, the gentlemen on the

124

other. For a few moments, observing the time-honored custom, the men crossed over to pay their compliments to the women. One lass down the line caught his eye, her lovely gown testament to the fact women oft wore their best garments to interments.

Alison?

She glanced at him then turned her face away, the feather plumage of her hat lifting in the rising wind, but not before he saw the ghost of a smile grace her flushed face. Tearing his attention away, bent on keeping his mind to the task at hand, he readied for the procession to begin. As he walked forward to take his place behind the casket, someone else caught his eye among the lasses. A solitary straggler near the back.

Wheest!

A second hard look and Everard nearly lost his bearings. The black veil attached to her bonnet fluttered, obscuring her features, but the sable dress could hardly hide her lithe form or queenly height.

Lady Hedley? For a moment he forgot so many eyes were upon him. Did they note his staring? What temerity the lass had. Though she was not bonnie, she was bold. And obviously intent on a long walk, however funereal. What would she do next? Seat herself at his table and discuss the next Jacobite Rising with David and Calysta?

Something akin to wry amusement lightened his mood. And then lightning-swift exasperation followed. The duke's daughter needed another talking-to, aye. But for the moment, he had a funeral procession to oversee.

Blythe knew the precise moment she was found out. Despite her hovering on the crowd's fringes, the laird's blue gaze found and fastened on her for an unflinching five seconds from across the rutted road. Another of his burning looks was sent her way. She deflected it by turning aside, her own gaze falling on the lovely woman he'd paid singular notice to moments before.

Alison.

She'd heard someone call her by that name, and it was as lovely as all the rest of her. In one beguiling gesture, Alison had smiled at the laird before tossing her head and turning away, a coquettish move Blythe had never been able to master.

The procession started, the women falling into step a respectable distance behind the Hume men. Dust rose like brown wraiths beneath the soles of their boots. And what men they were, so alike yet each so different but for the unmistakable twins. Four of the brothers bore the casket, all dark as the laird. Blythe wondered why there was no horse-drawn hearse. These Scots seemed to do everything the English didn't.

As the wind wreaked havoc with her veil, threatening to expose her further, Blythe spied who she guessed was Orin Hume walking alongside the casket, head bent, hands folded behind his back. Peg's words returned in a poignant rush.

"Though his brothers are braw and stalwart, he's not cut o' the same cloth. But a more charming lad ne'r lived, and we'd all be heartbroken should anything happen to him."

The lad's back was to her, so Blythe couldn't get a good look at him other than noting his hair was fair and his frame spare. Perhaps he seemed especially frail due to the vast, mostly treeless moorland ahead that lay split in half by a brown ribbon of road crowded by Scots as far as the eye could see. Surely so small a boy would find it hard to walk such a distance and then home again.

Onward they trudged. So far, other than the laird, no one had given her more than a cursory glance. With so great a throng she was easily overlooked. Not even Peg, walking with the servants, seemed to have noticed her yet. Surely such a large crowd was testament to the laird's character.

What had the former Lord Wedderburn been like? Perhaps there was a portrait of him in the Long Gallery that Peg had mentioned, though oil and canvas told only half the story. Had he loved his sons? Or had he been a distant, unapproachable father? Peg had not implied anything disagreeable like when she'd mentioned Calysta Hume. She'd spoken of him with utmost respect.

Blythe slowed her pace. Her slippers weren't made for distances. A blister or two would be her penance for this deception. The laird was in front of her, the women behind him. He stood out like a black sheep because of his height. His long coattails fluttered behind him as he walked, reminding her of ravens' wings.

Their arrival at the church came at last, offering shade beneath a bounty of oaks and elms. Time became a muddle of prayers and Protestantism so at odds with her Catholic upbringing. The old kirk had an earthy charm, having been built with a heather roof, and reminded her of their own chapel at Bellbroke Castle. Blythe kept to the shadows, out of sight of the laird and kin, mingling with the mourners who ringed the church. The sun came out, making the day less doleful, the June heat making her scalp itch beneath her borrowed hat.

Years from now, what would she remember?

Not the fickle weather, surely. Nor even the sorrowful look on the laird's face as the surprisingly simple coffin was lowered into the ground. Not the final prayer that was said, the Hume brothers bowing their coal-black heads.

Nay, when all was said and done, Blythe would never forget the way the new laird tenderly bent down and lifted his little brother, whose tears streaked his pale face, into his strong arms and carried him all the way home.

23

Death, they say, acquits us of all obligations.

MICHEL EYQUEM DE MONTAIGNE

O vercome with a nettlesome desire to have the last word, Everard arrived back at the castle and made his way unobserved to the tower. He'd not waited long by the turnpike stair. Winded and windblown, Lady Hedley soon appeared, her alarm at seeing him sketched vividly across her face. Removing her hat and holding the large hatpin in her gloved hand like a weapon, she faced him.

He stared at her, clutching his own hat behind his back. "Ye look ghastly in black, milady."

A beat of surprise followed. Had he set her a-simmer?

"How gallant, milord." She looked him over dismissively, faint scorn in her tone. "You yourself give new meaning to the phrase 'black as the earl of hell's waistcoat.'"

He stifled a wry smile. "Did you enjoy your long walk to the kirk and back?"

"Indeed, I did, despite the somber occasion."

"And how does your bonnie Northumberland compare with our barbarous Borders?"

She smoothed the veil of her hat. "I was too busy being discreet to pay much attention to the scenery."

"Nae doubt you'll rectify such in future."

"If you mean, am I anxious to go out again as I am tiring of my tower prison, the answer is aye."

"Have done with that," he said. "I am not your gaoler. Nor did I extend your stay by sending for your trunks and, um, spowe."

"*Spowe*? The Old English word for bird. I'm surprised you know it." Her full mouth curved upward, then flattened into a line. "You mean Pepys, my pet sparrow. Nay, you did not send for such. My father sent them, and for that I apologize, though my belongings are undeniably a comfort to me. Still, I have no intention of remaining here much longer."

"The duke obviously feels otherwise."

"I shall pen him a letter posthaste and press for a date of departure, then."

He held her determined gaze till she turned away and swept past him with a rustle of her skirts. Though she disappeared up the turnpike stair, her subtle rose cologne remained.

———

Still musing over his last encounter with Lady Hedley but determined to forget it, Everard entered the mews, the stone building facing open moorland that housed the Humes' hawks and falcons. The earthiness of hay and an almost melodic whistling and chirping on all sides were refreshing after so much company. Was it only two days ago they'd buried his father? It seemed an age instead.

The head falconer approached, his leather gloves always in evidence, a hooded longwing on his left arm. "Good morning, Lord Wedderburn."

"And to you," Everard replied, pulling on his own gloves. "I've come to see how the gyrfalcons fare, Dragonet and Bedivere in particular."

"Very well." He led Everard to their cages, enormous containers of iron with perches inside. "They've been enjoying a bit of sport along the hedgerows of late."

Each bird had an attendant, and Bedivere's was near at hand, feeding him finely minced wild game. The gyrfalcon, snow white except for slight markings on his wings, was calm. Only hungry birds were sent out. A sated bird was worthless as far as sport.

"Have ye come for a bit of hawking, milord?" the attendant asked.

"Nae. What I'm wanting is a kestrel to teach the youngest Hume hawking."

"Och, a sparrow hawk for Master Orin, then. The lad can learn to capture one if ye like, then name it and train it."

"Start small, aye. He's been studying the art of hunting with birds by book but has nae field knowledge. Tomorrow afternoon I'll bring him to the mews."

"We'll be ready, milord. And the same for ye if ye decide to go out yersel."

They knew him well. He oft cleared his head by going hawking. It was what he'd missed most while fighting on the continent. He was more about the birds than the chase, a constant point of contention between him and David. David was all about the kill. But he had left that morning for Edinburgh with Calysta, the both of them weary of country life.

Dragonet's keeper brought him forward, hooded and wary. Sharp talons gripped then slackened as the leather jesses tied to his legs were wound round Everard's extended arm. Never petted, these hawks were admired cautiously. The magnificent creature made a low *rrrrr* sound.

"D'ye want to dine, lad?" Everard said, lapsing into Scots. "Or fly?"

"He's not been out much of late."

"Still hood shy?"

"Aye, milord, but his dislike o' being hooded is some better."

They conversed a quarter of an hour more, and then Everard reluctantly left the mews. With the funeral now behind them, Wedderburn Castle moved forward without Alexander Hume's steadying presence and oversight. Everard felt the chasm acutely. It seemed he'd been handed a map with no directions or destination, no plan of attack. His father's illness had been sudden, with little preparation for the changing of the guard. Even the servants seemed tapsalteerie, still recovering from the weeklong lykewake and being up and down at all hours.

Everard headed toward the castle gardens. The yew hedge was in a full-blown June riot, the gardeners hardly able to keep it contained. Unwillingly, his gaze sought the tower, which was almost entirely smothered in ivy, an open window at the top. The dry moat beneath was abloom with wildflowers and weeds.

He'd not spoken with Lady Hedley since the burial. Odd what impressions lingered from that day. The sound of dirt clods hitting the lowered coffin. A woman's sobs, just whose he didn't ken. The scent of the wind and the warmth of the sun on his shoulders. He'd been the first to leave, finally carrying Orin home ahead of the funeral goers and leaving him to the care of his nurse.

Overriding all his scattered recollections was his terse clash with Lady Hedley afterward. He rather enjoyed riling her. How did she occupy herself on high? He passed through a side entrance, bypassing a maid carrying a bucket of ashes who curtsied hurriedly before continuing on her way.

That he'd best get used to, though he'd much rather remain Lord Fast. But lairds had a way of dying and lineages continuing. Wasn't that his father's final wish for him? A wife. A continuation of the Hume line. The ever-pressing heir.

He sought his father's study in a corner of the castle, the room that was becoming increasingly familiar and somewhat distracting on account of its expansive windows and views. Lately, he'd combed through account books and such, trying to grasp the complexities and inner workings of the estate. But there was much only a sleuth could decipher. If he only had his mother's ear. Her companionship and wisdom.

New correspondence sat stacked across his father's desk. Condolences, he wagered. Taking the top letter, he sat down, propping his boots on the low window ledge and leaning back in the worn chair. He swiped the seal and opened it, akin to uncapping a vial of perfume. Some spicy fragrance he couldn't own peppered the air.

Lord Wedderburn,

> *Our family expresses our deepest sympathies upon the passing of the former laird. We hope you will feel at liberty to call upon us at Landreth Hall in the near future.*

> *Believe me yours faithfully,*
> *Alison*

He looked up. Beyond the glass in his line of sight was Landreth Hall. Tall chimneys rose above oaks that gave the mansion both privacy and shade in warm Lowland summers. Sir Clive Landreth, a baron, was often away in London as a member of Parliament, leaving his wife and daughters in Berwickshire, though Alison often accompanied him. There she acted as hostess at their London townhouse and attended court functions. The baroness said it comforted her to know so many Hume men were near at hand just a few miles distant.

The temptation to visit was tempered by the tick of the mantel clock. Munro and Mrs. Candlish were due soon for their weekly meeting. But as the clock struck one, only the housekeeper appeared.

"Munro has been beset by the gout, milord," she said. "He is unable to take the stairs."

More than gout afflicted him, Everard sensed. He'd been especially downcast by the laird's death, having served him faithfully for thirty years or better.

"Is there nae stillroom remedy to ease him?" Everard asked. Munro was not a man to shirk his duties unless something was severely amiss.

"Naught seems to help, I'm sorry to say."

"Send for a physician, then."

"Aye, milord. I do feel 'tis time." She sat down in her usual place across the wide desk. The afternoon light called out the dark circles beneath her eyes and the spiderweb of wrinkles from forehead to double chin.

Munro wasn't the only servant Everard was concerned about.

The housekeeper had been in their employ even longer. "And you, Mrs. Candlish?"

"Me, sir?" She looked a bit startled. "Well enough after a lykewake and burial. I might ask the same of ye."

"Well enough, aye." He glanced at Alison's letter again before bending his thoughts to the matter at hand. "How goes it otherwise?"

"As for household news, the Edinburgh servants are in training, and 'tis fortunate since we've had one housemaid abed with a fever and another called away for a family misfortune. Cook has requested a summer's leave to visit her ailing sister in Berwick, so another cook has been secured from Glasgow with a character reference from Lord Buchanan"—she took a breath—"as his lordship has sailed to the American colonies and his return is unknown."

"Ah, fair Virginia," Everard mused. Buchanan was not only a Glaswegian but a tobacco laird to boot. "You are in need of leave yourself, are you not?"

Mrs. Candlish flushed. "Yer memory is rapier sharp, milord. But I cannot think of such now, not till matters settle down."

"Do they ever?"

"Never." She gave a rueful smile. "A household of this size has as much drama as a stage play."

"Speaking of drama, how are our guests in the tower?"

She paused, an amused light in her bleary eyes. "Lady Hedley is a most remarkable lass for a duke's daughter."

"How so?"

"I scarce ken how to answer, milord."

God's truth. "She is wanting to return to Northumberland."

"Indeed, but with matters unsafe for peers of the realm like the Hedleys, surely she should remain hidden here, at least till government troops withdraw."

"She attended the funeral."

"She . . ." Slack-jawed, Mrs. Candlish stared at him. Her shock was testament that the ruse had worked.

"In full mourning garb, which likely came from my mither's wardrobe."

"Well—I never—"

"She's clever. One step shy of scheming. But I don't want any harm to come to her on my watch. 'Tis the last thing Northumbria needs." He passed a hand over his jaw, unshaven since the funeral. "At the same time, harboring a Catholic Jacobite here casts suspicions on our loyalties and could well incur His Majesty's wrath."

"But, milord, you've proved yourself one of Britain's ablest soldiers. You were even knighted."

"Alas, Good Queen Anne is dead, and the memory of my service with her. The new king has nae such knowledge, nor can he speak English, let alone ken our prior history." He spoke slowly and carefully, reflecting on it all. "Loyalties change, as Hume history attests, and allegiances of both servants and masters shift too. I cannot urge caution enough to keep Lady Hedley's presence secret."

She fell into silence, then said, "Might there be a spy in our own household?"

He'd considered this. The *Scots Postman, Edinburgh Courant,* and *Gentleman's Magazine* were spread across the crowded desk, proclaiming the country's turmoil. Government troops sent as far north as the Highlands. Warrants served and arrests made for those who aided and harbored Stuart supporters. Rewards and bounties given to those who exposed them. The new king was trying to quell a rebellion before it began, by any means necessary and at any cost. There'd already been hangings and heads piked in public places.

"I would hate any harm to come to Lady Hedley . . . or to us," Mrs. Candlish said, eyes roaming the room as if she suspected someone might be listening. "She is highborn nae matter her circumstances—and altogether daring. A perfect storm for scandal."

"We must be continually on guard." Everard looked out the windows again, his tangled thoughts so at odds with the douce weather. "Wise as serpents and harmless as doves."

24

Fairies, black, grey, green, and white,
You moonshine revelers, and shades of night.

WILLIAM SHAKESPEARE

T was midnight. Time seemed to slow in Scotland, doubling the hours, the days. Unable to sleep, Blythe pushed back the bedcovers and tiptoed past Elodie, who snored softly in a corner bed. She approached the door to the turnpike stair, apprehension making her heart pound. Would the door be locked?

Her last skirmish with Lord Wedderburn had left her rather shaken. After he'd surprised her in the stairwell following the funeral, she suspected, perhaps unfairly, he might lock her in. But tonight, though she half expected it, nothing barred her exit.

Was he hoping she'd run away?

Breathing easier, she still trod on tiptoe, the stones cold beneath her bare feet though the June night was warm and inviting. Why did she feel a qualm? What harm was she doing in the dead of night?

From her tower perch she'd looked down upon and been deprived long enough of trellised roses and aromatic gillyflowers, ruffled cosmos and leggy sweet peas. The stone fountain splashed at the garden's heart, watery music night and day, making her want to trail her fingers in its cool depths. Prim beds of rue, sage, and other herbs abounded, even a lush canopy of grapevine and an old stone well.

A push of the heavy door at the stair's bottom led to a rusty groan so loud she winced. Was there a night watch? Moonlight silvered the garden, whose sweet scent was like perfume on the hushed air. This was simply the courtyard garden. Larger, more extensive formal gardens lay beyond Wedderburn's stony exterior. But nothing equaled the charm of this fragrant bower that had likely been here hundreds of years.

She kept to the shadows, feeling safe within castle walls. Even deer and rabbits and other marauding creatures were denied entrance. Outside the stillroom, the castle's hives hummed by day then faded to a slumbering lull by night. Her intent was a small bench she'd spied from all her looking out the narrow tower window. Discreetly, mind you. The last thing she wanted was to be found out. Few seemed to glance up at the old tower, but by going from window to window she had an enviable view from every direction at almost any hour.

She now knew when couriers came and departed. Which servants lived at the castle or in the village of Duns. What conveyances and horses were in the Wedderburn stables. How many gardeners there were. The location of the tradesmen's entrance and the coal cellars. Where the offices were—the stillroom and washhouse and poultry yard. She knew by heart the outer routines of the household from dawn till dusk, if not its inner workings.

Now, freed from her stony cage, she flitted about in the darkness like a captive bird. There was something utterly delightful about being alone and unfettered in a place usually denied her. She trailed her fingers through the splashing fountain, breathed in the scent of all the roses and lilies she could not gather for bouquets, and watched the moon creep across the skies till two of the clock.

She sat upon the bench, pondering her predicament and wondering why she'd not yet heard again from her father. Dare she ask the laird if he was privy to any news? He could be so forbidding . . . yet still tenderly toted his brother all the way home. She'd not seen this softer side of him, at least not in her presence. Nor had she seen him of late except by chance from her window. He obviously thought little of her or about her.

While she, oddly, found her thoughts increasingly full of him.

———— ◦❀◦ ————

The dining room had a new portrait. The tenth Earl of Wedderburn now graced the west wall. The likeness had been finished by artist Sir Godfrey Kneller before the laird succumbed to the illness that took his life, displaying the vigorous, ruddy-faced noble he'd once been. But at his instruction, it was not hung till his death.

Bernard gave the painting a stoic glance as he entered. Coming to the table, he looked at their father's empty place and then at Everard. "You might as well see it done," he said. "Faither isn't returning, and neither are you going anywhere."

Nay, he was not going away any longer. Not to war on the continent or their estate in Ireland or life as it used to be. Everard quietly changed places, raising the brows of his other brothers, who entered shortly thereafter and assumed their usual seats. Wee Orin appeared yawning and slow moving, taking his chair without a customary cheerful greeting.

"Since my word is now law," Everard said with a wink, "I want Orin nearer me than at table's end."

After a pause, Orin did as he bade, taking David's empty chair next to Everard. Grace was said and supper was served, dishes mounded with early summer fare from the garden, fresh salmon from the coast, and a great many bannocks.

"The sea fishing is fine," Ronan said, having caught their supper. "I've a new boat with a lugsail now that I'm overseeing the fisheries. Needs be we learn to cure herring as the Dutch do."

Bernard nodded. "We're better placed for North Sea fishing than even they. Faither always wanted our fisheries expanded."

Everard listened as they talked, glad the laird had insisted on an accounting of everyone's day around the table. Their mother had always been good at querying them and maintaining conversation, encouraging each one, when home, to take an active interest in the estate. David was the only one of the seven who had little involvement. Without him at the table, the mood was more congenial, the conversation less fractious.

Alistair and Malcolm would soon head to Edinburgh to train in medicine and law. Everard regarded them with affection. Highspirited, they kept Wedderburn from boredom and were known far and wide for their horsemanship, not only their soldiering.

"We've been invited to a ball," Alistair said, passing a dish. "At Addinston Abbey."

The auld pile was close to Wedderburn, near the Lammermuir Hills. The area contained several estates with an impressive collection of unmarried daughters. Bonnie Borders belles, all.

"Faither's passing has excused us Humes, aye?" Malcolm said.

"Aye, we've plenty to keep us occupied right here," Bernard said, helping himself to more tatties. "I have little time or patience for society."

Nodding, Alistair took a swallow of wine. "Needs be I get my lasses straight before I appear."

Ronan chuckled. "I, for one, would rather do anything than step the minuet."

"Shall we all grow auld and eccentric together, the *solitary* Spears of Wedderburn?" Bernard asked.

Alistair took another bannock and slathered it with butter. "The closest lasses are at Landreth Hall, though they're all a bit too young other than Alison."

"Dinna forget Lady Sirona of Merse House, Misses Lillias and Rose at Telford Abbey, Lady Janetta at Duns Priory. And . . ." Malcolm's hawkish features showed a telltale pleasure. "I dinna ken the last."

Laughter rumbled around the table. The last was Malcolm's favorite. He well knew her name. Countless letters had traversed the warring continent to her address, costing him a small fortune in paper and ink, sand and wax.

"The fair Honoree from Cranmuir Court," Everard said as he served himself another piece of salmon.

Malcolm flushed, managing to look delighted at the same time.

"Or have you set your sights on an English lass like our neighbor Mackay?" Everard jested.

"What?" all said in unison. "The bonnet laird?"

"He's recently taken a Lincolnshire bride. A distant cousin, I'm told."

Discontented murmurs ensued. All but Orin naysayed such.

"A sassenach? Is the man daft?" Alistair asked.

Everard tore his thoughts from the tower. What would his brothers think of their hidden guest? "So do we send our regrets about the ball or attend in mourning garb and risk putting a damper on the festivities?"

Silence was his answer. Orin shrugged and yawned again.

"Sleepyhead." Malcolm eyed his youngest brother before taking another bite. "Have your tutors been working you too hard?"

"Tutors? Nae, they're all on holiday," Ronan answered for him. "We've been in the mews training his kestrel for hawking of late. Smoking to calm the bird and keeping him in candlelight. I was smoking, rather. Orin minded the light."

"A kestrel?" Alistair asked.

"Aye, caught along the burn but a sennight ago."

"An eyas or a haggard?"

"Haggard," Ronan said.

"Remind me to give you another book I found in the library," Everard told Orin. "*De Arte Venandi cum Avibus*. On the art of hunting with birds."

"That is not why I am tired." Yawning again, Orin put down his fork. "I've been keeping watch at my bedchamber window when I come in from the mews. Betimes magic happens by moonlight."

"While the rest of us sleep?" Malcolm asked. "What means you?"

"There's a wraith in the garden," Orin said, his tranquil blue gaze undisturbed.

His brothers' eyes were upon him, utensils suspended.

"A wraith"—Orin picked at his bannock, chewing thoughtfully—"or mayhap a water kelpie."

Alistair's eyes narrowed. "You're jesting."

"She seems more water kelpie as she keeps by the fountain."

Everard felt a clutch of alarm. Studying Orin, he took another sip of wine. The lad's imagination knew no bounds. He was always authoring stories, his tutors said. Conjuring up fanciful tales and entertaining strange notions. Was his mind as weak as his body? Had their mother's death and now their father's left him a bit . . . unhinged?

"How many times have you seen this . . . um, creature?" Everard asked him.

Orin hesitated before answering. "Night after night."

"She does not frighten you?" Alistair asked.

A shake of his flaxen head. "She is douce, not ugsome."

His brothers were looking at Everard now, as if weighing his reaction. Orin's room was on the second floor facing the interior courtyard. He was usually abed by nine o' the clock, awake by six. Clearly he needed more sleep away from the mews.

Everard shrugged. "Dreams, mayhap."

"Nae." Orin turned toward him. "I am fully awake and watch by my window. Then when I cannot keep my eyes open, I return to bed and go to sleep."

"Do you see her come and go?"

He shook his head. "She just appears by moonlight. By day she disappears."

Alistair played along. "What is her name?"

"I dinna ken. But her hair is long and pale. And she is tall and willowy like a slender flower thistle."

Pale. Tall. Willowy . . .

Lady Hedley.

Everard nearly choked on his wine. Was he a simpleton, not realizing it in a trice? Tossing his napkin aside, he stood, wanting Orin's yawning to end. "To bed with you."

With a nod, Orin complied. The brothers resumed their talk of hawking and balls and comely lasses while he took Orin to his room, preoccupied by an Englishwoman who would have her way, come what may.

Even by moonlight.

25

Love built on beauty, soon as beauty, dies.

JOHN DONNE

Blythe watched the melted scarlet wax drip onto the letter before affixing her seal. It bore a woman's face in cameo but in no way marked her as the duke's daughter. She'd spent the morning writing letters in what she now thought of as the tower library, having moved the scarred desk beneath a window for better light. Pepys's cage was near at hand. Her beloved bird had been worrisome of late, hardly singing a note. Instead the clock Peg had brought ticked the time and helped orient her.

She leaned back in the chair, her gaze drifting from her letters to the lovely vista beyond the north window. She could not fault the view, though she missed the familiar upland fields and forest of home. For now, her nighttime revels in the garden were her secret pleasure, and she took additional delight in knowing the laird hadn't discovered her.

Sometimes she saw him ride out, down the long castle driveway and past the main gatehouse toward Duns or Moorkirk or across open moorland to unknown destinations. What freedom he had!

Sometimes she heard him outside. She was attuned to the richness of his speech even from a distance, all the rolling *r*'s and rich inflections of his Lowland Scots.

She searched for some physical flaw. *Spear of Wedderburn* wasn't far from the mark. Arrow-straight, he always stood tall and stalwart, his muscled bulk marking him as a warrior even in the garments of a gentleman. Quite simply, he stood out and drew the eye, like it or not.

She liked it not.

A twisting of the doorknob brought her to her feet. Turning, she faced the man she'd just been ruminating about, a flush warming her from the top of her head to her stocking-clad feet.

"Lady Hedley."

"Lord Wedderburn," she returned, schooling her surprise.

He left the stairwell door open behind him and came toward her, holding something in one hand. A letter? Nay, a package. Her gaze rested on it in question before rising to meet his remarkable eyes. She wanted to swim in their blueness.

He glanced at her desk, surely noting the stack of unposted correspondence, her many books and papers. She'd only posted letters to her father before now. What would he think of her messages to Oxford and Cambridge and abroad?

She tore open the paper and uncovered a book, the work of three long years. The printing had taken so long she'd nearly forgotten it. She set her jaw against the rush of emotion that followed, including feeling cheated of so personal a moment in the presence of a man she hardly knew.

"A book, Lady Hedley?"

"An antiquity I helped rescue for readers." Craving privacy, she turned her back on him, studying the specially cast Old English type and her initials on the cover beneath the name of an Oxford don's. Rifling the pages, she breathed in the fragrance of fresh ink.

She was at a loss for words, the achievement muted by the slight of her anonymity. Suddenly, Pepys burst into boisterous song, turning the moment winsome.

"Does your songbird always pipe such treasonous tunes, milady?" the laird said.

She turned round again. "What means you, milord?"

He held her gaze. "Is that song not 'The King Shall Come Round Again'?"

Understanding dawned and set her face aflame. Looking at the cage, she said sharply in Latin, "Tace!" *Be silent.* But Pepys had recovered his voice and was singing his heart out. Setting the book aside, she hastily covered the cage, and the music stopped. "Pepys's Jacobite leanings cannot be helped, milord. Besides, 'twas recently Restoration Day."

He let that pass, though she was surprised he didn't rise to the challenge. He had little regard for the Stuart kings. Liars and libertines, he'd once said. "Pepys, is it? Are you also a diarist, milady?"

"I do not keep one, nay. My diary entries would make you yawn, milord. What would they read? 'Transcribed fifty-four lines from Greek and Hebrew to Latin today, then paused for tea.'"

"You are an unusual lass, transcribing and translating Old English texts for publication."

He stepped around her to the desk, where he looked down at her work. The inked pages and various volumes, her many bookmarkers— some in Indian ivory, some silken ribbons, and others embroidered.

Feeling invaded, she couldn't help but quip, "Nothing remotely rebellious there, if you're wondering."

"What *are* you doing?" His *are* sounded like *air*. Would she never get used to his Scots lilt? How fickle she was. Rather, would she never tire of it?

She picked up her published work again, holding it to her bodice. "Translating Ælfric's ancient sermons, the homilies, from Anglo-Saxon."

"The auld monk?" One sooty brow raised. "An ambitious undertaking."

She covered a yawn with her hand, which led to his amused half smile.

"Is Ælfric boring to you, Lady Hedley, or are one too many midnight turns in the garden overtaking you?"

By Jove! She met his gaze again, a clash of green and blue. He knew. Pinpricks of surprise stole over her. She glanced at the window, craving fresh air, but the desk was blocking her way.

He took a seat on the settle, prolonging her disquiet. In the open doorway behind him, Elodie appeared briefly with an inquiring look, then vanished. Feeling tired and found out, Blythe sat down several feet away from him.

Would he reprimand her again like he'd done following the funeral? Studying him, unsure of his next move, she aimed for lightheartedness. "'You have such a February face. So full of frost, of storm, and cloudiness.'"

"Well played," he said, his eyes still stern. "Shakespeare. *Much Ado About Nothing.*"

"Act 5, scene 4."

He leaned back. "And you, milady, have a 'May face, full of caprice and whimsy and bordering on disgrace.'"

She couldn't place the verse, which was maddening. Had he made it up? Folding her hands in her lap, she refused to be unsettled by his poetic appraisal. Or yet another of his burning looks.

"My youngest brother believes you to be a water kelpie."

She paused. "I've no idea what a kelpie is, but I hope 'tis pleasant."

"Orin describes you as douce, not ugsome."

"*Ugsome* cannot be good. How is it our homelands are side-by-side yet I don't have a clue as to what you're saying? Though, by the intimation of it, *douce* does sound rather winsome, a bit in keeping with a water kelpie, perhaps."

He gave a nod, the light from the window falling across his linen shirt and dark jacket. "A kelpie is a fairy-like creature. A spirit. Sometimes evil, they can assume different shapes. Douce is indeed winsome. It means sweet, agreeable."

"I hope I didn't frighten him."

"Nae. He described you in complimentary detail around our dining room table, though his brothers think him a bit daft."

"Wee Orin."

He looked at her, a query in his eyes.

"I asked the maidservant Peg about your brothers. She's fond of Orin especially."

"All the household is. He had a hard start, our mither dying after his birth. He's been peely-wally ever since."

Her heart squeezed hard. This she understood firsthand.

Lord Wedderburn mentioned his mother in an entirely different tone. Regretfully and almost reverently. The countess had once been a vibrant, beautiful woman, Peg said. Her portrait hung in the castle's Long Gallery, a dusty chamber seldom seen, which piqued Blythe's interest if not her intent to go there.

"Our mothers were once friends," Blythe said with a trace of trepidation. Rarely did she speak of Clementine Hedley. Did he know her mother's history?

"The countess and the duchess, aye."

"Though they seldom saw each other after marriage."

"Except for your christening."

She sighed. "Which explains your unfortunate hosting of me here."

He regarded her as if she were a specimen under glass. "The gilded bird beats her wings against the iron bars of her humble cage."

"I hardly call Wedderburn Castle humble, milord."

"Compared to your Palladian palace in Northumberland it is, milady."

"How would you know?"

"I have spies, understand. Contacts."

"Then tell me how my father and home are. I've written to him faithfully and received but one letter in return."

"Your faither's well occupied keeping himself out of the hands of government men at the moment. He has little time for such niceties as letter writing." His face grew like February again. She daren't dig for details.

The tea she'd drunk for breakfast along with the bannock she was slowly becoming fond of twisted in her belly.

Oh, Father, you are in grave straits, indeed.

As she considered this new turn of events, the laird stood and walked away without so much as a by-your-leave, a great many unanswered questions in his wake.

26

She is a mortal danger to all men.

EDMOND ROSTAND

E verard left the stables atop Lancelot to clear his head from the morning's paperwork at his desk, tired of being so long indoors. The study's walls had seemed to close in on him. That and the memory of yesterday's meeting with Lady Hedley sat like a burr in his saddle. He leaned into the wind, Lancelot clearing a stone fence with ease, and headed toward the barn-building begun after the funeral.

The din of hammers met his ears, a welcome sound that bespoke a great many men from the surrounding glens and villages glad of work. One of his farm managers greeted him, his enthusiasm proof the effort was long needed and appreciated.

The auld laird's way was not the new laird's way.

His father, bless him, had resisted change. His lack of debt was testament to his Scots frugality, but the estate begged improvement. Aware of all the crumbling stone and peeling paint and damage done by time, Everard was intent on modernizing and beautifying his holdings, beginning with Wedderburn. His smaller, less significant properties could wait. He would, Lord willing, leave a legacy of which his descendants could be proud.

New barns, byres, and sheephouses were now begun at Wedderburn. A new dairy was proposed. Plans were drawn up to modify stables unchanged since the fifteenth century. Fallow and untenanted land was reviewed as to its best purpose. Crops were rotated. New grains were considered as farm records and accounting books were pored over. Tenants unable to pay their rents were not left mired in their debts but included in the improvements or given leave to go elsewhere. Everard worked as hard as his factors and farm managers. Let no one say he was idle or frittered his fortune away.

"Dinna be too ambitious," Bernard had said at breakfast. "You'll have Faither turning o'er in his grave."

"We're in a position to act, make better, even beautify," Everard replied with growing certainty, wanting his brothers to envision his plan or at least see the value of moving forward. "I'm nae spendthrift, but I'll see it done right during my tenure, at least till the next generation."

"The next generation?" Bernard had laughed. "Only Davie has wed and his union thus far has been less than fruitful."

Still vexed by the truth of his brother's words, Everard finished his rounds atop Lancelot. He came home and bathed, changed clothes, and was preparing to go out again when Boyd returned to give a report on his latest foray.

He looked askance at Everard. "Ye have the look of courting about ye, milord."

Standing before his shaving glass, Everard discarded a lace stock and wound a plain muslin one around his tanned neck. "Why does it feel like preparing for battle instead?"

Chuckling, Boyd admired a silver shoe buckle. "If it was the right lady, milord, it wouldna."

Everard chuckled. Duty or pleasure? "I'm to ride to Landreth Hall."

"Och, ye dinna look too pleased about it."

"I've been away too long. Such always makes for an awkward encounter."

"'Tis not ye who's been away, milord. Last I heard the Landreth lass was in London with her faither."

"She's since returned," Everard said. Alison's brief but alluring perfumed note was proof. Only he couldn't recall what he'd done with it. Buried beneath papers on his desk, likely.

Boyd muttered something under his breath while Everard knotted his stock. Alison, for all her beauty and breeding . . . Nae, he'd not give a nod to the wags who sought to besmirch her. It was mere hearsay. Best look to his own conduct and conversation.

He smoothed a strand of hair escaping his queue. The man in the looking glass seemed hollow-cheeked and red-eyed but was clean-shaven at least, his garments newly tailored and brushed. With a nod to Boyd, Everard left his rooms and returned to the stables.

Down the long drive he went at a canter, Landreth Hall's new Venetian windows glittering in its stone facade. Overlooking a small loch, the park-like grounds were a sharp contrast to Wedderburn's old-style Renaissance gardens and orchards.

Thinking of the gardens brought Lady Hedley to mind. Would she keep up her nighttime haunts?

Once he dismounted, a stable lad led Lancelot away and Everard approached the front door. It opened ahead of him, a liveried butler in attendance. Everard stepped into the cool, shadowed foyer. Every house had a certain ambiance, a fragrance, and Landreth was no different. Whereas Wedderburn was imbued with tobacco smoke and leather, Landreth bespoke beeswax and perfume.

The butler led him to a spacious drawing room. "Miss Landreth will soon join you."

Restless, Everard took a slow turn about the elegant chamber, noting the newly laid parquetry floors, the gilt mirrors covering oak wall panels, the sets of velvet settees and chairs and side tables. A silvery spiderweb clung to the plaster ceiling with its floral motif. Even so, the newest drawing room was a far cry from Wedderburn's worn grandeur.

"Milord." Alison's high voice was suffused with warmth. She approached him as he stood by the fireless hearth, her gown the purple of a thistle, her lushness spilling out of its silken confines at every turn. A beauty patch adorned one heavily rouged cheekbone, drawing attention to her eyes. Her hair was powdered snow white. She had the look of a courtesan. Perhaps that gave the wags fodder for gossip.

"Alison." He removed his cocked hat and tucked it beneath one arm.

"I shall dispense with Lord Wedderburn, then." She smiled up at him, the arch of her dark brows beguiling. "There seems no call for it, given we've known each other since we were in leading strings."

He took her hand, kissing the soft, blue-veined skin lightly. The eldest Landreth daughter, Alison was the beauty of the family. It was said the court painter, Sir Godfrey Kneller, had approached her father to capture her on canvas at his London studio. Whether she'd obliged or not, Everard didn't know.

"I thought you'd never come," she said, leading him to a settee. "The time is long without you. I daresay you're even handsomer than I remember."

Handsome. Not hellish as in Lady Hedley's estimation.

He sat down after she did, an empty space between them. With a graceful display of lace-covered arms and pale hands, she settled her skirts around her. The silken fabric brushed his leg and covered one of his shoes. An outright enticement. Alison did indeed have all the makings of a courtesan.

Placing his hat on an end table, he said, "I would have come sooner, but certain matters keep me to home."

"I can't imagine how much Wedderburn Castle has changed in so short a time. You barely home from the war. The twins returning soon after and preparing for university in Edinburgh. I've heard Bernard and Ronan have taken an interest in estate management, especially the fisheries and collieries. Surely that leaves you more time, does it not?"

He leaned back against the stiffly upholstered settee. "More time for what, pray tell?"

"More pleasurable pursuits." She took out a fan, swishing it open with a flick of her wrist. She smiled at him over its lace-tipped edges. "You mustn't miss the event of the summer season—Addinston Abbey's ball."

"With pleasure," he replied wryly. "We're in mourning, remember." Though he grieved his father deeply, he was glad it excused him from society.

"Nonsense, Everard. Last I was in London I saw a harlequin, a Scaramouch, a shepherdess, and a black-satin devil get into a mourning coach to go to a masquerade. You can also frequent the gaming table and be admitted to any club whilst in sable, among other things."

"I've nae desire to game or dance or club."

"Besides, you are attired in blue, not black. I daresay mourning is at your whim."

"I ken how you hate black."

"Truly." She laughed and swished her fan harder. "As for the coming ball, whoever shall I dance with if not you?"

"Be glad I'm not stepping on your slippers."

"We could practice right here." She smiled, two well-placed indentations in her cheeks making him nearly capitulate to her pleas. "Right now."

He winked. "And what would your faither say to such?"

"You're recalling his dislike of your soldiering. 'Tis a different matter now you're the earl." She sighed, eyes narrowing. "Besides, Father remains in London. My sisters are elsewhere. And my mother is—"

"Right here, my dear. You don't think I'd neglect to express my condolences to the laird, do you?" Lady Landreth entered the room, a Pomeranian on her heels. "How is it you've neglected to call for refreshments? Surely Lord Wedderburn would like a wee dram, Daughter."

Alison blushed at her mother's gentle chiding, looking more the prim miss she'd once been before London had its sway. "Would you care for whisky, Lord Wedderburn?"

"Aye, madam," he said. Getting to his feet, he turned toward the baroness in greeting and gave a small bow.

She curtsied as Alison summoned a maid, then took a seat opposite them, placing her Pomeranian in her lap. "How good of you to see us." She regarded her daughter with a secretive smile. "One of us in particular."

"How is Sir Clive?" Everard asked as refreshments were served.

"Still in London trying to pass the Septennial Act and reduce parliamentary expenses." The baroness's levity seemed to fade, and a frostiness crept in. "He was last home at Martinmas."

November. Everard took a swallow of whisky, the burn of it rolling down his throat as he recalled the baron had been in some sort of brow-raising incident of late. Everard paid little attention to scandal sheets, but London newspapers had tied Landreth to a certain courtesan there. Many men had mistresses, but he hadn't thought the aging statesman would be one of them.

"I've seen Father more recently, being in London till now." Alison sipped her drink, her face a mask of composure. "He is well. And busy planning his usual fall hunt here, to which you and your brothers are invited, of course."

Everard gave a nod. He'd missed the last one. "He was always one for sport."

"Truly, be it politics or wild game." Lady Landreth gave a sympathetic smile. "I'd rather talk of your family, milord. How are your brothers faring after so great a loss? Orin especially?"

"Dear Orin," Alison said. "He was quite undone at the funeral."

"He was close to Faither. The loss hasn't been easy." Orin's tear-stained face was uppermost in Everard's mind as well, though the rest of the day was a benumbed blur. "I've given him some time away from his tutors. Lately he's taken up hawking."

"Wise of you to give him a respite from all that learning," Lady Landreth said. "He shies from firearms if I remember correctly. Hawking might suit him better."

A patter in the hall ended their conversation. Three of Alison's sisters rushed in, their youthful exuberance excusing their behavior. Miniature versions of Alison, they smiled prettily at him, curtsying and jockeying for position. He'd forgotten their names as he rarely saw them. Lady Landreth reminded them to mind their manners before telling them to accompany her to the garden now that the sun had come out. They left, the Pomeranian trailing, its claws clacking against the parquet.

Left alone with Alison, Everard finished his whisky, mindful of the time. She waved her fan about again with practiced ease. Women and fans were not unlike men with swords, he decided. Hers seemed a blatant tool for coquetry.

"When shall I see you again?" Brushing his sleeve with the fan's lace tip, she looked to her lap, then up at him as if gauging the effect she had on him.

He met her seductive gaze and nearly lost his footing. Still enticed he was, yet oddly evasive for reasons he couldn't define. "Mourning is a hard taskmaster. Who can say?"

27

I am little acquainted with politeness,
but I know a good deal of benevolence of temper
and goodness of heart.

ROBERT BURNS

A storm of hoofbeats drew Blythe to a tower window. Lord Wedderburn? Down the castle drive he went on one of the handsomest dapple-grey stallions she'd ever seen. Earlier, from another window, she'd spied him crossing the courtyard to the stables. His attire had taken her aback.

Dressed in a deep-blue coat and breeches, with silver buckles at his knees that glinted like the silver buttons forbidden during mourning on his waistcoat, he seemed to have shed his sable. Silver lacing adorned his cocked hat. Not at all fit for mourning. Fit for courting.

Was he?

Depressed by the most recent news of her father and strangely unsettled by the laird's fine appearance, Blythe went to bed. Surely a nap would restore her low spirits. Her nights in the garden were catching up with her. And now that she'd been found out, future nightly escapades held less appeal.

She lay down on the immense bed, a prayer on her lips and her grandmother's rosary clutched in one hand. Slowly she slipped into a fitful sleep, broken by Pepys singing and the ebb and flow of castle life beyond the tower.

A door thudded closed.

"Have mercy, milady." Elodie's distressed voice brought Blythe bolt upright. "I'm sorry to awaken you, but . . ." She sank down on the foot of the bed, a hand to her bodice as if she'd suffered a fright.

"Are you all right?" Blythe asked, casting off sleep. Rarely was Elodie so discomfited.

Her flushed face bespoke alarm and regret. "Nay. I've—*we've*—been found out."

Blythe glanced around, expecting someone to rush in and demand an accounting. As if reading her thoughts, Elodie hastened to shut the door as Blythe sought the hearth's warmth.

"Peg came with a letter whilst you were asleep." Sitting again, Elodie still looked stricken. "On her way back down the stair she dropped a handkerchief. I thought to catch up with her, so I strayed beyond the turnpike stair into the corridor just as a boy came into it—"

"A servant, perhaps?"

"If so, a well-dressed one, though he hadn't the look of a Hume about him." Elodie took a breath. "Peg went on her merry way, none the wiser, and there I stood with the handkerchief, the boy looking back at me over his shoulder as Peg ushered him away. The laird's mood may be especially dark once he discovers we've been further found out."

Blythe envisioned it, feeling they were naught but a burden all over again. "Perhaps 'tis best. Confirmation we cannot stay here any longer. I shall ask for the loan of a coach. We can be home in two days' time."

"But Peg overheard the laird say your father is no longer at Bellbroke, which must mean he's gone into hiding. If so, 'tis no safer for us to return there alone with the servants, if any faithful servants remain."

Blythe's mind veered from home to the matter at hand. "The boy you mention might well be young Orin Hume. Though I've not met him, I saw him from afar at the funeral. He's fair and slight."

"'Twas him, then." Elodie sighed and began pacing before the hearth. "'Tis not possible to keep hiding from all those in the household."

Blythe slipped her rosary into her pocket. "Our three weeks here is a quandary for all involved." She looked toward the door, further perplexed. Was it ajar? She thought Elodie had closed it. "You mentioned a letter? Not from Father, I suppose."

Elodie went to retrieve the post from the table by the door. "Nay, from Cambridge, likely involving your work. But it's been opened and perused by the laird, of course, who must monitor all that comes and goes for our safekeeping."

Pocketing the post, Blythe glanced at the door again. A boy stood there, silent as a cat. She'd not even heard the door open. So pale he was but for his eyes, the same remarkable hue as the laird's. The same child she'd seen the laird carrying in his arms after the funeral. And now the Hume who'd foiled their hideaway.

She went to the door, hand outstretched. "Please come in, kind sir."

The boy regarded her closely, a query forming on his face. "You are the water kelpie."

She smiled despite herself. "I am merely Lady Blythe Hedley, a duke's daughter, though perhaps a water kelpie is something to aspire to."

He gave a charming little bow, and she sensed his disappointment that she was merely a duke's daughter.

He took a tentative step forward, eyes on Elodie, who had stopped her pacing. "I am the youngest Hume."

"Ah, Master Orin." Blythe gestured in Elodie's direction. "I believe you've already met my lady's companion? She seems to have been our point of introduction."

He gave a shy smile, then looked around the room so intently Blythe wondered if he'd ever seen it. "Why are you being kept in the tower?"

"A fair question." She hesitated, wanting to handle matters honestly. "But first a bit of history. When I was born, your parents were my godparents. And being godparents, they promised to look after me. Lately my family has become unpopular with the king, and so—"

"King Geordie?" His eyes widened. "Not the king o'er the water?"

"King Geordie is not fond of my father, I'm sorry to say. But the would-be king o'er the water and he are indeed friends. Alas, the Stuart heir has been away doing what deposed royalty do."

"Plotting to regain his faither's throne," Orin said with an understanding that belied his age. No doubt he was privy to more than a few political conversations between his elder brothers around the dinner table.

"So," Blythe finished, "I've been needing a place to stay while my father and King Geordie, as you call him, get things sorted out."

Pepys began to sing from the other room, a timely distraction, delighting Blythe. Immediately, Orin turned in the bird's direction.

Blythe smiled down at him. "You've yet to meet my feathered friend, Pepys. He has a repertoire of songs that are quite forbidden and may well pipe you a treasonous tune or two."

Orin listened, his solemn face transformed. She led the way into the other chamber, where the sparrow sang as if in symphony. The lad stood before the cage, enthralled. Had he never seen a tame songbird?

"To reward him for his daring performance, you might give him a bit of rapeseed. Here." Blythe poured some into Orin's open hand and showed him the narrow opening in the cage, where his fingers fit easily.

To Orin's obvious delight, Pepys began pecking at the seed and soon consumed it, only to resume singing again, so exuberantly Blythe finally said, "Tace!"

When Pepys fell silent at the sharp command, Orin grinned, revealing a missing front tooth. "Optimē."

"Your high praise of him might fluff his feathers," she teased.

He laughed. "I should like for Pepys to meet my kestrel, Sir Gareth."

Blythe pursed her lips in thought. "But what if Sir Gareth is hungry for a song sparrow?"

His brows arched. "Then I shall write a tale about them meeting. They shall be quite civilized Aves."

"Gentlemanly Aves, I'm sure." She laughed softly, the sound strange after so many melancholy days. "So your pastime is writing, is it?"

"On occasion, though my tutors discourage me all they can."

"Bah! 'Tutors' is just another name for depriving boys of their play."

He nodded, focusing on the sliver of window where the light was quickly fading, as if mindful of the time. Orin was cast in shadows, his profile a softer silhouette of the laird's more rugged one. But where had he gotten all that fair hair?

"'Twill soon be suppertime," he said. "Won't you join my brothers and me in the dining room?"

Blythe checked another laugh, envisioning the laird's thunderous expression if she accepted the invitation. "You have commendable manners, Master Orin, but Miss Bell and I had best content ourselves by partaking of supper right here."

He studied her as if still deciding whether she was a kelpie or a duke's daughter. "I must go, milady." He gave another touching little bow, then backed out of the room as if she were royalty.

For a few minutes, lost in the pleasure of his company, she'd nearly forgotten her predicament.

28

The hours I spend with you I look upon
as sort of a perfumed garden, a dim twilight,
and a fountain singing to it.

GEORGE EDWARD MOORE

T was Orin's turn to give an accounting of his day. Expecting him to tell about his kestrel or Wallace's latest antics, Everard was only half listening, lost in thought about his afternoon visit to Alison. When the dining room suddenly grew hushed, he thrust his musings aside. His fork stilled when Orin announced between bites, "I have met the water kelpie, and she is, in fact, a duke's daughter."

Wheest! His brothers' gazes swiveled from Orin to him. Setting down his fork, Everard took a long drink of claret. No doubt this meeting had happened while he'd been away at Landreth Hall. He swallowed. "So, what do you make of her ladyship?"

"She is verra bonnie."

Everard raised a brow.

"And clever."

Clever, aye. Lady Hedley was that.

"Her sparrow is clever too. He sang me several songs." Orin forked a bite of mutton, smiling. Everard had missed that smile. He'd hardly seen it since their father had fallen ill. "I told her about Sir Gareth."

160

Farther down the table, Bernard asked in Gaelic, "Has our wee laddie gone mad?"

"I fear so," Ronan said with a frown.

"Too much time is being spent penning fanciful fables and the like," Malcolm added. "His tutors said as much, did they not?"

Everard set down his glass. "Orin is simply telling you about our new houseguest, Lady Blythe Hedley, the Duke of Northumbria's daughter."

A sudden silence, and then . . .

"Come, Brother, what haver is this? A duke's daughter?" Alistair began to laugh so heartily he nearly knocked over his glass. "And from Northumbria, nae less, the den of Jacobites and Papists? Well, that makes a fine tale!"

"'Twas Faither who invited her," Everard said, unamused. In as few words as he could, he enlightened them on all that had transpired. "Her ladyship is lodged in the tower at present. I had thought to keep her there till Davie was gone, at least. And it seems safest given the sentiments of some of our neighbors."

Ronan pushed his plate away. "You are not jesting."

"Nae. Her ladyship's circumstances make her something of a prisoner here." Everard looked at his unfinished meal. "And she does not care for our Scots hospitality."

"You can hardly blame her." Malcolm resumed eating. "A lofty Northumbrian dukedom is a far cry from a rustic earldom in the Borders."

"We must meet her," Bernard said, a glint in his eye. "Is she fair as an English rose? Or more like a Scottish thistle?"

Orin sat up straighter in his chair. "She is verra douce to me."

"Then by all means send for her," Ronan said, looking at Everard again. "We must meet this secreted sassenach."

Blythe drew her spoon through her bowl of Scotch broth, enjoying the coziness of eating by the fire and not in a cavernous dining room. Across from her, Elodie poked at her salat, still dismayed by the afternoon's events.

"I do wonder what the laird will do once he learns we are found out." She took another bite, looking mournful. "I take all the blame. If I'd only let that dropped handkerchief alone . . ."

"What's done is done," Blythe said gently, secretly relieved. Being discovered seemed one step shy of departure. "If Lord Wedderburn storms in, I shall ask him for the loan of a coach, as I said. Surely his zeal to be rid of us rivals our own—"

A door creaked open. Peg appeared, looking a bit flummoxed. "Milady . . ."

"Do come in." Blythe smiled, bringing a napkin to her lips. "Supper is delicious, by the way."

Peg approached, appearing a bit downcast. "I'd be bringing ye dessert, but it seems the laird has other plans."

"What means you?" Blythe asked, setting down her spoon.

"He's requesting you meet him in the formal drawing room. With yer maid."

Blythe looked at Elodie, whose brows nearly touched her hairline. Peg's unspoken words resounded loud and clear.

Immediately. Without further ado.

Looking down at her gown, Blythe was glad she had on her best blue silk with the lace trim. Though she was plain, her gown was pretty. She raised a hand to the lace pinner atop her hair. Elodie had taken pains with her coiffure that morning, arranging a cascade of barrel curls. A pearl choker circled her throat, not the more dramatic royal gems she'd inherited from her mother, which were still at Bellbroke. Or had they been plundered?

"Very well, then." Fighting the dread of another encounter, Blythe stood, her supper grown cold.

Might the laird have more news of her father?

Elodie brought up the rear as Blythe followed Peg down the turnpike stair into previously forbidden realms. Shadowed corridors and door after heavy door piqued her curiosity. She breathed in the utterly masculine character of the castle, as if there'd never been a countess. What had Lady Wedderburn been like? Had she not left her mark on anything but her sons?

Peg paused before a grand door. No voices snuck past it, making their entrance especially unnerving. Once Peg opened it, Blythe summoned all the dignity of her grandmother, the dowager duchess, and crossed the threshold, Elodie in her wake.

Ringing the paneled chamber were four stalwart Humes in varying degrees of virility. She'd seen them only from a distance at the funeral. How striking they were up close. Black clad, they reminded her of specters, akin to something out of a Shakespearean tragedy. Hamlet or Macbeth.

The laird was standing by a window, his back to her. He had shed his fine courting clothes of that afternoon and returned to unrelieved black again. He turned around, though his brothers had already pinned her with inquiring eyes. She smiled, or tried to, the room so quiet one could hear the rain's patter on the roof. Her pulse was fast as Pepys's wings, stealing her breath, making her rue her too-tight stays.

Orin was sitting on a window seat. He came forward, smiling, obviously delighted to see her. She took her eyes off the laird and took Orin's outstretched hand. He seemed to be saying, *This is my friend whom I want you to meet.* The clasp of his small fingers was sweet. For a moment, the knot in her throat made her forget her skittishness.

One by one the brothers came forward, executing small, gallant bows in deference to her rank.

"Lady Hedley, I am Ronan Hume." The man who stood before her was most like Lord Wedderburn. Such eyes he had—even bluer than the laird's.

"I am Bernard, milady." This man's lithe frame was at odds with his sturdier brothers'. She saw a bit of Orin in him. He looked kind. Sincere.

"And I am twin to Malcolm," said the next. "Alistair Hume."

The twins were impossible to tell apart except one bore a slight cleft in his chin. Candlelight called out reddish glints in their hair. Wide of shoulder, they were nearly as tall as the laird.

Why must she measure every man against him?

"Davie is missing," Orin told her quietly. "He lives at Hume's Land in Edinburgh with Calysta."

For this absence Blythe was most grateful. The silence stretched a beat too long till she said, "I am pleased to meet you all. I'm here under unusual circumstances with Miss Bell. But"—she looked to the laird, who stood on the other side of Orin—"I come with a request. I can no longer impose on your hospitality." She squeezed Orin's hand. "The loan of a coach would be much appreciated. Traquair House is not far, to start."

"Forty miles," the laird said.

"Not so daunting a distance, surely, in a coach-and-four. Or a flying coach if you have that here. Perhaps the villages of Lauder and Galashiels have a stage." Could he tell she'd been consulting old maps in the tower library? "They are not so small as towns go."

"Stages are regularly attacked by highwaymen in these parts, milady," Bernard replied. "As for Traquair House, it has recently been sacked by a mob. Though the Stuarts are away, damage has been done."

A gasp escaped her as shock took root, bringing back the horrific night they'd fled Northumberland. "I am very sorry to hear it. Glad I am the Stuarts are safe. Which returns me to the coach-and-four. Will you loan one to us for a time?"

"Nae," Everard said matter-of-factly.

Nae. Was that all? She flushed, waiting. Orin squeezed her fingers gently as if telling her to take heart.

"He's right, milady. Highwaymen aren't the only ones to take heed of," Ronan said. "King Geordie's troops are crawling all over both Highlands and Lowlands. Even a lady of your rank and station isn't safe. Your Catholic Jacobite leanings mean mayhem, I assure you."

"Besides, our faither, God rest him, promised you safe haven."

This from Alistair, who'd crossed his arms and widened his stance. "What would we tell your faither if harm came to you?"

"Not only that," Malcolm said. "We've neighbors who are pro-Hanoverian and some we suspect to be spies. If they ferreted out you'd been here, there'd be Hades to pay."

Spirits sinking lower, trying to make peace with discarding her plans, Blythe stared at the green-and-gold-patterned carpet at her feet.

"Return to your cards," the laird told his brothers, "so that I might have a word with her ladyship in private."

They withdrew, even a reluctant Orin, though Elodie took a seat by the door.

The laird came nearer the hearth, where a low fire sputtered, and removed something from his weskit pocket. "I have a letter from the duke," he told her, eyeing her again before unfolding the paper.

Her soul stood on tiptoe waiting. Did he always do things with such infernal unhurriedness? When he passed the letter to her, she bent her head and devoured the heartbreakingly brief contents. Her father was concealed at various friends' and neighbors' homes, evading arrest. He would write again as time and circumstances allowed.

She craved more, but little must be penned lest it be intercepted. She sensed he was still plotting. Planning. Helping return the Stuarts to their rightful throne. His beloved scrawl swam before her eyes as tears rose. One spattered the paper she held, large as a raindrop. She could not help it. Did the laird despise a show of emotion?

Leaning nearer, he pressed a black-edged pocket handkerchief into her hands. She dabbed at her eyes discreetly, wishing she could turn her back on him like she had when he'd handed over her published work.

"Mayhap you need to reconcile yourself to staying here, milady." His steady gaze held shrewdness. "Earn your keep."

Earn my keep?

"'Tis obvious Orin is fond of you. He doesna take to many outlanders."

So not only did she need to earn her keep, but she was an outlander. A—what had Peg said? Sassenach? She'd uttered the word like one would an epithet.

"I mean nae insult. Once upon a time we Lowlanders were called that by Highlanders." He paused, something softening his intensity. "As long as you are here, I ken how to better pass your time."

"Then pray, tell me."

He crossed his arms. "Orin's tutors are an ill-willy parcel."

Ill-willy? Less than complimentary, she guessed.

"Not what a grieving lad needs. I sent them away for a time and would like to keep them away awhile longer. But I need something to fill the lad's hours." He returned the letter to his pocket. "You come well qualified."

So blunt he was. Such utter disregard for her title and standing. He might ask her rather than tell her. Her chin rose a smidgen higher. "Do you often assign houseguests such tasks, milord?"

"Only duke's daughters." Eyes alight, he continued, "You may find tutoring to be more rewarding than toiling for university dons who fail to publicly credit you with anything more than your initials on a work you obviously invested a great deal of time in."

She all but squirmed where she stood. For once they were likeminded. Had he somehow sensed her private frustration?

"Mightn't a grieving lad have more need of your scholarship than a passel of vauntie, vainglorious auld men?" he asked.

Again, he read her thoughts, but she couldn't resist a little needling of her own. "Perhaps I should apply my scholarship to your speech, milord. Labor over a dictionary of your peculiar language. 'Tis a great garble of words and growls, at least to my Northumbrian ears."

"Your Northumbrian *r*'s stuck at the back of your throat are little better, milady."

Suddenly weary, she looked away from him to the hearth's fire, wanting to sit down as the conversation continued. He reached for a pipe in a pipe stand on the mantel and bent to light it from the glowing coals.

Would he not even ask if she minded he smoke?

He gestured to the sofa nearest the hearth. She sat, gratefulness warming her as much as the fire.

Pipe lit, he drew in a breath, his chest rising then expanding as the bowl grew fiery. "Are you not aware that Northumberland was once claimed by Scotia? I do recall hearing something about the upland Hedleys, notorious Borders reivers beginning in the fourteenth century."

Ignoring that, she said, "If I am to tutor Orin, how would my presence be explained to the rest of the household?"

He shrugged. "You could take the form of a servant."

Her eyes widened. "I—what?"

"Did not Christ our Savior do the same? He made himself of nae reputation and took on Himself the form of a servant." He blew out a breath and held the pipe aloft, examining it. "We'd be wise to follow His example."

"You quote from Philippians." She looked hard at him. "It hardly applies."

"Och, but it does. To live is to give—serve—nae matter our rank or station. Yet we are all proud, milady. Sometimes pride even parades as humility."

Humility. Of which she had none. The pride of Lucifer, perhaps. Heat rushed through her like a rash. "Go on."

He gave her another of his burning looks. "Alas, your speech and demeanor are hardly servant-like and would give you away." Another lick at her pride, surely, though his tone was smooth as oil. "'Twould be wiser to have you here under the guise of hard circumstances."

"Like Elodie, my companion. She came to me in similar fashion."

He looked over her shoulder at Elodie still by the door. "As tutor, you'd have the run of the castle."

She softened, trying not to look at him overlong. "Indoors and out?"

"Not too far out of doors. Safety is our aim, aye?"

Our. What a wonderful word. While she was already fond of

Orin, she was far less sure of this unexpected arrangement. She studied the laird through the purling smoke, his pipe reminding her of home. The scent was unmistakable. Even noblewomen smoked at the French court, but few had this variety of tobacco. 'Twas her father's favorite.

"Orinoco," she said, ignoring the pang it wrought.

He gave a nod. "From Virginia Colony, aye."

She breathed in the fragrance even as she sent up another silent prayer for her father and returned to ruminating over the laird's startling proposal.

29

Glass, China, and Reputation, are easily crack'd,
and never well mended.

BENJAMIN FRANKLIN

Truly, a more contrary woman had never been born.

Everard smoked his pipe, wondering whether she objected. Virginia's fragrant Tidewater tobacco smoke spiraled between them. The half-moons beneath Lady Hedley's eyes didn't escape his notice. Was she not sleeping well?

Her skirt hem was alarmingly near the hearth's fire. Bending down, he gave a tug to the silk for her safekeeping. "I've ne'er seen a lass so besotted by fire."

"I've never had a man mind my petticoats," she returned.

"Silk and fire dinna mix well."

"Nor do we, milord."

He nodded. "A sorry circumstance, milady."

She smoothed her skirts. "So I am to be a tutoress in dire straits?"

"You'll be styled Lady Blythe," he said, having given it some thought. "For the time being we'll dispense with your surname and Northumbria title."

"Shall I remain in the tower?"

"'Tis distant. The household would find it odd if you stayed there. Needs be you remove to the guest wing, closer to the rest of us."

"And I'm to help tutor Orin."

"Nothing too rigorous. You can keep your own schedule. As much time out of doors as in." He drew on the pipe again, wondering if this was the plan of a simpleton and what her father would think of it. Or his.

He studied her in a way he'd not done since she'd come to Wedderburn in the dead of night. Looking down at her bent head, he began with the long, glossy curls pinned so artfully and interwoven with ribbon, crowned becomingly by a lace cap. Her aristocratic features were fine, her skin a most decided English rose. The pearls encircling her slender throat suited her. She had an ethereal fragility, all her movements remarkably graceful. She reminded him of a swan.

The mantel clock chimed in rapid succession, reminding him of the hour and breaking his concentration. "For now, since most of the servants are belowstairs, we shall quietly move you with the help of Bell and Atchison."

"Atchison? Peg's surname?"

He nodded. "If you're not too weary, I'll personally show you to your new rooms at ten o' the clock."

Her eyes reflected surprise. "Tonight, milord?"

He almost smiled. As if that were the most scandalous thing he could have suggested. "If you will."

"All right, then."

He told Bell to begin packing up their belongings in the tower, and she went out, shutting the door behind her.

"There's a back stair to the upper floor," he said to Lady Hedley. "My faither had a rule that nae servants were to be seen upstairs after ten o' the clock unless sent for."

She stood, her skirts rustling. "I wish I could have met him, if only to thank him for taking me in."

"He would have been fond of you," he said without thinking. It was true. His father would have admired her agile mind. Her way with dress. Her grace.

She looked at him most intently, as if his words begged explanation. Heat jumped from his neck to his face. Bending, he knocked the dottle from his still-smoking pipe and returned it to the pipe stand.

"Time to get up yon close," he said in Scots as he led her to a narrow door between bookshelves, glad to end her scrutiny.

"The stair you mentioned," she said quietly.

"Aye." Opening the door, he gestured for her to go first, and she did so on light feet, lifting her skirts to navigate the steep steps. A wall sconce had been lit, illuminating the stair made of oak, not shudderingly cold stone like the tower's turnpike stair.

He came after her, not so closely he trod on her hem, then realized all too late he'd forgotten to warn her about one uneven step. Her sudden cry erupted as she lost her footing and fell back toward him in a whirl of silk. In a trice they collided with a breathless thud. The jolt of his pulse surely matched hers as they crashed against the stairwell wall. He embraced her, her hair caught in his whiskers, her back pressed to his chest. He was aware of a great many things at once. How soft she was. How fragrant. Light as thistledown. The harried beat of his heart and her own nearness left him all a-fumble.

He breathed in her telltale rose scent. "Steady, milady?"

A breathless pause. "Nay, milord."

"Did you turn your ankle? Needs be I carry you the rest of the way?"

Her shocked expression proved his sudden gallantry was more jarring than her stumbling. "I— 'Tis unnecessary, though I'm glad you caught me before I tumbled to the bottom." With a little shudder, she peered past him to where they'd started seventeen steps down.

He looked up at the remaining steps to the top. "One final question."

She stilled, nestled against him, making mincemeat of his resolve not to query her further.

His mouth was near her ear. "What is that fragrance of yours?"

She sighed. A happy sound. "Queen of Hungary's Water. A distillation—or, rather, scintillation—of rosemary, mint, lemon, and rosewater."

Scintillation, indeed. Very different from Alison's heavy Asian perfumes.

She took a deep breath, her nose wrinkling. "And you, milord, are a credit to Aqua Mirabilis."

"Miracle Water, aye."

Recovering his wits, he set her back on her feet but kept hold of her hand, easing past her and leading her the remainder of the way. Once safely on the landing, he scoured the passage to make sure they were alone. His brothers, all but Orin, usually retired to a small sitting room and played All Fours or Lanterloo till bedtime. This wing was not used except for houseguests.

Taking a candle from a wall sconce, he held it aloft to guide her to the bedchamber of her choice. "There are four apartments to choose from."

They entered and exited them one by one, no sound other than the quiet opening and closing of doors and the movement of their feet. What would her preference be?

"The Garden Room," she said at last. "What do you Humes call it?"

"My mither named it the Larkspur Room."

He set about lighting other tapers, the scent of melting beeswax wafting through the cool space. Being in her chamber of choice seemed to delight her, and she went about the room, touching this or that as if making herself at home. Soon the maids came, Ronan in tow, bearing their trunks.

"You canna have all the amusement, Brother," Ronan said with a wink, taking one trunk into the adjoining dressing room. "'Twas either me or a nosy footman."

"Needs be I bow out," Everard said from the doorway, giving a last look at Blythe. "Is all to your satisfaction, milady?"

She turned away from a nightstand toward him, raising the heat in his face all over again.

"Indeed, it is, right down to the Chinoiserie daybeds and the whimsical trompe l'oeil touches throughout." Her voice held both weariness and warmth. "Thank you, Lord Wedderburn. Perhaps I shall see you on the morrow."

30

*Love is a canvas furnished by nature
and embroidered by imagination.*

VOLTAIRE

Elodie applied the final touches to Blythe's toilette the next morning, her smile evidence of her pleasure in both her efforts and their move. The new chamber was flooded with light, the morning sun pouring past the glass onto the floral carpet all the way to the door.

The Larkspur Room was well named, with its soothing blues and purples, the ceiling a floral masterpiece of plaster. Even the dressing table seemed made for her, its feminine flourishes and upholstered seat matching the trompe l'oeil wallpaper. She felt more a part of the castle, not a captive of it, all in a few scant hours. They'd already made use of the two daybeds at each end of the fireplace. Blythe hardly needed the sumptuous four-poster in the adjoining chamber. Even the artwork on the paneled walls delighted her. Landscapes, her favorite, filled beautiful gilded frames of all sizes.

But it wasn't only her new placement that enthralled her. Something had happened between her and the laird in the stairwell that had nothing to do with her misstep. Just what, she didn't know, but it seemed to have put them on more friendly footing.

She blamed her cologne. Eyeing the bottle, she hoped it was more full than empty.

Elodie set aside her brush. "Milady, what is that bruising on your wrist?"

Blythe looked down at the purple patch on her skin. "Whilst I was coming up the stair ahead of Lord Wedderburn, I fell backwards into him."

"Have mercy!" Elodie peered closer. "He's like a stone wall! 'Tis a wonder you didn't break your bones."

"He caught me very neatly or I might have," Blythe said, trying to make little of it. Still, had their collision not kept her awake half the night? Her heart had taken forever to settle. "I found him rather gallant . . . for a moment."

"Just a moment?" An amused smile wreathed Elodie's face. "His brother, the one who helped carry the trunks—what is his name?"

'Twas rare for Elodie to mention a gentleman. "Ronan," Blythe said. Of all the Humes he seemed the most sociable. "The fourth-born son, if I remember correctly."

"He has a merry way about him." Elodie fastened Blythe's pearls about her neck. "Do your lessons with Master Orin begin today?"

"I expect so." But would she ever find her way around the castle? "Now that we've been released from the tower, the laird might find me too much underfoot."

"If so, I'm sure he'll waste no time telling you," Elodie said.

Blythe smiled despite her trepidation. What if he found her tutoring skills lacking? Or she failed to keep Orin's attention?

"Well, no fault can be found with your appearance." Elodie stepped back, and they both focused on the looking glass.

"What would I do without you?" Blythe turned her head this way and that, admiring her lovely coiffure. "Now, can you make me less plain and a little more plump?" Though she was teasing, the dark-haired beauty she'd seen at the funeral rarely left her thoughts. "And a few inches shorter?"

"Beauty is more than skin-deep, remember," Elodie said gently. "Besides, the lad adores you."

"He's missing a mother foremost. One he never knew."

"The poor urchin. Your motherless heart goes out to him."

Blythe started as a light tapping at the door announced Peg, who seemed triumphant. "The other servants have been told of yer—um, arrival, mem. Nae need for us to go skulking about any longer." She looked toward the door. "And ye've a visitor, though the laird has told him he's not to bother ye in yer wing of the castle."

As Orin stepped into the room hesitantly, one hand behind his back, Blythe exclaimed, "He's no bother!"

"Good morning, milady." His smile was bright as summer sunlight. As he approached, he swept a bouquet from behind his back, a few petals falling to the carpeted floor.

Blythe caught her hands together in gratitude. "You gathered them from the garden?" At his nod, she took his gift, admiring the color and variety. "Roses, delphinium, daisies, Queen Anne's lace . . ."

"You've not been on another of your midnight rambles, so I thought you might be missing the garden. Mrs. Candlish said my mither, the countess, was fond of flowers in her rooms."

Blythe slipped an arm around his shoulders and embraced him. "Your mother sounds like my grandmother, God rest them both. My grandfather even built an orangery for her so she could have roses in December."

"We've nae glasshouse . . . yet," Orin replied. "But I want to show you the gardens beyond castle walls."

"When shall we go, then?"

"After dinner?"

"Perfect. For now I need to have a word with Lord Wedderburn. Can you show me to his study? Or help me find him if he's not there?"

Orin nodded, looking more pleased by the minute. "He's not hard to track at this time of day. Follow me."

Still holding on to the flowers, Blythe left the room, taking note of as many details as she could, including the doors and passageways. When they came to an immense cedar staircase she looked up, awed by the ornate white plasterwork framing a painted celestial sky, complete with Father Time, as if one were looking up into the very heavens.

"Alistair says my guardian angel is up there, keeping me from mischief," Orin told her with a shy smile. "Though Malcolm says small as I am, I've naught but a cherub to watch o'er me."

Down the winding staircase they went to a marble-floored foyer with the familiar Hume coat of arms in the center, a vivid green with a lion and three popinjays, which Orin told her matched the lion gate marking the estate's north entrance. A few maids and one footman hastened past, bobbing their heads and going about their duties. Wedderburn was indeed vast, the tower but one small, outdated part of it. When they halted before an official-looking door, Orin gave a respectful knock.

"Come in," the laird said.

Seated behind a large desk, he pulled himself to his feet at the sight of them. His gaze cut to the flowers Blythe carried, a slight smile appearing.

"Lady Blythe wishes to speak with you," Orin said, wandering to a large bank of high windows. Was that the formal garden he had spoken of, just beyond the glass?

"Good morning, Lord Wedderburn," she began, always unsure of him. "Might I have a tour of the castle today?"

"Now that you're nae longer in hiding, you mean."

Was he a bit mocking? He was a continual conundrum.

Orin turned away from the window. "May I come too?"

"Nae," Everard replied with an eye on a near clock. "You're expected in the mews at ten o' the clock."

It was five till the hour. With a little bow in her direction, Orin promptly did his brother's bidding. The door closed with a click, and Blythe and the laird faced each other, a chasm between them that seemed deep as a ravine and twice as uncomfortable. In her mind's eye was a clumsy woman hurtling backwards on a staircase into his arms like something onstage or penned in a romantic novel. Tall as she was, she'd have knocked a lesser man down. Truly, if Lord Wedderburn wasn't so stalwart of frame . . . The thought warmed her all over.

He gestured to the windows. Had he seen her looking at them?

Glad for the distraction and missing Orin's playful presence, she walked to the glass as she tried to collect her thoughts and settle her emotions. "A princely view."

"You've yet to be outside castle walls since you arrived, except for the mournful occasion of my faither's funeral." He came to stand beside her. "And knowing your penchant for gardens, at least by moonlight . . ."

She flushed again, clutching Orin's flowers so tightly her palms were damp. "I'm as much interested in your portrait gallery as your gardens."

His brow arched. "Dusty oil paintings of long-dead Humes."

"I beg to differ." She focused on a climbing rose wending its way across the upper pane, its showy scarlet blossoms pressed against the glass. "Your renowned ancestors, milord."

"We'll start there, then. But first surrender your flowers." He pulled on a bell cord to summon a servant. "A maid can put them in a vase."

Peg came and whisked the bouquet away. Touching Blythe's lace sleeve, the laird directed her out of his study and up the cedar staircase till they came to the Long Gallery in question. No flagstone floors and suits of armor here. Sunlit and still, it was a room to reckon with. Blythe stood on the threshold, reminded of their own gallery at Bellbroke, devoid of furniture but overflowing with portraits. Oak paneling, plush carpet, and ornate chandeliers studded the breadth of this chamber, the paintings illuminated by vast windows on an opposite wall.

She studied the first, a gilt frame reaching from floor to ceiling. The laird in Elizabethan dress, with the telltale raven hair and height of the Hume clan, was as dominating as the present Lord Wedderburn himself. The uncanny resemblance made her shiver. The Long Gallery was chill, though the sun streaming through the windows touched her back.

"Tell me about him," she said, unable to look away from the portrait.

"Alexander was the fifth earl. He fell at Flodden Field alongside King James IV and his son. My faither bore his name."

She recalled the old English ballad, hardly believing she stood alongside a descendant. "'When they encountered a strong Scot, which was the king's Chief Chamberlain, Lord Hume by name of courage hot, who manfully marched them again.'"

"Of courage hot, aye," the laird said. "Supposedly he took the king's body from the battlefield and hid it in an underground passageway to the well at Hume Castle."

"Hume Castle?"

"Our family seat in the broad lands of the Merse, the eastern Borders. Naught but a pile of stone now. You passed by it on your way here, but the hour denied you the pleasure of seeing it."

"I should like to visit and locate that mysterious passageway."

"Nae doubt you'd find the castle's territorial view of the Lammermuir Hills to the north and the Cheviots to the south unsurpassed."

They'd moved on to another painting, this one half as large but no less important, she sensed.

"Another of our chiefs, Sir John," he said. Was there a touch of pride in his tone? "He was called Willie with the White Doublet, distinguished as much by his garments as his military exploits."

"A memorable sobriquet," she said, admiring his distinct dress. "You do him proud. I understand your line is one of military merit."

"Borders lords. Rogues and cutthroats, some of them." He touched the antique frame. "Parliament once declared they and their fellow Borderers were free to rob, burn, spoil, slay, murder, and destroy without any redress to be made."

"The Debatable Lands, you mean, extending between my family seat and yours." British history had always shocked and saddened her. So much bloodshed, no family untouched. And a fractious dividing line that seemed insurmountable, its feuds lingering.

"Do you ken the treaty made back then?" he asked as if testing her.

She paused a moment, remembering her many tutors at Bellbroke. "The Treaty of York in 1237, the one with the impossibly long name."

"In Latin, if memory serves."

"*Scriptum cirographatum inter Henricum Regem Scocie . . .*" She resisted the urge to impress him, for he did not seem easily impressed.

"Something to that effect, aye, but still the raiding and marauding continued. 'Tis a wee bit more settled now." He gave her a wink, his lilt lighter. "Nae more stealing of heiresses such as yourself."

Her brows raised, more from his winking at her than the history lesson. "Of which the Humes took part once upon a time?"

"To their detriment," he said.

A little gasp escaped her as they moved on to another portrait in a giltwood frame. Before them stood a tall woman in Renaissance garb, sapphires and pearls adorning her embroidered kirtle, a long black braid dangling over one shoulder to her narrow waist. An astonishingly handsome woman.

"Why, she seems more like you Humes than all the rest," Blythe exclaimed.

"The seventh Countess of Wedderburn. My great-great-grandmither. You occupy her apartments at present, though they've been refurbished."

Blythe took a last look at the woman's unsmiling face. Those intense eyes seemed to follow her as she and the laird continued down the gallery. If only she could know more of these Humes' personal history—their preferences and habits, their loves and loyalties. Portraits, while intriguing, told little.

"How do you recall so much of your ancestry?" she asked.

"My parents required we learn it." He stood so near she felt, for once, like a diminutive woman. "There's little sense in having centuries of paintings with nae memory of who the sitter was—or the artist. Do you not recall all those dukes and duchesses whose blood-line is your own?"

His question fell flat. Like a wound it was, sore and never mending. Again that loss, that shameful sense of not being enough, shadowed her. But she must say something in reply. "Betimes I'd rather forget. Like your own lineage, not all my family history is praise-worthy."

My mother foremost.

At last they came to a portrait wall of children. Fascinated, Blythe took in the dozen or more frames and faces, searching for the laird's own. She gestured to a lad whose boyishness and blue gaze bore a striking similarity to the man beside her.

"You have a keen eye," he told her.

"Is there no portrait of you full grown?" she asked with more vehemence than she'd intended. "I mean—you are, um, worthy of being captured as the heir, and . . ."

His eyes narrowed with a devilish mirth, his broad mouth lifting ever so slightly. That flush she'd experienced since being at Wedderburn engulfed her anew and tied her tongue. Did he sense she found him . . . worthy of painting? Striking in the extreme?

"I believe I've had enough of the Long Gallery, Lord Wedderburn." She brought a hand to the pearls at her throat. "Fresh air would do me good."

"The gardens, then. Should I escort you?" he asked, appearing so concerned she nearly squirmed.

"Nay." She looked about for an easy exit. "If you simply show me the best way to reach them, I shall go alone."

31

Other men it is said have seen angels,
but I have seen thee and thou art enough.

GEORGE EDWARD MOORE

The laird led Blythe out, down a back stair to a small, octagonal chamber—a morning room?—and another door she'd not yet seen. It opened onto a small walled garden, a glorious panorama of color and disarray reflecting her present mood. Here there was no formality, just bed upon bed of flowers carefully tended of weeds but blooming with abandon.

Shading her eyes with her hand since she'd forgotten a hat, she looked beyond to more formal gardens hedged with yew, parterred as they were at Bellbroke, which brought a sudden, homesick start. These sloped to a distant watercourse—a burn, as the Scots said—spanned by a charming Palladian footbridge that matched the stone of the castle. Here and there were sundials, statuary, and benches inviting her investigation.

"Don't venture far, milady," he told her, eyes scanning the distant landscape as if ferreting out any trouble.

"I shan't, I assure you."

Once he took his leave, she strolled about, taking myriad paths through the formal gardens before taking a seat facing the rolling hills that made up Berwickshire. A warm wind rippled her skirts and her upswept hair with its lace pinner. Surely the original Hume Castle he'd spoken of could not boast better views.

As she oriented herself, another realization took hold. Unwittingly, she'd wandered into the part of the gardens the laird enjoyed from his study windows. And if he'd returned there, she was directly in his line of sight, was she not? Such scooted her off the bench and sent her walking briskly in another direction till she was sure she was at least partially hidden behind one wing of the castle. But it in no way dislodged the laird from her thoughts.

She breathed in the fresh air, trying to return to the woman she'd been before Wedderburn. Upheaval and uncertainty had matured her overnight, given her new insights. Whatever life dealt her, she must not be alone with the laird again. He was mercurial as the weather. Tempting as treacle. She'd seen a more engaging side of him in the gallery. Likely he'd be altogether different at next meeting. His dark intensity, his brusque manner, the uncanny way he summed up a situation in an instant, the utter disregard he had for proprieties and conventions . . . All worked to turn him absolutely enthralling. Dangerously so.

If she was comely or a true guest, she might indulge in a brief, albeit harmless flirtation. But she was neither. No doubt he found her as unappealing as yesterday's pottage. A nuisance.

"Milady." Peg hurried to her side, bearing a beribboned yellow hat—her favorite. "The laird said he doesna want yer lovely complexion spoilt."

Blythe stood thunderstruck, flushing in a way that had little to do with the sun. Could he not have said something less charming? Less endearing?

She took the hat with thanks, expecting Peg to laugh in jest, but she was entirely in earnest before disappearing from sight.

Doubly undone, Blythe stood by a sprawling yellow rose the same hue as her hat, tying her chin ribbons and breathing in the potent fragrance. An odd hurt pressed against her heart like a thorn.

Yes, her heart.

Might Lord Wedderburn manage to steal it?

Her defenses had been bridged, compromised. She should have continued to find him maddening, even infuriating. *Not* enthralling. Her ears had somehow warmed to his lilt. His fine looks had worn her down. His vitality and presence dominated a room. When he entered, no one else existed. When absent, he filled her thoughts to the brim. How had she become so enamored of a man she could never have? Her thoughts were decidedly unfit for a convent!

Squeezing her eyes shut, she bent her head. *Lord, inflame my heart and inmost being with the fire of Thy Holy Spirit, that I may serve Thee with chaste body and pure mind. Through Christ our Lord. Amen.*

Should the worst happen and Father was killed or imprisoned, all his estates and her inheritance forfeit, she would seek holy orders. What else could she do?

"Milady." A call across the garden made Blythe turn. Elodie hastened toward her, her face clouded. "I saw you alone from the bedchamber windows. Is Lord Wedderburn to blame for your downcast countenance?"

"On the contrary," Blythe said. "The laird and I passed an enjoyable hour in the Long Gallery but a short time ago."

Enjoyable and *laird* hardly belonged in the same sentence, Elodie's expression seemed to say. "Very well. I had thought to join you sooner, but I was . . . detained by Mr. Hume."

Blythe's good humor rebounded. "Which of the brothers might that be?"

A telltale pink shaded Elodie's high cheekbones. "Ronan."

"Our trunk bearer." He'd been noticeably obliging when they'd changed rooms. "Something tells me Master Orin is not the only Hume in need of feminine company."

Elodie sighed, looking out over the garden. "Shall I walk with you, milady?"

"Of course," Blythe said with a smile. "Needs be you should clear your head." She stemmed a sigh.

And I clear mine.

Everard returned to his study to find that one of his factors had left behind paperwork he'd requested on last year's crop yields. Sitting down with renewed purpose, he willed himself not to look out the window, but the farming report before him was no match for Lady Hedley's lithe form among the flowers. Or mayhap she made an impression because the gardens had been bereft of admirers for so long. Only on the rarest occasions did a lady venture there.

An abominable waste employing gardeners, his father once said, with so few to see the fruit of their labors. But as the grounds had been the countess's passion until her premature death, nothing was altered or much appreciated. Till Lady Hedley's coming.

Everard inked a quill and added up a few sums, only to find his gaze rising from his work. Lady Hedley had on her hat at last. The ever-present moorland wind seemed determined to pick at her tresses till he'd sent Atchison to the rescue. And such a hat! Wide of brim and dripping with lace and ribbon. Such became her. Her garments were so finely tailored they took his attention when he'd not paid attention to such before. Though she had few clothes here at Wedderburn, she always managed to add a special dash, changing sleeves and jewelry and shoes and petticoats so she always appeared fresh, even modish.

Aye, his growing interest in her was only a passing fancy. Merely surprise and gratitude for her ladyship's kindness to Orin and her appreciation for the gardens, all tempered by the obvious fact she did not relish his company. He'd intended to show her more than the Long Gallery. The plan had been to take her on a tour of the entire castle. But she'd endured his presence for less than an hour before fleeing out a side door. What had she said?

"Fresh air would do me good."

Mayhap Orin should escort her in future. Orin was charming whereas he was not. He'd still not mastered his surprise at Orin's bringing her flowers. Such a gesture wouldn't have crossed his mind. Might his younger brother be the gallant of the family?

"Brother." Bernard entered, finding him still staring out the window.

Everard set aside his quill. "What brings you inside at such an hour?"

"The day is too windy for the fishing fleet." He came to a stop at the desk, his attention on the windows as well. "Though it doesn't seem to keep our guests from the gardens."

Glad of his brother's company, Everard gestured to a chair.

Bernard sat, his back to the window, blocking Everard's view. "How long is her ladyship to stay on? You mentioned you'd heard from the duke again."

Gesturing to the latest letter, Everard mulled its startling contents. "Northumbria remains in hiding. He's secretly been supplying arms and funds to the Jacobites ahead of the rebellion. I sent Boyd back with a reply to keep us apprised."

"Boyd rivals the official post of late. Does her ladyship ken all that is at stake?"

"I doubt it. Matters change by the hour."

Bernard's expression tensed. "Is it true a number of Catholic Jacobites throughout Britain have been served warrants?"

"Aye, including the Hedleys' nearest neighbors, the Wellinghursts. Though word is Sir Jon has stepped away from his Jacobite involvement of late, Northumbria remains fully committed and at large."

"Is the man mad?"

"Lairds like Northumbria will nae more renounce the Stuarts than they will their Papist faith."

"Tower Hill will be busy, then," Bernard said of London's execution site. He motioned to the letter upon the desk. "May I see it?"

Everard handed it over and looked again to the garden where Lady Hedley had vanished. Was she even safe walking about with her maid? If word of who and where she was fell into the wrong hands . . .

Bernard grew still, his attention rapt as he turned to the letter's second page. "By all that is holy, the duke is proposing marriage." He met Everard's eyes, his own shot through with disbelief. "To *you.*"

"Such makes sense. His utmost concern is for his daughter's safety and well-being. And that of her fortune. Her future . . ." Everard left off, flummoxed by an increasingly complicated situation.

"'Tis a tidy solution, marriage." Bernard returned to the letter again, reading it aloud quietly as if wanting to be certain. "To a very tricky circumstance."

"More tricky than tidy."

"If you wed her, all of Northumbria's fortune—his lands and titles—would be yours. The Crown could not take them. They would be safe from forfeit."

Everard reached for the brandy decanter and poured a dram, then handed Bernard the glass before pouring another. "I could not in good conscience marry a lass under such circumstances."

"Circumstances aside, titles and inheritances form the footing of most matches among peers and have for centuries. Besides, if it helps safeguard her . . ."

Everard downed the spirits in two bracing swallows. "You do the deed, then."

"Wheest!" Bernard shook his head. "A duke's daughter wedding the third son of an earl with little to recommend him save the Hume name? Nae. But a reputable earl of some standing marrying a duke's daughter—aye."

He spoke the truth, but Everard aimed for levity. "Lady Hedley would nae more agree to wed me than she would the pirate Blackbeard."

"I am not so sure." Bernard stared at him. "Why not broach the matter with her? Determine what she has to say about it?"

"I'm sure she'll have a great deal to say about it," Everard said, amused by the notion. He reached for the letter again, though he'd already perused it half a dozen times.

"Everyone expects you to make an alliance with Landreth Hall, if for nae other reason than Alison has had her sights on you since she was first in petticoats." Bernard's face grew grave again. "But you ken what's said about her. She's reputed to dally with every man in breeches within court circles—"

"Regrettable." Everard fixed his attention on the windows again, wondering where Lady Hedley had gone. "Alison is not the lass she once was. And I, too, have changed. I remain a free man. Free to marry whom I please. Or not."

32

Hide not your Talents, they for Use were made.
What's a Sun-Dial in the shade?

BENJAMIN FRANKLIN

S unlight filled the morning room, dust motes swirling. Orin
bent over his desk in concentration, writing out a Latin verse.
For just a minute, Blythe breathed in the utter stillness save
his quill scratching across the paper. The small, gilded chamber
smelled of old texts and ink. A mullioned window was ajar for fresh
air. Her view was one of endless moorland when once it had been
wooded parkland in Northumberland.

Green pastures and still waters.

Peace. That was what she felt in this room, surrounded by the
things she knew best. Books and quills and paper—and a sensitive
boy who seemed to love the same. Peace was what she craved. Peace
for her restless, fretful heart.

Orin straightened in his chair and held the paper aloft. He read
to her in his childlike voice, almost musical in Scots and more lively
than ever before. He seemed to want to please her in all he did.
Touched, she found the last few days' worth of lessons as much to
her liking as his, even when pertaining to dry, dusty verb tenses.

"Fine work, Master Orin. Now let us move on." Taking a slate, she scrawled the irregular verbs across it, then turned it toward him. "The imperfect tenses of *to be.*"

"Eram," he replied. "Eras. Erat. Eramis. Eratis . . ."

She watched him carefully. He was but eight. A boy needed as much exercise as desk time. His paleness was concerning. He seemed almost otherworldly—hardly the stuff of most Humes. He'd nearly died at birth, Peg told her, but some miracle had preserved him.

Using the tenses, she made up a humorous Latin rhyme and they sang it together, their combined laughter spilling out of the room. When she turned round again, the laird stood in the doorway, watching them.

"Lord Wedderburn," she said, at once stiff and surprised.

He entered in, his gaze settling on the books open on every table, the writing implements and papers strewn about in haphazard fashion. The chess set lay where they'd enjoyed a morning's game. There was even a tray of empty teacups and bannock crumbs, for growing boys needed added nourishment, did they not?

She gave him a sheepish smile. "I can guess what you're thinking . . . a far cry from the usual tutors and routine."

He said nothing. Undaunted, Orin proudly showed him a rendering of a goldfinch that had been his unknowing subject in the garden just yesterday. "I should like to draw Pepys next."

The laird took the artwork from his outstretched hand. "The piper of treasonous tunes?"

Orin laughed, his paleness suffused with a sudden ruddiness.

Blythe removed her spectacles, a bit embarrassed the laird would find her so . . . bookish. "Orin shows talent for painting and drawing, not only storytelling."

"So I see," he said, examining the rendering.

Looking at the clock, Orin bid them both adieu and said in hesitant French that it was time for a brief visit to his kestrel at the mews.

"À tout à l'heure," Blythe replied with a smile, sorry he was leaving her alone with the laird.

Lord Wedderburn returned the watercolor to the desk. "Vous joindre à nous pour le dîner?"

Her heart stilled. A dinner invitation in flawless French. She felt that traitorous warmth only his presence wrought. "I had no inkling you spoke anything other than Scots."

"At breakfast Orin schooled me in enough French to ask you. So . . ." Crossing his arms, he sat upon the edge of the desk. "Will you?"

Torn, she looked to the window, fixing her gaze on anything but his striking face. "If you are asking me to dine with you and your brothers, I hardly think it appropriate."

"How so, milady?"

"Because . . ." Her usual rational train of thought took wing. She wanted nothing more than to sit at that dinner table. Alongside him.

And alone.

"You are our guest, are you not?" he asked. "Would guests continue to take meals in their rooms?"

"A tutor certainly would, being in that rather grey sphere of neither house servant nor family member, and usually welcomed neither below- nor abovestairs."

"A ruse, remember."

She returned her gaze to him. Steeled herself against the rich azure of his eyes. "You are not going to take nay for an answer, are you?"

"Nae."

An idea struck her. "Is Miss Bell invited?"

He smiled. "Ronan certainly hopes so. Mayhap you and I should conspire. Bell is nae lady's maid but an impoverished gentlewoman who had nae recourse but to seek service, aye?"

So he approved? "That she is. As for your brother, I've no wish to matchmake unless both parties agree to such."

"What about dinner, then?"

Toying with her spectacles, she said, "I must confess I find your frequent silences unnerving. What if we come to dine and you don't say a word?"

His throaty chuckle had the same mesmerizing effect as his eyes. "My brothers more than make up for it, as you shall soon see."

"Very well. We'll join you *once*. Your personal volubility shall determine future seatings."

"Milady, must I resort to carrying a dictionary whenever I encounter you?"

"Meaning I employ grandiose words and phrases."

"Aye."

"'Tis more entertaining, surely, than your muteness."

"That would be debatable."

His intent gaze forced her own to her feet. "Are you adept at fencing as well as languages, Lord Wedderburn?"

"I am."

"I don't doubt it, but I do find this verbal swordplay between us wearisome."

"Och, I am rather entertained by it," he said.

She detected that maddening hint of mockery again. Confound it, he confounded her!

She straightened her shoulders, feeling she'd been backed into a corner. First, a dinner invitation. Then this endless back and forth. She rued Orin had gone to the mews.

Everard reached into his weskit and withdrew two letters. Her heart gave a little leap. Once they were in her hands, her spirits fell. They were from Oxford and the Traquair ladies in France, sent to Bellbroke Castle and then forwarded to the laird from her father from wherever he happened to be. Usually they would have made her glad, but now nothing seemed to matter but her father's well-being.

She looked at him again, steeling herself against her blooming attraction to him yet determined to satisfy a niggling query that would not let her be. "Are you being forthcoming about my father's personal correspondence to you? Won't you let me read it?"

A flicker of surprise reached his eyes. "I've nae wish to worry you, though at the same time I would tell you what you need to know."

"But not all of it."

"You've nae need to ken all of it."

"I beg to differ. There's not another person on earth who deserves to know more about my father and his present struggles than I do. It might better prepare me for what is to come."

"Meaning?"

"If his title and lands are forfeit, I need to know. Such impacts me profoundly. I sense his very life is at stake. Nothing but the grimmest of circumstances would have led to him forcing me from the beauty and sanctity of our home in the dead of night." She put her spectacles aside and took a fan from her pocket, waving it to cool herself. "My father's life is likely in danger at every turn, while here I sit, playing your houseguest and tutoress, half-sick with worry."

He rubbed a hand over his jaw, a familiar mannerism of his. "Join us for dinner, then I will show you his latest letter."

33

Love comes with hunger.

DIOGENES

Elodie's eyes sparkled. "We're to join the Humes for dinner?"

"Yes, but I am thankful we shall still have supper as usual in our rooms," Blythe replied, more than a little flustered. Surely her discomfiture had more to do with the content of her father's letters than the unexpected dinner invitation.

"Dinner is the main meal at Wedderburn, supper simply an afterthought." Elodie began sorting through Blythe's meager wardrobe. "You must look your best."

"But this is a house of mourning."

"For the family and servants, not guests."

"Something subdued . . . My mint-green taffeta should suffice."

"Milady, suffice is not enough. You must shine."

"*Shine* is difficult for me," Blythe said ruefully. Again, the thought of Ronan Hume piqued her. Might there be a match in the offing?

"I beg to differ. You are positively regal in sapphire silk. With your height and slim waist, your bountiful hair . . ." Elodie took a Spitalfields gown from the dressing room's wardrobe. "This matches your pearls very nicely. All you lack is a crown to look like a queen . . . or a countess."

"Elodie!" Indignation was in Blythe's tone if not her spirit. "We've heard from Peg about Alison of Landreth Hall."

"The future Countess Wedderburn? I do wonder, given Peg's comment, if that honor might be bestowed upon someone else."

What had Peg told them? *"That one's had her bonnet set for the young laird a long time, she has. Everyone in Berwickshire and beyond has them wed in their heads if not their hearts."*

Was their pairing not warmly received in the Borders?

Blythe stared at the exquisite gown spread across the bed, then sat down at the dressing table reluctantly. Elodie promptly removed her cap and all the pins before rearranging and repinning.

"'Tis a wonder you need no white paint or rouge and that you wear your hair unpowdered." Elodie wound a bit of lace through Blythe's upswept hair. "I do think a more natural look becomes you."

Looking into the glass, Blythe recalled the beauty patches, or mouches, of France. Had the laird really called her complexion lovely? At least her skin bore no pocks or pimples, needing no artificial adornment. She had her mother to thank for that along with her deep-set eyes and long lashes, though she bore her father's other features.

In half an hour, Elodie had worked wonders. The looking glass reflected an unsmiling if outwardly poised woman at her best.

Dinner was at hand. Blythe rose from the table and took a deep breath.

Lord, help Thou me.

Everard had given notice to Mrs. Candlish and the kitchen. The dining room was polished and aired. Half-guttered beeswax candles were promptly replaced by new ones. He'd read the riot act to his brothers to be on their best behavior. No belching, bad manners, coarse talk, or unwomanly topics.

He wondered if anyone would say a word.

As two o' the clock neared, Everard stepped into the dining room to find all in readiness. Mrs. Candlish was carrying an enormous vase of freshly picked flowers for the centerpiece. "'Tis not every day Wedderburn Castle has a duke's daughter for dinner," she whispered, clearly delighted, as a footman entered the room with wine.

A duke's daughter, aye. Eight years of staring at his mother's empty place was at an end. He'd ask her ladyship to sit there, though he wouldn't tell her whose chair it had been.

He went to a window facing the long drive. Storm clouds gathered, amassing over Landreth Hall. What would Alison say about their dining arrangement? Competitive by nature, she'd no doubt dislike it. But for the moment she was the last thing on his mind.

"Brother." Ronan entered, his attire raising Everard's brows. Though still mostly black clad, he wore a colorful waistcoat and had taken pains with all the rest.

"You look like a courtier," Everard said, catching a hint of ambergris. "And you smell like one."

Adjusting his stock, Ronan chuckled and eyed the elegantly appointed table with open appreciation. "I suppose you've lambasted Cook to serve us more than brose and kale."

"You'll soon find out."

"But will her ladyship like it? The both of them, rather?"

"Why not ask them?"

"Surely Northumberland's fare is not so different. A great deal of meat, fish, fresh fruits and vegetables."

"A worthy conversation starter," Everard said, eyes on the doorway.

Orin appeared next in a freshly ironed shirt, weskit, and breeches, his face expectant. "Are they still coming?"

"Why wouldn't they?" Everard asked.

"Because they are lassies and we are used to dining alone," he replied, smoothing his tied-back hair. "I hope they won't find us boring."

Boring? Few Humes fit that description.

"We'll try to be so chivalrous they'll want to dine with us again,"

Ronan said as the twins appeared. "Though that might not be the case should Davie be here."

"Nae," Everard said. Davie could curdle fresh milk. Calysta was no better. "Where is Bernard?"

"Late, as usual," Orin said, pulling at the back of his chair in a bid to sit down.

"Stay standing," Everard told him. "You canna sit till the lassies do."

Orin darted a glance at the door. "I hope you keep all my tutors away for good. I've learned more from Lady Blythe in a few days than they've taught me altogether since they first arrived."

Ronan winked. "You've been beglamoured by her, then."

Orin smiled. "When I am with her I forget I am learning."

Everard felt a twinge. Orin's ancient nurse had one foot in the grave. Mrs. Candlish was too busy for any mothering, and her station prevented it. But Lady Blythe was a different matter altogether. Once she left, what would the lack do to such a vulnerable, open-hearted lad? And she might well leave immediately once she read her father's latest letter.

"We shan't hear any bad schoolroom reports of you, then," Alistair said, coming to stand by Malcolm near the fireless hearth. "Nae caning or taking the lash."

Orin laughed. "She is such a lady she would only tickle me."

"She is indeed a lady," Malcolm said. "I'd almost forgotten what the feminine sort was like."

"But she is not such a lady she is afraid to go hawking with me," Orin said. "She told me even Mary, Queen of Scots, was keen on hawking, as are some noblewomen in England."

Alistair looked impressed. "Indeed. When are you going hawking?"

"On the morrow."

There was a hush as two more footmen appeared carrying covered dishes. Not long after came their guests. Everard stood at the table's head, eyes alighting on Blythe as she entered ahead of her maid.

"How gracious of you to invite us to your table," she said with no hint of her discomfiture of before. Her colorful gown was finely made and snug to her slender shape, her fair hair arranged in a splendid display of curls framing her neck and shoulders, her hands folded at her waist.

"Welcome to our table," Everard said as Orin played the gentleman and led her to her chair.

Bell was seated across from her, Ronan doing the honors. He then sat down beside her in his usual place, a felicitous arrangement from all appearances. A moment of uncertainty ensued, and then all bowed their heads. Everard uttered the timeworn prayer of his father, wondering what sort of blessing Catholics gave.

"Our most merciful Faither, we give Thee humble thanks for Thy bounty, beseeching Thee to continue Thy lovingkindness unto us, that our land may yield her fruits of increase, to Thy glory and our comfort. Through Jesus Christ our Lord. Amen."

The footmen removed the covers on a dozen silver dishes. To Everard's right, Blythe took his cue as a white soup was served. He hoped the food was still warm, given the long haul from the castle's kitchen.

Blythe's smile hadn't dimmed. She was admiring the cut flowers, her gaze sweeping the unfamiliar room. She sampled the pigeon, ate all her veal cutlet, made much of the garden's asparagus and glazed carrots, and sipped her madeira with an ease that surprised him, not at all undone by his company, or so it seemed.

"Your new cook has outdone himself," she said to him as he finished his meal. "Everything is delicious, though I was expecting neeps and tatties and the like. And I am keen to try your haggis."

Smiling, Ronan lifted his glass in a sort of toast. "To our esteemed guest, who is as brave as she is beautiful."

Blythe pinked. "More brave than beautiful, I assure you."

"Is haggis not eaten in England?" Alistair asked.

Bell's tight smile indicated it was not, at least at their Northumberland table.

"Rich, savory, nourishing," Malcolm said. "An infinitely agreeable dish."

"'Tis my favorite pudding," Orin said with more gusto than usual, as if savoring his meal as much as the company. "I shall have Cook make it for you if you promise to sup with us again."

Blythe smiled at him from across the table. "How can I refuse?"

"Well, now is the time, as I do not think you'll think well of sheep's offal," Bernard said in his honest, self-effacing way. "Our mither abhorred it."

Blythe laughed, the sound so charming amid so much masculinity that Everard smiled. "I may well agree with your beloved countess," she said. "But I must try it."

Dessert appeared, a pyramid of fresh fruit. Exclaiming in delight, Blythe took a large portion and poured custard atop it. "'Tis like the fruiterers in France. A happy memory."

"A happy memory, indeed." Bell made much of it also as the dessert dwindled. "My father kept a lovely orchard at our home on the outskirts of Haltwhistle."

Everard noticed Blythe turn toward her in surprise. Did Bell rarely speak of her past?

Ronan looked out the window as if judging the weather, then in low tones asked, "Would you care to take a turn with me in the gardens, Miss Bell, before the rain?"

A slight pause made Everard tense. Ronan wasted no time with courting. Flushing, Bell glanced at her mistress. Blythe smiled encouragingly even as thunderheads loomed.

34

*She instills grace in every common thing
and divinity in every careless gesture.*

EDMOND ROSTAND

The dining room cleared. Blythe watched as Ronan led Elodie out a side door, their intent the garden. For a moment she felt another bewildering sense of her world shifting. Elodie had been with her for so many years. Why had it never occurred to her that her lovely companion might have an opportunity to be something other than in service?

What if she became part of Clan Hume?

Orin was chattering like a magpie across from her as his brothers disappeared one by one. "I'm to have a riding lesson soon, milady. Might you go with me?"

"I should like that very much, weather permitting," she told him a bit distractedly. "I miss my mare at Bellbroke's stables. I used to ride her everywhere. She was quite fond of oats and orchard apples."

"What's her name?"

"Guinevere," Blythe replied with a homesick pang.

Orin's eyes widened. "The wife of King Arthur?" His gaze sought the laird, who was rounding the table. "My brother calls his stallion a like name."

"Lancelot," Everard said.

The coincidence made Blythe smile. "I've always been partial to Arthurian legend."

"Perhaps it isn't legend after all." Everard accompanied her through open double doors into the next room—a large, dark-blue drawing room she'd not yet seen—then on to the smaller drawing room in a lighter shade of blue. Orin trod after them faithfully like an over-grown puppy.

"Guid day," Everard said as he shut the double doors soundly in the lad's smiling face. "Go join your other brothers."

Blythe pressed a hand to her lips lest she laugh outright. "I would feel sorry for him, but he is surely used to your ill-scrappit ways."

"Ill-scrappit, aye." Amusement laced his brogue. "Well done, milady. You've not been here long but are speaking broad Scots already."

She sat down on a settee while he took a chair across from her, the growl of thunder in the distance a dismal backdrop. The richly appointed room drew her notice, the crystal chandelier above their heads aglitter with no less than fifty beeswax tapers. She counted every one of them if only to keep her focus off of him.

Alas, tonight he was handsome. So handsome it hurt her. And freshly shaven. In exquisitely tailored garments, a snow-white stock wrapped round his sinewy neck. His gloss of hair caught back by black ribbon, tailing down his back between wide-set shoulders. He wore no wig, nor had he need of one. He rivaled the replica of Michelangelo's statue of David in Bellbroke's formal garden. Only he was vibrant flesh and blood, not cold, white marble.

He was reaching for something in his weskit, and the rising tick of her pulse at his nearness overwhelmed her. If the letter contained heartrending news . . . She snuck a hand into her gown's pocket to ascertain a handkerchief was there.

"The duke's most recent correspondence." He handed it to her, the thin slip of paper folded and creased and obviously reread more than a few times, the black seal telling.

To her great relief, he stood and walked to a window, his back to her, a courtesy that surprised her and gave her courage as she opened the post.

I trust this finds you and all in your safekeeping well. My prayers night and day include petitions for health and happiness. I have indeed come under suspicion with the king's men, and a warrant has been served for my arrest. Thus I am writing from various places as I elude my captors, who demand I forsake not only my Catholic faith but the Jacobite cause. If I do not, my land and title will be forfeit, and any inheritance also.

I would be errant, even foolish, if I did not broach the matter of matrimony. You well know advantageous marriages are often arranged among peers of the realm. I can think of no more desirable a match than that of my own and your distinguished house. I give you my wholehearted approval for the joining of our noble families, including all Northumbrian titles and estates therein.

Blythe swallowed, her heartbeat ratcheting harder beneath her tight stays. Nay . . . a thousand times nay! A blatant proposal of marriage. This was not what she'd expected. And now a warrant for his arrest. His continuance in hiding. Desperation driving him to rashness. Even his scrawl across the page looked hurried and forced.

She stood, dropping the letter, uncaring that it fluttered to the carpet. "So my father would further foist me upon you by forcing you to consider matrimony."

The laird turned toward her.

"As if I had no say in the matter," she continued, a crushing dismay weighting her. "He might have warned me of such first."

"'Tis a letter, Lady Hedley, a proposition," he said. "Not an order. Not law."

"A scheme of the utmost embarrassment," she replied, voice shaking. Tears clouded her view of him, and she blinked them back. "Lest you think I am one of those fawning, simpering females who would throw myself at your feet, I would sooner join a convent than be your countess!"

Her pointed declaration did not move him, at least not that she could see. She simply wanted to give him a way out, making room for his certain refusal of her.

He returned to his seat, his gaze holding her own. "I am not your enemy, Lady Hedley. Nor, as I've stated before, your gaoler. And lest you believe I have matrimonial designs, I do not."

"But my father certainly does, and so the unsavory matter is before us."

He took the letter from the floor and refolded it, then secured it beneath his weskit. "You would be wise to consider the matter, unpalatable as it is to you."

Unpalatable to me? What about you?

Sinking down on the settee, she released a pent-up breath, trying to gauge how he truly felt about her becoming a Hume, which, given his stoicism, was like scaling a stone wall. Her own feelings, carefully concealed, were so at odds with her heated speech. Could he sense her attraction to him? The long looks she sent his way despite her best intentions? How her vehemence about a convent was naught but smoke?

"Consider this," he told her as if laying out a battle plan. "You are one of the wealthiest heiresses in England if not all of Britain. You are also the last of your line. Do you seek to remain celibate and your lineage to end? Is that fair to your faither, your family legacy? Would you willingly forfeit hundreds of years of a peerage by government seizure or by casting it away of your own accord?"

She swallowed, balling her handkerchief in her fist. Looking to her lap, she allowed herself a forbidden thought. That the man across from her did not find her unworthy or unattractive—and was not enticed by her dowry.

"What do you advocate, then?" she asked, the fire slowly going out of her.

"That you weigh carefully what your faither is proposing." His lilt deepened when he spoke with serious intent. "Do not reject it out of hand."

Her heart squeezed hard, bringing with it an odd breathlessness. Dare she even entertain it? She couldn't believe *he* did.

"I ken the dilemma your faither faces. Is it not my own?" He raised an upturned hand. "If I believe in the divine right of kings, my allegiance is to the exiled Stuarts. They were Scotland's monarchs before they were England's. But in truth I have nae faith in another restoration. So do I join the doomed Jacobites and forfeit all, including my family name and the future of my brothers? Especially Orin, who has yet to grasp what sort of political upheaval he's been born into?"

"Nay," she said, having never heard the matter laid out so succinctly, so plainly. Orin, beloved by all, was reason enough to refrain.

He sat back, looking grieved. "I went to war and was knighted under the reign of Queen Anne. I fought with the English at Oudenarde and Malplaquet while the Stuart Pretender, as he's called, fought for France against us. What sort of man wages war against the people he professes he wants to rule? At the same time, I want naught to do with the present Hanoverian monarch. British kings and queens come and go, and such is out of my control. My purpose is here. Wedderburn is my legacy, my future."

A shiver ran through her. She quickly calculated all that was against him. The both of them. "And here I sit, a traitor in your midst."

"You are your faither's daughter, not a traitor. You've done nothing remotely rebellious except wear white roses on your garments."

She looked at him, unsurprised he hadn't missed those subtle details.

"And," he added, an amused light in his eyes, "own a sparrow of treasonous tunes."

Yes, but that was not all. He was treading lightly for once. Was it because he sensed she was fragile? About to shatter?

She took a breath. "Having a Papist beneath your roof is another strike against us both."

"You needn't answer to any for your religion but God Almighty," he said. "Certainly not to me."

She looked to her lap, fighting the appeal of his answer, trying to dispel this swelling yearning inside her. Nor did he allay her growing attraction with his next, low words.

"Would you allow me to call you by your given name, milady?" His query held no awkwardness. The request flowed out of him like treacle, wooing her with a few well-placed words, making mincemeat of what remained of her resistance. "At least when we are alone . . . in private?"

She nearly sighed aloud. If she didn't know better, she'd swear he was set on wooing her.

Had he any inkling the sway he had over her harried heart?

Even so small a step as the intimacy of names worked to ensnare her further. He was not a novice with women, surely. Discerning as he was, he knew them well. Knew, too, the power of his own attraction, his personal appeal.

Already she felt the pinch that preceded brokenness. Soon he would have her whole heart in his callused hands. And he would then break it if only because she had somehow, unwittingly, fallen in love with him and he could not return her affection.

Everard all but held his breath in the sudden silence that fell between them. He looked at Blythe's bent head, her lashes lying like pale fringe across her flushed cheekbones, her slender fingers knotting her lace handkerchief, a pearl ring on the little finger of her left hand. Gowned in blue silk in a blue room, she seemed to belong to it.

He lingered longest on her upswept hair. How would it be tumbled down around her shoulders? He felt an almost irresistible urge to remove her lace cap.

"You would call me Blythe." She looked up at him in that poised way she had, though he sensed she was ruffled beneath the surface. "And I would call you Everard?"

He nodded, moved by something he couldn't name. Her fragility, mayhap. The utter grace of her every move was as if he were watching a minuet, a dance. She had a wistful cast to her delicate features that was not only beguiling, it was . . . haunting.

"I should like that, Everard," she said softly.

"Blythe is a singular name." In a land of Janets and Agneses and Marys, it was as unique as the lass who bore it.

"'Tis a river in Northumberland," she told him, slowly unfisting her handkerchief and smoothing it out across her lap. "In Old English it means gentle, pleasant."

"The name suits you," he said, holding her green gaze. "At least in this instance."

She nodded, pensive. "'Twill be good to have a friend in this house besides Orin."

35

Cupid is a knavish lad, thus to make females mad.

WILLIAM SHAKESPEARE

Blythe returned to her room just as Elodie appeared clutching a single red rose, as bright and a-flush as the bloom in her hand.

"I know not what to make of this afternoon, milady." She brought the flower to her nose. "Picked by Mr. Hume."

"Such a rich scarlet. Surely the color is significant." Admiring it, Blythe sat down on a window seat, the chamber cast in shadows as rain began "pishing doon," as Peg said, and wind rattled the panes. "I'm glad you came in before the storm."

"I confess I did not notice. I'd have walked with him in a downpour if he'd wanted." Elodie spun the rose in a sort of awed agitation. "I fear I may have overstepped my station. Both concerning you and Mr. Hume."

"Nonsense," Blythe exclaimed. "If not for the death of your parents, you would have no station to overstep. I'll be glad of the day when you are lifted out of it and you can be a lady's companion no more and resume your rightful place."

"Whatever do you mean?"

"I've begun to think we've come here not for me but for you." The realization solaced Blythe. "Your happiness. Your future."

206

"'Tis happening so fast." Elodie settled on an upholstered stool. "My mind cannot take it in. Usually I am calm, even practical. But Mr. Hume puts me in a muddle."

"He has won your heart," Blythe whispered with certainty.

Tears stood in Elodie's eyes. "But, milady, how can that be? The gentleman and I have been together but a few fleeting times—"

"Love consults neither the clock nor the calendar."

"You speak as one who knows."

Blythe blanched at the observation. If not truly love on Blythe's part, it was a rather violent infatuation. Schooling her emotions lest they betray her, she said, "When my grandmother met my grandfather, she said she knew almost immediately he was the one for her. Their marriage was arranged, of course, but upon introduction something sparked. Do you not feel the same?"

"A spark?" Elodie gave a little laugh. "More an inferno. A blaze. But what of you? You are my first concern, my reason for being here."

"Perhaps the time has come for our parting," Blythe said gently. "My meeting with the laird this afternoon helped put things in perspective. I cannot remain here much longer and must make plans for my own future."

Alarm marred Elodie's delight. "You must not be rash, milady. What could Lord Wedderburn have said or done to cause this?"

What, indeed. Nothing at all except exist. That alone ensnared her.

"He was actually the most gentlemanly I've yet seen him," she said. She would not reveal that half an hour before, the laird had proposed marriage based on her father's urging. 'Twas hardly the love match of Ronan and Elodie.

"Then . . ." Elodie turned entreating. "Why this haste to depart?"

"I stand to lose my inheritance. Father is being hunted like a criminal, unable to even reside at Bellbroke or any of his other, smaller estates at present. A warrant has been issued for his arrest, only to cease once he swears allegiance to King George and forsakes all Jacobite activities."

Elodie fell silent, her misery evident.

"I've finally decided to pen a letter to the prioress at the Convent of Our Blessed Lady of Syon. We met while in France, remember."

"I do recall it, but . . ."

"'Tis clear Ronan Hume has set his sights on you. We'd be foolish—even coldhearted—to end it now. And the laird has given his approval, at least to me."

"Truly?"

"He spoke of us matchmaking for the two of you. But 'tis hardly needed." Blythe looked out the rain-smeared window to the south. "My letter to France shall take time, of course, then the prioress must write back. There may even be the chance she refuses me."

Lord, a way of escape, please.

France was becoming more of a refuge in her mind. Though she'd grown bored by her time at court and all the frivolities therein, she would be well occupied as a convent teacher and could continue her work with the universities and other scholarly pursuits.

"But, milady, whatever would I do here without you?"

Blythe pushed past her own heartache and focused on the faithful companion who'd stood by her for so long. "I foresee a bright future for you. We must do all we can to embrace it, given Mr. Hume's obvious and honorable intentions."

"He *is* quite chivalrous and attentive." Color still high, Elodie sighed happily. "He mentioned going riding with me next."

"I'm pleased to hear it. Felicitous timing, that, as you've just finished your redingote. And you simply must borrow the riding hat you made me."

"Enough of me. I'd rather talk about you . . . and Lord Wedderburn."

Blythe smoothed a pleat on her petticoat. "Whatever do you mean?"

"There is something between you."

"Indeed. A great deal of aggravation."

"Nay. Something else entirely."

Clearing her throat, Blythe cast about for an answer. Elodie knew her well. She would not lie and deny her attraction, at least in private, though it was hopelessly one-sided and might take her some time to admit it.

When she said nothing, Elodie continued in her calm, measured way, "Let us not talk maidservant to mistress but woman to woman."

"Very well."

"I don't mean to embarrass you but merely want to share an observation. Whenever you are in the room with Lord Wedderburn, he seems very, um, aware of you—and you him."

"'Tis only because he—all the Humes—are starved for feminine company."

"I feel 'tis more, milady."

"The laird simply doesn't know what to do with me." Blythe was finding the seam of her petticoat quite interesting. She would not meet Elodie's eyes. "And I am tiring of being a burden."

As lightning lashed the sky, she left the window seat and moved nearer the hearth's low fire. Thankfully, Everard was unstinting with coal and allowed her to indulge her constant whim for warmth. She took a turn before the fire, mindful of her dress hem and his thoughtful, almost playful tug at her skirts.

"If there's an awareness, 'tis entirely one-sided. I am—" Oh, how she must almost grit her teeth to say it. "I—well, I find the laird something of a distraction. Braw is the Scots word for it. He reminds me of the garden statuary at Bellbroke, only he is blessedly clothed."

"Blessedly, indeed!" Elodie laughed, dispelling the tension. "Lord Wedderburn *is* uncommonly handsome. I always wondered what sort of man would turn your head, and now I have my answer."

"There you have it, yes." With the confession came little relief. "I've grown so accustomed to French fops that when faced with a man of the laird's, um, attributes, it leaves me quite undone."

"The Humes are a far cry from French courtiers." Elodie watched Blythe curtail her pacing and come to a halt on one side of the marble hearth. "But again, I do not think this awareness is one-sided."

"If so, I am no more than a burr beneath the laird's saddle. A lump in his porridge."

Elodie shook her head. "I shall hush for now, but I urge you to not make light of it. Something is betwixt the two of you that has naught to do with burrs and lumps." With that, she went into the dressing room to attend to some task, leaving Blythe alone, her head and her heart overfull.

What else was there for her but a nunnery?

Life stretched out like a blank book, begging to be filled. Would she spend her days, her years, with bells and masses, matins and complines, all the while stifling her yearnings for a husband and family? Or accept a loveless offer and forge a marriage that might safeguard her fortune but leave her married to a man who would regret it in time? The tug-of-war between her heart and head was becoming intense.

If she did seek holy orders, never would she forget the enigmatic, irresistible . . .

Everard.

36

All that's said in the kitchen
should not be told in the hall.

SCOTTISH PROVERB

In the confines of his study suddenly absent of all people, Everard moved from his desk to the door. All morning he'd handled one matter after the next, feeling a bit like arbiter and judge. Two tenants involved in a boundary dispute. Improperly stored provisions in the kitchens. Munro's feuding physicians. Mrs. Candlish's dismissal of a scullery maid. An overdue bill from Hume's Land in Edinburgh as David racked up debts there. The quantity of dung needed for outfield lands and lumber for new barns, including preparation for lambing and kidding season. Even an offer of marriage for Alistair from a Highland clan, which his younger brother rejected out of hand.

Correspondence was stacked as high as boundary stones atop a silver tray. These could wait. Everard needed air.

At breakfast, Orin had announced his intent to spend the morning at the mews, Blythe with him. Several days of dreich weather had had them postponing it till now, and the wait had sharpened Everard's determination to join them. Blythe did not come to dinner every day, which left him teetering between anticipation and disappointment.

Blast the unpredictability of it all.

211

He found himself not having enough time. Or enough talk. Dinners flew past with increasing speed and a great deal more jollity with two women present. He hardly knew what he ate. It had simply ceased to matter.

His brothers plainly enjoyed Blythe's company, Orin especially. Not to mention Ronan being fond of her companion, Bell. Everard wasn't displeased or particularly surprised by their mutual attraction. Titles and pedigrees meant little to him. Another Hume marriage was overdue. Bell seemed a fine lass and was beneath their very roof, making courting all the easier.

He made his way across the castle courtyard in all its summer splendor toward the mews. The sun beat down upon his shoulders even as his cocked hat shaded his eyes. He'd barely set foot on the cobbled lane when Orin and a falconer appeared with Lady Hed—

Blythe.

What a sight she was, dressed in a fawn-colored riding habit, a darker brown feathered hat atop her head. On her left hand was the large leather glove used for hawking, which extended nearly to her elbow. Orin wore a glove as well and was busy chatting and walking alongside her, oblivious to all else.

Just how he himself felt of late.

Everard slowed his eager gait. Took a steadying breath. *Easy, mon.*

Seeing his approach, the falconer returned to the mews and reappeared with another glove. Attendants followed with the uncaged birds, intent on a freshly mown meadow. Two of the youngest hawks were in training, including a rare eyas peregrine from Wales, which wore a special ornamented hood.

In the distance a wooden block was set up. The birds would fly from the block to a gloved fist or gauntlet. Everard's heart gave a beat of anticipation. Few things fascinated him like falconry. He was intrigued Blythe was willing to hazard it. For Orin's sake, mayhap.

He caught up to them, surprised when she suddenly turned round. She came to a stop while Orin went on with the others.

"Lord Wedderburn," she said in greeting.

"Have done with that, Blythe," he returned quietly. They were out of earshot, were they not? Besides, he liked the way she said Everard. Softly and pleasantly in her crisp Northumbrian tones.

"Very well, Everard." She fell into step beside him, the feather in her hat dancing. "You are fond of falconry, I take it."

"Aye, in all its aspects."

"I think Orin may well follow you. He's quite enamored with his kestrel and wants to show me how Sir Gareth is being trained. But his interest reaches further than hawking." She smiled up at him. "He's also wanting a toy sword and musket. Yesterday during our lessons he drew up a battle plan after I told him about young Prince William, who formed his own unit of Royal Horse Guards as a boy."

"The late Duke of Gloucester?" The memory of the charming lad, a miniature model soldier, always made him melancholy. "He used to drill his wee men outside palace walls. A spectacle not to be missed. I met him shortly before his tragic death."

"Such an immense sorrow for his parents. And their only child." Hopefulness lit her pensive features, her voice soft. "I sense Orin is becoming stronger in body and spirit. I pray continually and fast for his well-being."

For his well-being if not hers. The irony was not lost on him. "Which is why you don't come to dinner every day."

She simply gave him a small smile. Hardly reassuring. How many fast days did the Catholic calendar hold? She was whip thin, alarmingly so, yet he'd seen her eat with relish at their table. And she was a born mother. Her every interaction with Orin confirmed it. Had she never reckoned with having children of her own? Built as she was, could she? Or would she be a casualty like his mother at the last?

He cleared his throat. "As your, er, guardian of sorts, I would caution you about your own health."

"Have done with that, milord," she said, giving him a sidelong glance. "I'm stalwart in soul if not body, far stronger than I look. And"—she raised her leather glove—"ready to go hawking. And riding."

"You are not intent on escaping my lair, are you?"

She laughed, her eyes a snapping green. "I cannot ride far, you mean."

"Not with Orin, nae. He prefers his pony cart. But I could show you Berwickshire. Take you places where you'd not easily be seen or raise suspicion."

"What mount would I have?"

"There's a milk-white Arabian mare that may suit you. Sleek and fleet of foot."

"And you?"

"A Darley Arabian from bloodstock that kept me alive on the battlefield. I've narrowly escaped capture a time or two owing to its superior speed."

"Lancelot."

"I could send for your Guinevere."

Her hopeful gaze returned to him. "Would you?" Then a sudden shadow crossed her face. "Nay, that shan't be necessary. I'll tell you why after dinner today."

Would she make him wait?

"Wheest, lass." He came to a standstill. "That is not how we Humes handle matters."

"Wheest, indeed! Kindly mind your rank, sir," she teased. "A duke's daughter takes precedence over an earl, does she not, Lord Wedderburn?"

"Not in Berwickshire." His formal title stuck in his craw, at least when she said it. "So you will make me tarry till afternoon to hear it." He fixed his eye on the master falconer by the far wooden block. "Promise me you'll join us at table, then."

She moved away from him to rejoin Orin. "I shall do both, milord."

———— ∞ ————

The brisk knock on his study door after dinner rivaled the ratcheting of Everard's pulse.

Blythe?

He sensed she was on the verge of announcing her departure. Would it not be better for all concerned if she were to have her way and leave Wedderburn? Aye, better for all but Orin. Though she'd been tutoring him but a sennight, he was becoming as attached to her as a lamb with its ewe. She herself became an altogether different person around the lad—especially tender and attentive. Unlike her no-nonsense way of dealing with him as laird.

And then there was his brother and Bell. If he had set fire to Ronan, the courtship couldn't have commenced any faster. And from all appearances, Bell returned his affections, while Ronan's devotion to farm and fisheries waned. Everard had said nothing, knowing such might be short-lived. If Blythe left, no doubt Bell would go with her, turning the couple's blazing attraction into a passing infatuation.

At a second sharp rap, he called for her to enter, then went to stand by the window. He didn't want the bulwark of a desk between them. They had enough obstacles to overcome.

She appeared, a tentative look on her face, something in hand. "I've brought you a letter to post."

He took it, wanting to look at the address but knowing she'd tell him in her forthright way.

She wasted no time, her gaze on the garden. "I've written the prioress I met in France. After much thought and prayer, it seems the best course is to return to the continent. If the prioress refuses me the teaching position I hope for, then I shall remain over the water with the Stuarts of Traquair, my lifelong friends. At least until my father's unfortunate affairs are sorted out."

Everard digested this in silence, looking to the letter he now held. "What would your faither have to say about it?"

A pause. "He would no doubt discourage me if not forbid it."

"Yet you expect me to give you my blessing."

She sighed. "Your blessing and your coach to the coast, not to mention the needed funds to see me safely there . . . which I would repay in full." She turned toward him entreatingly. "Which brings me to the matter of Miss Bell. Might she take my place as tutor?"

He placed the letter on his desk. "Why would I employ the future Mrs. Hume?"

She smiled. "And how do you feel about *that* turn of events?"

"Bell seems a fine lass, not of your caliber but a lady nonetheless. And my brother is so enamored with her, he'd cross swords with me if I agreed to her going with you or made mention of employing her. Which brings me to the disagreeable matter of your traveling alone."

"I could hire another maidservant."

"Maidservants are in short supply. Mrs. Candlish can confirm it."

"Why do I detect a nae in your tone?" She entwined her fingers at her waist. "Something tells me you may well send that letter not to France but to my father."

"You would be right."

To his surprise, she sat down on the window seat and looked up at him. "I would miss Orin more than I can convey."

"He would be sair-hearted by your going," he said in a rare maudlin moment.

And not only Orin.

He set his jaw, trying to return to the passionless place where reason ruled, that colorless landscape of old before her coming. A battle-worn soldier would not let his heart usurp his head, yet somehow, against his will, he'd given way to her. She stirred him in a manner he could not ignore. Or deny. Or admit.

And she was looking at him as if privy to this mounting battle betwixt his head and heart. A bit pensively, even a tad amusedly, as if she'd bested him somehow.

Or was it his imagination?

"Let us mull the matter for another day or so," he finally said, wanting nothing more than to go riding and clear his muddled mind. "Rashness becomes nae one."

37

In peace, sons bury their fathers.
In war, fathers bury their sons.

HERODOTUS

Everard left the castle to escape one lass only to run into several more. Too late to change rein and go another direction. He'd already been seen. Alison was nothing if not eagle-eyed.

She galloped toward him feverishly over open moorland without heed of fox hole or footbridge. She leapt flawlessly over a stone dyke, a trio of her younger sisters in close pursuit. If this was any indication of Alison's current temper . . .

He gave Lancelot his head, and the stallion found a meandering burn to slake his thirst. Everard had had an enjoyable hour's ride, covering his favorite parts of the Merse, and had been about to return to the stables.

"At last," Alison said as she drew up in front of him. "What an opportune meeting. I've not seen you in an age."

"Stretching the truth does not become you." He rested his hands atop the pommel. "I thought you'd be back in London by now."

"I'm needed more at home than in the city."

He gave a nod to her younger sisters, who smiled and blushed until Alison sent them packing. "Go on with you three. Mama will wonder why we've been out for so long. I must speak with Lord Wedderburn in private."

They departed in a fit of giggles, casting a last coy look over their shoulders. When they were out of earshot, Alison said, "Even a wee bit of their company wears on me."

"You rarely range onto the Merse. What brings you so far?"

"All this rain of late is tiresome and keeps me too long indoors." She studied him, unsmiling. "'Twas unutterably boring at the ball without you Humes. I'll be very glad when you're out of mourning, though you look quite dashing in sable."

He nearly smiled, again remembering Blythe's less charitable assessment. *Black as the earl of hell's waistcoat.*

Alison tilted her head, eyes narrowing beneath the brim of her riding hat. "You seem preoccupied."

He said nothing to this, just raised his gaze to watch a soaring hawk. The steeple of the Duns parish kirk rose up behind her in the distance, a welcome distraction.

"So, how goes it at Wedderburn?" she asked.

"I'm learning my faither was a verra busy mon."

"I'm sorry to hear it, though all of that business likely helps temper your grief."

"Aye." He ran a hand over Lancelot's thick mane. "And nae."

"You should confide in me, Everard. Those in positions of authority have few whom they can trust." Her piqued tone turned almost brooding. "I've been waiting for you to return to Landreth Hall so I might tell you something momentous, but now seems an opportune time."

"Speak freely, then."

"Father has news of your brother at Hume's Land. Ill news, I'm afraid. Though I can see from your expression you are not surprised."

"Davie has long been wayward. Edinburgh only adds to his vices."

"It seems he has come to the attention of the king's men not only in Edinburgh but in London. His Majesty has made inquiries as to who are the leading Jacobites in the Borderlands, and David has been named."

"The list is long."

"Long, yes, and too close to home. Or in this case, *Hume*," she said.

"I am not my brother's keeper."

"But you are now laird and can wield your power at will. The king is determined to put down any traitorous plots and intrigues. Father has lately been in secret meetings with His Majesty's councillors. They are, of course, weighing the best course of action. As Lord of Session, Father has His Majesty's ear." A clear warning was in her gaze. "And as a voice for the Lowlands, Father warns you to tread lightly."

Everard looked toward Wedderburn's turrets, fighting that extraordinary inward battle of wanting to return there when it had oft been the opposite before. "Sir Clive's concern is appreciated, but . . ."

"In a bid to deflect the attention given the Jacobites in our parish, Father has even told the king about your outstanding military service to the Crown."

His attention swung back to her, gravel in his gut. He had no wish to be made known to the king. Did she not ken what that might mean? Barmy, the lass was. But she talked on, insensible and obviously pleased at his having been singled out.

With a smug smile, she said, "We are not all treasonous, rebellious Borderers, and Father means for His Majesty, new to our country and customs, to know it."

Everard could only hope the German's dearth of English would save him any notoriety, doubly glad London was far removed from the Lowlands.

Alison's voice was proud. Brash. "Mother has decided to hold a soiree to foster goodwill as well as gain any news that might be of benefit to Father in London. Just a small gathering of local lairds. A few significant bonnet lairds have been invited also. Will you come?"

He could not ignore what was happening around him. As laird, he must learn to navigate parish matters as his father had. And determine how to best handle David. He would not follow his father's negligence in that regard, though much of what his brother did was beyond his control.

He gave a terse nod. "When is the gathering?"

"Soon. I'll ask Mother for details, then send a note round as a reminder." Her lovely face turned entreating. "Everard, please. I sense some change in you. I ken the earldom weighs upon you and your time, but surely you have a wee spot left for me and parish doings. This meeting might serve you well."

"I want little to do with plots and intrigues, however cleverly disguised, Alison."

She expelled a tense breath. "As I said, you seem almost a stranger of late, and I would ken the cause of it."

"Expect me at Landreth Hall when the time comes." His terseness did not sit well with her, he realized. Nor did he feel like tarrying as in days of old, something sure to raise her hackles too. "In the meantime, keep me apprised of matters in London."

38

The path to heaven passes through a teapot.

Blythe could sense when the laird had gone missing. The castle had an altogether different feel. Or perhaps it was only the hole in her heart? Though she hadn't seen Everard leave, she did notice the door to his study was open, the room empty. She'd gone back and forth tutoring Orin, riding in his pony cart, and walking about the gardens with Elodie. But the laird wasn't anywhere to be seen, and she daren't ask about him. 'Twas none of her concern how he spent his time and with whom, though her heart told her otherwise.

Blythe trod another silent passageway to the servants' wing, bearing gifts. Mrs. Candlish was on her mind today. She could not dismiss the housekeeper's harried state of late. Munro had recovered his legs and was again tending to his usual business, including his late-night violin playing, but still the housekeeper seemed tired. Might she be ill?

Blythe took a liberty seeking the woman out. Servants were not always glad to see members of the household in their domain, especially one posing as a guest. Still, an obliging maidservant showed her to Mrs. Candlish's personal sitting room not far from the kitchen and buttery. Blythe tentatively knocked on the door, hoping the woman wasn't napping.

"Come in," came the familiar voice.

When Blythe entered, the housekeeper abandoned her task at her desk and stood. "Milady, what a lovely surprise."

"Please, be at your leave," Blythe said with a smile. "I don't mean to impose on your time."

"Nonsense, mem. 'Tis an honor. Won't ye join me for tea?" She gestured to a chair. "'Tis almost four o' the clock. Polly brings it promptly. I'll simply call for another dish."

"Thank you." Blythe sat by a window overlooking the kitchen garden. "I've not come empty-handed. Orin has picked you some early blaeberries from our foray in the woods." She set the dish of fruit atop the tea table. "And here is another small gift."

Mrs. Candlish took the folded shawl, her expression rapt, even awed. "Milady, such fine cotton, surely imported cloth. 'Tis exquisite!"

"I do enjoy embroidery," Blythe said, hoping she found it pleasing as well as practical. "I've worked the flowers and butterflies in stem stitch and satin stitch for the most part."

"Such tidy hems and seams. Why, ye've even embroidered thistles amongst the lilies and carnations," Mrs. Candlish said. "And in cotton yarn too."

"Father kindly sent along my sewing kit, so I'm able to keep my hands busy. I can't always have my head buried in a book."

The housekeeper smiled. "This puts me in mind of the late countess. She was rarely idle. Winter and summer she spent at her embroidery along with Lady Howard."

"Lady Howard . . ." The name rang a dusty bell.

"A former maid of honor at King Charles II's court and one of the countess's closest confidantes."

Blythe froze. Did Mrs. Candlish know her mother's tawdry history? The joy surrounding the gift turned to ashes. Peg had said Mrs. Candlish was the most devout of women . . .

"Lady Howard never married and lived in the castle's gatehouse. Sadly, she passed away not long after the countess of a lung ailment. The damp Scottish climate worsens such maladies, I'm afraid." Mrs. Candlish draped the shawl around her plump shoulders before sitting down opposite Blythe. "Though I am a proud Scotswoman, I am never warm enough. The castle is chill except for the hottest summer days."

"I am glad for a generous supply of coal," Blythe said as a knock sounded and a tea tray was brought. "Though I'm quite curious about your country's use of peat."

"Ah, nothing quite like the smell of a peat fire. The stuff of my childhood."

Though Blythe typically took tea with Elodie in the privacy of their rooms, today seemed a special occasion, marking Mrs. Candlish's thirtieth year of service, or so Peg had told her. Blythe couldn't let the day go by without recognizing that fact.

A large porcelain teapot graced the table, the fragrance of hyson strong. Girdle scones covered a pretty china plate, butter and jam beside it. Slices of seed cake graced another dish.

"Would ye like to serve, milady?"

"Please, you do the honors as it's your special day," Blythe said, her stomach rumbling. "What is in this little jar here?"

Mrs. Candlish chuckled. "Potted hough. I do wonder if ye'll care for it."

"Is it like your haggis? I am fond of that."

"Are ye now?" Mrs. Candlish looked impressed. "Much like the laird. He's always been one for haggis and hough. Nae expense is to be spared in the kitchens on his watch, thankfully, including the finest tea. He's generous to those belowstairs, both upper and lower servants. 'Tis not every noble house can boast of such."

Hearing him spoken of so fondly lifted Blythe's spirits. She busied herself with her tea, stirring in cream and sugar while marveling the housekeeper took neither.

"'Tis a fine day when I sit down with a duke's daughter, though

I had tea thrice with the countess in her day." Mrs. Candlish eyed the half-open door, then got up and closed it. "There, we can talk at will with nae eavesdroppers in the hall."

Blythe felt another qualm. Would the housekeeper ask about her mother? "'Tis wonderful tea." She took another sip. "And company."

"Och, yer good for my flagging spirits," Mrs. Candlish said, sitting down again. "I've been right weary o' late, but the laird, bless him, has told me I'm to train a woman of my choosing to help me."

"Oh?" Pleasure coursed through Blythe, warm as the tea in her cup. So he'd taken the recent suggestion she'd made to heart?

"The auld laird's own health took a toll once the countess passed, so much so he wasn't sharp as he once was overseeing household matters. But the new laird is righting that now." She darted a sympathetic look at Blythe. "Speaking of faithers, ye must be missing yers terribly."

"Very much." Blythe reached for a girdle scone.

"'Tis cold comfort to be the sole bairn," Mrs. Candlish said. "Be it a humble croft or lofty castle."

"My father longed for a son."

"One day, Lord willing, you shall give him a grandson."

"I can only hope to marry and have more than one child." It was an honest admission, long mulled since childhood if only to be discarded in adulthood. Blythe took a bite of scone slathered with butter and jam, thankful for life's simple pleasures even if she was denied larger ones.

Mrs. Candlish sipped her tea, then sampled the seed cake. "D'ye not have a suitor somewhere, milady? Surely a comely lass of yer standing . . ."

How easy it was to confide in such an openhearted woman. "Lately I've been wondering if the Lord has instead made me for a convent."

"Losh, milady!" The cup of tea came down, rattling atop the table. Mrs. Candlish's vehemence was at odds with her usual circumspect demeanor. "Think not of any holy orders, I beg ye. There are four

Humes to choose from at present. Ronan is occupied with Miss Bell, and happily so. But one of the others might suit, though a duke's daughter could well have a prince."

Swallowing a sip of tea, Blythe took her time answering. "There's no suitor, prince or otherwise."

"A shame, milady." Mrs. Candlish pursed her lips thoughtfully. "Since ye appeared on our doorstep in the wee small hours, I've oft wondered why. 'Tis nae accident, surely—rather, a divine instance."

"I do wonder," Blythe said, thinking of Elodie.

"For one, wee Orin is all the better for yer coming. Everyone's noticed he's not so shelpit since ye've begun overseeing his affairs. The whole household speaks well of ye, from the laird to the bottommost scullery maid. Word travels, ye ken. And Boyd has brought back a good report of how well regarded ye were amongst yer faither's tenants, ever watching out for their well-being. This shawl and the berries ye've brought me are proof of a douce, generous heart."

Touched, Blythe said, "Boyd is the laird's manservant, is he not?"

"Aye, and a jack-o'-all-trades. He goes hither and yon for the laird, is another set of eyes and ears for Wedderburn."

"A trusted servant, then."

"Och, most certainly. Orphaned in his youth, he was a sad spectacle till the auld laird brought him to the castle from the collieries where his faither had perished. He even followed Lord Wedderburn onto the battlefields of Europe." Mrs. Candlish plucked a berry from the dish. "Ye've seen the world, then, same as the laird, with yer time on the continent."

"A bit of it, though I'd hazard a guess the laird has seen far more of it than I."

"He rarely speaks of such. He's not boastful like so many."

"Indeed, he is not." And she was growing used to his silences, no longer thinking of them as intimidating but more admirable. A man who weighed what he said before he said it was worth listening to.

"He's cut o' the same cloth as those who sired him, has the best of both his faither and the countess. The auld laird was very distraught when he went away to war. But with six other sons to bear the load if he didna return, what could he say?"

"So, Lord Wedderburn wanted to be a soldier?"

"From the time he was a wee lad. There's a long line of Humes who've fought, starting at Falkirk when William Wallace led the Scots."

"A proud, illustrious history, then."

"A great many of them died during the wars, and we feared the laird would meet with the same sad fate." Mrs. Candlish poured more tea while Blythe spied a kitchen maid through the window with a basket on her arm, picking herbs. "I do hope to see another generation running about before I'm too auld to enjoy them. This castle needs new life, new hope."

"Children always help make a house a home," Blythe said, remembering the many Wellinghursts and wondering how Charlotte's family was.

Mrs. Candlish nodded vigorously. "I do hope ye'll do nothing rash and leave us, Lady Hedley. Especially for a far-flung convent."

39

What worries you, masters you.

JOHN LOCKE

Bernard entered the stables, having recently returned from the Hume collieries a few miles distant. The staccato clip of hooves announced his coming, but Everard hardly noticed. Thoughts full of the *Edinburgh Courant*, he remained so preoccupied he hardly heard Bernard's greeting. David's continued exploits were hardly surprising, but to see them boldly laid out in ink before all of Britain . . .

"Good morning, Brother." Bernard dismounted, and a waiting groom saw to his lathered horse. "Are you riding out?"

"Nae, deciding on a proper mount for Orin and her ladyship."

"Ah, our guest. Then why do you have the look of our faither contemplating something dire about you?" Bernard plunged his hands into a water bucket and washed the coal dust from them. "Do you want to hear my ill news first or tell me yours?"

"Go ahead."

With a look around, Bernard reached into his weskit. The two of them passed beneath the stable's arch with its clock tower before he handed Everard a paper. "The factor wanted this brought to your attention straightaway. Your approval is needed before posting."

Beneath an eave, Everard perused the paper, recognizing the factor's bold hand.

The following bound colliers, belonging to Lord Wedderburn's coalworks along the Firth of Forth, having recently mutinied and deserted viz. Archie Hunter Factor, this public notice is given that no coal master may entertain them: Adam Duncan. John Shaw . . .

"A dozen men, then," Everard said, reviewing the list. "The Duncans are the ablest and longest-employed miners we have. Surely there's just cause for their complaint."

"Their chief grievance has to do with some malady the doctor can find nae remedy for."

"Send the doctor to me, then, so I can hear firsthand. I've not visited the collieries in some time but will do so if only to shut them down, at least temporarily, till the problem is resolved."

"Shut them down? Surely you jest."

"Faither deplored conditions there and called it the lowest form of servitude. He spoke of selling or leasing them if not quitting them entirely."

"Yet our coal exports are second to none."

"If we do continue, there needs to be extensive improvements to both ironworks and saltworks, not only the coalworks." Everard folded the paper and pocketed it. "But I'll undertake it slowly and carefully."

Bernard tugged at his neckcloth as if it was too tight. The day was the warmest so far but with a rising wind that rustled the thick-leafed oaks and elms about the stables. Looking to the castle, Everard noticed no smoke puffed from Blythe's chimney. He'd not seen her today and wondered if she'd appear at dinner.

"I passed Boyd at the south gate leaving for parts unknown." Bernard removed a flask from his pocket and took a long drink. "Any more news about the Jacks and their planned Rising?"

"Boyd is carrying correspondence from her ladyship to her faither."

"To the duke's secret contact in Berwick?"

"Aye, and on that subject, more government troops have been sighted coming over the border."

"I feel to my marrow a conflict is imminent." Bernard offered Everard the flask, but he declined. "This morn I heard directly from a Jacobite leader in Duns that Stuart forces are well supplied with the latest imported muskets and bayonets from Northumberland clear to the Highlands."

"I dinna doubt it. Redcoats have even been sent to Oxford, where riots have erupted in favor of Jacobites and against dissenters."

Bernard whistled. "Reports are being made of pillaging at will and without consequence."

"Keep a close watch on our own borders. I'll not have any mischief done us or any of our tenants." To say nothing of Blythe and her maid. Wedderburn was comprised of a great many men and only a few women, and he'd never been more glad of his small if lionhearted household army.

"And your own news?" Bernard studied him, expression dour. "Might it have to do with Davie?"

"Aye. He's apparently sponsored a Jacobite dance at an assembly room in the heart of Edinburgh. 'Tis causing something of a storm."

"I suppose his antics have seen ink." Bernard grimaced. "Nae doubt the High Street is a-crow from the castle to the Canongate." When Everard nodded, Bernard took another drink before capping the flask. "Sure ye dinna want a nip?"

"Nae." Everard turned toward the castle. A whole hogshead of whisky wouldn't soften the harsh realities of the present.

Blythe had excused herself and Orin for the afternoon, taking dinner out of doors, Mrs. Candlish said. Sitting down in the dining room at two o' the clock with three empty places made Everard more tapsalteerie than he cared to admit, if only because he didn't know Blythe and Orin's whereabouts or how far they'd roam. But after he heard that two armed footmen had accompanied them, his mind eased.

He studied the door, wishing Blythe would appear after all. He might have paid more attention to their going had he not been preoccupied seeing Malcolm and Alistair off to Edinburgh in the forenoon after he went to the stables. Their time at university was at hand, though he might well have need of them at home. But they'd vowed to keep an eye on Davie, at least, and send word if something else transpired.

For now, Everard dined with Bernard and Ronan, the latter noticeably quiet.

"Where are the lassies?" Bernard asked, spearing a piece of mutton. "The dining room feels deserted."

"Miss Bell has a headache," Ronan replied.

"'The course of true love never did run smooth,'" Bernard said with a long look at him. "Act 1, scene 1. *A Midsummer Night's Dream.*"

Ronan kept his eyes on his plate. "I well know it, tutored alongside you."

"As for her ladyship, she left in a pony cart with Orin a half hour ago, a victual basket between them," Everard said. He regretted he hadn't been the one to show her the part of Scotland that rivaled the luxuriant English Midlands, but he wouldn't begrudge Orin the pleasure. "They have a mind to take their dinner on a high spot overlooking the Merse."

Bernard looked at Ronan again. "I suppose Miss Bell could not conscience dining alone with us Humes without her mistress."

Ronan expelled a breath. "I hope that and her headache account for it, aye. Nothing more."

"Have nae fear." Bernard continued his literary onslaught between bites. "'All's well that ends well.'"

Ronan grimaced. "Is not that Shakespearean play about a woman of lower rank and a nobleman she wishes to wed?"

"So it is," Bernard said, reaching for a bannock. "But a comedy, not a tragedy."

"Bethankit," Ronan replied as Everard listened to their good-natured banter. "We've enough mourning at Wedderburn. Time for merriment . . . marriage."

Bernard stopped eating and stared at Ronan. "Your intentions for Miss Bell are serious, then."

"Serious as the attack on Flodden Field." Ronan cast a look at the portrait of the former laird. "I only regret Faither didn't live to see more of us wed. Mither often spoke of grandchildren. A true tragedy in hindsight that we've dragged our feet so."

"You'll wait until mourning ends?" Bernard asked him.

Ronan shrugged. "I canna answer yet, though I see no reason why. Faither never let the business of mourning trump the business of living."

Bernard grew grave. "You care not she's bereft of a dowry?"

"It troubles her mightily, though I've assured her she has need of none."

"You have my blessing, for what it's worth," Everard said, looking at Blythe's empty chair again. Since when had he stopped thinking of it as the countess's and started thinking of it as hers instead?

"Where will you live?" Bernard asked.

"Cheviot Lodge is what Faither meant for me, aye?" Ronan looked to Everard for confirmation. "Though Handaxewood in the Lammermuirs would suit."

"Cheviot is closer. Dinna go too far afield lest we seldom see you," Everard said. "You and your bride can have your pick of the two if she agrees to wed a barbaric Scot such as yourself."

Ronan chuckled. "We'll know soon enough. I intend to ask for Miss Bell's hand on the morrow."

40

My thoughts and I were of another world.

BEN JONSON

At sennight's end, Blythe stood in Wedderburn's chapel. Its relics were both Catholic and Presbyterian, a testament to the Humes' changing allegiances over the centuries. Soft afternoon light pressed past the stained glass and turned the hallowed interior into a rainbow of color. She felt more at home here, aware of a great many things at once other than the happy couple. The heraldic panels that bespoke the long Hume lineage were a pleasant distraction, as well as the shields of the Royal Arms of Scotland—even one of Saint Margaret, a former Scottish queen.

At some point over the centuries, a Protestant parish minister had replaced a Catholic priest. As Elodie was Protestant, no trouble was had on that score. A special marriage license had been obtained, dispensing with the reading of the banns three Sabbaths in a row. Blythe took her place at the front of the chapel, a bit thunderstruck.

These Scots, when something moved them, moved heaven and earth till it was done.

Though there had been a great deal of surprise and hustle since the marriage proposal a few days before, Elodie looked radiant, even elated. Clad in her best gown of pearl-grey satin trimmed with Brussels lace and carrying a bouquet of pink roses, she never stopped smiling. And Ronan had the look of a prince, trading his sable for a handsome tan suit, a sprig of white heather adorning his chest.

Beside the groom stood the laird, looking more pleased than Blythe had ever seen him. His usual intensity had lightened, and she watched him discreetly. As the ceremony progressed, she found herself surprised, amused, and moved by turns, noting how different were Scottish weddings from English ones.

Holy Communion was part of the service, the couple drinking from a shiny, silver, two-handed quaich. Ronan then produced his siller—thirteen silver coins—as a pledge to provide for and protect Elodie. Her open hands received them before returning them to her groom, who then passed them to the minister.

Not to be forgotten was the luckenbooth, a Hume heirloom that Blythe likened to a broach, pinned on the bride's bodice once vows were said. Crafted of silver, the entwined hearts boasted a crown and several small gems that winked gaily in the candlelight.

Oh, Elodie, blessed are you.

For a few fleeting seconds, envy intruded on Blythe's happiness. If only . . . If only the laird had proposed and not her father. If only she was the bride on this most hallowed occasion. Everard would make the brawest of bridegrooms.

Bells began pealing, sending a shiver down Blythe's spine. At the door of the chapel was a lad with bagpipes. As soon as the minister pronounced the couple man and wife, the piper filled the place with a soaring melody, then led them all to the castle's Great Hall for dancing and feasting. Two fiddlers awaited at one end of the enormous room, rosining their bows, a few notes escaping as they tuned their instruments. Even Munro plied his violin, joining them.

The entire household had gathered to greet the bride and groom, from the merest scullery maid to all the upper servants, including Mrs. Candlish. Blythe felt their excitement and read the good humor in all their lively faces.

Orin clasped her hand. "We must dance as we did at Faither's lykewake, only this is a happy occasion." His blue eyes sparkled like sapphires. "I hope we dance all night long."

Blythe felt a start, her hope to sit quietly by discarded. Orin, she realized, would have none of it, nor would the laird. The latter was looking at her from where he stood between Munro and Bernard, still in mourning but obviously intent on celebrating despite it.

"I should like another sister-in-law," Orin was saying overloudly. "I wonder if you might want to marry one of my other brothers?"

"Might I, indeed." Blythe squeezed his hand a bit harder than she intended. Thankfully, the piper's notes swelled and Orin's voice was lost in the music.

Or so she hoped.

Flushing, she sat down on a near chair against the paneled wall, her russet skirts swirling in a silken circle around her. Orin tapped his foot beside her, gaiety stamped in his every feature.

"Cook has made a wedding cake. Have you ever tasted one?" he asked her.

Blythe was glad for a diversion, her gaze leaving the laird and fastening on the table where the confection rested—a large, two-tiered, brandy-soaked fruitcake.

"Never a Scottish one," she said, noting the abundance of dishes both savory and sweet spread on other tables at one end of the Great Hall.

An early afternoon wedding left plenty of room for revelry. Blythe doubted the guests would see their bedchambers till midnight. A lively tune was struck, unknown to her but dear to everyone else, or so it seemed.

"'Tis the shame-spring reel," Orin told her. "The first dance, ye ken."

Out of the corner of her eye she saw the laird approaching, unaware of the trepidation in her heart. She could dance, of course. Her father had seen to that long ago with a dancing master, beginning when she was only five. Lately, she had danced her way through France. Rank was usually observed in more genteel circles, those with the loftiest titles dancing first. But did these Scots honor such protocol?

It seemed they did.

Everard stood before her, his gaze holding what seemed a challenge. He gave a flawless, courtly bow, and she found herself rising from her seat to curtsy deeply. Her pulse pounded as he took her hand, the swish of her stomach rivaling the swish of her skirts. The mere brush of his fingers—'twas the first time he'd touched her since their stairwell encounter—seemed more caress.

Ronan and Elodie looked on, smiling. The entire assembly was watching. It seemed everyone held a collective breath.

Everard was an accomplished soldier, but could he dance?

In moments Blythe had forgotten everyone but him and her own flying feet. Pleasure coursed through her as she gained confidence in the surety of her steps. The laird astonished her. For a man of his stature, he was as nimble and surefooted as any accomplished courtier, the perfect partner. He elevated a simple country dance to noble heights, his pleasure plain, his stoicism a memory.

Hot-cheeked and winded, she was next claimed by Bernard, then Orin. A great many were dancing now, all the servants in two longways sets, the fiddlers in a frenzy, the piper bravely keeping up with them.

Six dances later, so parched it hurt to swallow, Blythe made her way to an enormous punch bowl, her whole being one joyous palpitation. No longer was she the unchosen miss who hugged the wall or sought a solitary alcove.

Hands atremble, she held her punch cup and willed the silk roses sewn to her bodice to stop their rapid rise and fall as she recovered her breathing. But her emotions refused to settle, at least with the laird still beside her, intent on the punch to quell his own thirst.

"You are a dancing mistress in disguise," he told her, an admiring glint in his eye.

"You flatter me." She took another sip, tasting sugared limes and brandy. "I am thankful to not step the minuet."

He turned back toward the dancers. "A fussy, complicated exercise from the continent, foreign to us Scots and making fools of many."

She smiled at his assessment. "'Tis different from your country dances, more a duet between a single man and woman with a great many patterns and complexities."

"Akin to courtship."

"I wouldn't know," she said more wistfully than she wanted to as the punch spread through her languorously.

His voice dropped a notch. "Have you never been courted, lass?"

Lass. Somehow the wording turned the question more intimate. "Never."

"D'ye want to be?" His honest query, perhaps prompted by the tongue-loosening spirits, held her captive.

"It must be wondrous to be mutually in love," she said, having pondered it many times amid a world of infidelities and betrayals. "To remain there."

"I believe the bonnie bride and my brother may have found it."

She took another sip of punch, weighing his meaning, wishing life were not so fraught with the bittersweet. "I am happy for them."

"And yet at the same time it leaves a hole inside you," he said.

She stared at the whirling dancers. Tears stood in her eyes, making the room a colorful wash. Why was happiness so often elusive and tinged with sadness? Why could there not be joy untarnished?

"Are you still considering a convent?"

She clutched her empty cup. "I am . . . undecided." What had he done with her letter to France? Put it in his desk drawer or forwarded it to her father? At the moment it didn't seem to matter.

He stood so close his coat sleeve brushed her forearm, though his gaze remained on the dancers. "Would you consider becoming my countess?"

Her breathing stopped. Shock coiled round her like a serpent. A reel finished and a jig began. She had misheard him, surely. The music was playing tricks on her ears. She daren't turn to him, though she longed to look into his eyes. Would they be full of their usual intensity, underscoring his startling question?

Countess . . . or mistress?

Her mother's many sins came rushing back, entangling her. She was unworthy to be the wife of an earl. An honorable man would not want her. Had it not been the same with John Manners, Duke of Rutland? And she was a Papist Jacobite, to boot.

Munro drew nearer, speaking on the other side of the laird about some matter she wasn't privy to. Excusing himself, Everard left to attend to something beyond the Great Hall. She watched him go, shaken and rent with an indescribable yearning that was part physical ache.

But the bewildering moment was not long entertained. Orin gave a little bow and whisked her into a sprightly allemande. The old laird had not neglected his youngest son's dancing lessons. Orin's wholehearted enthusiasm was a delight to behold, even if she was, as the Scots said, sair-hearted.

41

My heart is sair—I dare na tell,
My heart is sair for Somebody.

ROBERT BURNS

The next morn was unusual for its quietness. Save for Pepys piping a bright tune, all lay abed and lessons were delayed. Upon awakening, Blythe was greeted by Peg, not Elodie, and the events of the previous day and night came rushing back, one memory uppermost.

What had Everard said to her amid the bustle of the Great Hall?

She stared at her reflection in the looking glass of her dressing table, the dark circles beneath her eyes testament to a near-sleepless night. Too much punch. An abundance of unfamiliar if delicious rich food. Endless dancing. A midnight toast. More dancing. And not another word with Everard, leaving his last question begging clarity.

"Would you consider becoming my . . ."

Did he think her only recourse was being someone's mistress because she was plain and had a shameful heritage? Was he offering her that dubious role, thinking it was all she might aspire to? She bent her head as hurt throbbed like an actual wound.

Lord, please steady my spirit. Reveal any untruths.

The mind could play tricks, especially mingled with the strength of the punch she'd partaken of. He might have been asking her something else entirely, yet her fevered mind and heart twisted it into a more damaging query. Given her lineage, she was overly sensitive. How she longed to settle the matter without a shade of doubt. How she wanted to hear him say clearly and unmistakably, "Will you be my countess?"

The mantel clock struck eleven. By now, Ronan and Elodie would be halfway to Handaxewood or Cheviot Lodge. What a wonder to be able to choose from two residences. At their leaving, Elodie had embraced Blythe tearfully, making her promise she would visit them soon once they decided where they would be. She had waved at them till their coach disappeared through the north gate.

Blythe almost couldn't take it in. To be a bride. To go away on a honeymoon. To anticipate children. To have new vistas and new friendships. To learn more every hour about your groom, down to the smallest, most delightful detail.

"Is Lord Wedderburn at home, do you know?" she asked as Peg placed clean laundry in a wardrobe.

"He usually takes a morning ride about the estate. I did hear Mrs. Candlish say he's to go to Landreth Hall tonight."

Landreth Hall. It rang an alarming bell.

"'Tis the baron Landreth's residence. Fancies himself king of Berwickshire, he does." Peg snorted, then colored the red of an orchard apple. "Beg pardon, mem. My tongue gets ahead of my wits betimes. His oldest daughter has long had her sights on the laird."

Alison.

Would the haughty Alison be his countess? Blythe's whole being cried out against the mismatch. "I believe I saw her at the funeral."

Peg chuckled. "I forgot ye were there. A braisant lass, ye are."

Blythe sighed. Such meant brash, surely.

Peg shut the wardrobe with a little thump. "Methinks Lord Wedderburn is hard-pressed to ken what to do with ye."

"Oh? His lordship doesn't seem to be much confounded about anything, at least in my estimation."

"Till yer coming, nae." Arms akimbo, Peg gave a chuckle. "But here lately there's a bit o' tittle-tattle belowstairs. Bets placed as to how long his lairdship will remain unwed."

"On account of Miss Alison."

"Hoot! Her Royal Loftiness doesna have much to do with it."

"What do you mean?"

"Glad I am his lairdship is distracted by yer presence here." Peg gave a devilish wink. "It may well bring all the wiles of Landreth Hall to naught."

Blythe drew her sultana closer and stared after Peg as she left the bedchamber, daring to hope.

42

All that glitters is not gold, nor all that sparkles silver.

ANCIENT PROVERB

The gardens solaced Blythe as little else did. In midsummer they were nearly at their peak. She often sat beneath an arbor of wisteria that was fragrant as perfume, Orin beside her, their watercolors before them.

Another winsome bird had emerged amid his paint and paper, this time a skylark. Orin's strokes were more deft than Blythe's, a claw here, a beak there. Downy feathers bore white streaks, and the crest sat proudly atop the bird's wee head like a miniature crown.

"If only art could sing," he said, studying his work.

"It makes one's heart sing just looking at it," she replied. "I can hear the lark's melodious music in my mind, all because of your watercolor."

"I hope to paint Wallace next. Only he willna stay still."

They laughed. Even now the pup cavorted about Orin's ankles, occasionally chasing a small leather ball or sampling a tempting flower. A half-chewed daisy lay at their feet.

Orin looked at her own work. A rose was in progress, a sunny yellow, the leaves a mint green. But how to capture the flower's delicate folds and ridges . . .

"I can nearly smell your rose," he said. "'Tis yellow as butter and makes me hungry."

"You didn't eat much at dinner." She'd been concerned at the time, though he seemed unaffected by it. A late night at the wedding frolic and too much cake, she'd decided. "Supper isn't long now. How about we partake together?"

He nodded and dabbed a bit more paint onto his brush. "It shall be just the two of us. The laird and Bernard are going out to Landreth Hall."

"Ah, yes." The fact was no more pleasant than it had been hours earlier when she'd first heard it.

"Sometimes Miss Alison comes here, though not lately. Once I heard her ask, 'Who is that sickly looking lad? He cannot be a Hume.'"

"Oh? People ought not to say such things."

"'Twas long ago. I was wee. But I have not forgotten." He set down his brush. "Needs be people speak kindly."

"Always."

He brightened. "Just this morn at breakfast I heard the laird say you're the bonniest dancer he's ever laid eyes on. And we all agreed."

Blythe's entire being stood on tiptoe. "He did?"

"And then Bernard said you have so light a step because there's so little of you."

Blythe laughed. These Humes, each so different, were amusing, every one of them. Except David. From all she'd heard, David had a darkness about him that boded ill.

Orin yawned and covered his mouth in his usual polite way. For a lad raised without a mother, he was remarkably courteous. "'Tis good to pass on pleasant talk, is it not?"

"Indeed. Pleasant words are as a honeycomb, sweet to the soul and health to the bones, as Scripture says."

He leaned closer, his head against her shoulder. She slipped an arm around him, her cheek resting against his silky hair. Together they looked out over the garden, and she tried not to think of the lovely Alison or the fate of her own father or Elodie's absence.

For the moment she was safe. Sound. Amid a world of color and beauty beside a lad she dearly loved.

And the laird had called her bonnie.

Landreth Hall's drawing room was crowded, the scent of tobacco and spirits strong. Several men were smoking in an anteroom—bonnet lairds, mostly, unaccustomed to the grandeur of great houses. Already, overweening voices and laughter rang out as Everard took stock of the company.

Like his father, he usually shunned such gatherings, but it was imperative he keep current on events and the people behind them. There was a great deal of empty babble on the whole, though occasionally a kernel of truth would emerge and prove useful. Tonight's company was decidedly in favor of the new German king. Though Everard had just arrived, he'd already heard the words *Jacobite* and *Papist* spoken with disdain.

His hackles rose when he laid eyes on a few Blackadders. Long-time enemies of the Humes if for no other reason than their enmity went back centuries, they eyed him warily in turn. Recently there'd been a complaint of sheep being stolen from the Humes' large flock on pastureland that bordered the Blackadders'. Everard had largely forgotten it, glad to forgo a potential grudge over so small a matter and let his factors deal with it as they saw fit.

The baroness approached him even before Alison did. "Lord Wedderburn, so good of you to come." She seemed relieved, as if she'd feared he wouldn't make an appearance. "My eldest daughter will be delighted too." She signaled to a footman. "We must start off on the right foot with some of our best brandy."

Glass in hand, Everard spied Alison coming toward him in a rustle of green silk that reminded him of a peacock, emeralds draping her neck and dangling from her ears. Color high, she curtsied, and they moved away from the entrance.

243

"Here you are," she said, looking triumphant. "Better tardy than absent. Where is Bernard?"

"Deterred at the last." Everard didn't envy his brother. He would rather attend this function than a fracas at the collieries.

"A pity." Her gaze roamed the room. "Or perhaps providential. I recall he is even less fond of the Blackadders than you are."

"'Tis a long, complex association," he said, tasting his brandy.

"What a feat to have both Blackadders and Humes in our very parlor, former Borders reivers and foes once joined by marriage. I well remember the Fraud of the Humes, as 'tis called."

"Of which I am not proud," he replied, having mulled it many times. "Though Flodden Field might be the worst of it."

Her smile dimmed, and she led him toward a small alcove flooded with the last of the daylight. "I must ask you, before you are overtaken by others here, about a certain matter." With a flick of her wrist she opened her fan, her voice holding the petulant edge he disliked. "How our servants talk. One of our chambermaids is kindred to one of yours at Wedderburn. She mentioned there is a lady of note who has come to tutor Orin, though she did not name her."

Everard stayed stoic as dismay nicked at his composure. Which servant's tongue had been loosed? Though he was surprised it had taken this long to become tattle.

"I cannot resist asking for details as to this intriguing circumstance."

"The lass in question is my parents' goddaughter."

Again that brittle smile. "Surely she has a name."

Blythe flashed to mind as he'd last seen her, wearing her spectacles beside Orin as he worked, a sunny silhouette in the morning room. "She's a sassenach. You wouldn't ken her."

"I might call on her. Introduce myself as your nearest neighbor."

"Nae need." The urge to protect Blythe rose up, lending a terse edge to his words. "She came to pay her respects at my faither's funeral." For once he was glad of Blythe's daring as he spoke no lie. At the same time he owed Alison no explanation. He glanced out the window toward Wedderburn, the peel tower climbing above oaks and elms against a gilded sunset. "Soon she'll take her leave of us."

He couldn't hide the feeling from his tone, mournful as a fiddle's lament. Blythe gone. Wedderburn empty. Orin sair-hearted.

And not just Orin.

At the back of his mind was the startling question he'd asked Blythe at the wedding reception, only she seemed not to have heard him. Or might she have chosen to ignore his startling proposal? True, 'twas a roundabout way to ask for her hand, but he remained unsure of her and her regard of him.

"I do wish you had confided in me." A fitfulness crept into Alison's gaze, her silk-clad shoulders squaring. "How you try my temper, Lord Wedderburn."

He took another drink, glad to be an aggravation, at least where Blythe's well-being was concerned. He was enjoying this rabbit trail Alison could not possibly trace, or so he hoped. "Next you'll be hearing Ronan has taken a bride."

Her vexation gave way to astonishment. "You jest!"

"He's wed, aye, and left Wedderburn."

Her brows arched. "A Scotswoman, I hope, of ample dowry and pedigree."

"Nae." Even as he voiced it, he marveled at the turn of events. "A simple English lass."

"One of no distinction?"

"My brother feels otherwise."

"I—well . . ." For once Alison was nearly speechless. "One of my sisters said she heard chapel bells pealing at Wedderburn yesterday . . ."

"At the conclusion of the ceremony, aye."

"Felicitations to the happy couple, then." Her voice lacked warmth. She was aggrieved to have learned of it secondhand. But murmuring and discontent were ever Alison's way, and it was becoming clearer the longer their acquaintance.

"Have you any news from London?" he asked.

"None of note. But the gossip from Edinburgh is rather scintillating. 'Tis being whispered your libertine brother has become enamored with a stage actress—"

"Lord Wedderburn." A bonnet laird stood before them, clearly intent on conversation, coming to Everard's rescue. "I've been wanting to discuss leasing land from you."

43

Out, out, brief candle!
Life's but a walking shadow.

WILLIAM SHAKESPEARE

Blythe turned over, sated with sleep and barely aware of a candle penetrating the darkness.

"Milady, I am loath to wake ye." Peg's anxious voice threaded through the velvety darkness. "'Tis Orin, mem. He's taken ill and is asking for ye."

Blythe came awake in a trice. She pushed back the bedcovers and fumbled for her sultana.

"He's retched twice and is hot as an iron." Peg's unwelcome words sent her rushing from her room. "The laird has not yet returned from Landreth Hall."

Should they not send for him, then?

Blythe wondered the hour. Not midnight, she guessed. She'd gone to bed right after Orin, before nine of the clock, wanting to make up for the recent festivities and little sleep.

She'd seen Orin's bedchamber but once. A small room, it adjoined the laird's and was at the top of the grand cedar staircase in another part of the castle entirely. Tonight it seemed to take an age to reach it, her heart a-thunder all the way. Orin needed a mother at such

247

times. But she was all he had other than his nearly blind nurse, who she hoped was abed sleeping peacefully.

At last Blythe reached him. His bedchamber was cold, and his heated skin seemed to sear her hand. He murmured and thrashed about, his beloved face beaded with sweat, the bed linens in a tangle. She called for a basin of cold water and soft cloths.

Merciful Savior . . .

She shied from illness. She'd not yet moved past the horror of her grandmother's sudden death, all the nostrums and bloodletting, the smell of decay and the bewildering despair.

The basin was brought, and with Peg's help they removed Orin's soiled nightshirt. Gently Blythe began to cool him with a damp cloth, laying another one across his brow.

"He needs water," she said. "Cold well water."

Peg vanished, and in minutes the laird was bending over Blythe, surprising and relieving her at once. Candlelight called out the concerned slant of his features.

"When did he fall ill?" he asked her, his palm on Orin's reddened cheek.

"I'm uncertain, though he seemed lethargic at afternoon lessons and had little appetite at supper. I was hoping a night's sleep would restore him."

"I'll send for the doctor." His hand fell away. "He's here too oft of late."

He left the room only to return moments later. Pulling up a chair, he sat down as she perched on the side of the enormous bed that seemed to dwarf so small and sick a boy.

Water was brought, and together they tried to trickle it down Orin's throat, Everard holding him up so he wouldn't choke. How tender he was with the boy. How . . . unsoldierly. There was no doubt of the love betwixt them.

She took a breath. "When the doctor comes, I beg you to dispense with any bloodletting. I fear it weakens rather than remedies."

He looked at her, a query in his dark-blue eyes as they moved from her face to all the rest of her. Only then did she remember she was in her nightclothes, a sultana wrapped round her, her loosened hair spilling down. Her braid had unraveled, its tie lost in her bed linens. His buckled shoe accidentally penned her trailing hem and tugged at the silky garment.

Stricken, she stood, righting it. "Milord, forgive me. I'm not fit to be seen—"

His fingers wrapped round her wrist like a bracelet. "I beg to differ." He swallowed, his voice falling to a rumbling whisper. "Such becomes you."

Tearing her gaze from his, she sat back down as that peculiar melting rush sacked her stomach. No matter that she kept a vigil beside a sickbed in complete dishabille, he'd paid her some sort of compliment.

Her attention returned to Orin, and she plunged her hands into the basin of water again with more force than she'd intended, if only to dispel the effect the laird had on her.

Everard watched Blythe, aggravated that at such a time he was distracted by womanly things. His hand itched to move to her hair and sink his fingers into the wealth of its waves, aching to know how it felt against his callused palm. Like tangled gold, it fell free in all its glory as she bent over his brother.

With effort, he returned to Orin, the sight of his suffering creating a fierce burning in Everard's chest. Candlelight did not hide the lad's distress. He gave a whimper now and again like a wounded animal. Everard's own gut cramped when Orin clutched his stomach as if the pain centered there.

Too much death. Too much suffering. Wedderburn felt like a tomb.

"Another careful drink." Blythe's low words inspired him to action. Together they managed to get a good amount of water down Orin without his sputtering.

Everard sat back, watching as she wiped down Orin's fevered face with cold cloths and replaced the one on his brow. Orin was oft ill, but not like this. Since birth he'd fought for his very life on more than half a dozen occasions. Always the fearsome question arose. Would this malady prove too much for him?

Was Blythe wondering the same? She looked at Everard again, a bit wild-eyed. "Pray with me . . . please."

The plea in her eyes—and her words—rattled him, and he was not easily rattled. Did she sense this was a mortal illness?

He reached for her hand as she slid to her knees beside the bed, tipping her head to rest against the feather bolster. "Pater noster, qui es in cælis . . ."

The Latin words did not escape him. The Lord's Prayer. His own days in the schoolroom returned, and he murmured it with her, her fervor washing over him and removing all weariness.

At their combined amen, he opened his eyes but kept hold of her. He studied the soft, pale fingers in his own, unwilling to let go. And half forgetting their prior exchanges, often barbed and fraught with heat.

She stayed on her knees, though she lifted her head. Her free hand brushed Orin's damp hair, her profile in the flickering light visibly moved, a single tear sliding toward her chin. 'Twas clear she loved the lad. Leaning nearer, she kissed Orin's cheek, then rested her head on his pillow and whispered words Everard wasn't privy to in his brother's ear.

The poignant whole of it reached deep into his battle-scarred soul and shook him. Without thinking, only feeling, he bent his head and pressed his lips to her upturned palm. A surge of gratitude mingled with desire overcame him, tempering his worry. Turning the sickroom bittersweet.

And erasing the last of his resistance.

44

No more tears now; I will think about revenge.

MARY, QUEEN OF SCOTS

I t befell in the days of Uther Pendragon, when he was king of all England . . ."

Blythe read from the legend of King Arthur, her voice carrying in the August breeze. Tucked into a fragrant corner of the garden, she and Orin sat with their backs to the castle's stony exterior. He was beside her in a cane chair, Wallace asleep in his lap. His gaze was riveted to the book's colorful illustrations, though this was not their first reading.

In a quarter of an hour, likely lulled by her voice and the warmth of the sun, Orin dozed. Stifling a yawn, she closed the book and shut her own eyes, the thankfulness she felt at his recovery overcoming her weariness from a sennight's vigil. Though Everard wanted her to go to her rooms and rest, she had steadfastly remained by Orin's bedside till the fever had broken. Once, she'd gone to sleep in a crisis, and her grandmother had died. The regret of it never left her.

This was her rich reward, Orin's prayed-for recovery filling her heart nigh to bursting just when she'd feared all was lost. But it was more than the lad's well-being and the garden's sunlit beauty that consoled her. The laird was near at hand. Just beyond the mullioned windows was his study. She could hear him even now speaking with

251

various members of the household. Munro's gravelly lilt contrasted with Mrs. Candlish's high-pitched tones and the new assistant house-keeper's milder, more tentative ones.

"Bide awhile in the garden nearest my study windows," Everard had told her that morning when she'd mentioned she wanted to take Orin out into the fresh air. "There I can keep an eye on things."

The way he'd said it seemed to imply it was more than Orin he was keeping an eye on. He'd given her another of his long looks, leaving her again at loose ends, cast back to the wedding frolic and what he'd asked her there.

Even the memory of his keeping vigil with her in Orin's shadowed bedchamber warmed her all over, especially the lingering brush of his lips on her palm. Everard had stayed up with her that first endless night, but she'd insisted he rest the second, comforted that his own bedchamber was reached by the adjoining door.

The doctor finally came. Orin wasn't bled but dosed with a tonic that seemed to relieve him. When the worst seemed to pass, Blythe lay down at the foot of his bed, and when she awakened she found a plaid over her, the laird dozing in the chair he'd occupied at first. She felt the thrill of his nearness even now.

A bird trilled shrilly by the fountain, striking a warning note in her soul. Her head cleared. How rash one's thoughts could be when met with unbridled emotion. 'Twas perilous to confuse gratitude for affection or desire. Gentlemen kissed ladies' hands all the time. Why must she make too much of it?

Any romantic notions vanished as she looked to the lad who bound them together in a sort of threefold knot.

Steeling herself against the hurt of having lost her heart, she shifted her attention to the long drive besmirched with dust. A rider was approaching. He disappeared briefly as he passed through the gatehouse that marked the halfway point, then came near enough that Blythe realized it was a woman intent on the castle's entrance.

She wore a large hat with pluming feathers, her habit brick red, black boots encasing her feet. Her stride was confident, even purposeful. From all appearances she was a superb horsewoman. At the same time, Blythe realized the laird's study was quiet. Had he gone to meet her?

Alison from Landreth Hall?

"Methinks Lord Wedderburn is hard-pressed to ken what to do with ye. Glad I am his lairdship is distracted by yer presence here. It may well bring all the wiles of Landreth Hall to naught."

Blythe hadn't pursued Peg's cryptic wording or asked her meaning. A true lady did not indulge in gossip any more than scandal.

Reaching into her skirt pocket, she fingered her rosary, feeling far afield from her faith. Deprived of mass and Holy Communion, her family's priest and all the familiar trappings, she felt adrift. Watching the Humes leave for their parish church on the last Sabbath had fueled her longing to worship. To be free and open with her faith, not hunted down and called a Papist as if it was some dread disease.

Oh, heavenly Father, please protect my earthly father. Where is he and is he well?

Her musings vanished when the door to the laird's study leading to the garden opened. The woman Blythe had seen riding—the same woman she'd seen at the funeral—stepped out, shutting the door behind her and coming toward them. Not wanting to wake Orin, Blythe stood and walked toward a fountain where water flowed from a dragon's mouth into a lily-padded pond.

She was keenly aware of Alison's sharp gaze, her eyes sweeping Blythe's figure and pinpointing everything about her person like a mantua-maker taking her measure. "You must be the goddaughter Lord Wedderburn told me about."

Blythe was thankful she wore a simple linen gown with its bosom knot of rose ribbon. Since Elodie's leaving, she'd dressed herself, her hair less styled. Peg wasn't trained as a lady's maid and had other obligations. If Blythe had been richly clad like a duke's daughter, would such not give her away?

"Yes, I am the former laird's goddaughter," she replied, stopping at the fountain's edge in full view of the laird's study windows. Where was he?

"And your name?" Jade eyes fastened on Blythe and wouldn't let go. Alison was as persistent as she was beautiful.

Blythe said nothing. Every British peer knew of the Duke of Northumbria if only because he was in trouble with the Crown. And this woman whose father was oft in London was surely no exception. A search of names might lead to Blythe's discovery and harm the Humes in some way.

"You are obviously English." Alison's riding whip stretched taut in her gloved hands. "If the former Lord Wedderburn was your godfather, the countess your godmother, you must also have a title."

Blythe worked to hide her annoyance at such blatant bad manners. "I am a simple English lass."

"And a very modest one. Your genteel breeding is evident. Not for a moment do I believe you to be a mere tutoress. I would know more. A little mystery always piques me."

"Oh? Then I shall remain elusive."

"So must we play hide-and-seek?" Alison laughed, but it lacked warmth. "The laird was nae more forthcoming about you than you yourself are, though he did say you will be leaving soon."

Had he? The words seemed to shut another door with their finality. Suddenly sad, Blythe trailed her fingers through the fountain's water. She merely wished an end to this uncomfortable, untimely meeting.

Alison sat down on the fountain's wide edge. "Where in England will you be returning to, perchance?"

A voice rang out behind them. Orin had awakened, his face absent of his usual smile. He approached, expression sleepy but as chary as Blythe felt.

"Master Hume," Alison greeted him.

"Miss Landreth," he replied, flicking a honeybee from his shirt-sleeve.

"You are looking more pale than usual, I see. And missing your frock coat. Have you been ill again?"

"Aye." He came to stand beside Blythe, his voice flat. "Have you come seeking the laird?"

"Indeed." Alison's eyes rolled heavenward in annoyance. "Your new housekeeper showed me to his study, but he is elsewhere at the moment. I stepped into the garden to sweeten my wait."

Sweeten was hardly the word Blythe would assign.

A footfall near at hand ended the discussion. Everard appeared, leaving the door to the study open behind him. He came toward them, and Blythe saw the hard line of his jaw. He cast a look her way, and she knew for once she was not the cause of his consternation.

"The housekeeper showed you to my study, did she not?" he said to Alison. Blythe detected an edge of reproof in his tone.

Alison stood. "How can I resist so lovely a garden?"

"Come, Miss Landreth. Nae games." He looked to Blythe. "If you'll excuse us."

Alison swept past him, obviously bedeviled by his terseness. Blythe turned to Orin, splashing a bit of water on him to lighten the fractious moment. With a laugh, he splashed her back with gusto, wetting her skirts. The laird looked back at their play and smiled over his shoulder, stepping around Wallace, who was perpetually underfoot.

The door to the study soon shut. If Blythe ever wished to be a fly upon the wall, 'twas now.

45

*There is little that can withstand
a man who can conquer himself.*

LOUIS XIV

D avie is in the tower."

Bernard stood at the edge of a shuttered mine, hands on hips, and looked at Everard atop Lancelot for a full thirty seconds as he obviously grappled with all the implications. "Edinburgh Castle?"

"Aye, arrested day before yesterday," Everard said. "Alison brought word from her faither this afternoon."

"Brother, of all the sore news . . ." Bernard all but cursed. "Now we Humes are most assuredly cast under suspicion. And harboring the daughter of an avowed Rebel to boot."

Blythe's mention in such terms did nothing to lift Everard's mood. Nor did the acrid smoke of numerous pits and coal wagons that spread before them in all directions as colliers went about their work with blackened bodies and grimy faces. The runaway miners were still missing, weighing on those who remained, his factors included. In their absence the very air seemed laden with a seething discontent.

Though out of earshot near an enormous rowan tree, Everard was still attracting attention. When he came round, the pace seemed to slow, all wondering what his presence meant. Bernard had been visiting the mines with the doctor, talking with colliers and their families in the village the auld laird had had built for them. Their houses were end to end on cobbled streets, a larger residence reserved for those infirm or too aged to work. The day was nearly done now, the doctor gone, and Everard needed to give Bernard warning before he rode to the coast to manage a fisheries matter.

"You'll go to Edinburgh, of course." Bernard no more relished the task than Everard did. "Meet with our jackanapes of a brother."

"I leave at dawn," Everard said. "Nae doubt he's being told to take an oath to King Geordie to gain his release. Knowing Davie, I ken what his answer will be."

"I do not envy you." Bernard grimaced. "Be wary yourself. Dealing with Calysta will be difficult enough."

"She's likely already left for the Highlands."

"Och, of course. Endie as she is, she'll not stay on in Auld Reekie and play the longsuffering wife, nae."

Everard looked toward the biggest mine, where men were coming up out of the ground as a bell sounded to end the day. "I hope to return by sennight's end."

"Do what you need to do regardless of the time. Boyd should be with you, aye?"

At Everard's nod, he seemed easier. Boyd was usually beside him at such times, while Bernard was most needed at Wedderburn.

Bernard stroked Lancelot's nose. "I'll manage with Munro and the factors as best I can in your absence, and pray for protection and a speedy resolution to what now concerns us."

Everard left him and took the most direct route back to the castle, ruminating all the while. He'd told Munro and Mrs. Candlish he'd be gone by morn. Now to pack and bid goodbye to Blythe and Orin.

One tugged at him more than the other.

———⚮———

In the gloaming, Wedderburn Castle seemed to take a breath and come to a standstill. Since Elodie's leaving, Blythe's evening routine had changed. At nine of the clock, Orin went to bed, but first prayers were said. 'Twas as easy as breathing for Blythe to be on her knees like her grandmother before her. The childhood memory resurfaced each time she clasped her hands and knelt by Orin. This was how faith was passed down, surely, though the clasped hands were those of a Catholic lass and a Protestant lad.

Together they said, "Now I lay me down to sleep, I pray Thee, Lord, my soul to keep. If I should die before I wake, I pray Thee, Lord, my soul to take. If I should live for other days, I pray Thee, Lord, to guide my ways."

Orin sighed before he continued, "Thank You, heavenly Faither, for Lady Blythe, and keep her near always. Please bless Ronan and Elodie, and help them to not miss us like we miss them. Help me not be afraid of the new gyrfalcon in the mews." His petitions touched her with their honest innocence. He paused as if gathering his thoughts, his words especially earnest. "Please help Davie guard his tongue and obey the king. And let not the king's men be angry with the laird when he goes to Edinburgh in the morn . . ."

What?

Blythe's eyes flew open, and she bit her lip. 'Twas a torment to wait till Orin said amen. He yawned, still looking peaked, and reason rushed in. Such weighty matters for a wee lad. She would not press him. What all had she missed in the hours since Alison's coming? Everard and Bernard had both been absent at both dinner and supper, a rare occurrence, leaving her and Orin to dine alone.

Orin climbed the bed steps to lie down, and she tucked the covers around him, bending low to kiss his brow before snuffing the sole candle. Wallace burrowed in beside him for the time being, soon to be whisked away by a footman and returned outside. The laird's orders.

Stepping into the corridor, she drew the door shut softly only to hear a footfall on the cedar staircase. Everard? Her heart did a little dance, and then a thought curbed her. Often he appeared to bid Orin good night. Forever unsure of him, she walked slowly toward the stairs, the corridor's wall sconces hardly needed as a bank of windows flanked the opposite wall, offering the last of daylight.

He mounted the top step, his gaze holding her own. "Blythe."

She came to a stop, *Lord Wedderburn* always on the tip of her tongue. "Everard."

His hand rested on the newel post, his signet ring glinting. "Orin is abed?"

"Abed but not yet asleep. We've just said our prayers."

"I won't disturb him, then."

"Your good nights are never a disturbance but rather a benediction on his day."

At that he moved past her with a low, "Tarry here till I return."

When he did, he led her to a deep window seat well away from Orin's door. She sat, minding her petticoats, but he sat so near that their silky profusion covered one of his boots. Alison seemed to hover, a disapproving presence, her memory troublesome.

As usual, he was not dissembling. "I leave for Auld Reekie at first light."

She felt a beat of amusement. "Is that what you Scots call your great city?"

"You'd better understand if you visited."

She took a breath. "Then take me with you." Dismay at his leaving made her bold. Never had she been so beseeching. "Please."

Her request seemed to catch him by surprise. He turned toward her slightly, then looked out the window glass, his thoughtful features in profile. "So, you want to go to Edinburgh."

The burr in *Edinburgh* left her stomach somersaulting. She wished he would say it again. She couldn't possibly echo it with the same force or richness. "Miss Landreth said you told her I would be leaving soon. Let it be to Edina."

"Edina, as 'tis Latinized." His eyes narrowed. "What else did Miss Landreth tell you?"

"As little as I told her, though our curiosity about each other was evenly matched. She knows I'm the goddaughter. Little else."

They lapsed into silence. A pair of doves could be heard cooing outside. Soothing, Blythe always thought. Not so the present company or conversation. The laird always put her in a tangle, tonight especially so.

"Orin prayed for your brother in the tower." Though numerous families were riven with Jacobite and Hanoverian tensions, she sensed this matter with David Hume was serious indeed. "I'm sorry to hear such."

He shook his head in a sort of resigned disgust. "Davie has ever courted disaster."

Was life not challenging enough, that one would seek opportunities to worsen it? She worried the pearl ring on her finger, her voice more whisper. "Do your brother's misdeeds place you in jeopardy?"

His pause unnerved her further. "I plan to stay in the government's good graces. Harm only comes to those who naysay the king or supply and take up arms with the Rebels and renounce the reigning monarch."

"Like my father."

He looked at her, his eyes so darkly blue in the fading light they resembled black onyx. "On that score, my manservant has recently returned and brought word your faither is said to be in France with the king o'er the water."

Her hand moved to her bodice, covering her heart. "France . . ." She'd begun to fear his cause was hopeless, the potential losses ruinous and far-reaching, including his very head. "Can it be true?"

"Hearsay, mayhap." With a shrug he returned to looking out the window. "A lie is oft halfway roon Scotland afore the truth has its boots on."

Her spirits sank as she realized she might never see her father again. "I pray he's no longer on British soil. France is his best refuge. He might send for me. I could return to St. Germain."

"At the mercy and benevolence of the French king, who is said to be dying."

"C'est pas possible," she murmured, disbelieving. Would the Sun

King's long reign end? "Father and I would be together, at least, come what may. He is all the family I have."

"There are Hedleys across England, aye?"

"Family who've shunned us because of my mother's reputation."

"'Twas years ago. Another century, even."

"Animosity and grudges linger long."

He was looking at her now in that intent way he had, making her feel like a fox before hounds. Yet somehow it loosened her tongue.

"Some relatives sought to be enriched through her role as maîtresse-en-titre and were disappointed, even angered, when that did not happen. Others felt her scandalous behavior unforgettable—and unforgivable."

"Yet she returned to Bellbroke."

Blythe nodded, moved anew by the enormity of such a gesture. "Some called Father weak. A spineless cuckold. But I think him brave, even Christlike in his forgiveness. He said he would honor his wedding vows till death even if she didn't."

"How is it you ken so much about your mither?"

She hesitated. Never had she revealed her source. "She kept a diary of her time at court." Not even her father knew she possessed such. Or rather that it possessed her. She was cast back to the very day she'd uncovered it. "I found it in my grandmother's desk after her passing. To my astonishment, my grandmother forgave her. Prayed for her. Even welcomed her home after the king died."

The case clock at hall's end tolled nine dramatic times, punctuating her words. She felt an odd relief confessing the diary, as if it was a sin that must be expunged.

He shifted, arms folded. "Have *you* made peace with your mither's past?"

Had she? Throat tight, she could not answer. A rush of long-banked emotion made him a blur of sable. Was that not an answer in itself? Feeling for her handkerchief, she brought it out of her pocket and dried her eyes.

His voice was extraordinarily gentle. "The diary grieves you."

She hesitated. "I hardly know how to answer. Sometimes it seems I'm reading about a stranger, not my mother. 'Tis my one tenuous tie to her." Other than a few impersonal gems, what did she have of Clementine Hedley but a diary?

"Tell me something good about her."

Good? Stunned, she looked straight at him and then away as shame gained the upper hand. Was not her mother's life story tawdry and unmentionable?

"Surely there are praiseworthy things about her, as she was made in the Lord's image."

She all but recoiled from his unexpected if carefully broached question. It forced her to regard her mother in a different light. The silence stretched long as Blythe groped for what little she'd read or heard.

"Aside from her uncommon beauty, she seemed to be kind to those outside of the court if not within it. She especially loved children." Blythe stumbled on. "She had a lovely singing voice. She was witty and made others merry."

"Then think on those things. You cannot change the past, only how you regard or respond to it. Nor should you dwell on it." He seemed remarkably free of judgment in regard to her mother or herself. "What became of the diary?"

"When the mob stormed Bellbroke and I came here, it was left behind." She'd not thought of it much since, but she'd begun to suspect home and its contents might be lost to her forever. "As for Bellbroke, shall I ever return there? Or will a French exile be my portion?"

"You're at a crossroads." Tenderness laced his tone, his brusqueness subdued. "France might not be the answer. For now, Wedderburn is."

Had he made peace with her presence? He seemed to be telling her she was not alone. That he was her protector. A refuge. Or was she once again reading into things? She tried to see him as a soldier, a sword at his side. Waging war. Killing men. Her spine tingled as she imagined it. He was her unlikely knight.

"You regard me so intently, Blythe. Do you trust me?"

Heat rushed to her face, and she looked away toward the sunset burnishing the western moorland red-gold.

I do not trust myself.

Tonight he was so close, the closest he'd ever been. The two of them were completely alone. All the servants were belowstairs. He was the canniest of men. Could he see straight through her? To her suddenly wayward heart?

If she dared, she could reach out and touch his bewhiskered jaw, savor the feel of his dark hair between her fingertips. Even sitting here with him in the quiet left her . . . wanting. She clasped her hands together in her lap lest she give in to the desire that swarmed her tip to toe, that mad need to be in his arms, to feel his lips on her skin. To have him claim her completely.

If they could not be married, might she be his mistress for the time remaining to them? 'Twould be their secret. None would be the wiser . . .

None but God Almighty.

"Do you, Blythe?"

Did she trust him? She met his unwavering gaze in a sort of ecstasy, stunned to sense the struggle was not hers alone. His long look told her he found her far from plain. Far from undesirable. Each second they tarried in this shadowed hall seemed to ensnare them further, a palpable, smoldering enticement nudging them ever nearer a dark moment that would forever mark them and leave them undone.

In a blinding flash the years fell away, and she stood in her mother's place as past and present melded and she battled for her very being. She understood as never before the power of irresistible attraction and the ruinous sway of unbridled desires.

Dear Jesus, I beg You to defend by Your grace the chastity and purity of my mind, body, and soul . . .

Everard stood abruptly, ending the intimate moment. "I'll have Atchison pack your trunk for Edinburgh."

46

We do not stop playing because we grow old;
we grow old because we stop playing.

GEORGE BERNARD SHAW

The next morning the Hume coach lumbered north toward Edinburgh, a stretch of more than fifty miles. Blythe sat by Orin, who was so excited he looked continually out the window and talked by turns. It was not only her first time to the city but his. She was not surprised he was accompanying them lest she travel alone with the laird, who sat across from them, saying little, his manner reserved but obliging. Though he must have a great deal on his mind with his brother in the tower, he seemed entertained by their ongoing delight.

As the miles stretched north, her and Everard's emotional tryst the night before faded. Gone were his burning looks in Wedderburn's corridor, as if she'd imagined their tête-à-tête. Or were they simply heading toward another intimate encounter in Edinburgh? She took pains not to regard him overlong, giving her attention almost entirely to the lad beside her. 'Twas far safer.

And far less scintillating.

They overnighted at a bustling coaching inn, the rooms of quality, the fare adequate. Blythe was so impatient to reach the city she had never seen that time seemed to lag. Or was it only the time she spent away from Everard? Fleeing to France was no longer uppermost in her mind.

In the forenoon the next day, she raised the coach's shutter and took in the breadth and height of Arthur's Seat. Edinburgh! From its great heights on a fair day, one could see clear from the banks of Forth to the hills overlooking Tweed.

"Once upon a time 'twas home to the sleeping dragon," Orin said from the other window. "The beast who terrorized the city then fell asleep atop its rocky crags and troubled them no more."

"Rather the realm of King Arthur and his knights," Everard said.

"Camelot," Blythe mused, never taking her eyes off the mountain.

"I should like to behold Excalibur." Orin turned toward his brother. "Is it like your sword, I wonder?"

"Alas, I cannot draw my sword out of stone," Everard replied with a smile, looking out his own window. "But cut steel, aye."

Blythe preferred the other version of the tale. "Excalibur might have been given King Arthur by the Lady of the Lake."

"I stand by the stone." Orin settled back on the seat and looked hard at his brother. "You've brought your Doune pistols, aye? Both of them?"

The laird nodded. "I rarely travel without them."

A bump in the road bounced Blythe to the right, her stomach somersaulting with it. They'd lost a wheel in the muck near Dalkeith, but the journey since had been steady if teeth rattling. No highwaymen troubled them, perhaps because of their unmarked coach. What assailed them now on Edinburgh's outskirts sent her digging for her hartshorn vial. Orin was not so discreet.

"Crivvens! I thought you were jesting about the reek of the town." With a groan, he covered his nose with his coat sleeve. "It stinks of fish and chimney smoke."

"Don't forget the dyers and tanners and chandlers. A smelly business, all." Everard shuttered the window and leaned back against the upholstered seat. "We'll stay at our residence in the Canongate near Holyrood Palace. Less crowded than the High Street or the

Lawnmarket. Hume's Land is up the hill near the castle and reeks all the more."

Such interesting names, so different from London. The Hedleys' terraced townhouse in St. James Square had never felt like home as they'd been there so seldom.

Numerous sedan chairs winged by, hefted about by chairmen. Liveried footmen ran ahead and announced the important personages within, crying, "Have a care!" or "By your leave!"

"Such a clamor!" Orin said with all the fervor of an eight-year-old. "I must ride in one with Lady Blythe. But nae running footmen, please."

Their talk faded as the coach slowed before Reid's Close. The Hume residence rose up with its forestairs and balconies and turrets, a garden surrounding the mansion. Carved corbels bore Latin phrases, but there was no time to puzzle over these as they passed beyond high gates into the forecourt. Blythe's admiring gaze lingered on one significant detail.

Above the main doorway, the Hume family crest was carved in stone with its lion and shield, the words "True to the End" above it. The initials of a former laird and his countess were in monogram below, a charming detail.

Blythe gave way to a wishful thought. How would it be to intertwine the initials *B* and *E*?

She wondered how long they might stay, already feeling a kinship with this strange city and its rich, colorful, oft tragic history.

They alighted from the coach and entered the front hall. A housekeeper was on hand to meet them, expressing surprise but obvious pleasure at seeing the laird. "Welcome, Lord Wedderburn. And this must be Master Orin." She beamed at him, then looked to Blythe and curtsied. "An honored guest, I see."

"Goddaughter to my late parents," Everard said. "Lady Blythe, this is Mrs. Rennie, our prized housekeeper."

Blythe greeted her, her gaze pulled to the beautiful stair that hugged one wall. Beneath it rested a cream-colored sedan chair, its door open as if inviting one in. A lady could be carried about the city without setting foot in a grimy street. Its doors bore the Hume coat of arms, its painted panels a work of art, the upholstered interior regal.

"Ah, yer admiring the countess's favorite means of transport," the housekeeper said with a smile.

"Beautiful—and practical," Blythe said. "It has a French flair with all of that lacquer. So like the chaises bleues of Versailles."

"Alas, licensed chairmen are needed to carry it. We had four well-trained Lowland lads when the countess was in residence."

Orin climbed in and out of the conveyance, examining every stud and seam down to the gilded carrying poles as if searching for some flaw.

Watching him, Everard chuckled. "For now, we need our chambers and refreshments. The Royal Room should suit her ladyship."

"Of course, milord," Mrs. Rennie said. "All is kept in readiness. Please come with me, milady."

Up another staircase they went to a floor reserved solely for guests, the housekeeper said. A blue-and-lavender bower came next, the ornate plasterwork ceiling with its griffins, flowers, and fleur-de-lis stealing Blythe's breath, as did the canopied bed swathed in blue silk. Three windows overlooked the garden, a charming, antique summerhouse amid the blooms. Another window overlooked a busy wynd, a balcony beckoning.

"'Tis enchanting," Blythe said. "A Royal Room, indeed."

Mrs. Rennie smiled. "'Twas the countess's favorite. She selected all the furnishings and linens herself. 'Tis reserved for our most distinguished guests."

"So different here than in the country."

"And very different from Hume's Land up the High Street, Mr. David Hume's residence." At the mention, Mrs. Rennie's brows knit together. "I shall have tea sent up. And hot water to cleanse the dust of the road." Brightening, she gestured toward a fringed bell pull near the hearth. "Please don't hesitate to summon me. And if ye've need of a lady's maid, there's Mari, who was trained in a noble house."

Mrs. Rennie went out, and the promised hot water and tea soon followed. Glad for time alone if only to gather her wits, Blythe sat down and savored a cup, knowing Orin would soon appear. As for the laird, he'd seemed increasingly preoccupied on their journey, and she found herself wishing she were privy to his thoughts. But with a brother at odds with the king, how could he not be distracted—and most unpleasantly so?

Or was he mulling Alison? What *was* their relationship? She knew not, though she was certain something was betwixt herself and Everard, just as Elodie once said. Would he dally with her, then marry Alison?

Lord, perish the thought.

She did Everard a disservice. He was a principled gentleman soldier, was he not?

She poured another cup of tea, aware of the hubbub on the street below as hawkers shouted about their wares and sedan chairs and carts vied for position on the busy thoroughfare. It was an oddly comforting sound, full of life and movement and excitement.

She felt an overwhelming urge to step out into the melee. No one would know who she was, nor care. She would cease to be a troubled duke's daughter besotted with the laird. She'd simply be another Edinburgh lass making her way up the High Street on a sonsie summer's day.

47

Edina! Scotia's darling seat!

ROBERT BURNS

Early the next morn, before Blythe and Orin were awake, Everard made his way up the High Street on foot at break of day, feeling a bit unguarded without Boyd by his side. But in truth, he craved Blythe's and Orin's company far more. Dawn colored the August sky dragoon red, and the stench was like a blow to the nose. At ten o' the clock the night before, chamber pots had come pouring out countless windows onto cobblestones. Scavengers had been at work since then, clearing away the worst of it and leaving the rest to be washed downhill by the frequent rains.

Ignoring the odor and watching his step, he kept up a steady stride, his thoughts not on the shops and stalls opening all around him, nor the bakers and weavers and fishmongers and various craftsmen readying for the day's business. His mind returned to the night before, to the simple supper of colcannon and bannocks, he and Blythe and Orin talking and laughing before exiting the dining room to have hot chocolate in the small parlor. As if coming to the city was naught but a lark.

Today was an altogether different endeavor, less convivial and far more complicated. First, he'd visit Hume's Land and determine if Calysta was still there or had fled as he suspected, and further determine the state of the household.

Up the turnpike stair he went, speaking briefly with a city minister who lived on another floor as he made his way down. Soon, Hume's Land's butler and housekeeper, clearly anxious at all that had transpired, spilled their tale of woe. They gathered in the formal parlor, and Everard listened without surprise. Calysta had indeed fled with many of her belongings as soon as the sheriff appeared, leaving no word or note as to where she had gone.

"To her Highland clan, nae doubt," Mrs. Archer said, looking more relieved than regretful. "She's been gone ever since Mr. Hume was taken to the tower."

"Your brother put up a bit of a fight when the authorities came for him," Simms said, explaining the damage done to the foyer. "But they soon had him in irons, and off he went with them."

Bellowing all the way, surely.

After seeing to a few matters with household accounts, Everard again sought the turnpike stair and the High Street, which was growing more congested by the minute. But his mind remained on the Canongate mansion and Blythe. She'd expressed interest in the garden's summerhouse, and Mrs. Rennie promised to serve her tea there. He'd promised to take Blythe and Orin into the city once he returned but hadn't decided where. Somehow knowing they were waiting bolstered him and made the task at hand more bearable.

He stared ahead at the stone fortress that crowned the High Street. Edinburgh Castle was grim no matter the weather, and today's fiery skies gave it a particular menace. A series of formidable gates denied him entrance, the castle garrisoned by the British army.

At his approach, a guard asked his business. Another guard recognized him from his prior military service and admitted him without requiring further proof. So many soldiers boded ill, the new barracks speaking to the Jacobite unrest sweeping all Britain.

He passed through the Portcullis Gate and wondered if the chamber above it held David. Entering the esplanade, Everard saw a group of soldiers playing bullets, his brother among them. Even David's diversions were dangerous. Everard knew men who'd died from being struck by the heavy ball. But David hadn't a care.

Canny as a fox, David likely knew the moment Everard stepped onto the esplanade, though he didn't acknowledge him till he'd had another turn. Wagers were being placed as to who could throw the weighted iron ball the farthest. No doubt David's guards wanted to take advantage of his purse. Bribes and betting were commonplace. The rapidly dwindling coin in Everard's own pockets was proof. He watched from the sidelines, well out of harm's way.

Finally, David swung round with a grin. "The more mischief, the better sport."

Together they left the yard and climbed a stair to one tower, an armed guard following. Into a round, windowless chamber they went, David reaching for a pitcher of ale before he sat down.

Everard tossed the guard a gold guinea. "Leave us."

With a nod, the man bowed out, taking his weapon with him.

Putting his boots up on a near stool, David leaned back and studied his older brother by the light of a single candle. "Welcome to my humble abode, yer lairdship."

"Humble, aye," Everard said, pouring his own drink.

"Why in the world are ye here?" David asked, slaking his thirst.

"Play nae games with me, Davie. I've nae time for it," Everard said. "How do matters stand?"

David snorted. "Tolerably well, though I refuse to take an oath of allegiance to the Rebel king."

"Which means your stay here will be ongoing."

David shrugged his thickset shoulders. "All for a bit o' sculduddery at the assembly room. I'm not the only Jack locked in, ye ken. My fellows also refuse the oath. Others are being rounded up and held in the Tolbooth as we speak."

Everard well knew who'd been arrested and who hadn't. The papers never ceased reporting it. "I stopped at Hume's Land before this. Mrs. Hume is not there."

271

"Calysta was nearly arrested too, but I put up a bit of a fight. I told her to return to her clan."

"The foyer bears testament of your undying devotion, aye." Everard couldn't keep the scorn from his tone. Theirs was not a happy union, as David's carousing attested to. He reached into his coat, withdrew a book he'd found while going through David's papers, and placed it on the table. *Edinburgh's Complete List of Ladies of Pleasure.*

A smirk lit David's sullen features.

Next Everard laid out a stack of unpaid debts. "'Twill be debtor's prison for you next," he said, taking the lurid book and letting it catch the candle flame. The paper flared, and Everard let the book burn down to his fingertips before he dropped it to the stone floor, grinding it to ashes beneath his boot heel.

David snorted and poured himself more ale. "You'll settle all my accounts, of course, as Faither did."

"We've had this conversation before. And my answer remains the same. Nae."

David looked at him with outright loathing, a deep cut on his jaw and a welling bruise over his left eye telling. Unshaven, he seemed more the rogue than ever.

Everard took a drink of the watered-down ale. "I did, however, pay the wages of your servants, who, through nae fault of their own, have a drunken bundle of iniquity for a master."

Rearing back, David laughed, slamming his fist upon the crude table. Ale sloshed onto the scarred top and dripped onto the floor.

Used to his outbursts, Everard remained perfectly still. "'Tis hardly a laughing matter. Take care lest the king make an example of you. Your cause is lost, any word of Jacobite forces overcoming His Majesty's armies a fiction."

"Jack spies swear otherwise." David's jaw jutted, and his injury began to bleed anew. He swiped at it with a soiled sleeve. "When the Stuarts triumph again, 'twill be the laird of Wedderburn who'll be known for standing back and letting Geordie play king while his Hanoverian puppets—"

"Listen hard. The head of Rebel forces is none other than Bobbing John, Earl of Mar, whose allegiances shift as the wind blows. Mar is more fit to command a passel of pipers than a regiment. He declared for the monarch in the '07 Rising, remember. To aid him in his present, precipitous downfall is the honorable but misguided Earl of Derwentwater and Thomas Forster, not to mention other lairds sure to lose their heads when this debacle is over."

David's sneer was becoming commonplace. "So you are a seer, Brother, as well as laird and can foretell the future?"

"I am a seasoned soldier who kens how the battle will play out. I fought alongside General Wills on the continent, who is now in command of government forces. He is a canny, experienced officer who will fight to the death and take as many of the enemy with him as he can."

David lifted his ale and made a toast to the king o'er the water. "Even Wills cannot stand against all the gold, swords, musketry, and gunpowder that make up a consignment now headed to the Jacks."

"Mark my word, he can and he will." Everard leaned forward, done with his drink. His thoughts veered to Blythe's father, said to be among the foremost suppliers. "For God's sake if naught else, consider what it is you do to your wife—and your kin—with such rashness. Have you nae care about anyone but yourself?"

The door opened and another guard appeared. "'Tis time, yer lairdship."

Everard rose from the table, leaving with the bitter frustration that had long tainted anything to do with David. If it had been any of his other brothers, they would have embraced with respect and affection, bidding each other goodbye with a "Haste ye back."

But not this prideful Jack.

48

Blushing is the color of virtue.

DIOGENES

O rin tugged on Blythe's hand, and they paused to watch a puppet show at a fair in the Grassmarket. The marionettes, Punch and Judy, behaved outrageously, jerking about on their strings across the elaborate painted stage as the audience laughed uproariously. Even the laird found it amusing, though he seemed most entertained by Orin's mirth.

Up and down the High Street and through the wynds and closes they went, eating flaky meat pies and steaming hot cross buns and iced gingerbread. They admired the goods displayed in the luckenbooth around St. Giles Cathedral, even tarrying at a glover and then a hatter on the High Street. All was a whirlwind of novelty and delight.

As they lingered at a bookseller, Blythe's gaze snagged on a newly printed offering at the front of the shop—*Lives of the Court Beauties* by Captain Alexander Smith. Bound in blue leather with gilt lettering, the book was as alluringly packaged as its contents. Looking over her shoulder to make certain Everard and Orin were elsewhere, Blythe reached for it, curiosity overtaking her.

Opening it, she eyed the frontispiece. A portrait of her mother looked back at her, her name and title beneath. The Duchess of Northumbria was not, however, the only court beauty therein. Charles II's entire seraglio seemed to be between its blued pages. Blythe stared down at the print, awash with revulsion. She snapped the book shut and hid it beneath another tome, but the tainted feeling remained.

"Are you all right?"

How had she failed to notice Everard's approach? Or forgotten to school her dismay at her discovery?

"I need fresh air." Lowering her eyes, she moved toward the door, wishing they'd never spied the bookseller in the first place.

Thankfully, other distractions soon won out. Orin got his wish to ride in a sedan. The muscular Highland chairmen carried him and Blythe to Greyfriars Kirk while the laird hired a hackney coach and met them at what was said to be the grandest building in Edinburgh, Heriot's Hospital and gardens. After a delicious punch seasoned with freshly ground nutmeg, they moved on to the Royal Botanic Garden to admire the new glasshouse and all the medicinal plants.

By this time Orin was yawning, Blythe's shoes were pinching, and the laird seemed ready to end the outing. Another hackney coach was hired to transport them to the Canongate, the mansions there a startling contrast to the rest of Edinburgh with its medieval essence.

"Oh, do come in out of the heat and hustle," Mrs. Rennie exclaimed, greeting them in the cool, shadowed foyer. "A fine supper is being prepared if yer hungry."

Orin presented the housekeeper with oranges and Blythe gave her gloves, while the laird looked on with a smile at Mrs. Rennie's flustered appreciation.

After excusing herself, Blythe went up to her rooms to refresh herself before the meal as a maid brought hot water and fresh linens. The buxom young woman curtsied, her round face alight at Blythe's greeting. "I'm Mari, milady."

Blythe smiled. "Pleased to meet you, Mari." Missing Elodie, she turned toward the dressing table noticeably absent of perfumes and cosmetic pots. "As you can see, since my own maid recently wed, I'm left to my own devices."

"I shall remedy that, mem. I served a viscountess in Chancellor's Court till she died, then came here."

In under an hour, a newly pressed silver-brocaded gown was readied, and Mari had worked magic with her toilette, making Blythe wonder how she'd done without a lady's maid even briefly.

"If only I could take you with me . . ." Blythe's voice trailed off as she realized once again she was no surer of where that might be than when she'd arrived on Wedderburn's doorstep.

"I'd be honored, milady. I'm kept on here for guests, but there's been precious few since the auld laird died and all is in mourning."

"Do you have family in Edinburgh?"

"I'm niece to the housekeeper, Mrs. Rennie. Nae other near kin to speak of."

Blythe stood and Mari arranged her skirts, plucking a pin from a pincushion to better secure her stomacher before applying a dab of jasmine perfume to her wrists.

Looking forward to supper with the mischievous boy who'd stolen her heart, not to mention Everard, Blythe went downstairs to the dining room, a little thrill of anticipation rivaling her appetite. Even after spending a day with them both, she'd not had enough of their company. Orin's presence guaranteed her nerves would stay settled.

Stepping into the unfamiliar candlelit room, she found it quiet and empty save her growling stomach. Supper was laid on the damask-clad table in covered dishes with a charming sugar-paste centerpiece of fresh fruit and flowers. Moving to a window, she looked down upon the garden, further intrigued by the summerhouse there. The gloaming was at hand, gilding the luxuriant walled space and making her wish they could take supper outside.

Everard's voice sounded in the corridor, and Blythe turned toward the doorway. He entered, having changed garments himself, his scruff of beard shaven. Her gaze trailed behind him, anticipating Orin.

What? No beloved boy?

Her surprise must have been plain, for he looked at her apologetically and said, "The lad is worn out—fast asleep."

"Asleep?" Her lighthearted query belied her sudden skittishness. Everard had just spent the day with her. He'd find more of her company tedious, surely. "Then you'll have me to put up with."

"Put up with, nae." His eyes held the humor she'd seen flashes of lately as he seated her to his right, nary a footman in sight. "Rather, you must endure my company."

Suddenly timid, she put her serviette in her lap and waited for him to sit down at the head of the table and bless the meal. When he extended his hand, she clasped it, just as she'd done when on her knees by Orin's sickbed. A rush of thankfulness swept through her that the boy was only sleeping and all was well.

"Father in heaven . . ."

Though she bent her head and closed her eyes, she scarcely heard his prayer, so great was the tumult inside her. They released hands, but his mesmerizing hold on her remained. She stole a look at him as he reached for a dish. She wondered at his wearing grey. Might it somehow reflect his mood, a subtle shift away from mourning?

"So how does Edinburgh strike you?" he asked as he passed her another dish.

"'Tis infinitely more amusing than London." She took a spoonful of neeps and tatties, following his lead. "Though the Thames provides endless amusement with all the watercraft." His searching look loosed her tongue. "I was last there long ago, but I remember a great many theaters and coffee and chocolate houses."

"If you want to go out again, there's a reputable theater in Carrubbers Close." He speared a piece of beef. "And an assembly room in the West Bow for dancing."

"Or we could remain right here, repeat playing triumph or whist in the parlor, and have another dish of chocolate." She'd enjoyed last evening to the utmost. "You might even show me the French pears in the garden Mrs. Rennie told me about."

"The woman you completely won over with your gift of gloves."

"'Twas a small if heartfelt gesture."

"'Tis unusual and moved more than the housekeeper."

Did he approve, then? "One must always strive to be kind, honoring of others."

"Said by a duke's daughter."

"My grandmother set the example. I simply follow it."

"Her Grace was a remarkable woman, then. Duchesses, especially dowagers, have a knack for remembering their place and everyone else's."

Nodding, she brought her serviette to her lips. "There are no titles in His kingdom, Grandmother used to say, just worshipful sons and daughters." In contrast, her imperious mother, said to have wielded her title and position like a whip, leapt to mind. Dismissing the sore thought, she asked, "So . . . an evening at home or an outing about town?"

"Home may well win." He studied her as he set his goblet down. "I'm surprised, scholar that you are, you've not found the library."

How could she have forgotten? For once, books were the furthest thing from her besotted mind. "Am I free to roam your entire abode, then?"

"If it suits, aye."

She forked another bite, eyes down. "How long are we to stay on here?"

We. She must be careful of that. It sounded too . . . intimate. He mustn't think she'd begun to regard them as a pair, as entwined as the monogrammed initials at the mansion's entrance and elsewhere.

"I've business to address for a few more days. Time enough for you to explore the city if you want to. You're still missing Northumberland, nae doubt."

She looked up at him in surprise. "Hardly. At least since coming here." Fingering the pearls at her throat, she said, "I've become a student of your moods, Everard, and you are at your most charming of late. Edinburgh agrees with you if only because it's a blessed diversion like it is for me."

He chuckled. "Meaning we have other, more pressing matters on our minds that beg for a distraction, lest we fret our guts to fiddle strings."

49

There is a garden in her face
Where roses and white lilies grow.

THOMAS CAMPION

Fretting your guts to fiddle strings is not how I would describe you," Blythe said with a laugh. "Rather, I admire your fortitude. Could it be any more complicated? A new, grieving laird. A brother in the tower. And a sassenach thrust upon your very doorstep. Yet you weather it all well."

"Nor are your circumstances any less nettlesome, yet you handle them with a great deal of grace." He signaled a footman and asked that a coal fire be lit in the small parlor. "I ken how you like to be warm." He didn't miss her look of appreciation.

"So shall we play cards? Or must I trounce you at chess instead?"

Amused, he pushed away from the table. "First the garden, aye? Before it grows too dark to see it properly."

A double doorway off the dining room led to stone steps and a rectangular terraced garden of two acres. Daylight hadn't eroded completely, but an ethereal fog hovered, wrapping the garden and its high walls like a scarf.

"Haar," he told her, sending for a shawl. "Sea mist."

Blythe raised upturned palms as if she might touch it, her skirts flowing in the cool night wind driving the haar in from the coast.

Once the shawl was around her shoulders, the fabric bore tiny drop-lets of mist.

Everard regarded everything with new appreciation through her eyes. He'd been at the Canongate townhouse many times as a child but far less as an adult and not at all since he'd become laird.

""Tis a knot garden like we have at Bellbroke," she said, circling the garden and admiring a tall-stemmed patch of blooming lavender and hyssop.

He was more interested in the ornamental trees and the bee boles built into a terraced wall. A raucous fountain divided the upper garden from the lower one, several green chairs and stools scattered about. When Blythe discovered a copper can, she began watering a cluster of drooping plants in an ornamental pot.

"Meadow rue," she said admiringly. "Though your gardener may not appreciate my help, I cannot help myself."

"When I was a lad, I wanted my hands on the wheelbarrows and stone rollers. The spades and shears in particular."

She smiled as if imagining it. "Even then you had the makings of a soldier." Setting down the can, she rejoined him, and they took another whitewashed walkway that led to an elaborate archway at the back side of the south Canongate.

He slowed his pace and watched her escape round a hedgerow, glad he'd hired a second gardener. Even in the gloaming their pains-taking efforts were apparent, new plants and trees thriving. He sampled a gooseberry, finding the fruit more tart than sweet.

His gaze swept his surroundings, searching for a flash of silver brocade. She was a minx. How had she eluded him?

A taper flickered in a fanlight over the mansion's rear door. Mrs. Rennie, ever alert, intended to light their way back to the house. He looked up at Orin's bedchamber window, willing the lad to stay asleep.

He walked on, wanting to find her. Nothing moved in the orchard except the haar and the night wind. At the back of the garden sat the barely visible summerhouse.

Was she there?

A well-maintained relic from another century, the brick building had a timeless appeal, its ogee roof crowned with a weather vane bearing the Hume coat of arms. He pushed open the door with a screech of rusty hinges and stepped inside as a sudden volley of flower petals filled the air.

Blythe stood to one side of the doorway, laughing, threatening to dart away from him again. He reached for her and clasped her wrists before she could.

"Aies pitié!" she said. *Have mercy.*

She gave no resistance, and he let go. Her hands lay flat upon his shirtfront, her floral essence—or was it the flowers?—settling over him. She plucked a speck of lavender from his hair, then brushed a rose petal off his shoulder. The warm, close chamber pressed around them as if melding them together in the near darkness.

Her lips parted as she looked up at him. There was a purity—an innocence—about her that struck him hard. His heart beat a cadence that left him slightly winded. In the light of her presence, every burden he'd brought to Edinburgh fell away. From the open doorway, a song thrush broke the stillness with its achingly sweet notes that somehow reflected his fullness of soul.

Gently, he drew her into the circle of his arms, his hands splayed against the brocade fabric at her back. He expelled a low breath as she laid her cheek against his chest. Tall she was, yet she still fit neatly beneath his jawline. His lips brushed her hair, every bit as silken as her gown. Eyes closed, he drank in the solace of her. The beauty. He willed time to stand still. She nestled closer, achieving a hallowed intimacy he'd never known. And then a palpable shudder passed through her. Stiffening, she took a step back before fleeing the warmth of his arms and the summerhouse, her shawl falling to the stone floor.

He retrieved it and buried his face in its folds, riven with something he'd never experienced. Something so intense it left him unsteady and shaken. It was not simply the timeworn pull of attraction and desire. Nae . . .

Love.

50

We are asleep until we fall in love!

LEO TOLSTOY

Yer quite flushed, mem." Mari removed Blythe's pearls and plucked the pins from her hair as the clock struck ten. "A bit odd with the chill of the haar outside."

Blythe reached for a fan, wishing her every emotion didn't stain her features. Had anyone seen her running across the garden? "Perhaps some cold water will help."

Mari hastened away to bring both a cup and a whole basin of well water. "Ye've not the lad's fever, I hope. I overheard the laird telling my aunt upon arrival that Master Orin's been quite ill of late."

"No need to worry," Blythe said. "I'm just . . . out of sorts." Taking the linen cloth Mari brought, she dipped it in the water and cooled her face and neck. How would she face Everard come morning?

"Would ye like the windows onto the garden open, mem? There's a refreshing night wind blowing."

Blythe nodded absently and continued to cool her skin. But there was no cooling the fire within. She shut her eyes, recalling his touch, the precise moment his lips brushed her hair . . .

As for herself, there was no hiding her growing feelings for him. Try as she might, she communicated it in every glance his way. Though she'd always prided herself on being modest and self-controlled, all of that vanished in his presence. A coquetry overcame her, a warmth and a wooing that propelled her forward and into his embrace.

Yet she had run.

Bewildered, she stared at her still-flushed face in the looking glass. She would not mimic her mother. Nor would she become involved with a man tied to another.

———— ❦ ————

After a restless night, Blythe stood by a window as Edinburgh stirred to life. A low fire burned in the grate, warming the lovely room as dawn lit the sooty sky. It was too early for Orin to be on his feet. Even too early for the laird, though she heard someone belowstairs.

Mari entered with a cheery smile, bearing a tray. She set it on a small table before Blythe, who blinked at the offering. A blue porcelain teapot with a matching cup sat alongside a plate of crisp buttered toast and gooseberry jam. And a perfectly ripe French pear.

"Lord Wedderburn picked the pear himself, milady. He said ye have a fondness for them."

"How thoughtful. I must thank him." Truly, he behaved like a man confident of her affection. Or perhaps needlessly apologetic for what had happened between them. Pondering it more objectively in the light of day, Blythe poured tea and ate her breakfast, saving the fruit for last.

It was a luscious pear too, sweet as marzipan, the juice dripping down her chin. She'd overlooked the pear tree last night.

Gardens in the gloaming were dangerous trysting places.

———— ❦ ————

The laird would be away all day on business, Mrs. Rennie told them. So Blythe and Orin took a walk about the Canongate, exploring the closes or courtyards on all sides, Mari accompanying them lest they lose their way or meet with a pickpocket or other unsavory person. Blythe missed Everard, feeling safest with him. It seemed he could take on all of the High Street and remain unscathed.

Mansion after mansion sat back from the street, most adorned with gardens, but none so lovely as the Humes'. At two of the clock they returned and had dinner without the laird, followed by a game of chess that proclaimed Orin the winner.

"Checkmate!" Orin's concentration broke as he moved his queen and rook, hemming Blythe's king in completely.

"Well played," Blythe said with a smile.

"Dukes' daughters are hard to best." His blue eyes narrowed in thought. "Did you let me win, Lady Blythe?"

"Whatever do you mean?"

"You seem, um . . . somewhere else."

"Ah." She sighed. "My head is full of a great many other things presently, but you did win fairly and squarely, promise."

He slid from his seat, smiling. "I am going out in the garden to play with my soldiers. Shields says there's to be a war."

"Shields?"

"The butler. Have you not met him?"

"Not yet, just Mrs. Rennie and Mari," she replied, her high mood dimming at any ominous talk.

She'd seen the headlines of the *Edinburgh Courant* and other papers just that morn. Dire news of spies caught and letters deciphered and government troops raised and reviewed in France, England, and Scotland. Even in Edinburgh, some as close as Holyrood Palace grounds. Again she wondered how close her father was to the action.

"Perhaps the laird will take me to see the soldiers' parade here in Auld Reekie!" Orin turned and waved from the doorway before he ran off, leaving Blythe free to roam the townhouse.

She walked the main floor, continuing to listen for Everard in the background once he returned from town. Everything echoed rather emptily. Servants here were few compared to Wedderburn Castle, ever ready to assist but mostly out of sight. Not one person did she see in her perusal of the immaculate, elegant rooms.

Late afternoon found her in the library, which was charmingly situated in one corner of the mansion. She tarried by the portrait of the fourth laird of Wedderburn between two windows overlooking the Canongate. Muscular and dark and in full military dress, he bore the Humes' distinctive mark.

She drifted toward a section of poetry, amazed by the breadth and scope of it. Titles swam before her eyes in gilt lettering, some volumes quite worn, even frayed. A bookbinder would have a heyday here, restoring the oldest texts.

When the door clicked closed behind her, she hardly heard it though she sensed who it was. A quick look over her shoulder confirmed it.

"Greetings, milord." She turned toward him, suddenly woozy and wondering what the closed door signaled. "We missed you at dinner."

"And you were missed," he said with a long look she could only describe as enigmatic. "Neither the company nor the fare at the George in Parliament Close is your and the townhouse's equal." He removed his cocked hat and cape, both reminding her of the stylish domino attire at French masquerade balls.

"You have the look of a highwayman about you," she teased despite her best intentions to remain aloof. "All you lack is a Venetian mask."

"A gentleman highwayman." He draped his garments over a chairback. "If so, I shall be exceptionally courteous lest you flee from me a second time."

She turned back to the bookcase, any witty repartee dissolving. Should she apologize for her flighty behavior? The heartfelt words stuck in her throat.

"Are you looking for anything in particular?" he asked, coming up behind her.

He stood so close she felt light-headed and breathless. Reaching out, he touched several spines on the shelf, then lingered on John Donne's poems.

Her heart gave a little leap. Did he know Donne held a special place in her heart?

"There's no poet who pleases me more," she said softly.

"Which of his are you partial to?"

"The romantic ones. So full of lyric grace." She shut her eyes, aware of his right hand resting against the bookcase and hemming her in, his left hand at the small of her back.

He bent his head, his breath against her ear, and spoke the verses she knew by heart. "'I am two fools, I know, for loving, and for saying so.'"

You are no fool, Everard.

In a rush of longing so acute it nearly buckled her knees, Blythe turned toward him. Light from a near window fell across his beloved face, his gaze holding hers before traveling to her lips and then meeting her eyes again.

Was he seeking her approval before he kissed her? Sensing her hesitation, her halfhearted resistance?

All that was within her cried yes, but . . .

"Milord." Desperate to put distance between them, she shook her head. "I—we—cannot."

His hands fell away. "Why do you hesitate?"

"Because of"—she swallowed, the lovely face firmly in mind—"Alison."

Understanding lit his features. "I should have made myself more clear. There's nae Alison between us, Blythe. There's only you and me."

She knotted her hands at her waist. Could it be?

"You're still unsure." His eyes darkened with concern. "Unsure of my intentions."

Even as she said it she knew the disservice it did him. "I feared you had something else in mind."

He took a breath. "Like a . . . mistress?" The firm shake of his head shot down the notion. "Never that, Blythe. I am not that sort of man, nor are you that sort of woman. I'll have you honestly and honorably or not at all."

Honestly and honorably. The truth swept in, shifting the shadows of her mother's memory. Reaching up, she caressed his cheek, her palm resting there, her lips parting in anticipation. At the touch of his lips to her own, she tasted something sweet. A honeyed kiss not unlike the French pear he'd picked for her that morning. He was gentle, even restrained, but at her wholehearted response, he clasped her tighter. Their first kiss was lost in so many there seemed no end to them.

When he drew back slightly, she felt a loss. He was looking down at her so tenderly she melted like candle wax again. "Now you know how I feel about you. My intentions are as plain as they are honorable."

Her thoughts returned to the castle's Great Hall when she'd been far less sure. "So I didn't dream you once asked if I'd consider becoming your countess."

"That was nae dream, though I wasn't sure you heard me above the music. You are hard to woo if not eventually win."

The sudden vulnerability in his face turned her heart over. 'Twas her turn to remove all doubt. "You must know by now, Everard, I am yours completely."

"Then I am the most blessed of men." He drew her close again. "That night you came to Wedderburn, little did I ken what it meant."

"Nor I." She leaned into him again, a beloved Scripture leaping to mind in the warm intimacy between them. *Delight thyself also in the Lord: and he shall give thee the desires of thine heart.* "I don't quite know what to say . . . I only feel. Which is why I fled the summerhouse last night. I've never been in love before, and it leaves me quite undone."

"Undone, aye. And I'd be even more undone without you. We've much to discuss of our future—"

The library door opened with a little click. Everard stepped back, as did Blythe, and they turned toward Orin, who poked his head in.

"Has knocking gone out of fashion?" Everard asked him.

Despite the laird's gruffness, Orin smiled and opened the door wider, a wooden soldier in hand. "I heard you came back."

"And I bring glad news. Alistair and Malcolm have permission from the university to dine with us tonight." Everard pulled a silver watch from his waistcoat. "Which means you have a quarter of an hour to ready for their arrival."

Orin's smile widened. "Did you tell Lady Blythe you want to take her to the theater?"

"Nae, you just did." With a wink, Everard pointed toward the ceiling. "Do I need to carry you to your chamber?"

With a laugh, Orin darted off, taking the steps so fast they heard his furious footfall.

Mindful of the open door, Blythe caught her breath and said not entirely in jest, "I'm feeling a bit faint, Lord Wedderburn. If you don't mind, I shall sequester myself with my joy and have a quiet supper upstairs while you Humes gather for a gentlemen-only evening."

He regarded her intently, eyes shining. "I understand. But will you accompany me to a Holyrood Palace play on the morrow, Countess?"

She smiled and squeezed his hand briefly before exiting the library with a smile. "The king and all his men couldn't stop me."

51

I saw Hamlet, Prince of Denmark, played; but now the old play began to disgust this refined age.

JOHN EVELYN

I rather like the anonymity of Edinburgh," Blythe said as they took seats in a private box in Holyrood Palace's tennis court turned theater.

"Don't be fooled," Everard told her, his attention on the gallery and pit below. "You may remain a mysterious English lass, but there are a great many Scottish nobles here tonight I recognize."

Blythe relaxed in her velvet-upholstered chair next to his, Mari seated discreetly by the closed door behind them. The coach ride to Holyrood Palace, located near the Hume mansion, had been short and unhurried. Never had Blythe seen a fairer evening, stars spangling the skies and mirroring her own romantic mood. The chill haar had disappeared and summer had returned.

Tonight the long, narrow chamber and its parade of theatergoers, especially the ladies in brilliant gems and silks, rivaled the drama of the play to come. A great many men in formal dress wore their small swords, Everard included.

The clamor around them heightened, and Blythe's focus turned to the comely orange girls peddling their sweet China fruit as well as carrying private messages to theatergoers in the pit and elsewhere.

289

The very air swirled with ribaldry and intrigue. As darkness descended prior to the first act of *Macbeth*, Blythe recalled her mother's adoration for the London stage and that one of her rivals had once been an orange girl who caught the king's eye. But in light of the love of the man beside her, the memory failed to hold the usual pinch.

Everard reached for her gloved hand. "Have you been to the theater?"

"In London and Paris, yes. The French court has always been theatrically minded, especially Versailles."

"I prefer books and periodicals."

"As do I," she said, thinking of their future library. "Though I am glad of our outing tonight."

The tragedy unfolding before them was riveting, and when lightning and thunder flashed and a lifelike battle ensued, she gripped Everard's hand tighter. In that tender way of his she loved, he simply lifted her fingers to his lips and kissed them, making her completely forget the Scottish king and his mortal enemies onstage.

The hour was late when the play ended, Mari dozing by the door. All at once a great many men stood up in the audience. Blythe felt Everard tense. He shifted and leaned forward in his chair as a well-dressed gentleman below got to his feet and shouted, "Let us not leave till we sing, 'The King Shall Enjoy His Own Again!'"

Blythe snapped to attention, instinctively wanting to stand, but Everard's firm hold of her hand kept her from doing so as the song swelled to the rafters.

"'And we never shall be free till the time we do see that the king shall enjoy his own again . . .'"

A great cry of support sounded, only to be drowned out by a roar of furious nays. As swords were drawn and chaos erupted all around them, men rushed the stage, some even jumping from boxes to the galleries below to join the fight.

On his feet now, Everard hurried Blythe and Mari out of the theater and down a set of back stairs away from the melee. Such quick action gained them their coach, and they left the palace grounds ahead of anyone else at a pace far faster than when they'd arrived. But not fast enough.

Suddenly light-headed, Blythe struggled to breathe. Thoughts of another night not so long ago assaulted her anew. Angry, harsh shouts. Shattered glass. Frantic steps through the priest's hole to the stables.

"Are you all right?" Everard's voice seemed distant. She could feel the pressure of his hand as he took hers.

She pulled out her fan, snapping it open and stirring the air. "I'm reminded of that night at Bellbroke, when the mob came in the dead of night."

"You're entirely safe. My Doune pistols are at hand, if that's any consolation."

She squeezed his fingers, his calm presence reassuring.

Once back in the safety of the townhouse, Everard stood with Blythe in the foyer while Mari hastened upstairs. Blythe's heart had hardly settled when he kissed her thoroughly and set it racing again.

"Not the evening I'd envisioned for my future bride," he murmured.

"You saw us safely past the fracas." She smiled despite it all. "I suppose this is good night."

He released her slowly and unbuckled his sword. "To my everlasting regret."

She felt the same. In spades. Would this sweetness fade in time?

She started up the stairs. "At the risk of sounding like a lovesick lass, no doubt I shall dream of you tonight."

In the sconces' low light, his smile was a flash of white. "Needs be we do less dreaming and more planning. With a wedding posthaste, you'll be a proper countess."

"I don't seem to recall a smitten laird on bended knee," she half jested.

"I would do a great deal more than bend my knee." He followed her up the stairs where she'd halted, his arms slipping around her again. "I'd rather kiss you soundly instead."

"That you do verra weel, as you Scots say."

His lips grazed her temple. "My heart is entirely yours. I love you and you alone. Without a doubt you're the bonniest, most confounding lass I've ever known."

"And you are more a prince than Lowland laird. I nearly curtsied when I first saw you."

"Yet you outrank me. And would deign to marry a man not your equal."

"If he asked me, yes." She sighed, wanting to slow the tender, candlelit moment. "Though I would argue against your being my inferior in any way."

"Will you marry me, Blythe?" The emotion in his voice underscored his words, as did his kiss, long and lingering, making her light-headed all over again. "Cast your lot with a man wholeheartedly devoted to you, come what may?"

"In truth, I've already wed you a thousand times in my imagination in Wedderburn's chapel."

"Then I'm ready to leave the city and have it done."

"When shall we see Berwickshire again?"

"Do you miss it?"

"I'm rather enamored by Edinburgh. 'Twill always be the place where our courtship commenced, though the country has its charms."

"In future we can return here whenever you wish."

"As your countess."

"The next Countess of Wedderburn, at long last." He looked proud. Inordinately pleased. "As for time, I've a few more matters to take care of in the city. We'll likely depart by sennight's end."

52

A rule that may serve for a statesman, a courtier,
or a lover: Never make a defense or apology
before you be accused.

CHARLES I OF ENGLAND

How different was her second trip to Wedderburn Castle than her first. Blythe easily recalled her terror of less than three months before and the breakneck speed at which their unmarked coach traveled across the border in the dead of night. This time, with Orin and the laird and Mari, her new lady's maid, she felt almost as if she was coming home.

Orin slept most of the way, his head against his brother's shoulder, lulled by the motion of the coach. The landscape held considerably less appeal. For Blythe, looking at the laird was far preferable to looking out the coach window. Occasionally he'd wink from his seat across from her, their newfound intimacy a bone-deep delight. For the time being, no more kisses or embraces, no tender, murmured endearments. At least till the next highly anticipated private moment.

Now late summer, the countryside had never been more serene or sweeping. Along the roads and lanes of Berwickshire, wildflowers and wild roses grew everywhere Blythe looked.

Finally the turrets of Wedderburn came into view. Down the long

293

castle drive they went, the coach wheels churning up so much dust she closed the window.

Mari was visibly excited, two days of travel hardly dinting her enthusiasm. "My aunt tells me 'tis a grand house, even grander than the Canongate mansion. And far older."

"Eleventh century, aye." Everard closed his own window. "I'm the next laird in a long line of them, several of them cut down by war."

Blythe thought of her own family history and wondered at what points the Hedleys and Humes had intersected over the centuries. How thankful she was her mother and Everard's had become friends.

At last they came to the castle. A letter from Elodie was waiting, but first the grime of the road needed cleansing. Since they'd arrived at four of the clock, tea was sent for, and Blythe was touched by Mrs. Candlish's warm welcome of Mari, as she'd known her in Edinburgh. Bernard was on hand to greet them, wanting to speak to Everard in his study. Watching their exchange, Blythe hoped it wasn't anything concerning. After the tumult in the theater, she knew the political unrest was growing.

Once in her bedchamber, she sat in the window seat and read Elodie's letter, hardly believing they'd soon be related by marriage and she had her own glad news to share.

Dearest Blythe,

I am beside myself with happiness except I miss your company dearly. Ronan is the tenderest, most attentive of husbands. We are settling in well at Cheviot Lodge, having chosen the larger residence as we hope to fill it with a family in time. Please write as soon as you are able and tell us when you shall visit . . .

Blythe read on distractedly, her tea growing cold. No word from Father. The delay chafed, all the implications gnawing at her.

Mari's and Peg's laughter erupted in the other room as Pepys began singing, surely the cause of their amusement. Turning toward the window, Blythe looked out over the garden to the very spot where she'd met Alison. Brash as she was beautiful, Alison would surely object to the laird's choice of a bride.

—⸙—

Everard entered his study. He'd been gone long enough it felt foreign, the desk considerably and unsurprisingly more laden than when he'd left for Edinburgh. But it hardly lessened his high spirits, his thoughts firmly anchored to Blythe. And Bernard, especially canny, did not overlook his buoyant mood.

"Something happened in Auld Reekie, something that made even Davie's plight less dire." Settling into his chair, Bernard waited for an answer. When Everard hesitated, he added, "And I ken it has to do with Lady Hedley."

Unable to suppress a smile, Everard sat down behind his desk.

With a chuckle, Bernard said, "I've witnessed the both of you trying in vain to avoid the other since her arrival, when it's obvious you'd rather do otherwise."

"I cannot hide it." Still smiling, Everard poured them both a dram of whisky. "A toast to our future union. Lady Hedley has agreed to become Lady Wedderburn."

Bernard lifted his glass, pleasure suffusing his ruddy features. "Despite the complications her family and faith bring, she is a very worthy choice. Far worthier a lass than another I have in mind."

Everard took a long drink. "I never intended to form a misalliance in that regard."

"I'm relieved." Bernard expelled a breath. "Though I didna expect you to follow so hard on Ronan's heels, I'm heartily glad of it. Wedderburn needs a mistress as much as you need a wife. I believe Faither would heartily approve of Lady Hedley. Mither certainly would."

The knot of grief that had begun to soften since Blythe took hold of his heart loosened further. "Little did I ken where meeting Northumbria in an oyster cellar would lead."

"Interesting, too, it was you who had to go in Faither's stead to take care of the matter. As if he had matrimony in mind from the first."

"We'll never ken." How he wished he could have asked his father if that was indeed his intent, as well as take back the hasty words he'd spoken of wanting no sassenach for a wife. "Life is full of twists and turns, aye."

"Speaking of such, a letter came yestreen from the newly married Humes, inviting us to Cheviot Lodge."

Good news, that. He'd not been to the Cheviot Hills in some time. Still . . . "Let the newlyweds enjoy their privacy awhile longer."

"Which you're unlikely to do here as laird," Bernard said.

"I regret the earldom came before marriage, but it cannot be helped." Everard looked out the window as a gardener passed by with a wheelbarrow. "Her ladyship understands, being a duke's daughter."

"Speaking of Northumbria, have you any news of late?"

"Not since confirmation came he safely crossed the channel to France and it's not just a ruse to throw authorities off his trail. Boyd has yet to return from his last circuit, gathering what intelligence he can. From what I saw, there's a noticeably stronger military presence at Edinburgh Castle and Holyrood. Even the town guard has increased their number. 'Tis likely the same all over Britain."

Bernard gestured toward a stack of paper. "The newspapers and broadsheets are full of war talk, though sorting fact from fiction is nae easy task."

"How was it here in my absence?"

"There was a bit of a clamor the day after your leaving." Bernard grimaced. "The Duke of Argyll paid us a visit accompanied by some of his officers, though he left his dragoons in Duns. Said they'd been scouting both Highlands and Lowlands."

"Johnnie Campbell?"

"Aye. General Johnnie was quick to remind me you'd served with him on the continent and distinguished yourself."

"Rather he distinguished himself, having recently been awarded

296

Scotland's commander in chief and also the colonelcy of the Horse Guards, if memory serves."

Bernard nodded. "He wasted nae time telling me."

Everard checked a wry smile. How arrogant these officers could be. Special appointments and titles, even if well deserved, oft went straight to their heads.

Bernard grimaced. "Which means he's a favorite of King Geordie, nae doubt."

"Short-lived, I'd wager, as he has Jacobite sympathies. Or once did."

"He said more than once he regrets your resignation."

"If he does, which is questionable as it cleared the way for his promotion, I do not. He said nothing of Davie?"

"Nae. He and his officers joined me for a dram in the small drawing room while the stables saw to their horses. Then they were on their way."

On their way having made a significant detour. Even though Everard was a fellow soldier, it was highly unusual to decamp on a man's doorstep. His mind turned, weighing all the implications, none of them pleasant.

Blythe.

Would he never cease to worry about her? Tie every happenstance to her well-being?

He ran a hand across his eyes, which were still stinging from the dust of the road. "On a lighter note, the twins are enjoying their studies, one more than the other."

The tense mood lifted as Bernard laughed. "Let me guess. Malcolm is the true scholar."

"Aye, but I encouraged Alistair to hold steady. The end result will be worth the pain of the present."

"And Davie?" Shooting a glance at the door as if to ascertain it was indeed shut, Bernard continued, "How goes his time in the tower? I'm loath to ask as I'm fairly certain of the answer."

"Our second meeting met with nae more success than the first. I told him the Jacks' cause is doomed and his own life is in danger, but all warnings fell on deaf ears and always have." Betimes he believed David had a death wish. "As it stands, he's done damage to Hume's Land in his scuffle with the authorities and sent Calysta packing."

"He may well lose his head, depending on His Majesty's mood." Bernard poured another dram, looking weary of the struggle. "But better that than something happen to you. God forbid he become laird in your stead."

God forbid, aye.

Everard had oft grieved Davie's obstinance and willfulness over the years and wished he weren't the second-born. Bernard was far more worthy. "He's akin to the parable of the prodigal in the book of Luke, but there may never be a day of redemption."

"All of Faither's and Mither's prayers seemed to come to naught regarding him. But I'd rather talk of more agreeable affairs like weddings." Bernard made his usual effort to bring cheer. "You'll marry here, of course, by special license. Nae banns read in kirk. Nae fanfare."

"'Tis complicated. The kirk requires our names. Blythe's identity will nae longer be secret, though we will keep it as quiet as possible. Then there must be nae objection to our union within the parish or beyond it."

"A clandestine marriage is not to be had as in some cases." Bernard frowned. "If you dinna go through the proper channels, the reverend will be fined heavily if found out."

"The entire business must be legal in the sight of the Almighty and man."

"What will you do?"

"Risk declaring who she is. Pray for protection and favor. I feel an urgency to wed her not only because of the devotion I feel to her. The sooner she becomes my wife, the safer she'll be."

"Is she aware she must forsake her Catholicism to wed you? Become Protestant or the kirk won't perform the marriage rites?"

Was she? Rather, would she? Amid their being in love, such concerns seemed small. But as he discussed the details with Bernard, his high spirits nearly deserted him. Even one of these obstacles could keep them apart.

Would he stand on his faith or his fears?

He looked at the tray of letters to be read, mostly condolences with black seals, the brevity of life ever before him. "I believe the Almighty led her ladyship here for many reasons, one of which is to become my wife. He will make a way."

53

That which is striking and beautiful is not always good,
but that which is good is always beautiful.

NINON DE L'ENCLOS

T was exhilarating being on horseback again. Though she missed Guinevere and oft wondered how she fared at Bellbroke, Blythe had her pick of the Wedderburn stables. On their second day back from Edinburgh, she decided on a brown bay mare, fifteen hands high, as fleet of foot as she was docile.

Riding out with the laird for the first time, she tried to embrace the present and keep all worrisome thoughts at bay. Everard had to restrain his high-spirited stallion as he didn't want Blythe's mare at a gallop till she'd learned the lay of the land. His gentle protectiveness touched her. Side by side they rode at a gentle canter, toward a sunny horizon indicative of their future, or so she hoped.

Such happiness ahead. Such joy. Still, in unguarded moments, doubts assailed her like poisonous darts. Would he be true to her? What of her inheritance? Her Catholicism? Must uncertainty and heartache cloud their plans?

As if sensing her inner turmoil, Everard drew up beneath a rowan tree alongside a burn. He helped her down from the saddle and spread a blanket for her to sit upon, the landscape before them like a painting, Hume acreage as far as the eye could see. Here all was private. Peaceful. They leaned back against the tree's broad trunk while their horses grazed by the rushing water.

After removing one of her riding gloves, he took hold of her hand, his tanned, callused fingers entwined with her pale, delicate ones. "You're pensive today, Countess."

She smiled to reassure him. "My thoughts are but those of a foolish, lovestruck lass. Hardly worth mentioning."

"I would ken them anyway."

She bit her lip. How straightforward he was. How . . . untangled. If only she could banish the awkwardness that came with such honesty!

"My mind goes a great many directions lately," she said. "So much to consider."

"Such as?"

"I don't doubt your intentions, Everard, nor your heart."

"Nor have I any qualms about you, Blythe."

"But I do." She fixed her eye on a haze of fragrant purple heather. "Alas, I am not a beautiful woman. A man of your standing and stature could choose amongst a great many noblewomen who are infinitely more pleasing in face and form."

He kissed her fingers in that gallant way she loved. "You are beyond bonnie to me, Blythe. So bonnie, in fact, it blots out any other woman of my acquaintance, including the lass I sense you still have in mind."

She nearly sighed. Was she so easily read? Alison was now the least of her concerns. "What of my dowry? I may well lose it. In fact, I may have already lost the whole of my inheritance, including my title. Then there is the matter of my dubious parentage. My mother's reputation."

"You are a lady through and through, with or without a title and nae matter who your mither was. Nor am I greedy for gain or some penniless peer depending on your dowry. Such makes a shaky foundation for marriage."

"Yet you ken me little. Suppose you tire of me in time? Suppose you rue the day you wed me?"

"Call it virtue or vice, I am a canny man. An experienced soldier learns to take someone's measure in a trice. You are, without a doubt, a worthy woman." His voice lowered, a teasing lilt lending to his brogue. "Let's put the shoe on the other foot. Why would you agree to marry a man who at first sight had a knave's manners and nearly turned you out?"

"I expected no less from a Scottish laird in the fractious Borders." She smiled. Hindsight colored it amusing. "And you must admit I gave you no quarter."

"You made a formidable prisoner even though you were half in love with me from the first."

"Half? I was *wholly* yours from the moment I set foot in Wedderburn's foyer." She leaned into him, her head against his shoulder. "I daren't ask when the tide turned for you, when you began to regard me as something other than a nuisance."

"When I came to the tower and saw you wearing your spectacles and poring over your books."

"Surely you jest."

"Nae." He smiled. "A most fetching sight. And then later when you partnered with me for a reel, all was lost."

She sighed, the delight of it unfading. "Orin told me you said I was the bonniest dancer you'd ever seen."

"'Tis truth."

She grew quiet, saving the sorest, most formidable hurdle for last. "You are willing to wed a Catholic, an abomination to many."

"Not to me. You are devout. We worship the same Lord. 'Tis all that matters."

"I have longed to attend your kirk, watching from the window as you leave as a family on the Sabbath. I would worship anywhere openly and in freedom."

"You're willing to become Protestant, then? Our marriage seems to hinge upon it."

She knew this was the case and felt a sudden sadness that had nothing to do with forsaking her family's faith. "So many pretend to be pious yet live unholy lives. The French court is rife with it. All those masses and confessionals full of those who continue to savor their sins."

"'Tis the same for any faith. Wide is the gate, and broad is the way, that leadeth to destruction. In the same vein, rigid Puritanism and Protestantism are full of folly, forbidding one to dance or even look long in the mirror without judgment and damnation following."

"I think Christ would forbid both extremes were He among us."

"He is among us."

"Indeed, He is." The hardships dealt her of late had shown God's rescuing hand the clearest. "Our Lord has been more real to me here than ever before. So long as we both believe in Christ as our Lord and Savior, what does it matter what we call ourselves except His own?"

He reached for a flask, uncorked it, and offered her a drink of water. She took a sip, another memory taking hold.

"Not long after I stumbled upon my mother's diary, I found some sermons written by Isaac Watts."

"Watts the dissenter?"

"A man of profound intellect and integrity. He writes that the book of God is his chief study and his divinest delight. I would know that kind of faith better." She handed him back the flask, her solemnity turning playful. "I would know *you* better."

"As husband and wife, aye." Leaning in, he kissed her long and lingeringly before helping her to her feet. "I'd wed you today if there was nae license to be obtained. As it stands, I'll ride to the kirk tomorrow and see what remains to be done."

She pulled on her glove as he called for the horses. "Then I'll pray there's no impediment. Surely God is in this. I never dreamed I'd be your countess, but there's nothing I want more."

"We're of one accord, then." He looked down at her with undisguised adoration. "And I hope to find Reverend Johnston of the same mind."

54

Let no day slip over without some comfort
received of the Word of God.

JOHN KNOX

ord, be Thou my defense.

Everard removed his hat and bowed his head before the kirk's heavy door. As he did so, the bells in the tower began pealing, a reminder of the gift his father had made in memory of his mother upon her death. They'd always sounded mournful to Everard, a continual reminder of his loss. Their variations comprised the first true peal of any church in the Lowlands. At the moment, they were proclaiming eleven o' the clock—the hour of his attempt to marry the woman he loved more deeply by the day.

Once in Catholic use, the Duns kirk was now firmly Presbyterian. His family had their own history within its hallowed walls, not all of it holy. A hundred years before, the Humes had burst into a Sabbath service to sword-fight the Cockburns of Langton, wounding more than a few parishioners and ending up prisoners in Edinburgh Castle.

Mayhap Davie had a double dose of the fighting clan spirit.

Laurence Johnston wasn't expecting him, but Everard knew he'd be here rather than at the nearby manse. The man's habits were well known after his twelve years among them. Before making his rounds to visit the sick and infirm most afternoons, he attended to kirk business in the mornings, sometimes even acting as gardener to the grounds. Though a sexton could have been had, Johnston's fondness for the outdoors endeared him to his parishioners.

"Welcome, Lord Wedderburn." The reverend's resonant voice rang out from the nave, much as it did from the pulpit. He looked not at all surprised to see him, though Everard rarely came round except for Sabbath services.

"Reverend Johnston," Everard replied.

The balding man came forward with a brisk step that belied his age, his plain garments indicative of his station.

"I've come about a personal matter, if you have the time," Everard told him, placing his hat beneath his arm.

"But of course. Would you rather meet at the manse?"

"Nae," Everard said. "The kirk is fine."

With a nod, the reverend gestured to a side door that led to a courtyard hemmed in by a tall yew hedge offering both privacy and shade. A long stone bench akin to a pew proffered seating.

"I'll cut to the heart of it," Everard said once they'd exchanged a few pleasantries. "I wish to wed a lady from Northumberland. She is Catholic but agrees to become Protestant. I'd like the matter managed discreetly, honorably."

Johnston looked taken aback. Had he expected a Scots lass? "When might I meet your future bride, Lord Wedderburn?"

"Whenever you prefer. Her ladyship happens to be at the castle. You might remember Lady Hedley from my brother's wedding ceremony. Her companion is Ronan's bride."

"I do recall a tall, slender lass. As for my visit, will tomorrow suit?" At Everard's aye he continued, "How is it your intended is living at Wedderburn?"

Everard paused. Did Johnston think they'd made a clandestine marriage and now wanted it legal? "There's been nothing untoward in our arrangement. My faither and mither were her godparents.

305

Her own faither—the Duke of Northumbria—is abroad, and she is at Wedderburn in his absence."

"Ah." Johnston leaned forward, hands clasped on his knees. "Jacobites, I suppose, not only Catholics. Many Northumberland nobles are."

"As it stands, we are both above the age of consent. But if it matters, her faither the duke broached matrimony in a letter before leaving for the continent."

"Very well. There should be ample time ahead of the ceremony to be assured of her conversion and instruct her in matters of our faith—the catechism and the like. I also have a psalmbook that will suit if you want to take it to her beforehand."

"Lady Hedley is a learned lass. Have you any of the spiritual writings of James Durham or Elizabeth West?"

"Excellent suggestion. My copies are on loan at present, though they can be had for a half a merk Scots at the market if you don't want to wait."

"The market suits."

Johnston's apparent surprise shifted to concern. "Let us be perfectly clear, milord. You desire to bypass the reading of the banns to the congregation? Obtain a license instead like your brother before you?"

"I do, aye," Everard said. Johnston hadn't brought up the notion of his waiting till mourning was past. He'd wed Ronan and Elodie without complaint in that regard, though Elodie was Protestant, not Catholic. "A license is preferred. I'd rather it not come before the kirk session if it can be helped."

Who knew how the governing council would react to such? Not all landowners in Berwickshire would take kindly to a Catholic Jacobite neighbor, no matter how titled or converted. His fellow peers who sat on the session and decided parish matters might well deem the match an impediment, Sir Clive Landreth foremost. Having the ear of the king might mean trouble in Berwickshire as well as London. Everard would not see Blythe suffer for her father's political loyalties or his religion.

"I see nae harm in bypassing the banns and seeking a license instead." The shadow cleared from Johnston's face. "So long as I answer to the Almighty and obey the laws of the land, all should be well."

Blythe took the religious booklets from Everard's hands eagerly. She'd all but abandoned her own scholarly works of late, so to read someone else's writings was surely welcome. "I shall devour them. How thoughtful of you. Did all go well?"

He hesitated. "I want it to go faster. Expect Johnston on the morrow for tea. I doubt he'll catechize you so soon, but . . ."

She smiled. "I shall be ready nonetheless. Perhaps I'll even answer him in Latin."

She left him to sit in the garden alcove near his study window. He often joined her, glad to escape his desk work. He liked having her near as she read, worked embroidery, or dealt with some small task alongside Orin or her new maid. With her guard down and their feelings aired, there was now a striking life and sweetness in her face that matched the grace of her form. He was not a man easily beglamoured, but that remarkable quality drew him.

With a last look at her through the glass, he left his study and went into the entrance hall, where the Humes' family Bible lay in an ornate carved box. Worn from hundreds of years of hallowed use, the guid book was something Blythe would cherish. When he opened it to the page where his father's handwriting dominated, he found his beloved's name and the date of her christening days after her birth. He felt a little start.

Lady Blythe Hedley, Bellbroke Castle, 29 March 1687.

Who but the Almighty could have designed such a circumstance as her coming to Berwickshire after so many years? And despite his own foolish reservations?

He paged through the old tome till he came to the record of marriages. His own parents' had been recorded more than thirty-five years before in another century. Sorrow tugged at him, but he concentrated on the blank page where Blythe's and his names would be written following their own nuptials. Such joy ahead. No looking back.

Only forward.

55

But it is pretty to see what money will do.

SAMUEL PEPYS

An Edinburgh mantua-maker was summoned to sew Blythe's wedding attire. Katherine Murray had but a sennight to create a worthy gown. Mouth full of pins, brow puckered, she left no hour of daylight idle and even worked long into the night despite Blythe's overtures to rest.

"I must create a gown worthy of the laird of Wedderburn's bride," she said. "'Tis not every day I'm summoned from the city for such an important task."

Hastening around the sewing table in the multiwindow room provided for her, she continued her work, sending for Blythe for fittings, determined the gown would fit like a glove. "You are slender as a fairy and this fabric is sumptuous. You shall look like a princess when I am finished. Your groom has certainly paid a princely sum for it."

Mrs. Candlish took Blythe to the locked chamber that held the family jewels. Secreted behind a hidden stairwell in the old tower not far from where Blythe had first stayed, it was akin to a safe, housing several jewel chests.

"Some of the pieces are quite auld," the housekeeper said, opening one of the chests with a key dangling from her chatelaine. "The

Renaissance jewels are abundant. There's even a broach or two that reflects the Humes' years as Catholics."

And what a collection! Bejeweled small swords with gold and silver hilts. Pearls of all sizes and hues. Cameos with women's portraits. Enameled pendants and bow broaches. Earrings. Even tiaras.

"Feel at liberty to choose whichever ye wish for yer wedding day." Mrs. Candlish opened yet another velvet-lined chest. "The former countess was partial to small gemstones and this tiara with a fleur-de-lis design. 'Tis a work of art, is it not?"

Blythe lifted out a delicate creation of pearls and diamonds set in a floral framework. Not ostentatious yet every bit as regal as it was small. "Since it had meaning to the laird's mother . . ."

"A lovely choice, milady."

Blythe set it atop her head for just an instant, letting the reality of their wedding day take hold, the day she'd long dreamed of then almost discarded. Giddy didn't describe what she was feeling. It ran far deeper. Love and wonder and gratitude coursed through her like the blood in her veins.

"I shall take the tiara and polish it for ye," Mrs. Candlish said, locking the room after them. "Not much longer now. I've not seen the laird so happy since he was a lad. A new countess is an occasion to celebrate to the utmost!"

Five days before the wedding, Everard entered the red drawing room to find Sir Clive waiting. It was rare that Alison's father would appear at his own country seat, let alone Wedderburn. He and Everard seldom crossed paths. Alison was the liaison between them, though he'd not seen her since that regrettable day she'd come calling and surprised Blythe in the garden.

"Lord Wedderburn." Sir Clive stood, his girth wider than Everard remembered, his pockmarked features concealed by powder, his elaborately curled periwig a starker white.

Everard greeted him cordially, schooling his dislike. "Obviously, you've returned to Landreth Hall."

"For a brief time only. London rarely allows me leave. A certain matter concerning you necessitates my coming here today."

A footman brought brandy, an expected courtesy Everard wanted to wave aside. But custom prevailed.

Sir Clive settled on a sofa while Everard remained standing by the fireless hearth. "But first, I must convey my daughter's discomfiture that you remain so closely closeted in mourning."

Meaning Everard had not seen her, no doubt. "Is your family weel?"

"All but Alison." Sir Clive's soft, almost womanish voice belied the cunning and conniving he was known for. "She may return with me to London if matters don't improve."

Was she truly unweel, or did her malady stem from Everard's perceived neglect?

"My best wishes should she choose to do so," he said quietly.

"That is merely an aside." The baron's eyes narrowed. "I've come regarding matters pertaining to the king."

Everard took a sip of brandy and said nothing, always the best hastener of conversation.

"His Majesty is carefully selecting men of merit and experience to serve as his chosen officers should there be another Jacobite revolt."

"As expected. But what has that to do with me?"

Sir Clive looked startled. "If you were one of my daughters, I'd accuse you of playing coy. But since you are one of Britain's most celebrated soldiers, I ask *you* what such means."

"I cannot serve, if that is your intent. I have personal matters to address, including mourning my faither, which makes any military appointment impossible."

"I am well aware of that sad fact. But His Majesty mentioned you by name as did several of his cabinet members, including fellow officers you've served with in the field."

Everard swirled his brandy. Flattery, especially political, failed to move him. Besides, as the king could speak no English, Everard doubted his name was being bandied about. "If so, I am unable to comply."

"Comply, milord? As for His Majesty, 'tis a dangerous denial you make." Sir Clive stared at him in open rebuke. "Will you bypass another chance to curry favor? Earn His Majesty's ire with your refusal instead? You would be wise to count it your unavoidable duty, especially in light of your brother's treasonous activities."

"Currying favor is not in my nature, nor do I wish to earn the king's ire. I can only assure His Majesty of my fidelity. And my prayers." Everard felt a shade deceptive voicing what felt like thin platitudes. But was it not the biblical mandate to pray for leaders, even one that needs be dethroned? "I have nae control over my brother's conduct or allegiances. My ambition is to live a quiet life as laird and continue my faither's legacy."

"And you expect me to return to London with that answer."

Ire overtook his irritation. Had he not made himself abundantly clear? "I have nae more to say on the matter."

"I beg you to reconsider." Sir Clive downed his drink, then stood. "I shall remain in Berwickshire till sennight's end. Send word to me there should you change your mind." He walked to the doorway, his bearing stiff. Offended. "Our Hanoverian king is not one to be crossed. Remember his former wife, Sophia Dorothea, whom he repudiated and even now languishes in her tower prison these many years."

"A blatant hypocrisy, given the king's own conduct."

To his surprise, Sir Clive chuckled. "Ah, the Maypole and the Elephant now on English soil. I've met both mistresses and find them insipid at best. Hardly the caliber of Charles II's seraglio."

Was it his imagination, or did the baron aim a subtle insult at Blythe? On the other hand, how could he ken?

Everard finished his drink. "As for the imprisoned queen, one would hope she takes solace in the fact the king must give an accounting when he meets the Almighty."

No more was said. Sir Clive went out without a backwards glance.

56

*In appearance, at least, he being on all occasions glad
to be at friendship with me, though we hate one another,
and know it on both sides.*

SAMUEL PEPYS

wo days before the wedding, as Blythe, Everard, Orin, and Bernard sat down to dinner to say grace, a great fuss went up at the castle's entrance. Who might it be? Blythe's hopes for her father to suddenly appear had been put to rest. This was a different, altogether unexpected surprise. Blythe nearly cried when she spied Elodie and Ronan step down from the coach. Everard had not told her he'd sent word to Cheviot Lodge ahead of their wedding.

"Did you think I'd miss your nuptials?" Elodie exclaimed as they embraced, joy suffusing her features. "I shall stand up with you or perish."

They returned to the dining room with their guests for a delicious dinner, which would pale next to the wedding feast to come, Mrs. Candlish announced gleefully. They all joined hands and bowed their heads, wishing the twins could be among them at such a time. As for David, news had not come he'd been released from the tower.

Talk turned to other matters, the laird presiding at the head of the table. "Reverend Johnston will be here at ten o' the clock day after the morrow. The wedding feast will follow with dancing."

"I, for one, shall be dancing," Bernard told them, raising his glass in a toast. "Two brothers married within a month. Faither might well rise from the dead."

"Poor Faither would be very unmerry if uncasketed." Orin's grimace turned to a grin, caught up as he was in the jollity of the moment. "But I shall be verra glad of another countess."

Ronan winked. "I suppose this means you shall nae longer have Lady Hedley as your tutor."

Orin's levity vanished, and he looked at the laird. "Are my tutors to be brought back?"

"In time. Our countess will have other matters to concern herself with, though she'll continue to oversee your studies."

Blythe smiled to encourage him. "We shall keep at our painting and storytelling and all the rest. And you'll have plenty of time to go out riding and hawking, not just be at your books."

Orin's gaze was nothing short of adoring. Bernard elbowed him. "I do wonder who is most in love with our fair Lady Hedley."

"If I wasn't eight, I would marry her myself," Orin said, his words meeting with their laughter.

"I dinna doubt it," Ronan said, turning to Everard. "What is this I hear about your improving the castle?"

"Bythe and I have been conspiring," Everard answered. "We've decided on an orangery among other things."

"I won't argue," Bernard said. "We must leap forward from the Middle Ages at some point in time."

"What exactly are you proposing?" Ronan asked.

"A new wing as Mither once envisioned. Fireplaces in every room. Venetian windows. Mayhap even a new Palladian bridge that spans the burn."

"I am, truthfully, most enthusiastic about the colliery improvements," Blythe told them. "Better housing and care for the miners and their families. A physic and place of recovery as well as a large community garden."

"We've also laid out plans for another village at the farthest and largest mine," Everard added. "My bride-to-be has helped shed light on the malady among the runaway colliers, given her faither's operations in Northumberland. Apparently, 'tis due to lack of light."

Bernard looked relieved. "The Duncan clan's complaints weren't unfounded. Some of those runaways have returned of late. Lord willing, we'll keep the malady and any unrest from happening again."

They talked of parish matters for a few minutes, and then Munro appeared. His aging features wore a heaviness Blythe did not miss. He usually ate with Mrs. Candlish and the upper servants belowstairs. Had his own midday meal been interrupted?

He cleared his throat, and every eye turned toward him. "Milord, pardon the interruption, but Mr. Hume has arrived unexpectedly."

Before the last word was uttered, a commotion occurred in the hallway. At once all convivial talk and laughter ceased.

David?

Blythe's gaze swerved to Orin, who sank down in his chair as if wanting to hide. No one need tell her he was afraid of his own brother. Mightn't he be excused? Blythe bit her tongue to keep from doing so. She wasn't the countess yet.

Everard stood, now looking wary, as the errant Hume strode into the room and came to an abrupt stop halfway round the table, his gaze puzzling over Elodie and then Blythe. Indulgence sat upon his fleshy features, his eyes bloodshot, his words slightly slurred as he half shouted, "Why are there two unco lassies at our table?"

"Have done with your ill-scrappit manners and introduce yourself," Everard replied just as forcefully. He came to stand behind Blythe's chair, hands splayed on the chairback.

With an exaggerated bow Blythe and Elodie's way, David rolled his arm in a little flourish, stains on his sleeve. "David Hume, at your service."

Everard stayed standing as if a fracas might break out at any moment. He gestured to Elodie. "This is Ronan's new wife, Mrs. Hume." He touched Blythe's shoulder. "And this is the future Countess of Wedderburn."

David stared at Blythe openly, his cold eyes reptilian in their appraisal. Would he complain of her being plain next? Was he thinking of Alison?

She took a breath, forcing cordiality. "Mr. Hume."

"A sassenach." Contempt rode his surly features. "And a scourie Northumbrian from her speech."

"She is our faither's goddaughter," Everard said, warning in his tone as he returned to his seat.

David continued to regard her. Blythe sensed she'd best not back down lest he abuse her further.

"Can you be my intended's brother?" she said with a half smile, faint contempt in her tone. "If so, a preen-heidit ablach if there ever was one."

Astonishment gave way to robust laughter around the long table. All but David's.

His eyes flared wide, a smirk on his tanned face. "Did the heidie lass just call me a mangled carcass?"

"She did indeed," Bernard said to more laughter as all stared at Blythe. "Spoken like a true Scotswoman."

The laird gave a wink, easing her. She'd not trespassed too far, then. Just the other day she'd overheard a stable lad abusing another with those same words and had asked Peg what they meant.

Apparently unshaken by her setdown, David walked—nay, strutted like a banty rooster—to the other end of the long table, where he pulled out a chair. Eyeing the dishes whose contents were dwindling, he didn't signal a footman to fetch him a clean plate but simply took the meat platter and made it his dish.

Blythe schooled her astonishment as Everard remarked, "Obviously, you've either escaped the tower or the king granted pardon."

"The latter, though I did attempt the former," David answered, taking a huge bite of mutton. He waved his fork at a footman to fill his wine glass. When the servant was too slow to suit him, he muttered what sounded like an epithet.

Watching him consume his food with less grace than a common

field hand, Blythe was aghast. Would he drag his bread across the juices on his plate next? As she thought it, he did so. Grease dripped down his beard-stubbled jaw. No serviette in sight.

Somehow David managed to say around another mouthful, "So, we've one brother married and the laird about to be wed. Felicitous congratulations to you both."

"What are your plans now that you've been freed?" Ronan asked, continuing his own meal and obviously used to his brother's crudities.

"On my way to the Highlands to join my wife. But I wanted to see Berwickshire first."

"Cawdor Castle, then?" Ronan asked as the footman refilled his own glass.

A nod. "The king commands I leave Edinburgh and forsake all Jacobite leanings."

"So you'll trade Auld Reekie for Cawdor," Bernard said. "But likely retain your rebelliousness."

"The Highlands suit my purposes better at present." David sent a dark look the laird's way. "I'm at ebb water, but at least I've escaped my creditors in Edinburgh."

An uneasy silence descended. Blythe had lost her appetite and craved a cup of tea and a quiet corner. How long must they endure this man's offensive presence? Orin looked near apoplexy. He had hunkered down till his eyes were barely visible over the table's edge. The easy conviviality of the meal early on had been replaced with what she could only describe as malevolence. She herself disliked David on sight.

Do not return evil for evil.

Scripture's truth was never less welcome . . . but never was a man more in need of grace. A man soon to be her brother-in-law. And in a fit of pique, she had hurled an insult at him upon his arrival. Would he bear her a grudge?

Oddly, David's temper seemed to settle. On account of the meal or the wine? He leaned back in his chair and studied the former laird's portrait on the opposite wall, stifling a belch.

Everard stood with his usual equanimity, bringing the meal to a blessed end. "Let's adjourn to my study, Brother, and discuss your stay."

---⊃∞⊂---

Blythe retired early, her disappointment at not spending a leisurely evening with Elodie and Ronan due to David's arrival tempered by the excitement of the coming wedding. Mari snuffed all the bedchamber candles one by one as a soft knock sounded at the door.

Peg entered, locking the door behind her. "The laird has sent me to yer chambers for the night till Mr. Hume leaves in the morn."

Blythe climbed the bed steps, the weighted words sinking in as she settled down atop the thick feather mattress. So David was soon to leave. Had the laird sent him packing, or would he go of his own accord?

Peg patted her pocket. Did she carry a pistol? "Nae collieshangie, ye ken."

Blythe lay down and pulled the covers up to her chin. "I'm glad you're here, but I'd rather you sleep."

"I'll sleep like a bairn right here by the bolted door." Peg proceeded to lie down upon the pallet atop the carpet with a little sigh of contentment.

"At least take a pillow and blanket," Blythe said, handing Mari both. "'Tis drafty near the floor especially."

Mari passed them to Peg, a look of understanding between them. "I'll be in the dressing room as usual should ye need me, milady."

Blythe had been tired after supper but was now wide awake. Her ears pricked at the slightest sound. She listened to the great house settle with the sweet realization that this chamber would soon be empty and she'd move in with Everard and nearer Orin. That could not come too soon.

Another creak in the corridor had her at sixes and sevens. "What is that noise outside our door?" she whispered.

"One of the footmen, mem," Peg said with a yawn. "He's armed too."

Would this now be the protocol when David visited? Blythe took comfort in the fact Everard had her best interests at heart even if his brother was a force to reckon with. She'd not press Peg on the particulars that had led to the laird sending her to her chambers. Suffice it to say Blythe would breathe far easier when Mr. Hume was on his way to the Highlands.

57

Many might go to heaven with half
the labor they go to hell.

BEN JONSON

The next morn, David left in such a hurry it seemed Hades itself was on his heels. The entire castle seemed to exhale with relief. Blythe certainly did, watching his departure from the morning room. Late August sunlight streamed through the high windows and pooled on the carpet at her feet. Unusually subdued, Orin was behind her, working studiously on his sums. At the retreating hoofbeats on the drive, he raised his head.

"Davie the Devil, most call him, even in Duns and beyond," he said.

Blythe left the window and came to stand beside him, her eyes on his work, her hand on his shoulder. "I'm sorry."

"'Twas right of you to put him in his place lest he bedevil you too."

Was that why Everard had sent Peg and her pistol—and even an armed footman—to her bedchamber? "I thought better of it once it was said. I don't want to make an enemy in my own household."

"He's not really one of us Humes," Orin said. "Some swear he was snatched by fairies at birth and replaced by something monstrous."

"But we know better, do we not? Fairies are fine for make-believe stories, but David seems beset by some very real vices."

"Ronan says he has a death wish. And Bernard said 'tis better *that* than he become laird."

"Why ever would he become laird?"

Orin gave a shiver. "The king has summoned Everard to fight the Jacobites."

What? Blythe sank to the seat beside him. Surely, he'd misheard. "But there's no Rising to speak of, just rumors."

"There will be. My brothers swear to it. And the king has called for the laird to fight when the time comes. If he falls in battle, then Davie takes his place and Calysta will be countess." He looked at her with those impossibly blue eyes that were wise beyond their years. "I'd rather die than see such."

"No need to trespass on trouble, Orin, or worry about what may never be." Blythe spoke more calmly than she felt. "Think instead of the joys of summer, our wedding day on the morrow. Not war." Even as she said it, she heard the faint strains of a fiddle.

Orin's face darkened anew. "Munro's fiddle weeps."

She listened to the lament, wishing for a sprightly jig instead. The mood in the household seemed suddenly grim. Why had Everard not told her about the king?

Leaning in, she kissed Orin's knotted brow. "You've worked diligently for over an hour on your sums. Why not pause from your studies and see to your new pony? We might go riding this afternoon if the weather continues fair."

He brightened and pushed away from the table to head toward the door. She followed after him to seek out Everard. But as soon as she stepped into the corridor, he appeared.

She forced a smile, determined not to be a scold. "I was just coming to find you."

"You look troubled, my love." He stepped into the room and opened his arms to her, nudging the door shut with his boot. "I was waiting for Davie's departure before I sought you out."

She laid her head against his chest. "He's a troubled soul."

"And a dangerous one. I sometimes think his conscience is so seared he'll become more so." He held her close, her upswept hair catching on his bristled jaw. "His unexpected appearance raises a great many questions. I have reason to believe his release from the tower has more to do with me than him."

The solace and safety she always felt in his arms vanished. "What means you?"

"His release might stem from a bid to curry favor by the king's ministers. An attempt to sway me to join His Majesty's forces should there be another Rising."

"Oh, Everard—"

"I kept it from you because I hoped it would not matter. But now I think, with Davie's coming, it might matter very much. I even wonder if the king and his ministers released my brother on the condition that he act as government spy."

"But he's a Jacobite."

"One easily swayed by money and power, and now headed to the Highlands, a Jacks' nest." He released a breath. "Though I do wonder if he'll reach Cawdor."

"Meaning it might be a ruse?"

"Aye, and in that vein, I have other news." He looked down at her. "I've just heard your faither remains in the country but continues in hiding. The France rumor was likely put forth to end the search for him."

She was unsurprised. Such intrigue and dissembling and subterfuge. She absently fingered a button on his weskit. An age seemed to have passed since she'd seen her father. "If only he could learn of our wedding. Yet I know not where or how he is. I can only pray."

"Prayer may be the best weapon we have."

Her arms stole about his waist. "Tell me more of the king wanting your services."

"Sir Clive brought word to me from London, though he is not entirely trustworthy and rarely does anything but further his own ends."

"There are many ambitious men like him, but what do you think His Majesty's response will be when he hears your answer?"

"My refusal will likely get the king's nose out of joint, mayhap incur his wrath. But who can say? Only God knows, and I refuse to dwell on it." His lips brushed her brow. "What occupies my mind at present is tomorrow and my bonnie bride."

"Has the Duns tailor finished your wedding suit?"

"Aye, and I promise it's not black."

She smiled, imagining it. "Nor is my lovely gown, thanks to you. I had a final fitting with Mrs. Murray just this morning."

He regarded her intently. "Nae last thoughts of joining a religious order?"

"Surely you jest."

"And your books? Will you return to your translating and studies?"

"I doubt it. Though they kept me pleasantly occupied, they were, in hindsight, more a way to fill the hours and find fulfillment. What I most covet is a castle full of children."

"A good half dozen should do, Lord willing. Nine months hence would be . . ."

"Springtime." That telltale flush he'd invoked from the first climbed up her neck in a warm rush.

"For the time being," he said, "there's but a few hours left till we're man and wife. The servants are in high spirits, and the garden has never been better in terms of your bouquet."

"I shall pick a sprig of white heather for the both of us, then. A charming Scottish custom."

He looked thoughtful. "I'd be willing to wager a great deal more practice is needed ahead of tomorrow's nuptials, which calls for a kiss, if I remember correctly."

She shook her head and stepped away from him. "No more kisses or seeing the bride before the ceremony."

"Wheest, lass." He laughed, pulling her close again. "Have done with that."

Wheest! Her Northumbrianness embraced the Scots word anew.

At her sigh, he bent his head, his lips leaving a teasing trail from her brow to her throat.

What a mere kiss could do. For a few breathless moments there was no more David. No more missing fathers or talk of war or kings or spies or intrigue.

Just a man and a woman thoroughly in love.

58

Three can keep a secret, if two of them are dead.

BENJAMIN FRANKLIN

Had there ever been a more beautiful wedding day?

After a wee smirr of rain during the night, cleansing the air and cooling the gardens, the sun shone down. Fully gowned, Blythe stood by the windows of her bedchamber looking out on the moorland she was to call home and hearing kirk bells in the distance. A little thrill coursed through her. Pealing for them?

The castle fairly ticked with anticipation. Mari had gone below to gather the bridal bouquet. Peg darted in and out, announcing that Reverend Johnston had just arrived, that Orin insisted on picking the white heather, and that the chapel was all in readiness, having been bedecked with so many blossoms it appeared the gardens had come indoors. Even the musicians hired for the occasion were enjoying a celebratory dram ahead of tuning their instruments in the Great Hall.

A knock at the door gave Blythe pause. Elodie entered, clad in pale yellow, her own wedding gift of a luckenbooth adorning her bodice. Her eyes widened when she saw the bride. "Milady—" With a little laugh, she amended, "How hard old habits die, *Blythe*. Rather, *Lady Wedderburn* in public."

Blythe turned in a slow circle to show the gown to the best advantage. It was fashioned from blue-and-cream silk damask, the neckline and sleeves embellished with silk ribbon and bobbin lace.

A remarkable sewing feat in so short a time. Elodie's sigh was testament to its beauty.

Mari soon appeared with the bridal bouquet—roses of every hue—and Peg came in from the dressing room with the polished tiara. It rested upon a small velvet cushion, all aglitter.

Sitting down at her dressing table, Blythe cradled her bouquet while the tiara was placed on her head, the curls Mari had spent the morning on cascading from the back of her head to her shoulders.

"Shall I tell Lord Wedderburn you're ready?" Peg asked her.

"I lack white heather, is all," Blythe said with a smile, just as a noise in the hall announced its timely arrival.

Orin appeared, slightly winded as if he'd run all the way, and helped her tuck the sprig into her bouquet. The women tittered as he gaped at her.

"You look more a queen than a countess," he said at last.

"I do feel like a queen," Blythe said, bending down to kiss his cheek. "But mostly I feel very thankful."

"I must give your groom his heather." He held up a second sprig.

Her heart beat faster. "Then please tell him I am ready when he'd like to escort me to the chapel."

She returned to the window, the view no longer barren to her but beautiful. The maids dispersed, Elodie with them. Did they mean to give her a moment of privacy?

She felt so . . . tranquil. In the tumult of the past weeks—months—she'd forgotten how lovely tranquility was. She even felt lovely, perhaps for the first time in her entire life. Bending her head, she breathed in the perfume of her bouquet and felt the slight weight of the tiara while listening for the laird's footfall.

Heavenly Father, I owe Thee endless thanks.

She looked out the window again, her attention drawn to the castle's approach. The main gate and sturdy gatehouse were now clouded by a storm of dust. It took her half a minute to make sense of the unwelcome sight . . .

British dragoons?

Nay. Stricken, Blythe whirled away from the window, her hard-won peace shattering. Breathless with distress, she made it to the door to find Everard striding down the corridor, the maids in his wake.

His eyes were alive with alarm, but his voice was calm. "Go with your women to the chapel and wait for me there." It was no less than a command.

He turned away, and she did the same, hastening toward the flower-strewn building where Reverend Johnston surely waited.

But would there be a wedding?

Everard stood at the foot of the cedar staircase, having summoned Munro and Boyd and his most able-bodied footmen at the dragoons' first sighting. When their clamor reached the castle's entrance, Everard strapped on his sword as Boyd and Munro went outside to ask their business.

Returning, Boyd told him, "Captain Agnew of the Royal Regiment of Horse Guards requests to see you, milord."

Requested? Rather, demanded, Everard wagered. "The Blues," he replied, on account of the distinctive color of their uniform.

"Aye, milord. And the captain seems in high temper. They're a large body, some eighty or so, all armed to the teeth."

"Let him in, but only Agnew, ye ken."

With a nod, Boyd moved toward the castle door, a dozen servants behind him lest the entire company try to force their way in. Munro stood just outside the main entrance to keep an eye on them lest they try to gain access another way.

In minutes, Captain Agnew stood before him, the door locked behind him, the castle's wary footmen on either side.

Everard faced him, twenty feet from the flagstone entrance. "What brings you unannounced to my door?"

The captain drew up stiffly. "I am here at the behest of His Majesty and his ministers to apprehend Lady Hedley of Northumbria."

"On what grounds?"

"Her father is an enemy of the Crown, a traitor at large, and needs be her ladyship answer for his conduct or serve as proxy till the duke's own arrest be made."

"'Tis a fool's errand." Everard rested his hand on his sword hilt. "I would be cut to pieces first."

At once Agnew drew his sword, but not before Everard's steel tip had slashed away a button on the captain's coat sleeve. It fell to the flagstones with a staccato pop, a none-too-subtle warning.

Fire flared in Agnew's eyes. Still, he seemed to hesitate before he engaged. Everard immediately parried, the ring of steel nigh deafening in the echoing chamber. At the captain's next thrust, Everard caught his sword by the hilt and flipped it into the air. The weapon clattered onto the cedar staircase behind him. He kept his eye on Agnew lest he reach for his pistol. At Everard's signal, Boyd confiscated the fallen sword.

A bit breathless, Everard sheathed his own sword, his mind on Blythe and this untimely interruption on so hallowed a day.

"Lord Wedd . . ." With a low moan, the captain swayed, took a step backwards, and collapsed.

"Wheest!" Boyd said as the intruder landed in an ungracious heap.

Kneeling, Everard found the captain's pulse. Agnew was the white of his sweat-soaked linen sark. "He's likely been in the saddle since dawn and needs to slake his thirst, among other things."

Turning the captain on his side, Everard carefully examined him. The plaited hair on the back of his head was warm with blood. Not a serious blow, it seemed, though there was a slight gash from the flagstones, giving rise to veiled amusement among the hovering footmen.

"Ye scairt him tae death, milord, yer sword aside," Graham said, his words meeting with muted laughter.

Everard stood and called for clean cloths and water, not wanting to delay a moment longer. "When Captain Agnew comes to his senses, bring him a dram of our finest whisky and keep an eye on him here in the foyer. If he has a hankering to eat, feed him. I've a wedding to attend."

59

If passion drives you, let reason hold the reins.

BENJAMIN FRANKLIN

Blythe waited near the chapel's altar, her senses swimming in the perfume of countless blooms as Reverend Johnston paged through the Bible with unsteady hands. By her side was Elodie, Ronan opposite them alongside Orin and Bernard. The chapel was still, but Blythe could not quiet her own rapid heartbeat. Head bent, she prayed silently but passionately.

Lord, deliver us. Let us at least be united in holy matrimony, no matter what happens.

Who could have anticipated their wedding day beset by dragoons? 'Twas like a fairy tale gone horribly awry. Opening her eyes, she prayed on, her pleas for her groom's protection foremost as Orin fidgeted and Bernard cast anxious glances at the chapel's narthex, where Everard would likely enter.

Or wouldn't he?

The creak of a door alerted them. When the laird finally appeared, they all seemed to heave a collective sigh. He walked toward them with a slight smile, his eyes for Blythe alone. She took a few steps in his direction, assessing every inch of his person to ascertain he was all right.

"Everard . . ." Her anxious gaze fell from his composed features to his suit. A telling crimson stain dotted his buff-colored coat sleeve, doubling her fears. "You've blood on your fine garments."

"My apologies." He looked at the stain absently. "All is well."

Taking her free hand, he returned her to the front of the chapel. At his urging, the reverend commenced the long-awaited ceremony.

Blythe tried to be fully present. She tore her gaze from the soiled jacket, thinking not of dragoons at their door or what might happen next. Had he sent them away—with a warning?

". . . promise to keep her, to love and entreat her in all things according to the duty of a faithful husband, forsaking all others during her life . . . to live in holy conversation with her, keeping faith and troth in all points . . ."

She marveled at her groom's calm. His apparent joy. She fixed her gaze on the white heather adorning his coat, a token of protection, good fortune, and wishes coming true. But at the moment they needed far more than Scottish lore to bolster them. The flowers in her own hand trembled slightly, the petals shivering as if from cold.

When Everard placed a ring on the third finger of her left hand, she marveled. She'd not known he was to give her a ring. And what a ring it was, of gold with the Wedderburn crest encrusted in tiny, glittering diamonds. A seal of sorts. His eyes told her there was no mistaking who she belonged to.

Never in her wildest imaginings had she dreamed of this day, or so noble a groom. A happiness she'd never known shimmered inside her as she looked into his eyes. She'd never felt more alive, her full heart near bursting. She was so moved by turns she almost couldn't speak.

The vows were finished, the final blessing given. Was it her imagination, or was everything conducted a bit more hastily than usual? Increasingly wary, Blythe returned her groom's kiss with the realization that this might be their last embrace.

The intimacy ended all too soon. Everard kept hold of her hand and told the reverend how matters stood as his brothers left to see how the captain was faring at the entrance. With a reassuring squeeze to Blythe's arm, Elodie followed Ronan.

"I believe I shall take you up on your gracious offer to enjoy the festivities with some of my flock," Johnston said with an admirably calm smile. "Let me know if I can be of assistance with your, um, uninvited guests."

Alone now in the narthex, Everard looked down at Blythe. "I will not lie to you, Countess. Matters are grave."

"Meaning I must continue my sojourn in the school of calamity," she replied, steeling herself.

"Your wit becomes you and will stand you in good stead."

"Let me guess. The head of the dragoons displeased you and you put him in his place."

"Aye. But 'twas not enough to rid us of him and his fellows."

"They have come either for me or for you. Which is it?"

"They have come for you in the name of the king, determined to flush your faither from hiding. But I believe this also has to do with me, forcing my hand to join government troops against the Jacobite threat."

"Am I to be their prisoner, then? If so, where will I be taken?"

He seemed more grieved than she'd ever seen him. "Either Edinburgh or London. The captain has not yet told me."

"Where is he?"

"Cooling his heels at the entrance with a guard of footmen and the like—and as much whisky as he can hold." His fingers grazed her flushed cheek. "I shan't leave you. We may be separated at some point, but I'll do all within my power to free you, including riding to London and demanding an audience with the king."

London. Some four hundred miles south. But what recourse did they have?

"I would go quietly if unwillingly," she said. "One does not defy the king without grave consequences."

"Mayhap it behooves us to comply at present, aye. Though I put up a merry fight at first."

"No wonder the king wants you on his side."

"Taking my bride from me is not the way to go about it."

"From all accounts, His Majesty is ruthless and will force your hand if only to have his way."

"I refuse to give in to their demands. You have done nothing wrong." He looked toward a near door. "I could have you hidden. There are secret rooms. Let them tear up the castle and they'd not find you—"

"Nay." She pressed a finger to his lips. "I would be as hunted as my father, then. Such would only incense the dragoons and put yourself and others here in danger."

His eyes glittered. How handsome he was, even riled. There was a steely determination about him, as much as a desire to shield her at any cost. Even to his own detriment or demise.

She breathed in the heady scent of her bouquet, suddenly sad. "Unfortunately, we are dealing with a king whose own wife has been imprisoned for years on what many believe is a false charge. He is not in his right mind. His treatment of his enemies is merciless. Let us not add to their number."

He expelled a breath. "We are wed. That cannot be taken from us."

"I'd best ready myself, then." She began to remove her tiara, but he stayed her hands, his warm gaze admiring.

"Leave it. Let them be reminded of the noblewoman you are. The bonnie Countess of Wedderburn."

⸺∝∾⸺

Even as strains of fiddle music erupted in the Great Hall, Wedderburn's coach hurtled down the long castle drive, Blythe and her maids within, the laird riding alongside on Lancelot. Surrounding them were dragoons, a full military escort for all the wrong reasons. Back to Edinburgh they went, traveling a different road than they'd taken before, this one as rutted and jarring as their shifting circumstances.

All the elation of the morning had drained out of Blythe, her final memory upon leaving that of the gaily decorated Great Hall and the servants who'd been given leave to start celebrating. Naturally,

332

many of them appeared doleful as the Hume coach was brought round to the front of the castle and the bride and groom departed on something other than a honeymoon.

Captain Agnew, florid of face, his hand bandaged and his uniform missing a button, hardly looked at her when she came into the courtyard, her women trailing. "Lady Hedley, I presume," he said, giving a nearly nonexistent bow.

"The Countess of Wedderburn," Everard corrected.

Agnew inclined his head as Blythe glanced over his shoulder to the mounted dragoons. "Am I truly a prisoner, Captain?" she asked, testing the waters.

"On the order of His Majesty the king, aye." He had the grace to look a tad shamefaced. "I am simply doing his bidding, milady. The matter has to do with your father, an avowed enemy of the Crown."

She took this without flinching, having had time to come to terms with all the implications, as Mari packed some of her belongings in a small trunk.

Now, as she tried to sit comfortably atop the upholstered seat, her voluminous wedding dress seemed to take up more of the coach than it should. Opposite her, a dressed-up Mari and Peg eyed her with a mixture of shock and sympathy.

"I'm heartily sorry you cannot stay for the wedding festivities," Blythe told them, meaning every word. They served unstintingly and without complaint. They deserved some merriment, not this.

"Milady, think nothing of it," Mari told her, tears in her eyes. "I was bound and determined to accompany ye."

Peg sniffed, yanking her petticoat free of the door. "I'm praying those dragoons have an ill-scrappit time of it all the way to Auld Reekie."

"Who could have done this to yer ladyship?" Mari asked, digging for her handkerchief.

"I know not," Blythe said, sorting through the persons and suspicions in her mind.

Her father had been named as the cause for her arrest. Was all this truly a means to lure him out of hiding and thereby deprive the Jacobites of one of their foremost supporters and activists? Had David Hume something to do with it? His recent appearance left her wondering. But Everard told her he'd given no hint of her identity, nor did David ask. Might Reverend Johnston have said or done anything, even unwittingly, ahead of their nuptials? Or had Alison and her father found out?

Blythe opened the coach shade, unmindful of the dust. Her eyes fastened on Everard flanked by Bernard and Boyd, all armed and looking grim. Aggravated.

Blythe wondered the hour. She had not thought to bring her timepiece. With Edinburgh still distant, they might overnight at some coaching inn along the way.

Her wedding night.

Surrounded by soldiers was not how she'd envisioned spending it.

They rode on past dusk, the lights of East Lothian piercing the gloaming. After so many miles the soldiers seemed weary, even restless. Captain Agnew's color remained high, perhaps on account of the whisky's lingering power. Or his humiliation? At full dark he called a halt to their journey before an inn, and the laird and Bernard dismounted under the watchful eye of the dragoons.

She looked on as Everard spoke with Bernard and Boyd beneath the lantern-lit eave. Everard was no stranger to the proprietor, who'd greeted him by name and apologized that he lacked better accommodations. Blythe emerged from the coach and was led upstairs by a tavern maid to the inn's best room, a cramped if clean chamber overlooking a well and the Mercat Cross at the heart of town.

Supper was brought up to her, and though she tried to eat of the well-seasoned mutton and tatties, she had little appetite. All the while she listened for Everard's footfall. In the tumult of their arrival, she'd wondered if they might have separate lodgings. Then she overheard the captain's cryptic comment.

"I'll not deprive your lordship of both his wedding day *and* night," Agnew said after posting a guard outside the inn's main doors and windows. Like as not, he didn't want to earn the laird's ire should he find himself serving under him in a Jacobite rebellion, so, mindful of his rank, he allowed this concession.

Glad she'd bathed that morning, Blythe washed the dust away when warm water and fresh linens were brought. Mari helped her undress while Peg readied her nightclothes. A special nightgown had been sewn, the creamy linen edged with the most delicate lace. A tiny sponge and mint paste freshened Blythe's teeth. Amazingly, Mari had thought of everything, as if this were none other than a proper wedding journey.

"Halfway to Edinburgh," Peg said, hanging up Blythe's wedding gown in the wardrobe. "Mari and I shall be across the hall should ye need us, mem."

Mari gave a small curtsy. "Take heart, milady. God goes with ye. And ye've got the ablest of earthly protectors besides."

Such heartening truths. Blythe smiled at the maids as they shut the door, their soft footsteps giving way to more pronounced ones. Suddenly self-conscious, Blythe climbed into the bed that did not look near big enough for both her and the laird. A sole candle flickered on the mantel. She lay back upon a bank of pillows as the doorknob turned.

Everard?

She held her breath. To be alone with him at last, though in a noisy, overflowing inn . . . Thankfully, the taproom was at the other end of the building and they'd been given a quiet corner.

Everard came in, locking the door behind him, his head nearly touching the low ceiling. "And how is my bonnie bride?"

"Mightily glad to see you," she said.

He drew near the edge of the bed, shrugging off his stained wedding coat. After draping it across a chairback, he began to unbuckle the linen stock about his neck.

"Are you tired?" she asked.

"Nae. Crabbit. And you?"

"Bewildered." She bit her lip. "I suppose there are guards posted."

"Thankfully not outside our very door, though there's a sergeant dozing at hall's end. Most of the dragoons on watch are on the ground surrounding the inn or bedding down in the stables."

"I'm sorry, Everard."

"Dinna be." He lapsed into broad Scots, which she now better understood and found charming. He went to the washstand and poured fresh water from the ewer to the basin. "They canna stop me from enjoying my bride. I'm going to lie down and put my arms around you. And pray."

She nearly laughed. "How like a Puritan you sound."

"Wheest." He gave her another of his old searing glances before he snuffed the candle. "I feel very unpuritanical tonight."

In the semidarkness the tick of her heart grew loud as the mantel clock. Clasping her palms together, she found them slightly damp and cold. But all that was forgotten when Everard sank down beside the bed instead of atop the feather mattress. She blinked, thinking the darkness deceived her. Never had she seen a grown man other than a priest in so humble a posture. Much less a nobleman.

Did desperation drive him to his knees? Or was this his usual practice? Her heart squeezed with a tenderness she'd never known. How much she had to learn about this new husband of hers.

"O Lord, open Thou our lips and our mouths shall shew forth praise. O God, make speed to save. Lord, make haste to help. Glory be to the Faither, and to the Son, and to the Holy Ghost. As it was in the beginning, is now and ever shall be, world without end. Amen."

She echoed "Amen" as the bed groaned beneath his weight. Turning on her side toward him, she pillowed her head atop one arm. He rolled toward her, and the bed settled. Nearly nose to nose with him, she shivered with delight at his nearness.

"You wear a lovelock," he murmured, looking at her hair worn over one shoulder and tied with a ribbon rosette.

336

"An auld custom I find romantic," she said softly. "The tiara is hidden away in my belongings."

He pulled gently at the ribbon, and her hair fell free onto the linens between them like an ell of yellow silk. His fingers stroked the length of it, then he kissed her bare shoulder where her nightgown had slipped. "Soft as a rose petal. How is it you carry the scent of roses all about you?"

"I would be at my best for my bridegroom." She touched his own nightshirt, the linen smooth against her searching fingers. "If I am a rose, then you are . . . Castile soap and mulled cider."

The cares of the day began to fade in the unspeakable joy of his presence. From somewhere below, a distant fiddle struck a robust tune, but she hardly heard it.

Everard kissed her long and lingeringly, his words coming between caresses. "I promise you . . . a proper honeymoon . . . in time."

"This moment is all that matters," she said breathlessly. "I shan't be your countess in name only."

60

London is the devil's drawing room.

TOBIAS SMOLLETT

rapped in thick haar from the windswept coast, Edinburgh Castle loomed over the city in shades of funereal grey. Rain washed down, turning the streets into a running river of mud. Blythe alighted from the coach with the laird's help, her windblown skirts held above the muck once they'd gained admittance to the castle's courtyard. To be inside rather than outside those high gates lined her soul with lead. That David Hume had been here before her somehow made matters worse.

"Have nae fear," Everard said, watching over her like one of the king's Life Guards.

Bernard and Boyd looked on, their hats pulled low against the rain, their cloaks sodden. The castle's dark stone was a dismal backdrop. Through the rain and haar, a little stone chapel embraced by fortress walls was visible, its stained-glass windows the only bit of color about them. Blythe wished that was their destination.

Everard noticed her scrutiny. "Built for the young queen of Malcolm III, a Northumbrian lass."

"St. Margaret, known for her kindness and charity." Blythe knew the history well and was struck by its irony. "'Tis said her unread warrior of a husband so loved her he kissed the books she cherished and had them ornamented with gold and jewels." The touching memory was eclipsed by their sad fate. Had not her beloved husband and son died in battle and she died of heartbreak not long after? Tears close, Blythe dared not make more of the sad tale than she ought.

In moments, the castle's governor greeted them respectfully but tersely. He closeted himself with Captain Agnew while Blythe and Everard waited in an antechamber. A servant brought refreshments that were meager but still appreciated.

Blythe regarded her bridegroom, the pleasures of their wedding night still uppermost in her mind and heart. Some of the most blissful hours of her life had just been spent in an inelegant little inn, surrounded by soldiers. Never would she forget it. The bittersweet memory would bolster her in the days to come.

The castle's governor entered the antechamber. "Lord Wedderburn, may I speak with you?" They in turn were closeted, leaving Blythe alone with her women, a guard at the door.

"I do wonder what they're going on about," Peg said in low tones, eyes roaming the chamber.

"Perhaps we shall be told to return home—*all* of us," Mari whispered. "Perhaps there's been some terrible mistake."

Blythe forced a smile, determined to not fail Everard but face what came with fortitude and dignity.

"How are ye keeping, milady?" Mari asked, digging in her pocket for a vial of hartshorn and taking a whiff of it.

"Better than I've ever been," Blythe said, admiring the ring encircling her finger. "Nothing can mar the joy of being happily married to Lord Wedderburn."

"Spoken like a true countess," Peg said, admiration in her eyes.

The men reappeared with a bailiff, the keys at his waist making a dull clanking.

Everard came to her and took her in his arms. "Your women will stay with you at all times. If you lack for anything, alert the castle's keeper. Bernard will lodge in the Canongate mansion and come to the castle daily while I'm away to make certain all is well with you. I'll ride on to London as there's nae time to waste."

To London could mean but one thing. He would seek an audience with the king. She rested her head against his chest for an instant, trying to come to terms with his leaving and his mission. "Safeguard yourself. Return to me as soon as possible."

He tipped her chin up with one gentle hand, looking for all the world like he wanted to kiss her but for their audience. "Remember whose you are."

"Yours," she replied without hesitation.

"Mine without question. But the Almighty's foremost."

And so I must bide awhile in the tower.

Blythe's gaol was as stark as practicality could make it. A single bed. A chair and desk. An arrow slit of a window. In winter, the small hearth could offer but meager warmth, another reason to give thanks she was here in summer instead. Oddly, she slept soundly that first night, her maids near at hand atop pallets on either side of her.

She awoke early to the sound of a dove cooing. The wind had risen, the sighs and groans of the old castle foreign. She'd grown used to those at Wedderburn and had begun to anticipate the creak of a door or a stair. But here . . .

She had fresh sympathy for all those before her who had been hemmed in unjustly by these walls.

Never had London seemed so distant. Four hundred miles stretched endlessly south on the well-traveled Great North Road, haunt of highwaymen and dubious coaching inns. Everard rode like a man possessed, pressing Lancelot nearly beyond endurance. At last a beleaguered Boyd begged him to stop.

"Milord," he said, breathing hard, sweat spackling his features.

"Ye'll do yer cause nae good to arrive undone even if King Geordie has got yer affairs in a fankle."

Everard slowed, swallowing the dust in his mouth with a swig from his canteen. Hard-pressed to contain his mounting fury, he gave way to a rare rant. "Here is my reward for a decade's service to the Crown. Flying to London to beg mercy of a foreign king while my bride bides her time in a tower fit for felons."

Lancelot spun around, kicking up more dust, ever attuned to his master's mood.

"Never have I regretted Queen Anne's death more, and this ensuing debacle."

Boyd expelled a breath and eyed him gravely, clearly shaken. Everard rued the outburst and felt no better after. Mumbling a prayer, he took in the steeple of a distant kirk with the latent realization they must eat and tend to their horses. Again. He'd begun to lose track of time on the road away from Blythe. She was beginning to seem like naught but a dream.

He was weary. Hungry. Heartsore. All a-tangle. In no mood to bow and scrape before courtiers and king. But bow and scrape he must.

———

Someone bore the Countess of Wedderburn neé Lady Hedley a grudge. Her first meal was served on a rude tray, a thin gruel with a moldy biscuit. Peg's and Mari's were the same. All stared down at the fare, hard-pressed to give thanks.

In the ensuing shock, Peg finally said, "Och, such treatment of a duke's daughter and now a countess!"

Blythe held her spoon aloft, more nauseous than ravenous after the tumult of the last hours. "I am most sorry for the two of you suffering on my account."

Both maids were quick to protest, but no one ate, which only insulted their gaolers, Blythe suspected. Would another meal be forthcoming? If so, it couldn't be any worse.

That afternoon after Bernard visited, they were denied the customary walk about the prison yard in fresh air and sunlight. A dismayed Peg stood by the window watching other prisoners allowed the liberty. Blythe bit her tongue to keep from complaining. It would earn her no favors.

Meanwhile they took their embroidery nearer the window. Tallow candles smoked and sputtered, emitting their rancid odor, which sharpened Blythe's appreciation for Wedderburn's finer beeswax tapers. The light barely penetrated the gloomy chamber, the sun refusing to shine.

Everard.

Never did he fade from her thoughts. She stitched and kept his memory close. Her prayers seemed strung together like rosary beads, though she'd forsaken her Catholicism.

Lord, please hedge my husband in behind and before and place Thy hand of blessing on his head.

Reduced to ruins then slowly rebuilt after the great fire almost fifty years before, London had a shine and polish Edinburgh lacked. Britain's largest city was laid out upon the River Thames, its medieval origins muted, its crown jewel the lofty St. Paul's Cathedral with its distinctive cupola and towers. Among the spreading cobbled streets and narrow alleys were a great many tradesmen and silk producers but far more of the poor. Destitution ruled the day, causing Everard a few pangs and more than a few pence.

"Ye'll soon become empty-pocketed here," Boyd said. "The king himself couldn't save all the beggars."

Everard recalled the Hedleys had a terraced townhouse in St. James Square—or once did. If not for their present predicament, he'd go there. For now his lodgings would be the King's Arms. He looked at the timeworn Latin inscription on the lintel.

Constrivssit. Rest awhile.

Boyd heaved a sigh. "Exceedingly fine words tae this wearied Scot."

But Everard could not rest till he had seen the king and won Blythe's release. For now, another night was to be had while he wondered how Blythe fared in Edinburgh. If only she could have lodged under house arrest at the Hume mansion in the Canongate or moved to nearby Holyrood Palace. But his request had fallen on deaf ears.

God Almighty, what am I to do?

Many seek the ruler's favour; but every man's judgment cometh from the Lord.

The Scripture seemed to hang upon the inn's smoke-filled air, convicting and comforting him in one swoop. He rested his hand on the hilt of his sword as the innkeeper entered his name in the ledger.

28 August 1715, Earl Wedderburn.

Everard and Boyd took their supper in the inn's crowded dining room, then passed into a smaller, emptier parlor. Periodicals lay on tables, numerous headlines in boldface. Boyd reached for the latest issue of the *Proceedings*, the published trial accounts from the Old Bailey. The fireless hearth bore testament to the sulky weather, sweat still limning his brow.

Feeling a foreigner amid so many Englishmen, Everard selected an old issue of *The Spectator* and took a seat near a half-open window, unwilling to retire to his room just yet. A parliamentary clock ticked along one papered wall, and his attention drifted to the Thames just beyond the window. Watermen ferried back and forth on the rain-dimpled river, their passengers hunched against the damp in hooded cloaks, a few lasses holding parasols.

Unable to concentrate, he watched as a burly printer selling picture cards packed up his wares while an aged woman displaying hand fans remained. She looked a bit downcast, silken cords dangling from her wrists, the fans fluttering in the damp air.

Blythe had a fondness for fans.

With a word to Boyd, who sat immersed in his reading, Everard left the parlor and passed through the inn's hall to the front door. Coaches and sedan chairs hurried past beyond its stone steps at breakneck speed. Navigating the crowded road was no small feat, but Everard schooled his patience and awaited a lull, avoiding horse droppings and mud puddles. Street traders continued to shout in chorus all around him.

"Fair lemons and oranges!"

"Four for sixpence, mackerel!"

But a fan was all he wanted.

The wrinkled seller smiled at him. "Have you come for a fair lady, sir, who covets a treasure from the Worshipful Company of Fan Makers?"

"My countess, aye," he replied, eyeing her many wares.

"Ah, and a Scottish one from the sounds of it. This artistry from the Strand might do." She opened a fan with a map of London in vivid hues on its leaves. "Created by a master fan maker. Ivory sticks. Painted vellum leaf. With a scene of St. James Palace and the Thames on the other side." With a little flourish she fluttered the extended fan and showed him. "Worthy of your lady, surely."

He examined others in her collection, then decided on the first after all. She produced a rectangular case and carefully returned the fan to its velvet-lined box. Despite the gnawing anguish of his missing Blythe, buying her even a small token somehow assuaged him.

61

*In private life he would have been called
an honest blockhead.*

LADY MARY WORTLEY MONTAGUE,
SPEAKING OF GEORGE I

At dawn, a waterman ferried Everard and Boyd down the serpentine Thames past the ruins of Whitehall. The immense palace was once said to have been the largest in Europe but had been reduced to ruins in the previous century. The abode of Blythe's mother, so she'd told him. Kensington Palace now reigned supreme, its gardens spread over acres where courtiers and London's elite promenaded in warmer months. Everard walked the distance to it, turning a blind eye to the beauty, his thoughts firmly fixed on Blythe.

What had transpired in his absence? He craved her conversation. Her softness and scent. The profound comfort of her presence.

Red-coated guards admitted them to the palace once Everard stated his rank and his business. He'd dressed carefully as befitted his station, knowing lesser-dressed men were denied entrance no matter their rank. His sword hung heavy, reminding him of his confrontation with Captain Agnew on his wedding morn.

He climbed the staircase that led to the king's apartments with Boyd in his wake. In time they gained the privy stairs, which connected to endless rooms and corridors and antechambers, before reaching the presence chamber where the king would grant him an audience.

Or not.

Was Sir Clive in London? If so, he'd likely be in this very palace or in Westminster, the seat of government and Parliament. As it was, the most important personages seemed grouped by rank. Everard was not the only earl present and waiting, but he was among the first. Around them were a great many ministers of state, nobles, and courtiers, even the two Turkish servants the king was said to prefer.

An hour passed. Then two. Boyd fidgeted and his stomach rumbled. Everard fought his compulsion to constantly check the clock.

When it seemed their time had finally come and the line behind them grew longer than the line ahead of them, a liveried servant appeared and announced in loud tones, "His Majesty is fatigued and will have no further audiences today."

The next day brought a repeat of the day before. Everard's every nerve was on end, his ongoing prayer that they gain access and not be sent away a second time. Slowly they inched nearer the palace's gilded door, and a prim-faced page acknowledged them at last.

The bewigged servant looked Everard up and down, clearly inspecting his person. "You are aware, Lord Wedderburn, that you must observe the three reverences."

"Speak plainly, then, lest I offend His Majesty."

With a little huff, he returned to a look of boredom. "Upon entering the king's presence, you must bow low from the waist. Once you have advanced halfway across the room, you bow again facing His Majesty. A final bow is required directly before the throne. Once your audience has concluded, you repeat the three reverences as you leave. At no point whatsoever do you turn your back on the king."

"And will His Majesty speak to me in English?"

"Nay, Lord Wedderburn. He communicates in French and German, the latter being his preference."

George of Hanover would never make sense of his Scots. And he himself would never make peace with palace protocol. "An interpreter is needed, then," Everard said.

"Of course." The page signaled to another servant and then turned back to Everard. "A final caution. Your valet must remain directly outside the chamber until you exit."

"Good, that." Boyd scratched his ear and murmured, "If not for Lady Wedderburn, I wouldna bow and scrape to any but God Almighty."

Everard tucked his hat beneath his left arm as custom required. The gilded double doors opened. There was no one before him now. With a prayer on his lips, he eyed the poker-faced footmen on either side of him and entered the presence chamber.

After performing the requisite reverences, Everard came face-to-face with the reigning monarch of England, Scotland, and Ireland. For all his regal attire and the enormous wig that added height and covered his supposedly bald head, the Hanoverian king was squat, heavy-jawed, and middle-aged. Unsmiling, he looked up at Everard, his bulging blue gaze falling to the sword at his side.

Was he somehow privy to Everard's swordplay with Captain Agnew?

Also armed, His Majesty's Life Guards were near at hand. The king was not popular. Since his coronation, rioting continued in parts of the kingdom, though two things remained in his favor. He wasn't Catholic and he certainly wasn't a Stuart.

The king said something in German. The interpreter to his right seemed amused. Everard waited, wishing to come to the heart of the matter, but protocol forbade him to speak unless spoken to. Rank ruled within and without palace walls, and he himself was but an earl.

"His Majesty says you have the mettle of William Wallace about you."

So the German knew their stormy history. The legendary Scottish knight, a formidable soldier known for his height as well as his battlefield exploits, had been an avowed enemy of the English Crown. "I can but claim Somerled, king of the Scots, in my lineage."

The interpreter translated clumsily and appeared exasperated. "Can you speak no German, French, or Italian, Lord Wedderburn?"

"Not well enough to state my case. My wife, however, is fluent in them all, and I am here on her behalf."

The king took his time answering. "Who is the Countess of Wedderburn?"

"The former Lady Blythe Hedley of Northumbria," Everard said without expression—or apology.

A spattering of German volleyed back and forth between the king and his interpreter. If Everard ever longed to speak the strange, guttural tongue, 'twas now. George of Hanover looked displeased, which made his countenance all the more repugnant.

At last he said, "Not all Scottish marriages are recognized as legal under English law in English courts."

Everard schooled his temper. "The rites were performed by a recognized church official but five days ago."

"Scottish clergy." The interpreter turned as sour as the king. "The very legitimacy of your children is in question, Lord Wedderburn."

Children. This gave Everard pause. After one wondrous night at the inn, might Blythe be carrying his child?

The interpreter continued in clipped English tones. "Upon His Majesty's orders, Lady Hedley resides in Edinburgh Tower."

Everard kept his attention on the king. "I have come here seeking her release." He spoke slowly and respectfully. "I would have her return home to her rightful place at Wedderburn Castle in Berwickshire as soon as possible."

Silence. And then another side conversation. The king blinked rapidly at the interpreter's frequent pauses. Never had a language barrier been so painful, so prolonged and infuriating.

"Lady Hedley's father is an enemy to the Crown, a threat to the kingdom. She has been taken prisoner in lieu of Northumbria, who has eluded arrest. Until he surrenders himself, she will continue as a prisoner in his stead."

"Lady Wedderburn has done nothing deserving of Your Majesty's displeasure," Everard said.

"Still, she must answer for her father. And you, Lord Wedderburn, must take your place against the enemies of this kingdom who would see a return to Catholic rule under the Stuart Pretender, a traitor who seeks to reign with the aid of the enemy French."

"I have proved my loyal service during the reign of Queen Anne. Recently bereaved of my faither, I seek nothing more than to return to Scotland and live quietly as laird with Lady Wedderburn alongside me."

"As a knight of the Order of the Thistle, you are required to take up the standard of your rightful king." The king's German grew louder and more insistent, as did the interpreter's English in turn. "Return to Berwickshire and raise men enough to assist in the coming Jacobite suppression, and prepare to march with your battalions to join the Duke of Argyll when the moment presents itself."

God forbid.

"I shall do as Your Majesty desires." Everard's tone was amiable but insistent. "Upon the condition my wife be returned to me beforehand."

The king stared at him as the words were translated. A moody silence ensued, and then he signaled the meeting was at an end.

Everard and Boyd left London as the heavens opened and another summer downpour pelted them. Soon sodden, Everard barely felt the rain, his heart full of Blythe, his head full of the king. His audience at Kensington Palace was only hours old, but his desire to leave the city as soon as possible and return to his beloved was foremost.

There was no way to measure the king's whims and dictates. If he released Blythe, when would he? If he didn't, what then?

Everard laid out a plan as he galloped up the Great North Road.

He'd reside in the Canongate mansion till her release from the tower. If her freedom was contingent on his raising troops, he had no choice but to raise them.

But first, Blythe.

———— ∞∞ ————

Moonlight limned the castle's forbidding exterior, the stone black by night except for tiny pinpricks of light. Everard's head was a-thunder, his throat parched. If not for Boyd, he'd have hardly eaten or slept. Half-crazed he was, haunted by another woman in another tower over the water. England's lost queen, some called her.

It bespoke cruelty. Vindictiveness. Abuse of power.

With effort, Everard pushed the thoughts to the back of his conscience, intent on the tower on the hill. Though it was nearly midnight, the city pulsed with life. Horse hooves and carriage wheels clattered past as alehouses overflowed.

All he wanted was to retire to the Canongate mansion and find his beloved waiting.

Boyd held the horses outside the gates while Everard announced himself to the night guard. A clank of keys and rusted hinges admitted him. He looked up from the cobbles to the tower where he'd left her. No light shone. She was abed, likely. But he couldn't wait. He needed to see her. To hold her if only for a few moments and reassure himself she was all right.

He started toward the tower.

"Lord Wedderburn." A voice behind him made him turn. Hamilton, the castle's governor, walked toward him.

Light shone in Everard's eyes as the man held his lantern high to identify him. Mud-spattered from the weather, he was hardly presentable for his bride, let alone the governor.

Hamilton lowered the lantern to his side. "Lady Wedderburn is nae longer here. Two days after you departed, word came from London. At the king's command she was removed from Edinburgh to an unknown location by appointed guards. I know not where she is."

The unexpected words held the force of a fist. "You ken nothing?"

"Nothing."

"Does anyone else here ken anything?" Disbelief and raw, overwhelming anguish colored his searching words. "Anything at all?"

"Nae."

"Who was in charge of Lady Hed—the Countess of Wedderburn's removal from this place?" Everard's voice was louder than he intended, but he no longer cared. Every frayed nerve widened to outright desperation and a fury that threatened to pummel any in his path. Stepping forward, he raised a fist. "Who, I ask you!"

Hamilton took a step back, lantern swinging. "'Twould seem, your lordship, that the king is determined your wife's father come forward. Her bondage is but bait to secure it. That much we understand. And lest that not happen soon, Lady Wedderburn's future is grim indeed."

62

We are twice armed if we fight with faith.

PLATO

Everard rode down the High Street to the Canongate mansion as if in a trance. Edinburgh's town guard roamed, seeking cutthroats and vagabonds in the myriad wynds and closes, but Everard was only aware of the weary horse plodding beneath him and his own shattered situation.

Boyd usually followed close on his heels, always on the lookout for trouble in the wee small hours. But no other rider plodded alongside Everard until, in a huff, Boyd caught up with him.

"Milord—" The words came in winded bursts. "Ye ken the blether around the castle? That the Landreth lass and her faither found ye out and betrayed ye to curry favor with the king."

Everard looked hard at him, weighing the ugly accusation. "I dinna doubt it."

A lantern burned at the front of the townhouse, and Boyd's loud pounding of the iron knocker roused the butler. A stable lad saw to the horses, saying little as if sensing their mood.

Everard entered the hall with a few wooden words of greeting, inquiring about Bernard.

"Your brother is abed," the housekeeper said. "He sent word to

London about the countess's removal from Edinburgh. Did the message never reach you?"

"Nay," Everard said, jaw clenched. He went up to his bedchamber, knowing sleep could not be had this night even though he was stretched at the seams with exhaustion.

Every nook and cranny seemed full of Blythe. Blythe as she'd been at their last visit. Blythe dining with him. Blythe roaming the garden, the summerhouse particularly. Blythe in the library, where they'd overcome their hesitations and indulged in a heated embrace. Blythe who'd kept him up half the night with the realization he'd finally found his countess.

Never had he anticipated this turn of events.

A knock at the door admitted a footman with a tray containing whisky. He disappeared again as the clock struck one. Everard looked away from the window to the aqua vitae, his legs splayed out in front of him, his bulk sunk into the Windsor chair. No amount of spirits could dull the ache that twisted and writhed inside him.

He was a warrior without a weapon. A noble without a plan. A besotted husband in need of his bride. He did something he hadn't done since his mother died.

He wept.

Stirling Castle. 'Twas said to be akin to a large broach clasping Highlands and Lowlands together. Blythe mulled its hilltop perch and immense gatehouse with a growing desperation. It seemed the twin of Edinburgh Castle, another grey stone bully atop a cliff overlooking a picturesque watercourse she had no name for.

"'Tis the River Forth, milady," Mari said.

Travel there had taken two days over bad roads that left Mari ill and Peg wheezing. Hot and cold by turns, Blythe sat wordless in the lurching coach. She was a state prisoner, the mounted guard all around her making her feel like a criminal. Ashamed, hunted, and reviled.

As the coach approached the castle, Peg slammed the window shut, her mood more volatile the longer they were away from Wedderburn. For truly, were she and Mari not captive too? Blythe had entreated her Edinburgh gaoler for both women's release, but her plea was ignored. And though she wanted them to go free, she was exceedingly glad of their company. Peg was more zealous watchdog while Mari was more lamb, the one forever watchful, the other comfort and consolation. Both of them sorely needed.

"I wouldna dream of leaving ye, mem," Peg told her between fits of fury.

"Nor would I, Lady Wedderburn," Mari said quietly. "We shall share yer captivity—and yer return home. His lordship would expect nae less, nor would we."

Blythe tried to bring her wayward thoughts to heel. What would her father do once he learned of her plight? Surrender himself? And Everard? His pleas to the king may well have met with resistance. She could only imagine what would happen upon Everard's return to Edinburgh to find her gone. She sensed her whereabouts would be denied him.

When the coach rolled to a sudden halt, Blythe emerged into a stony courtyard, the sunlight lifting her spirits. There seemed to be some confusion among her guards, and she and her maids were made to wait while a soldier summoned someone within the castle.

In time, a tall, spare officer with russet hair appeared, flanked by two shorter men. His grey eyes met hers briefly, and then he gave a small bow. "Lady Hedley, I am told."

Captain Agnew stepped forward. "Now the Countess of Wedderburn, Colonel Campbell."

Straightening, Campbell regarded Blythe with thinly veiled surprise. "Is that true, your ladyship?"

"My husband is indeed Lord Wedderburn." She gave a nod, hoping she appeared more dignified than she felt. "We were recently wed in Berwickshire."

That date was easily recalled. Who could forget one's wedding day? But all the days since were a beleaguered blur.

"Has your husband any knowledge of your presence here?"

"I think not, sir. We were lately parted at Edinburgh Castle against our will. He rode on to London to meet with the king about my release."

Campbell turned aside to confer with the captain in low tones. She understood but a word here and there, new worries fraying her strength. At last he gestured to the three-story building to the left of the gatehouse. "Show the Countess of Wedderburn to the royal apartments."

At that, all seemed to regard her with new respect. These men were soldiers. Did they know Everard? Perhaps they had fought alongside him in the long war on the continent?

"So ye shan't be lodged like a common criminal," Peg said beneath her breath as they were escorted inside the castle.

"Such bodes well indeed, milady." Mari trailed behind her, relief trumping her obvious exhaustion.

Faded tapestries. Furniture spanning several centuries. Their heels tapped against the old wooden floorboards as they walked from room to room. Though she was thankful to be free of the cramped carriage, Blythe's stomach rumbled. What she'd give for a cup of tea and a bath.

She tried to put down the lovely image of her rooms at Wedderburn Castle. Though royal, these apartments were old and smelled of dust and disuse. She'd not shared Everard's chambers yet, and the longing she felt each time she thought of him tightened.

Peg, ever efficient, asked for hot water and tea before the guards left them. In time a maidservant appeared, bringing more than what they'd asked for. Blythe thanked her, good manners never amiss. She'd not be thought haughty but obliging, whatever their circumstances.

A tray held meat, cheese, bread, and the largest teapot Blythe had ever beheld, steam curling from its pewter spout. After washing, the women all but fell upon the fare before them, a veritable feast compared to the inedible victuals of Edinburgh.

Finished eating, Blythe went to a window, familiarizing herself with her surroundings and wondering if Stirling was as old as Edinburgh Castle. Stone lions and unicorns decorated the roof's ridge, and across from her sat a bright yellow building within castle walls, resembling a Great Hall. It stood out like a merry monarch among all the somber stone.

"Yer smitten with the color, nae doubt," Peg said. "Fit for a king or queen."

"A royal ochre, yes," Blythe replied. "'Tis startling against all the drab."

Her gaze traveled around their royal apartments, all her book learning returning to harass her. Stirling Castle was haunted, some said, by Mary, Queen of Scots, and her women attendants, the four Marys.

Blythe shivered, wishing for a fire in the hearth. This might well be the room of her doom. Hopelessness hung in the air along with a chill sense of foreboding. It gripped her like the fiercest of talons, making inroads where none had been before. She pressed cold fingers to her temples. She would go mad thinking such thoughts. She must not give way to the spirit of fear.

Strength and honour are her clothing; and she shall rejoice in time to come.

63

My heart keeps watch for one that's gone.

MARY, QUEEN OF SCOTS

As the days crawled by, the weather turned windy and held an autumnal chill. Peg demanded tapestries be brought to cover the drafty windows of their apartments. A pail of fresh milk and marchpane cakes appeared with their tea, and warm if smoky peat fires were lit. Also Peg's doing, no doubt.

Fingers sore and eyes burning from so much needlework, Blythe sat down in a velvet chair before the hearth while Mari served tea and Peg regarded Blythe with her usual searching gaze, as if her well-being was her special charge.

"Yer going to put yer eyes out with that needle." Peg's frown gave way to a snicker of devilry as she pulled something from her pocket. "So I've wheedled a deck o' cards from the guards."

"But we've no guineas or gaming table," Mari said, eyeing the well-worn stack.

"Hoot! Such doesna prevent us from a bit o' sport."

"'Twill be a welcome change," Blythe said, tasting her tea while Mari sampled the marchpane. "I played a great deal of whist and ombre while in France."

They lapsed into silence, the clip of horse hooves and the jangle of harnesses and the drone of soldiers in the courtyard never ending. Day or night, Stirling Castle never quieted.

Peg drew her plaid closer about her shoulders with a shiver. "If only the cold kept any war away."

Blythe didn't miss the disquiet in her tone. Peg was frequently among the guards in her comings and goings, always alert for news of the inevitable conflict and how it might play out for them personally.

"So, pray tell, what have ye heard this morn?" Mari asked yet again.

Peg huffed out a breath. "As of September's end, Lord Derwentwater—the Northumbrian earl—has taken charge of both Scots and English forces in the Borders."

James Radcliffe? *A friend of my father's,* Blythe didn't say. She waited, certain the gleam in Peg's eye promised more.

"'Tis said Davie Hume is leading a detachment of a thousand or more Highlanders preparing to march south to meet up with Lothian Lowlanders headed for Lancaster. A movement is afoot to secure the Borders against King Geordie's troops, who are said to be ten thousand strong."

As the words left her mouth, bagpipes skirled beneath their nearest window, gaining strength with every winded puff. They were followed by a cacophony of drums.

"Worse than a wailing sheep." Peg grimaced. "Surely Colonel Campbell has a better piper to lead a charge than that!"

The piper gained strength, the music smoother by the second as if demanding she take back the hasty criticism.

"More troops are gathering every day," Mari said, sipping from the pail of milk. "I watch the windows, I do, and have lost count of how many are camped around the base of the castle, thick as thieves."

Indeed, each moment seemed to draw them closer to some calamity, to the acrid stench of gunpowder and clash of basket-hilted broadswords. Blythe's head throbbed from more than a headache as questions pummeled her day and night.

Where in all this was her father? Was he even still alive, or had he been hunted down by the king's men by now? Had she herself been forgotten, if not by Everard then by the authorities who had the power to determine her fate? Where was her beloved husband?

"I'd rather talk of Wedderburn," Blythe said at last above the howling pipes. "And what a Berwickshire autumn is like."

"Och, 'tis a wonder once the heather ceases blooming and the winds sharpen." Peg's face softened. "By then the castle's stillroom is as abuzz as the bees whose honey has been stolen. A great many mushrooms are gathered, and the fruit trees are picked clean of ripe plums and apples and the like."

Blythe's longing to return sharpened. Everard had shown her the orchards stretching out beyond the south castle wall, planted in the auld laird's youth.

Mari sighed. "October in Edinburgh means oysters. Fresh or pickled, take yer pick. I'm as fond o' them as haggis."

Peg's head bobbed in agreement. "My hope is to be back at Wedderburn by the first frost. Christmastide and Hogmanay will delight yer heart, mem. There's nae better place to be."

Blythe's attention wandered to the tapestry she was working for her and Everard's bedchamber, perhaps to place over the mantel. The lover's knot of their initials was more pleasure than work, bringing her a quiet contentment, as did her wedding ring proclaiming her a Hume.

Blythe Hedley Hume, Countess of Wedderburn.

No matter what, she mustn't forget it. Peg, bless her, was determined the guards didn't either. But how conflicted was her standing! Wife of a respected soldier and peer of the realm, yet daughter to a man branded a traitor to the Crown.

Which had the most sway?

A knock at the door brought Peg and Mari to their feet. Blythe stayed seated while a well-dressed Colonel Campbell opened the door and stepped inside.

"Lady Wedderburn." He gave a courtly bow. "Might I have a word with you privately?"

Mari and Peg hastened into the next chamber and shut the door behind them. Campbell came nearer the fire, the table between them. His gaze fell on the empty cups and mostly eaten marchpane.

"Are your quarters comfortable, milady?"

"I've no complaint," Blythe said, the marchpane aswirl inside her. "Please, have a seat. Would you care for some tea? I can call for more hot water."

"What I need is a great deal stronger than tea, your ladyship." He took the chair Peg had vacated with a certain stiffness. From an old injury? His lean, aristocratic features bore a mapwork of fine wrinkles. Though he seemed no older than the laird, his years of soldiering were more telling.

"Aqua vitae, then." She reached beneath the table and produced the flask Peg kept for medicinal purposes. "The best of the Borders, Colonel."

"Thank you, milady." He took it, a brow lifting in amusement. A swallow later he even chuckled, the somberness in his face easing. "So here we sit, the Earl of Islay and the Countess of Wedderburn."

"Your title as well as your literary interests and achievements are not lost on me, milord. You're said to have one of the most valuable libraries in all of Britain."

"Which I am missing the longer I am away from it." He looked about the chamber, his gaze lingering on the books atop a side table. "Is that Dante I spy amid your reading?"

"*Paradiso*, yes. From the castle library."

He nodded, his grey gaze returning to her. "'Amor di vero ben, pien di letizia; letizia che trascende ogni dolzore.'"

His flawless Italian was easily translated. "Love of the truth, full of delight; delight that transcends every sweetness." She drew an uneasy breath. "Surely you haven't come here to discuss my taste in literature, Colonel."

"Nay, but I am after the truth. And I have an unswerving loyalty to my fellow Scots officers." He paused, leaving her on tenterhooks. "What an interesting conundrum we find ourselves in, milady. You a prisoner of the Crown and your husband commander of His Majesty's forces for Berwickshire."

Blythe stared at him. Everard had once refused to take up arms against the Jacobites. Had the king forced his hand? Had he then agreed in an effort to gain her release?

"Lord Wedderburn has raised four hundred men in Berwickshire—a Royal Regiment of Scots dragoons—to assist in putting down all treasonous Jacobites."

"Treasonous, sir?" Blythe countered. "'Tis only treason if they lose."

Surprise snuck past Campbell's stoicism, and he gave a smile that struck her as dark. "Well played, milady." He crossed his legs. "I thought you would want to know that Wedderburn and his men will soon join me here at Stirling under the command of my brother, the Duke of Argyll."

Could it be?

Joy sang through her, bright as a rainbow after a storm, and then other, less noble notions rushed in. She bit her tongue, willing her warring emotions to settle. Relief at Everard's coming. Fear of the impending fight. The uncertainty of not knowing whether they'd ever be reunited.

Tears gathered in her eyes. "You will make my husband aware I am here . . ."

"I haven't yet decided. So personal a matter might distract him from his duties."

A harshness crept into his tone, which made her own defenses rise. Here was a man clearly conflicted about his loyalties to king and countrymen. She'd taken heart that he had approached her. She'd thought him a literary spirit, at least. Perhaps foolishly she'd tried to win him over with her gracious manner.

And failed.

Blinking the tears away, she kept her voice steady. "Then I beseech you to keep me informed as to my husband's safety and well-being."

The colonel's fingers tapped on his chair arm as if keeping time with the drumming outside. Without another word, he rose and left.

Peg reappeared, her steely eyes fixed on the door he'd just passed through. Through gritted teeth she said, "Ne'er trust a Campbell. Slippery as eels, the whole infernal clan."

Blythe went to the window overlooking the courtyard and watched as the colonel wended his way through the throng below. Her heart seemed to beat double since she'd been apprised of Everard's coming.

"I've good news, if Lord Islay is to be believed," she said, turning away from the window. "Lord Wedderburn is on his way here with his own regiment."

"Praise be!" Mari clasped her hands together in delight.

"Hoot!" Peg cried. "Though the laird keeps himself in check, methinks he'll show a wee bit o' Davie's temper once he learns his bride's locked in here!"

"Colonel Campbell may not tell him."

Peg's reddened face took on a calculating air. "*He* may not, the wretch, but I'll make sure the laird learns of it by and by."

"Please . . ." Blythe turned her hands up entreatingly. "Do naught but watch and wait with me. And pray. We want to be God-honoring in all we do."

"Amen," Peg said with sudden reverence. She crossed to the window facing the open countryside with a hopeful air. "Come, Lord Jesus, come. Or," she all but crowed, "send the laird in Yer stead."

64

I can not be a traitor, for I owe him no allegiance.
He is not my Sovereign; he never received my homage;
and whilst life is in this persecuted body,
he never shall receive it.

WILLIAM WALLACE

verard was glad of the coming cold. Engaging in battle in the heat was a special misery he'd not wish on his sworn enemy. As he rode toward Stirling, certain he'd soon be fighting his own brother, his thoughts often veered to the moment when one side or the other would be the victor. So much hinged upon a win. Defeat was best not reckoned with ahead of battle.

The long march from Jedburgh where he'd raised his troops was rife with a howling wind and rain. Eighty Scots miles took time as they were oft intercepted by envoys from other commanders and spies who flew about the country like flocks of starlings, carrying all manner of information. He'd traded Lancelot for a war saddle and a blood horse fitted for the fray of battle. Recently lamed, Lancelot wasn't fit for the task. Everard had already told Bernard to give the stallion to Orin if he didn't return.

"Colonel Hume." Gordon, his lieutenant colonel, rode up alongside him, rain slicking his sunburned face. "Will we billet in the next village?"

363

"Nae, continue on to Tarnton Castle, where Argyll's troops are garrisoned."

"How far from Stirling, sir?"

"Five miles or so. I'm to meet with Argyll at Tarnton, then proceed from there." Everard mulled the latest intelligence. "As it stands, Mar's Jacobite forces outnumber us three to one, and they'll likely attempt to take Stirling Castle on their way south. We're to provide reinforcements should that happen. I want every soldier fed, rested, and ready."

Gordon rode off to alert the rest of the miles-long train while Everard's mind circled back to Blythe. Always Blythe. Lately she came to him in snatches like he was waking from a dream. Time wedged between them, tearing at the fabric of their union, putting countless people and places and events in their way.

He swiped a trickle of rain from his brow, wishing she'd materialize before his very eyes. He found himself wanting her to have the powers of the fabled kelpie and change shape and locations at will. One of his fondest memories was Orin declaring her a moonlit fairy in the garden not so long ago.

Odd what recollections stayed steadfast. Blythe at the Canongate mansion, standing before the bookcase where he'd first kissed her. Blythe in the corridor at Wedderburn, when Orin lay ill and he'd wanted to take her in his arms. Blythe on their wedding day, resplendent in a gown the likes of which he'd never seen. Blythe on their wedding night . . .

Pain knifed him, carving up his heart before moving to his middle. He'd lost a stone since her capture. Eating seemed to be the concern of those whose hearts were whole, who didn't live with the paralyzing uncertainty of where a loved one was and if they'd ever be reunited.

He rode on at the head of the long column, glad when he sighted the River Teith, a quiet and comely water. The castle situated along its narrow banks was immense, auld as Wedderburn if not as well-kept. Soldiers surrounded it, making it look under siege, but they were only encamped there while awaiting orders from the Duke of Argyll. Heavy artillery reinforced a growing military presence. Rumor was the castle would hold Jacobite prisoners, though it had no dungeon.

Everard lifted his gaze. The high Gatehouse Tower rose up as if impaling grey skies, and with reluctance he tore his thoughts from Blythe to the matter at hand.

———— ∞∞ ————

Blythe listened to the drone of rain upon the hammer-beam roof, the castle courtyard below a chocolate-brown quagmire. Peg was seldom within their apartments, scouting for fresh information ever since Colonel Campbell had told Blythe four days ago that the laird was on his way. Mari kept Blythe company playing cards or doing needlework, staying near the fire as the weather turned. The phantom-like haar moved in to stay, curling around castle corners and misting the green landscape grey. Though eerily beautiful, it obliterated Blythe's view.

"If ye stay at the windows so much, milady, yer sure to catch cold," Mari said, draping a plaid around her shoulders, the warm wool dyed royal blue and black.

But Blythe's thoughts were far afield. Where was Everard in all this heavy weather?

As she thought it, Peg appeared, her face lit with satisfaction. In her apron were apples ripened to a burnished gold. Yesterday she'd found them brambles—blackberries.

Mari smiled. "The loot ye bring us!"

"I'm nae prisoner, I remind the guards," Peg said, depositing the fruit on the table. "It's gotten so they open doors as soon as they see me coming."

"Glad I am of it," Blythe said, selecting a particularly large apple.

"I've brought more than fruit." Peg poured herself a cup of cider and slaked her thirst before she said another word.

Eyeing her, Blythe bit into the apple, finding it honey-sweet, much like the pear Everard had picked for her in the Canongate garden.

Peg set down her cup and swiped her mouth with her apron hem. "I have it on good authority the laird is due to arrive at Tarnton Castle but a few leagues from here. He's to join the rest of the government men there before marching to Stirling. If Mar and his Jacks don't get here first."

Blythe swallowed, the fruit forgotten. Her gaze fixed on Peg, hopes rising like the haar before sun. "Are you certain?"

"Aye. He's with his regiment, part of Portmore's Dragoons, the best of King Geordie's men." Peg was studying her as if hatching her own battle plan. "If the laird comes and isna told yer here beneath his verra nose, I've a mind to clothe ye as a washerwoman and sneak ye to him by night."

Blythe felt a bit breathless considering it.

"But yer too tall, I fear, and would be found out. As it stands, crankie Campbell has suddenly decided to reinforce the guard. They're thick as May midges at all the entrances and exits."

Blythe grasped at possibilities. "Can you arrange for a note to be carried in cipher to Tarnton?" She had paper and ink, at least. All the letters betwixt her and her father had been written in cipher before her captivity. Everard knew how to decipher it.

"Mayhap." Peg took another drink, clearly weighing the matter and all its implications. "If yer found out, I shudder to think what might happen."

"I want no harm to come to Lord Wedderburn."

"Seems he could ken yer whereabouts and be nae worse for it."

Mari looked from Peg to Blythe, her face drawn with concern. "I'm sure the carrier would be well rewarded, at least on the laird's end as we have nae coin."

Blythe was already at the desk. She took a seat and prepared to write, pondering what she should say. The hearth's fire crackled, warming her back, the rain turning to a torrent over her head.

Her beloved was near at hand.

Lord, help me reach him.

Everard stood in the vaulted Lord's Hall, his back to the roaring fire in Tarnton Castle's brazier. Argyll had just made a speech near the double hearths at hall's end, apprising his commanders of the latest intelligence regarding the position of Jacobite troops and recent arrests throughout the kingdom. All waited for word of the landing of the Stuart who would be king, rumored to have left France with French troops and ships.

Head full of war talk, heart full of Blythe, he was assailed by a dozen different sights and scents. Saddle-worn soldiers. Earthy peat and woodsmoke. Roasting beef and spilled ale. Ancient, rain-slicked stones. He stared down at his muddy boots, aware of someone approaching from his right amid the garrulous, restless officers.

"Lord Wedderburn."

Everard looked up, meeting the eyes of a humbly dressed lad new to him. Few were allowed into the Lord's Hall, but somehow he'd gotten past the castle's sentries, perhaps due to his small stature. Something in his bearing alerted Everard even before he reached into the folds of his plaid and produced a folded, sealed paper.

"From Stirling Castle, milord."

His bloodshot eyes and muddy clothes bespoke much. Everard reached into his coat and produced a silver crown.

Gratitude lit the lad's thin face. "Bethankit, sir."

Everard watched him depart, memorizing every detail about him before breaking the seal. As soon as he set eyes on Blythe's cipher, a warmth engulfed him from head to foot. All else in the hall was blotted out save the feminine inkings he carefully deciphered.

Dearest husband,

I trust this finds you well. Presently I am being held at Stirling Castle in the royal apartments, though there has been talk of moving me at any moment to another fortress unknown to me. If this reaches you, please know my heart is yours completely no matter how near or far apart we are, though every day away from you feels like a decade, the uncertainty of the present a torment. My prayers that we are soon reunited are unceasing. At the same time, do nothing to endanger yourself where I am concerned. I simply want to tell you I am well and my women remain with me. There is much talk of war here. I pray you will not see battle or come to any harm.

Ever thine,
B

He read it thrice, savoring every stroke of the pen, every poignant sentence. Stirling was but a few miles distant. Every fiber of his being pulled him there.

He refolded the letter and tucked it inside his uniform coat as his gaze pinned Argyll across the hall. Did Johnnie Campbell ken Blythe was being held at Stirling under the command of his own brother, Archie, Lord Islay? Rather, the question was . . .

Did they expect him to do nothing about that loathsome fact?

65

Love seeketh not itself to please,
Nor for itself hath any care,
But for another gives its ease,
And builds a Heaven in Hell's despair.

WILLIAM BLAKE

Blythe lay awake, knowing the precise moment the rain ended and the moon escaped its veil of clouds. Cold silver light spilled through the one window left open for fresh air, falling across the counterpane of her bed. She was wide awake, but Peg's soft snoring and Mari's mumbling reassured her they were asleep on their pallets near the door. Even at rest they continued to guard her, if they could.

Just yesterday Peg had brought word there were more murmurings of moving Blythe to another location, given a Jacobite attack on Stirling was imminent. Glad she was she'd put this possibility in her message to Everard. But had the message been delivered? Peg had seen no sign of the lad she'd coerced as courier since. The wait chafed. Wouldn't Everard send word back to her?

Pushing aside the bedclothes, Blythe got to her knees. Her fretting was exchanged for praying until her spirit calmed again.

Once the maids were awake and they breakfasted together, one of

Colonel Campbell's equerries appeared. "Prepare to depart within an hour, milady," he said in terse tones. He left as quickly as he'd come.

The ensuing silence reflected their unspoken fears.

"Jings! 'Tis happening though I prayed against it!" Peg moaned, abandoning her breakfast to pack their few belongings. "And nae word as to where we'll be carted next!"

Blythe refused to give way to worry. "At least the rain has stopped."

"Still, the coach wheels will be sunk to the axles in mud," Peg said. "And I've prayed night and day the laird would get here in time and set all this nonsense to rights."

"He might yet." Mari dabbed at her damp eyes with her apron hem. "Mayhap he'll meet us on the way to wherever."

Wherever sounded mournful indeed and further out of reach.

By daybreak they were hustled into a waiting coach in the courtyard, a mounted guard surrounding them on black geldings. Colonel Campbell did not appear, and Blythe was relieved. He made her uneasy, and she might have abused him with questions in a weak moment. As the coach pulled out with a great clatter upon the cobblestones and on through the gatehouse Blythe hoped she'd never see again, she tried to take stock of her blessings.

At least she was presentable, having bathed the night before and having dried her hair by the fire. While clean, her gown begged ironing, though her cloak hid the worst wrinkles. Mari had woven a bit of ribbon into her upswept hair. One glance in the looking glass told her she'd grown thinner and paler. There seemed a new, resigned strength about her. Though much was beyond her control, she could still rejoice the Almighty ruled over earthly kings and military commanders.

The three of them seemed to hold their breath as the vehicle revealed their course.

"North!" Peg grew more distressed. "Into the Highlands. We might as well be entering the bowels of Hades!"

"The Almighty made the Highlands, did He not?" Steeling herself against Peg's outcry and preparing for a lengthy journey, Blythe leaned forward and looked out the coach window beyond the mounted guard. "Look how the foliage is turning to rust and gold. Autumn is everywhere."

Free of Stirling's forbidding walls, Blythe found the countryside picturesque. Distant mountains dominated the landscape and pine-scented woods abounded, reminding Blythe of home. When the coach lurched, pitching them hither and yon, all came to an ungracious halt.

"'Tis nae better than a mud wagon!" Peg said as a dragoon yanked open the door to ask if they were all right.

Blythe assured him they were, and soon whatever had gone wrong had been righted and they were on their way again. To where, she knew not.

An hour passed, the scenery ever changing. When a tall stone tower came into view along the river's edge, the guard seemed to slow.

"There's a lovely watercourse to our right," Blythe said, determined to raise their spirits.

"'Tis the River Teith, I heard one of the guards say," Mari told her.

Soldiers lined the riverbanks and horses were everywhere, some drinking from the river's edge, others standing hock deep in the rushing current.

Through another wood the coach traversed, ever nearer the castle that was clearly a garrison. There'd not been this many soldiers at Stirling. The coach halted again briefly as papers were shown and words were exchanged, then they passed through a gate and into a courtyard. Peg had turned contemplative as a monk while Mari seemed agape at the tower's height. The castle courtyard was oddly empty, the military presence mostly beyond the high walls.

Wary, Blythe stepped down from the coach, gaze on a set of stairs rising alongside the tower to a door on the second floor. An unknown soldier escorted her up them, her maids following. A turnpike stair came next, gashes in the curved stone walls indicative of fierce fighting in days gone by.

"You'll lodge in the duchess's rooms over the kitchen. 'Tis warmer due to the ovens," her escort told her as if a lady prisoner was a common occurrence. He took out a key and unlocked a round-topped door.

Blythe stood on the threshold until he gestured her inside. When she turned back around, he was gone, as were Mari and Peg.

Am I to be all alone now, Lord?

A stab of disquiet didn't steal her appreciation of the splendid room. Unlike Stirling, it showed none of the wear of ages past. At a glance she sensed the bed linens were new, the furnishings a striking mix of French and English. Thick, colorful carpet was beneath her slippered feet, staving off the cold as much as the fire that crackled merrily in the grate, a welcoming chair and footstool before it. Fit for a duchess, truly.

She closed her eyes, her hands clasped at her waist. She'd not felt her best of late. A little woozy and dull-witted. Too many sleepless nights and less-than-healthy fare. Soldiers seemed to prefer a great quantity of beef—

"Countess."

Her eyes flew open. A beloved voice sent her stomach somersaulting even before a familiar figure filled the doorway. The sight of Everard nearly buckled her knees. Was it naught but a dream? How handsome he was, yet so different in his crimson coat with blue facings—and such pathos in his face!

With a little cry, she ran across the room and into his open arms. Catching her up, he held her tightly for a long moment. When she looked up at him through tear-filled eyes, his own eyes were damp.

His voice was a bit ragged, so fraught with emotion her own throat closed tight. "I left nae stone unturned to find you, yet if not for your note I doubt we'd be here now."

"The note . . . I wondered if it would ever reach you."

"It arrived under rather odd circumstances. A disheveled lad got past the guards and came into the hall that is all but forbidden to any but officers. I read your note in the presence of other soldiers, none of which seemed to see the courier or question his presence."

"An angel, perhaps. At least to me." She smiled through her tears. "I pray we're not parted again." Her cold fingers fisted the fabric of his coat as if he might somehow slip away from her. "I'd follow you into battle if I could."

"Some lasses do. But not my countess."

He kissed her, so sweetly yet so thoroughly she lost all sense of time and place. She'd nearly forgotten his strength and the sheer force of his presence.

When the storm of their reunion quieted, he led her nearer the hearth's fire. His fingers trailed down her cheek, drying her tears, his keen gaze dissecting as if searching for any change their separation had wrought.

"I hardly know where to begin . . ." Her voice trailed off. "No harm has come to me, though I stand amazed at this turn of events."

"You're here at my req—nae, command." His wry smile told her much.

"'Tis a gift, every precious second." Even as she spoke, her heart ached at the coming separation and what it might bring. "Colonel Campbell came to my apartments at Stirling. He told me you were near, but I never dreamed we'd have this."

"Scots ties are thicker than those to a foreign ruler. We have till morn, you and I, then I march."

There seemed a foreshadowing to his words, a darkness she prayed she'd not live to remember.

She rested her head upon his chest. "If you march in the morn, a battle must be imminent. I've heard Jacobites are on the move and may take Stirling at any moment."

"Stirling will soon be reinforced like Bristol and Plymouth and Southampton."

"Will I remain here at Tarnton?"

"If I have anything to do with it, you will. 'Tis the safest stronghold in the kingdom at present."

"Is it true that desertions are rising by the day and even government officers are siding with the Rebels?"

"Hearsay, mostly." His gaze darkened. "Argyll has managed to destroy the Rebels' latest manifesto printed at Perth that encouraged officers to come over to the Pretender's service, countering it with a ten-thousand-pound reward for his capture."

She laid a hand against his bristled cheek. "I fear you'll face your brother at some point."

"Davie and I are overdue for a reckoning. It may not be the same battle, but I've nae doubt he'll be my adversary wherever he is."

"How I miss Wedderburn. Orin. Our life there."

"I feel the same. But let nothing intrude on our present happiness."

He unhooked the clasp of her cape, and the garment slipped from her shoulders to the carpet. She pushed back a wayward tendril of her hair as he shrugged off his uniform coat. Down to buff waistcoat, blue breeches, and black boots, he'd shed half his intimidating presence, at least.

"You are still my English rose," he said, laying their clothing over a chairback. "While I remain your Scottish thistle."

"I would have you no different than you are." She felt a bit breathless at his nearness, the startling events of the day catching up with her. "You are as much a soldier as laird."

He cradled her face between his hands, concern marring his joy. "And you are as lovely to me as you ever were but more slender . . . and even more pale."

She lowered her eyes, in a sudden quandary. "If I am peely-wally, Lord Wedderburn, you might be entirely to blame."

"What means you?"

"It may be too soon to mention . . ." She flushed. She'd missed her monthly courses twice. Mari had caught her falling asleep over her embroidery, and on a few occasions she'd cast up accounts in the middle of the night. Sometimes she had a fierce hankering for sweetmeats. "I am not myself of late."

His stunned expression moved her. For a long moment he said nothing, his gaze growing more tender. "That night—our wedding night—in so cramped a bed . . ."

"I hardly noticed," she said with a smile.

"The heir to Wedderburn conceived at an ordinary."

"Well, the babe shan't be born in one, Lord willing, but at home where he or she belongs."

"This makes me all the more eager to put any battles behind me and return you to Berwickshire."

"'Tis early yet." She still waited for a quickening, but as she knew so little about infants she wasn't sure when to expect such. "I could be mistaken."

With a swift, sure move, he picked her up as he'd not done on their wedding day to carry her over the threshold. "Let's relive our wedding night and hedge our hopes, then."

66

True to the End.

HUME CLAN MOTTO

Blythe stood at the tower window looking down on Everard as he prepared to march. They'd not left their chamber from the time she'd arrived yesterday morn till now, and she felt his loss like a blow. In his wake, Peg and Mari returned, but not till she and Everard had knelt and prayed for protection and blessing and a swift end to the conflict. Their combined amens left her so afraid it might be their last meeting that she feared her heart would burst as they said their goodbyes.

Dawn gilded the sky a curious crimson. A portent of foul weather? At a rooster's crowing the castle came awake, and the aroma of baking bread and more sordid smells like the emptying of chamber pots filled the air. Soon the military presence about Tarnton was reduced by half as the Duke of Argyll led out, Everard beside him, bound for Stirling.

While Mari bit her lip and tidied the bed linens, Peg stood motionless in a rare maudlin moment. "Suppose this is the last we see o' the laird," she said. "I canna bear that it might weel be Davie who'll soon lord it o'er us!"

Lord, nay. Banishing propriety, Blythe did the unthinkable and put her arms around the distraught maid, which made her cry all the harder. "Soon you shall be back in Berwickshire. I know you're missing your sister and your ailing grandmother in Duns."

Head bobbing, Peg accepted Blythe's handkerchief. "But what if the Rebels plunder and burn Wedderburn to the ground? 'Tis happening all around us by rogue Jacks!"

"Tea is what's needed," Mari said briskly, heading to the door.

Blythe nearly laughed at the ludicrousness of such, but she watched as the maid left in haste without consulting the guard outside their door. Unlike at Stirling, it seemed they were now being guarded from harm, not to prevent escape.

And given war swirled all around them, where could they escape to safely?

When Mari returned with a full tray of not only tea but butter, bread, and bramble jam, Peg ceased her crying, though her face was puffy and her expression no brighter. Silently she sat and watched Blythe embroider. As she was unable to read or write and was not fond of handwork, Peg's entertainments were few.

"Tarnton is a far cry from Edinburgh Castle, I'm pleased to report." Mari poured the tea, as hopeful as Peg was grim. "There's a small army of cooks and bakers in the kitchen. Provisions are aplenty."

"We shan't starve, then," Peg muttered into her dish.

"Nor will the king's men." Mari spread butter on a thick slice of bread. "Even the tea is quality. Big bricks of bohea with a fancy design pressed upon each as if made for His Majesty himself."

"Humph," Peg said. She took a first sip and seemed pleasantly surprised.

Blythe stirred cream and sugar into her tea, finding the aroma especially fragrant. All was delicious, and she'd even overlooked a generous wedge of cheese hiding beneath a linen cloth.

"I canna wait to see what's for supper," Mari said.

"I pray 'tis more than boiled beef and biscuits," Peg replied. "Though I saw the army leave with droves o' black cattle and sheep."

"Where do they spend nights, d'ye reckon?" Mari asked.

Peg assumed a knowledgeable air. "The main body encamps while the laird and officers billet in towns and houses. Boyd is with the baggage guard, which numbers three hundred or so. I had a quick word with him afore he left. He told me Dutch battalions are about to land with upwards of six thousand men, who'll soon join Argyll's army."

Blythe envisioned Everard with such a large army, relying on repeated intelligence from a large spy network. Peg's confirmation that Boyd was with him made her doubly glad.

"'Tis the number of Jacks I worry about," Peg said in low tones.

Mari raised a brow. "Suppose we're considered traitors supporting the wrong side?"

"Our prayers will do more than our worrying ever will," Blythe said as much to herself as to them. "Though I do hope, Peg, you'll keep us posted about anything you hear regarding the action, especially Argyll's and Lord Wedderburn's whereabouts."

"'Tis a wonder ye got to spend a day and a night together." Mari winked at Peg, who'd shed her black mood for the time being as they tittered like schoolgirls. "The laird is sae verra braw in uniform and surely swept ye off yer feet."

Blythe smiled. "You don't blame me, then, for being a bit addled after."

They chuckled, leaving her guessing they'd seen her and Everard's prolonged, passionate embraces in the corridor prior to his leaving. It had been the hardest parting of her life.

"The laird adores ye, he does." Peg looked supremely satisfied. "He's nae one of them nobles who has a mistress *and* a wife."

As the fire popped and sparked, Blythe drank her tea and reveled in the hours of stolen ecstasy they'd shared. Everard was as tender as he was fierce, as consummate a lover as he was a soldier.

And now a devoted husband.

67

A man is a lion in his own cause.

SCOTTISH PROVERB

November 13, 1715
Sheriffmuir Moor, Scotland

Everard was not a man given to fear, but as he looked out from Stone Hill across the white-frosted moor where the Rebels were arrayed, he wished he wore the bronze chain mail of the knights and men-at-arms of his ancestors. The Jacobites' stalwart appearance on both horse and afoot beneath ironlike skies, their banners a shock of color in the leaden landscape, seemed especially menacing. Everard squared his shoulders, his breath pluming like white feathers as he sat atop his horse, whose coarse black mane and tail fluttered like the distant flags.

Nearby, the Duke of Argyll, the distinctive Star of the Garter on his coat, barked orders to government troops as if the Pretender's rumored landing on their shores with a French fleet wasn't fiction but fact. Their own regimental flags flapped fitfully in a November wind that seemed to slice to Everard's bones. Not even his woolen uniform coat staved off the chill. It didn't help that his mind returned repeatedly to Blythe wrapped in his arms near Tarnton's hearth fire, the hours they'd spent there almost warming him in retrospect.

How was a man besotted supposed to keep his mind on battle?

His musings ended when Argyll rode abreast of him on his sleek war horse and apprised him of the latest intelligence. "I wish to God for His Majesty's service that the Irish and Dutch troops were here now." His cheeks were pinched red, his voice hoarse from cold. "We are unfortunate in having so very few men to oppose such multitudes, even with artillery and cannon."

They scarcely had three thousand, some of them ill. The enemy strength was thrice that. It cut Everard to the quick that he would fight his own countrymen. The regret of it took root, the little he'd eaten at dawn twisting inside him. Already his mind was torn with the shadows and bloodshed to come, the carnage doing untold damage to a great many souls, not just his own.

"There rides Lord Mar within musket range." Everard inclined his head, his eyesight keen enough to need no spyglass. A council of war seemed underway among the officers and lairds on the plain below them, the regiments assembling into battle formation. "Lord Marischal looks to be leading the advance force."

At that, Argyll issued an order that rippled through the ranks as the drums beat out the same. In seconds the bloodcurdling cry of enemy bagpipes carried on the knifelike wind. So many Highlanders, their bonnets and plaids marking them, their sharpened broadswords capable of slashing a man to bits in a breath. 'Twould be a horrendous fight on a field barren of all but a few scattered farmhouses and a peaty bog sure to mire their horses. And on the Sabbath, God forgive them.

No one conquers who does not fight.

His heart wasn't in the battle. The soldier had drained out of him amid the bloodbath of Malplaquet. But for Blythe he would fight. For their child. Their future.

God Almighty, help us all.

The castle's fires did little to stave off autumn's chill. Still, Blythe would not complain, knowing many soldiers bedded down in sheep cotes of straw. How long had it been since she'd whispered to Everard the suspicion she was now sure of? Because of it, joy colored her days. When worry threatened to intrude, she would pray. Sometimes it seemed she did nothing but pray, even as she stitched or read or was supposed to be sleeping.

She tried to recall the little details time worked hard to dim. Everard's rich lilt. The brush of his lips against her skin. His stoic humor. The stubble of whiskers that seemed to defy a razor. How his eyes shifted color depending on the light—clear as a spring one moment, then a bottomless sea blue.

The memories sweetened her work as she embroidered, holding close her secret of the babe she reckoned would come in late spring. Thankfully, provisions remained generous. Fresh bannocks and fish, neeps and tatties in abundance, and broth of all kinds. For this she gave thanks, if not for herself then for her babe's health, and ate all she could.

Stifling a yawn, she counted time in her head. 'Twas now November. Across from her, Mari scratched out a letter to her aunt in Edinburgh. Peg had gone missing an hour before.

With a loud groan, the door burst open. Peg hastened in, carrying a piece of paper. "I canna read a word o' it, milady, but 'tis the list of the killed and wounded."

Blythe stood, her pulse beginning to thrum, her breathing tight. Setting aside her needle, she took the paper, a prayer on her lips. "A battle, then."

"Aye, just Sabbath last." Peg's chest heaved as if she'd run up the turnpike stair. "I begged it off an officer, who said I'm to return it posthaste."

Blythe scanned the well-perused list, dread in her belly. So many soldiers. So many grieving families. Lord Forfar's name was scrawled at the top, all the nobles and officers who comprised His Majesty's army listed first.

"There's prisoners o' war who aren't listed," Peg said, jarring Blythe's nerves further. "Some say we won and some say they won, but all agree the Royal Greys chased the Rebels down and gave nae quarter."

Blythe read on, nauseous, her heart growing heavier.

> *Earl of Forfar—missing and presumed killed*
> *Colonel Hawley—shot through the body but hope of his recovery*
> *My Lord Islay—shot through the arm and the right side but his wounds are not mortal*

Blythe paused. *My Lord Islay* . . . Colonel Archie Campbell, the red-haired commander at Stirling.

She continued, the list becoming dangerously personal. And then . . .

> *My Lord Wedderburn—shot through the shoulder and left hip but hope of his recovery*

Blythe's hand went to her mouth as her other hand shook, the paper trembling so hard she barely made out the rest. Tears spotted the list, making the ink swell and run.

> *We compute that there lay killed upon the field of battle about seven or eight hundred of the enemy.*

⸻

Everard attempted to rise from his pallet, shaking and sweating by turns. The pain in his shoulder and hip nearly gnawed him in two. He'd had other wounds in past battles, but none that festered like fire and foretold blood poisoning. He raised himself on one elbow, determined to swing his booted feet to the floor, but he wore no boots, only blood-spattered stockings, and his efforts collapsed. Rolling onto his side, he further tore at his hastily stitched injury, sending that searing ache up his back and neck and down his arm before it rumbled down his leg. Holding back a moan, he closed his eyes.

God Almighty, be Thou near me.

The plea swirled through his befogged brain. Whisky saturated his sark, the only available medicine at hand, keeping him conscious even as it stole stealthily through his limbs. Soon he was lost in a netherworld where the past and present collided.

"Spare the poor blue bonnets!"

Argyll's anguished battle cry resonated between the whiz of bullet lead and the acrid smoke of black powder, the heavy, fatal striking of the claymores and bayonets slicing through his ranks and echoing on and on. A hellish half hour . . . so many men dead.

But here was a quiet contrast. A burst of pleasure. His pain seemed to ebb ever so slightly as her face swam before him. Smiling. Beglamouring . . .

Blythe.

The next morning a knock on the door rattled Blythe further. Peg answered, and the commander of the garrison at Tarnton stepped into the room. With a little bow he told the maids to remain, though he looked directly at Blythe.

"I bring your ladyship sore news." His grave demeanor made his gruff soldierly exterior more fierce. "I've just received word by express that though your husband acquitted himself with honor at Sheriffmuir, leading the Scots Greys to overtake the Rebels at the River Allen, he has since succumbed to wounds received in battle."

The needle and thread fell from Blythe's fingers to the floor. As all the breath left her lungs, she stared at him. Peg gave a sharp cry behind her, and Mari began weeping into her apron, strange discordant sounds on the still air.

All my prayers have been for naught.

Blythe's lips moved, but no sound came forth. Then a half-hopeful, "There is no mistake?"

"It awaits confirmation, but we have it on good authority from Stirling, where a wounded Argyll is once again quartered with his troops." He stepped toward the door. "My deepest apologies, Lady Wedderburn. Your husband was a fine soldier and a nobleman without equal."

Was.

The room tilted and spun, threatening to draw Blythe into an abyss of darkness. Stomach flipped, she eyed a basin then gripped a chairback, fearing she'd retch—or faint.

Mari was beside her instantly, her hand light upon her back. "Yer ladyship, let us get ye to bed. Yer undone with this grievous news."

Blythe leaned into her, her body and mind so numb they seemed to belong to someone else. Anguish pressed down on her as shock held fast, snatching her breath and squeezing her heart till she thought it would stop.

Mari led her to the bed where she'd last lain with the laird. The memory crushed her. Their time together had been so sweet—never to be regained—and she put a hand over her mouth lest she cry out.

A drink was brought, more tonic than tea. She drank it slowly with Mari's help while Peg paced before the hearth. Finally, Blythe slept, but when she awakened, hoping the news was but a horrendous dream, the frozen, starless night was as black as her spirits.

68

Journeys end in lovers meeting.

WILLIAM SHAKESPEARE

Blythe wore a sable gown, somehow gotten by Peg from Tarnton or the near village. Wearing a veiled mourning bonnet, she stepped slowly into the coach that would return her to Stirling. Once she was settled on the upholstered seat, a slight quickening gripped her middle. The babe? She'd lost track of time since Everard's death. Now she placed a hand upon her bodice, the sensation overriding her great grief. But only for a moment, and then the heavy darkness swept back in.

Peg and Mari sat across from her, their faces red and swollen from weeping. Since the news of the laird's passing reached them two days past, they'd all done their share of crying. But at the moment, traveling the road that had brought them to Tarnton Castle, Blythe was dry-eyed, worn to the nub from sorrow, her hopes trammeled beneath her feet. She felt nearly soulless. God seemed far off, adding to the agony of the present.

"Brace yerself, milady," Peg said when Stirling's battlements came into view.

Blythe looked out the window as snowflakes sifted down like tiny goose feathers. She knew what death was like, but nothing could prepare her for Everard's. Though she'd seen her grandmother lying in her magnificent coffin before burial, an engraved silver coffin plate on her chest, the dowager duchess had been old and full of years, ready to relinquish her long earthly life. But this . . . this was entirely different.

Peg alighted first upon arrival, saying to the guard, "Lady Wedderburn is here to see"—her voice cracked, but she forged ahead—"her husband's body."

The guard consulted another red-coated soldier, and then another came and led them through wending stone corridors down steps into what appeared to be the castle's dungeon. Holding a handkerchief to her nose, Blythe walked head down, Mari and Peg in her wake. So many bodies here, both Jacobites and the government's men, all so shatteringly still. In a far corner lay another linen-covered figure. Near tears, unsure how she'd make it through the next moment, Blythe prayed with desperate earnestness.

Lord, be my stay.

With admirable stoicism, the officer turned back the sheet, and Blythe heard a gasp before she even stole a look at the body.

"'Tis not the laird!" Peg exclaimed from behind her. "'Tis Davie Hume, his ill-willy brither!"

Mari's gasp echoed Peg's as Blythe looked down at the man who'd blackened the Hume name. His face was frozen in a sort of death grimace, his chest wound bespeaking an agonizing demise.

Shaking more from emotion than the cold, Blythe turned to the guard. "Where is Lord Wedderburn? This man is not he."

The man looked at her blankly, his ruddy color reddening further. "There's so many dead, milady. And a great many wounded, including Argyll himself. All's a heap o' confusion at present."

"May I speak with the duke, then?"

This request seemed to tax him. He re-covered David with the cloth before leading them up the way they'd come. "If you'll wait in the annex, milady . . ."

Blythe stood in a knot with Peg and Mari, waiting. *Chafing.* The drafty room had no fireplace, and the wind pressed against their skirts, stirring Blythe's dark veil. A bewildered uncertainty gathered round them, and the clock seemed just as frozen.

Blythe's mind spun with possibilities. Might Everard still be alive?

At last, another uniformed man appeared. "Lady Wedderburn, I presume?" At Blythe's nod he inclined his head. "Follow me, but leave your women here."

Clearly reluctant to be so dismissed, Mari and Peg remained behind. Head bent, Blythe walked a long ways, trading one section of the castle for another. Again that quickening stirred inside her, giving her courage to go on. The laird would live on through their child, Lord willing.

A door groaned open. The officer didn't enter in but shut the door so that she had complete privacy. Blythe cast a look at the bed across the room. Other than a small window and a hearth that crackled noisily, the light was dim. Camphor laced the air. Even whisky. Something wasn't right. Why the fire and medicines? Had she been taken to the right place?

Swallowing hard, still feeling woozy, she stepped toward the still figure, half expecting him to be laid out like David and covered in linen. Would she be able to turn back the sheet and look at her beloved a final time?

Shaking, she dropped to her knees beside the narrow bed, so riven with anguish she could barely breathe. Here lay her crushed hopes. Her dreams. The love of a lifetime.

Lord, I cannot bear it—

"Blythe . . ."

Her head came up. Dazed, she blinked back tears before tearing off her hat, pins and all. Everard rolled toward her, his blue gaze locking with hers, keenly alive if beleaguered, and full of feeling. His hands reached for her. Strong, capable hands that stroked her unkempt hair and drew her off the stone floor onto the bed.

Overcome, she gave way to quiet, shuddering sobs, sure she was dreaming and she'd awaken to the next nightmarish moment. She leaned into the man whose arms she'd never expected to wrap round her again, finding him not cold and lifeless but warm and joyous.

"Blythe, my love. I told them to send for you, and at last you've come."

"I thought you were dead of your wounds. They took me to David—" She closed her eyes to block out the shocking sight. "Will you live? Are you much hurt?"

Her hands and eyes roved over him, gently probing, grasping for assurance. His heavily bandaged hip and shoulder were not lost on her, nor were the multitude of scrapes and cuts on his hands and face. He was unshaven, even bearded, the smell of sweat and blood still clinging to him. His loose hair lay lank upon the pillow behind him, black as overturned ink.

"I look a fright and smell worse." He kissed her fingers. "Battle becomes nae one."

"You've never looked more braw to me." She laid her head upon his chest, where his heart pulsed in a reassuring rhythm beneath her ear.

"Weel, to be blunt, I canna help but repeat . . ." His breath came labored but was laced with humor nonetheless. "Ye look ghastly in black."

Something shifted inside her. She began to laugh, a high, merry sound that rang about the small chamber like a pealing bell.

He joined her, the effort clearly paining him, but the sound was rich and deep and held healing as well. "Are you ready to go home, Countess?"

"Is the fighting over?"

"All o'er, aye. The debacle at Preston yestreen ended the matter." She scarcely believed it. "Can you be moved?"

"The sooner I'm free of Stirling, the better I'll be."

"But the king—"

"Argyll has sent His Majesty an express telling him of the battle and that I have been relieved of my post and am free to return home."

"I shan't leave your side for an instant, then."

His eyes clouded. "You saw Davie . . ."

She nodded, hating that she was not truly sorry, just sorry it had come to this. "He's below in what looks like the dungeon amid a great many other corpses."

"A prisoner of war who didn't live to see his execution." He expelled a low breath, then sought her eyes again. "But all that has passed. How is my bonnie bride? My bairn?"

She slipped a hand over her stomach, the black fabric scratchy if warm. "We both are well and in need of you and home. But I don't want you moved. Not till the surgeons say 'tis safe to do so."

"I can manage some eighty miles with you by my side."

"In a coach, then."

"Let us make the arrangements posthaste." He smiled, more like the laird she loved. "Christmas will soon be upon us, and I want to be well and on my feet for the festivities by then."

"Our first Christmas together." She sighed. "'Tis like a dream. An answer to all our prayers."

69

O Bride, Brideag, come with the wand
To this wintry land;
And breathe with the breath of Spring so bland,
Bride, Bride, little Bride.

TRADITIONAL SCOTTISH SONG

Their return to Berwickshire took an unhurried sennight. Blythe watched over Everard with the diligence of a doctor, his comfort her only concern. Word was sent ahead of their arrival to Wedderburn. Boyd had left the day before to make sure all was ready for their coming. When at last they turned safely into the main gates of the castle, Blythe's tears were entirely joyous.

Everard leaned forward without a grimace, surely testimony of his recovery, and opened the window. Snowflakes wafted in as if proclaiming it the first of December. Never had the castle looked so majestic as in snow, every turret and battlement iced white as sugar glaze. For a few moments Blythe forgot her own stiff fingers encased in wool mittens and the dying coals in the brazier beneath her feet.

Home!

At the main entrance, the coach door opened and Blythe alighted first, then the laird, Mari and Peg just behind. Munro and Mrs. Candlish rushed through the winter's blast to meet them, the latter nearly slipping on the cobbles. Orin came next, barreling toward them with his pup, Wallace, who seemed full grown.

"You're home!" Orin cried, catching Blythe about the waist and burrowing his head in her cloak. "I feared you'd never come back."

She smoothed his pale hair, touched by the relief in his voice. He eyed the laird somewhat fearfully, as if having learned of his brother's injuries.

"Still standing," Everard said with a wink, embracing him no less heartily. He drew himself to his full height, his gaze rising as if he was surprised to see Wedderburn still standing, given the breadth and animosity of the conflict.

"Hasten in out of this snowstorm!" Mrs. Candlish half shouted above the wind, discarding her reserve. "I sent for refreshments as soon as I saw ye pass the gate."

They all piled in, capes and hats discarded on their way to the smaller blue drawing room. A brilliant fire lit the chamber, and Everard and Blythe stood by the hearth, glad to stretch their limbs after hours of coach travel. Bernard joined them, telling them the twins were on their way from Edinburgh and would be home for Christmastide. Ronan and Elodie were expected on the morrow.

"I suppose we'll continue in mourning awhile longer, then," Bernard said. "Though I hate to say it, Davie's end doesna surprise me."

"We'll not let it overshadow our joy," Everard replied. "I'm more glad of life than I've ever been."

Kneeling, Orin let Wallace have a bite of biscuit. "Having you home is the best Christmas gift I could have asked or prayed for."

Meeting Blythe's eyes, Everard said, "There's another gift to be had in spring."

All looked at him in question, then at Blythe, who smiled, her hand instinctively touching her waist. "You'll soon be Uncle Orin, Lord willing."

Astonishment washed his face. "A bairn?"

Laughter erupted when he gave a little whoop of pleasure. More questions were asked as to the nursery and names, and Blythe and

Everard fielded them with pleasure. Spring couldn't come too soon, but for now snow was filling in all the frozen nooks and crannies of the landscape.

Chocolate and tea, fresh bannocks, and a small feast of all the laird's favorites appeared. In time, conversation turned to other matters. Blythe was handed a letter from her father. She broke the seal, aware of Everard watching her. As if sensing privacy was needed, Orin and Bernard excused themselves till supper, and the two of them were left alone.

Blythe devoured the contents and looked up at Everard. "My father writes from France, perhaps to stay. I know not what that means for my inheritance."

"You are the only inheritance I need," he said. "All that matters is he lives. Mayhap he'll welcome news of his grandchild."

"He'll be overjoyed." Setting the letter aside, Blythe imagined his reaction. "I doubt he even knows we've wed."

Everard stood. "Will you do me the honor, Countess, and step a post-wedding, pre-Christmas reel with me?"

Concern marred the moment. "But your hip . . ."

"Is in need of exercise." He extended a hand.

Rising, she curtsied, her wide smile matching his own. "One of many married dances to come, my love."

He took her in his arms, looking down at her with undisguised tenderness. "But first, a kiss."

At the touch of his lips, she murmured, "Kisses without end. Amen."

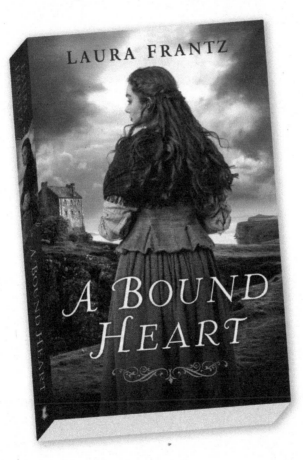

1

Nae man can tether time or tide.

ROBERT BURNS

Isle of Kerrera, Scotland, 1752

As the sun slid from the sky, Lark pressed her back into the pockmarked cliff on the island's west shore. The sea stretched before her like an indigo coverlet, a great many foam-flecked waves tossing gannets about. A south wind tore at her unbound hair, waving it like a crimson flag, as crimson as the fine cloth she'd seen smuggled ashore the previous night. These free-trading times were steeped in danger. Countless moonlit liaisons and trysts. Sandfilled shoes and sleepless nights. How oft she'd prayed an end to it all.

On this breathless May eve, the only aggravation was the sting of tiny midges as night closed in—and the thickset Jillian Brody as she bumped into Lark and nearly sent her off the cliff's edge.

"Look smart, aye? There's tax men about."

"I pray not," Lark breathed, craning her neck to take in the sweeping coastal headland that could only be called majestic. She wouldn't tell Jillian she was more addlepated about the handsome captain of the *Merry Lass* than the chancy smuggling run, and that she braved the midnight hour to gain but a glimpse of him or his ship.

"Yer not out here for the same reasons as the rest o' us." Jillian managed to stand akimbo, hands fisted on her ample hips, despite the path's ribbon-like lip. "What's this I hear about ye refusin' to help bring in the haul?"

"My conscience smote me," Lark told her. "I canna be in the business of stealing even if it betters the poor."

"Hoot!" Jillian spat the word out as the night wind began a queer keening, lifting the edges of their plaid shawls. "Yer fellow islanders are not so high and mighty. Be off wi' ye, then."

The dismissal, though said in spite, was gladly heeded. Lark turned and hastened away, stepping ably along the path though 'twas nearing midnight. Darkness didn't fall till late, which left precious little time for the free traders to do their work in the smothering safety of night.

Tense, she climbed upward, casting a glance over her shoulder at the beach now and again. But this long, miserly eve brought no goods ashore, nor a handsome captain home again, and so she entered the wee cottage no bigger than a cowshed, its humble stone her home since birth. Only she and her granny fussed with the peat fire and kept a-simmer the kettle of porridge or soup, which always seemed to taste of smoke. She washed up before donning a worn nightgown, then all but fell into the box bed, exhausted.

Early the next morn she trudged through the mist to Kerrera Castle. Glad she was to have gotten even a snatch of sleep.

Once on castle grounds she quashed the urge to steal into the walled garden and drink from the spring that bubbled forth in a stony corner. Like ice the water was, even in the heat of summer. Most servants weren't allowed in the formal garden. Kerrera's mistress did not like the help to be seen. Her fragile constitution could not bear it. The glorious bower was reserved for Lady Isla and Kerrera's infrequent guests.

Bypassing humble beds of herbs in the kitchen garden, Lark came to the beloved bee garden. Here she could stay content forever. Against one ivy-clad bricked wall were numerous bee skeps. Made of thick coils of straw, they were fashioned into golden domes, a wee door at the bottom of each. Even now their inhabitants hummed a lively tune, already at work among enticing calendula and borage, awaiting a feast of bee balm and snapdragons and cosmos in summer. Come August she would take a hive or two into the heather, making the coveted heather honey of which the laird was so fond.

Her gaze swung to the bee bath she'd created years before, a chipped, shallow dish for fresh water. Beach pebbles were scattered about for the busy creatures to perch on while drinking lest they drown. Their droning seemed to intensify with her coming. The bees sensed her, their singing rising and falling as she moved among them. They did not favor everyone, merely tolerating the head housekeeper yet circling the maids benignly. But they stung Cook in a fury. The laird of Kerrera Castle moved calmly and respectfully in their midst, much like Lark, both of them spared the piercing pain. She'd always wondered about their reaction to Lady Isla. But the laird's wife rarely ventured near the bee skeps.

Seeing all was well, at least in the gardens, Lark turned toward the castle.

"There ye be, Lark."

Was she tardy? Mistress Baird, the stern housekeeper, never greeted her, only made her feel guilty. In the bowels of the castle came the liberating chime of the case clock in the servants' hall.

Not late. On time.

From her chatelaine, Mistress Baird removed the key to the stillroom. Lark took it, murmuring thanks, and turned to go. She took the crushed-shell path to the small stone building attached to the castle's orangery, which had been damaged in a storm, a few panes of glass broken. The few awakening plants within were seeking summer, showy bright blossoms adorning one glassy corner.

The stillroom door creaked open. The scent of damp, cold stone and pungent peppermint embraced her, a reminder of yesterday's tasks. She reached for an apron dangling on a hook, tied it around her waist, and set to work.

Out the back door she soon went into the kitchen garden, mindful of her mission. The basket on her arm overflowed with herbs before she returned inside again, consulting the receipt book open on a near table though she knew the tincture by heart.

"Good morning to ye, Lark." The laird stood in the open doorway, startling her. He was in finely tailored Edinburgh garments, his hands caught behind his back.

Seldom did he come here. She hadn't seen him for a fortnight or better. He was mostly in Edinburgh at the courts of law. Once the distance had chafed. Now she was schooled to its pain. Close as twin lambs they'd once been, beginning when her mother was wet nurse to him. Only back then she'd not known he was a MacLeish, laird of Kerrera Castle. For all she knew he was one of the servants' children. A ruddy-cheeked, sable-haired barrel of a lad. Nor had he known she was merely a servant's daughter. Together they'd been weaned then toddled about before running together over the braes like unbridled colts.

Seeing him now, she nearly dropped her basket. "Yer lairdship—"

"Be done with that, Lark."

Sunlight spilled into the space between them. And an unseen wall of reserve. She would not—could not—call him Magnus ever again.

"We arrived late last night. I sent word ahead to ye. Did ye not receive it? About the needed tonic?"

"Nay." She sensed his distress. His stoicism did not fool her. His very presence bespoke something dire.

"To Hades with the post," he said with no small exasperation.

"Dinna fash yerself," she said as in days of old, hating that he seemed so vexed.

He looked skyward, his somberness unchanging. "There's to be no heir for Kerrera."

Her soul went still. Not again. What could she say to this? Six losses. 'Twas the reason the mistress was so gruamach. Kerrera desperately needed a babe, an heir. But no remedy or tincture could be had if one's womb was closed, Granny said.

"The doctors have sent Lady Isla here to recuperate. Beyond the stench and noise of the city."

Her hands nearly shook as she blended the herbs at hand. What a predicament! 'Twas no secret the mistress didn't care for the western islands. She found Kerrera uncivilized. Remote. A hue and a cry from her Edinburgh roots. Yet the doctors had sent her back.

The laird ran a hand through unkempt hair, gaze fixed on the sea that gleamed more gold than blue as morning bloomed beyond the castle walls. "What would ye advise?"

"Something calming." Her gaze lifted to the crocks and jugs on a shelf overhead as her thoughts swirled and grappled for answers. "Chamomile. Lavender oil. Lemon balm."

"How soon can ye ready a tonic?"

"Some things canna be rushed," she said. "Ye dinna want a false remedy. Besides, I've more than one tincture in mind." She bent a knee before she brushed past him, leaving the stillroom for a forgotten herb.

"I have faith in ye, Lark," he told her as she reentered the stillroom. "Mayhap more than in the Edinburgh physics."

"Yer faith is misplaced, mayhap." She met his azure eyes for a moment longer than she should have, if only to delve the depths of his pain. "Prayer is oft the best remedy. But this shall help in the meantime." She handed him a small glass bottle. "Have her ladyship's maid steep this in the hottest water, then wait a quarter of an hour before drinking it down."

"What does it do?"

"Rests her ladyship's womb." She flushed, hands busy with the next task. 'Twas awkward discussing such matters, but she forged ahead. "Returns her courses."

He was looking at her expectantly, no hint of embarrassment about him. But clearly flummoxed. Even disappointed. Did he think she could produce a child?

His gaze shifted. Studying the concoction in hand, he merely said absently before leaving, "Bethankit."

She mulled his bad news the rest of the afternoon, her reverie interrupted when she shut the stillroom door for the day and heard a rustling close behind her. She startled, her heartbeat calming at the sound of an unrefined yet familiar voice behind the hedge.

"Prepare for tonight. The *Merry Lass* is expected. When ye return to yer croft, stretch a bedsheet over yer peat stack once ye get the confirmation of landing. If the coast is clear, I'll shine the light. But beware. There's talk the tax men are about."

Another smuggling run? "I canna—"

"Wheest! So the blether I hear is true, then? Ye'll not help? The captain is dependin' on ye!"

Lark sighed, torn between bowing out or doing her part as a fellow islander. The least she could do was spread a simple sheet, aye? *Lord, forgive me.*

Giving the news bearer a reluctant "aye," she took the path down the cliff. The mere mention of excise men was enough to stop her cold.

⁂

"The *Merry Lass* will be bringin' a load of salt, ye say?"

"Nay, Granny, I didna say. We can only hope."

"God be praised if so!"

Together they sat at their small table, partaking of nettle kail and the last oatcakes slathered with crowdie, before a smoke-stained window. The view was wide and jaw-dropping, even to Granny, who'd lived there the longest. Perched on a cliffside, their humble croft seemed in Kerrera Castle's shadow. The castle was above them, the crown jewel of the coast with its splendid pink harled stone and profusion of towers and turrets, a sea marker for ships coming ashore.

"Who's the captain of the *Merry Lass*?" Granny asked.

Lark's stomach somersaulted. "Captain MacPherson . . . Rory MacPherson."

"Och! Mad Dirk's lad?"

"Aye, Granny, all grown up."

"Reckon he'll spare us a sack of salt?"

Lark swallowed another bite of supper, used to her grandmother's repeated questions. "The whole village is in need of such if we're to make it through another long winter."

"The laird willna let us starve." Granny poured tea with a steady hand that belied her age. The steam whitened the air between them, the aroma laden with guilt. Smuggled Irish tea it was, like the smuggled salt to come. "The last lugger brought only whisky. We have no need o' that but for medicine—or to befuddle the excise men."

Salt, on the other hand, was a necessity for preserving the fish to sustain them. And none could afford salt—or tea—since the Crown taxed both nigh to death.

Granny took a sip. "How are matters at the castle?"

'Twas the one query Lark had no heart to answer. "Lady Isla has lost another babe."

"God bless her." Granny's dark eyes narrowed to apple seeds. "The laird too."

"Is there nothing to help beget an heir?"

A faraway look came into Granny's eyes. Lark waited for some remembrance to kindle. In her day, Granny had been the stillroom mistress like Lark's mother had been the wet nurse. "My feeble mind has too many dark corners. I canna ken much."

"Well, if ye ever do . . ." Lark kept her eyes on her tea, wishing babies were as easily gotten as salt.

Where was the *Merry Lass* this twilight eve? Even if she looked hard, the ship eluded her. Painted black with dark sails, the sloop was nearly invisible on a moonless night. For now, the sun rode the western sea like an orb of fire, casting tendrils of light across their empty bowls and full cups.

'Twas calm. Warm. Lark's gaze sought the expanse of beach where the first tubmen were gathering to bring in the cargo. Soon the sand would teem with horses and carts, island women armed with cudgels and pitchforks to accompany the goods inland.

But before the *Merry Lass* put on all sails and headed straight for them, lookouts must be posted. Then Lark would stretch a bedsheet over their peat stack while someone else onshore shone the light.

———— ✖✖ ————

The immense sea cave boasted only a few ankers of brandy to one side and empty, shadowed sleeping platforms at the back. As midnight deepened, cold water licked Lark's bare feet and teased the toes of the captain's boots. With the incoming tide, there was precious little time to talk. 'Twas always the way of it. No time. Little talk. Great disappointment.

"So, lass, what have ye need of? Be quick to ask." Dressed in long boots, trews, and a striped jersey, Rory MacPherson had the look of a pirate, pistol and cutlass at hand. He made light of the tax men by calling them names, but the wariness remained. "I'll see no treasure fall into the hands of the Philistines, aye?"

She smiled, Rory's grin infectious. Tonight, the excise men had been outwitted by the free traders once again. The haul had been a roaring success. Forty chests of tea. Thirty mats of leaf tobacco. Eighty ankers of brandy. Two casks of figs and sweet licorice. A great quantity of salt. Oats.

"Salt and oats." Lark imagined Granny's glee. "Molasses, mayhap."

"Aye." Could he sense her delight? Her reluctance? She swung like a pendulum between the two. She nearly said *tea* but feared appearing greedy.

"Tea?" he stated with vigor as if sensing her longing. "A few bricks or a chest?"

"I canna haul a chest—"

"I can. I'm on my way to the Thistle. Ye take the rest."

Weighted down they were. But she was strong and fleet of foot, oft taking the craggy path in the dark by the lights of Kerrera Castle. Soon the tide would wash away their footprints and return the *Merry Lass* to sea, the braw captain along with it.

For now, breathless, her shawl slipping, Lark followed him up the cliff, the elation of a full larder eaten away by the coming separation.

Rory never stayed long. Though he stood hale and hearty, surefooted in his upward climb while dislodging a stone now and again, he would soon be gone, a ghostly memory. It seemed she lost another piece of him whenever he left, till the essence of him was no more substantial than the mist that hovered over the water.

She'd felt that way about the laird when he'd wed. Such a part of her life he'd been till Isla had turned his head. Rory had taken to the sea soon after, and she felt rent in two by both losses. While these men made their way in the world, she stayed the same, bound to croft and castle.

She looked up, the sound of the thundering surf in her ears. Tonight Kerrera Castle shone bright as a lantern just above. She glanced down quickly, then took her eyes off the path—off Rory's broad back laden with the tea chest—to rest her eyes on the castle's largest window.

There in sharp relief stood the laird, Magnus MacLeish, looking down at them. She resisted the impulse to throw up a hand. His tall silhouette was more familiar than the captain's sturdy shadow in front of her. She looked a tad too long. Her foot slipped. Pain seared her turned ankle. Noisy pebbles scattered like buckshot, causing Rory to turn around.

The castle's cellars sometimes held cargo secreted away when the threat of excise men made it too risky to move the goods inland. But tonight, with no hazard at hand, they walked free and cargo laden. Breathing hard, she stood taller when they crested the cliff and left the trail, favoring her turned ankle.

"Ye still with me, lass?"

She shifted her burden, the leather straps digging into her back. "Indeed."

"*Indeed*?" He cast the mocking word over his shoulder. "Why so fancy? Are ye getting above yer raising when a simple *aye* will do?"

She went hot, glad the darkness hid her flush. 'Twas a word she'd heard the mistress say in her crisp, aristocratic tones. Ever since, *aye* seemed too common, like dirt—much like the ancient croft ahead, turned a beguiling white in the moonlight but still simple. Unadorned.

Once there, Rory released the tea chest and Lark gave up her own burdens. Granny cracked open the door, her smile wide despite her missing teeth. "Such as ye give, such will ye get."

Rory gave a little bow at her hard-won words, to which Granny's cackling laugh was short-lived. Only during a run did Granny seem to forget her dislike of the captain.

Lark looked about for any lurking shadows as rain began spattering down, promising Rory a wet walk to the Thistle. Granny began taking the goods inside one by one to secret away in a hole beneath a hearthstone while Lark faced the captain. "I thank ye."

"Is that all ye'll give me?" he returned.

Used to his teasing, she sweetened her goodbye with a curtsy, but the merry singing of Granny's teakettle did little to banish Lark's melancholy as Rory began backing away from her, hat in hand.

"Someday ye must tell me of yer travels. If the French ladies are as comely as they say. How green Ireland is," she called after him, her voice falling away in the damp dark.

Small wonder he wanted to be away. The Thistle did more than wet his whistle. She'd heard tales of him charming the tavern wenches there with satin ribbons and bits of lace from foreign ports. He'd not given her such fripperies, naught but salt and tea and oats, a fact that held the appeal of curdled milk.

But her own charms were few. She had no power to hold him. No ale with which to entice him. He was less inclined to talk than the laird of late. But even if he'd paid her attention, her spirit stayed unsettled. All this smuggling—ill-gotten goods—squeezed the very life out of her.

Granny hovered in the croft's open door, as if chaperoning their parting. "Take thy tea, Lark."

And so she did.

Author Note

In the spring of 2022, I traveled to Château de Saint-Germain-en-Laye in France and then to Versailles. Both places were far more grand and expansive than I'd expected. It was easy to imagine Lady Blythe Hedley walking through those extensive gardens in her elegant gowns along with other French courtiers. Though the Saint-Germaine-en-Laye gardens are a shadow of what they once were in the eighteenth century and the grottoes no longer exist, I still sensed their enchantment. I also gained a deeper appreciation for Mary, Queen of Scots, when she left France and returned to her homeland. What a transition that must have been!

It wasn't until I set foot on the grounds of Wedderburn Castle in the Scottish Borders that I fully realized the magnitude of what my Hume ancestors had lost. At what point did the exiles realize they'd never see Scotland or their families again? Did they have regrets?

Wedderburn Castle and the Lowlands today are unimaginably peaceful, even idyllic. Held by the Humes since the fifteenth century, the present castle dates from the later eighteenth century and was built around an older tower house. An earlier fortification, Hume Castle, is just down the road and sits on a hill with an unsurpassed territorial view. Fast Castle on the Berwickshire coast was also once held by the Humes. I was unprepared for just how beautiful and bittersweet being in these ancient places would be.

According to Colonel David Milne Hume,

> For centuries, the Humes of Wedderburn were one of the most predominant families of the Merse. Scions of a warlike house and posted on the border as if for the very purpose of guarding the "in country" against the incursions of the "auld inimies of England," they were ever ready to venture their lives in the fray, and indeed they had their full share of the fights and forays of the border strife of old. Few of the older Lairds are known to have had any other death-bed than the battlefield, and their first funeral shroud was generally the banner under which they led their retainers to the fight, and which has come down to their descendants stained with their blood.[1]

Sir George Hume of Wedderburn Castle (my sixth great-grandfather) was a commander of Jacobite forces in the Jacobite Rising of 1715. Captured and imprisoned, then pardoned rather than executed, he died not long after. His son George Hume was also captured at Preston, imprisoned at Marshalsea, and finally arrived in Virginia at the age of twenty-three in 1721. There he joined his exiled uncle, Sir Francis Hume. Francis's wife and children remained in Scotland and never saw him again. He became a factor to "King" Carter at Corotoman Plantation as well as the Germanna settlement, only to be buried along the Rapidan River a few years later.

In a letter to family in Scotland, "Immigrant" George writes, "I find there is nothing to get here without recommendation. Tho mine was good yet it did me no manner of service." He referred to Virginia as "this Indian countrie" and always thought of Scotland as home.[2] He was, however, related to a lieutenant governor of Virginia (Alexander Spotswood), and his freedom was purchased by Captain

1. David Milne Hume, *The Report to Parliament on the Manuscripts of Col. David Milne Hume, of Wedderburn Castle* (London: Mackie & Co., 1902), 2.

2. "Letters of George Hume, of Virginia," *William and Mary Quarterly* 6, no. 4 (April 1898): 254.

Dandridge, kin to Martha Washington. Eventually he attended the College of William and Mary and is credited with teaching surveying to a young George Washington.

This novel is stitched together with a great deal of Hume history and a little literary license woven in. The true Humes were barons, not earls. Not all the Humes were Jacobites. Lady Blythe was an echo of the medieval English heiresses who married into Clan Hume, some of them kidnapped. The angelic bedside visitation happened not to Alexander Hume but to my maternal great-grandmother in her final hours. It came to mind when I was writing and seemed to fit Alexander's last hours too.

I was happy to stay in Scotland for *The Rose and the Thistle* so that the Humes did not have to forfeit all. *A Bound Heart*, my first Scottish novel, was inspired by the exiled Humes coming to America in the eighteenth century and tells of the travails faced by so many back then.

If I could rewrite history, I'd gladly be Lady Laura of Wedderburn Castle. Those of you with similar ancestry might dream of having never left Scotland too.

Acknowledgments

To readers everywhere who've embraced my books—you're a gift, each one of you. I'm very grateful. Thank you.

Thanks also to . . .

Revell, who has published all of my novels starting with *The Frontiersman's Daughter*. When I signed with them in 2008 I had no idea what I was getting into, but time has proved them to be top-tier over and over again.

Laura Klynstra and Revell's art team for designing a stunning cover that captures the spirit of this novel so well. Two covers, actually! I'm thrilled we chose this one.

To Rachel of Clan McRae. Your love of history and authors really shines. I never thought our Lifeway connection would transform into an editorial one, but I'm thankful it did.

Another extraordinary editor, Jessica English, who has such a keen eye and makes a book so much better. If this novel's dates and days eventually line up, it's entirely to your credit, not mine. Add the extra challenging Gregorian and Julian calendars at play in the eighteenth century and you're a genius!

Michele Misiak for your extraordinary savvy with all things marketing, Karen Steele who is able to plug authors into amazingly visible places, and Brianne Dekker who makes Revell's Beyond the Book club fascinating and fun, in addition to all the other hats you wear! And last but not least, the savvy sales reps who carry the weight of getting books into readers' hands in times like these.

Janet Grant, you continue to amaze me with your knowledge of the industry, writing, and publishing. Our every contact teaches me something and makes me wiser.

To those whose prayers are powerful—Patti Jones, Lois Bryen Williams, Cindy Reynolds, and Karen Wiley. You are priceless.

Pepper Basham, you have many friends yet are still willing to take time to do crazy things like travel when no one else is traveling. Your grace, good humor, and storytelling abilities, in addition to all the other things you do, really leave me in awe. I'm so blessed to call you a longtime friend.

Lydia Basham, map maker extraordinaire. Thank you for my first ever map but hopefully not my last!

To those intrepid, Scotland-loving souls who went on our recent adventure, not all of them lassies in hats—Pepper, Cheryl, Tawny, Sarah, Jennifer, Nicia, Julie, Amy, Heather, Angela, Alissa, Stephanie, Jim, Debi, Heather, Michael—you are an absolute gift to travel with. I'll always remember your many kindnesses, inspiring conversations, and bursts of hilarity! Thank you.

And Randy—there would be no books without you.

Soli Deo gloria.

Laura Frantz is a Christy Award winner and the ECPA bestselling author of fourteen novels, including *A Heart Adrift*. When she isn't researching and writing, she's cooking, taking long walks, gardening, and traveling. Her greatest joy is being the mom of an American soldier and a career firefighter. Though she will always call Kentucky home, she and her husband live in Washington State. Learn more at www.laurafrantz.net.

Can Love Survive the Secrets Kept Buried within a Tormented Heart?

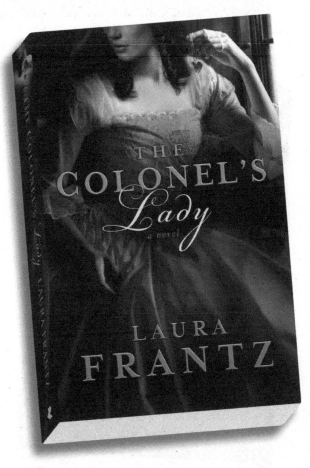

In 1779, a search for her father brings Roxanna to the Kentucky frontier—but she discovers instead a young colonel, a dark secret . . . and a compelling reason to stay. Laura Frantz delivers a powerful story of love, faith, and forgiveness in *The Colonel's Lady*.

"This tale of second chances and brave choices *swept me away.*"

—**Jocelyn Green,** Christy Award–winning author of *Shadows of the White City*

A colonial lady and a privateering sea captain collide once more after a failed love affair a decade before. Will a war and a cache of regrets keep them apart? Or will a new shared vision reunite them?

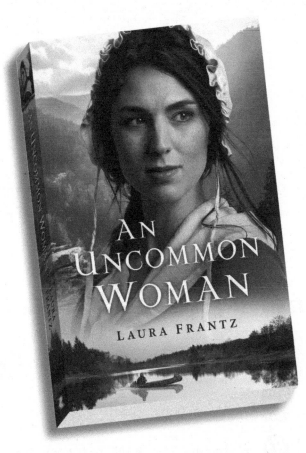

MEET

LAURA FRANTZ

Visit LauraFrantz.net to read
Laura's blog and learn about her books!

 enter to win contests and learn about what
Laura is working on now

 tweet with Laura

 see what inspired the characters and stories